RAVE REVIEWS FOR PAM CROOKS!

"Pam Crooks is destined to become a powerful voice in historical romance."

—*Romance Readers Connection*

LADY GYPSY

"Pam Crooks has written another fascinating tale of the Old West. *Lady Gypsy* will steal your heart."

—*Romance Reviews Today*

"Stirring passion, deep-seated prejudice, and hidden danger make Pam Crooks's *Lady Gypsy* an unforgettable treasure you'll want to take out again and again."

—*Rendezvous*

"This love story is outstanding!"

—*Romantic Times*

WYOMING WILDFLOWER

"Powerful emotions boil over in this gripping epic. Lyrical prose, complex characters, and clever plot twists combine for a perfect blend of romance and adventure. . . . Ms. Crooks is a writer of immense talent."

—*Rendezvous*

"*Wyoming Wildflower* is a complete Western with all the right ingredients. [Ms. Crooks] is an author to keep an eye on."

—*Romance Reviews Today*

"Pam Crooks writes a much different, but very interesting take from the usual Western fare . . . filled with a lot of emotion . . . a lot of love. [This is] a very satisfying book."

—*Affaire de Coeur*

A HEATED CHARADE

"Hannah is mine." Quinn's voice rasped from the depth of his rage. "Look at her. All of you."

He lifted her arm high about her head, firmly, and twirled her. Presented them her back, her side, her front. So there would be no question.

She was his. Untouchable. By any of them.

Hannah's eyes closed tight.

He stopped turning her. Her eyes opened again.

His gaze smoldered, stroked her with its growing heat. Her mind emptied. She thought only of the role they played. Of the deal they'd made. She thought nothing of brown habits and a convent that seemed forever unreachable.

She thought of Quinn, the man.

He filled her senses. She knew his intent even before his head lowered and his jaw nuzzled her temple.

"You mustn't do this," she whispered.

"Convince them, Hannah," he murmured. "Make them believe."

His chin brushed her cheek, then lowered to her jaw. She waited for what would come next, the anticipation building within her with every frenzied beat of her heart. At last, warm and firm, his mouth slid over hers.

Happy Reading — Aunt Rita

PAM CROOKS

HANNAH'S VOW

*Enjoy — Pam Crooks
5/02*

LEISURE BOOKS NEW YORK CITY

A LEISURE BOOK®

April 2002

Published by

Dorchester Publishing Co., Inc.
276 Fifth Avenue
New York, NY 10001

ISBN 0-8439-4986-4

The name "Leisure Books" and the stylized "L" with design are trademarks of Dorchester Publishing Co., Inc.

Printed in the United States of America.

Visit us on the web at www.dorchesterpub.com.

HANNAH'S VOW

Chapter One

New Mexico Territory, 1895

The rage burned within him. From betrayal. From abuse. From being locked up in prison for a lifetime. He fed on the rage, clung to it, until rage was his one desperate link to sanity.

He sat on the cold floor of his underground cell, his knees drawn up, his back pressed against the wall, darkened from the blood of nameless inmates before him. He listened.

It was happening again.

Voices. In the middle of the night. Heavy footsteps. The creak of the iron grate opening over one more cell.

Missing prisoners. Never seen again.

The rage pulsed inside him.

His brain sifted through the muffled sounds. The moans and grunts. The chink of ankle chains from one

1

more victim dragged away. Foreboding settled over him. Black and ominous.

He could be next.

A grate whined on its hinges, then clanged shut. Silence fell. A grim, gruesome silence.

The cell closed in on him. Lack of ventilation, his own sweat and filth, choked the air in his lungs.

He stared up at the grate, nine feet above. Unreachable. He fought the claws of despair, refused to give into its mastery.

Instead, he nurtured the rage, stoked it, kept it pulsating inside him.

He'd find a way to escape.

Or die trying.

Christmas Eve
One Week Later

Their song filled the convent chapel with a reverence that rivaled the seraphim, and for each of the eighteen good sisters kneeling in the pews, the words came from deep within her heart, pure and fervent.

But none more so than Hannah Benning's. She had much to thank God for, and even more to ask of Him, and thus she sang the Latin hymn with all the piety she could muster.

She was trying very hard. It had not been in her at first to pray like this, almost all day every day, to sing and be meek and silent to those around her, but it suited her now. She would live this life forever. She had to, for Pa's sake.

"Te Deum Laudamus," the ancient hymn of praise and thanksgiving, ended. The chapel plunged into com-

plete darkness. Hannah closed her eyes and savored the silence.

The midnight Office was her favorite of the vespers. The most dramatic. A fitting welcome to the new day when once she'd been afraid of the dawn. But she wasn't afraid anymore. She was safe here, a newly vowed novitiate, loved and protected.

But safe, most of all.

Sister Evangeline nudged her gently, and Hannah's eyes opened. Mother Superior emerged from the vestibule carrying the Paschal candle. She held its flame high, and guided by the flickering light, strode solemnly down the length of the chapel to the altar. She enshrined the candle and lit a smaller one, then turned toward the front pew, passing the flame to each sister holding a candle of her own. Soon, the chapel glowed with golden candlelight, with the joy of prayer and peace, and the air filled with their lyrical voices, praising and rejoicing the glorious season of Advent, the birth of the Christ child.

Too soon, the ritual ended. Hannah tried not to think of Christmas, her first without Pa, but instead blew out her candle and left the pew. Her knee touched the cold stone floor in a deep genuflect. She crossed herself and stood to leave.

Mother Superior led the sisters in silent formation from the chapel, their single line practiced, perfect. The block walls, bare from adornment except for a simple crucifix, cast a chill into the dim hall, and Hannah shivered beneath her brown wool habit.

The corridor angled past the main door to the convent and wound toward the sisters' sleeping quarters. Over the hushed shuffle of sandal soles, the outside bell tolled unexpectedly, sending a startled ripple through the women.

The toll announced someone at the gate; an oddity, for the clock had not yet chimed the first hour of the new morning. Hannah exchanged a puzzled glance with Sister Evangeline.

The ringing grew more forceful. The iron gate rattled. The bell clanged again and again.

Mother Superior pushed aside the muslin curtain covering the window. "It's Father Donovan." She made the sign of the cross. "Thank our Lord he is safe. He should have been here hours ago."

She lifted the latch and tugged the door open. Cold air drifted inward.

The clanging stopped. She rushed outside. The gate squeaked, and within moments, she reappeared with the priest, aged well into his fifties, breathing heavily from his exertions.

Black robes flared about his ankles; a knotted rope wound about his plump waist. The wisps of hair remaining on his balding pate stood in wild disarray.

His arms were laden with baskets filled with fresh-baked bread and jars of preserves, holiday gifts for the less fortunate. Hannah herself had helped fill them. He set the baskets aside.

"Forgive me for my tardiness, but—" He paused to catch his breath. A ruddiness colored his cheeks.

"Slow down, Father. Has Lucifer been chasing you?" Mother Superior's eyes crinkled, and she patted the priest's arm.

"Lucifer has no time for me, it seems," he answered. He cast a hesitant glance toward the sisters, their perfect line gone hopelessly awry in their curiosity. "He's been busy elsewhere."

Her humor gone, the abbess frowned. "What are you talking about?"

"It's the prison. Something is wrong. Graves are being dug. Now. At this very hour. Too many to count."

"Graves?"

"I first noticed them on my way to deliver the holiday baskets," he explained. "The sight troubled me, and I had to return for a second look." He shook his head in puzzlement. "More graves have been added. I knew I must come back for help." He emitted a slight moan of dismay. "I can't help feeling the warden has engaged in some form of illicit behavior."

The abbess pursed her lips. "Warden Briggs has a heart of stone, it's true, but I can't imagine him doing anything that would jeopardize his position at the prison. Surely the inmates suffer from an ailment. Influenza or stomach poisoning, perhaps. The food served there is atrocious."

"If it were a treatable illness, why wasn't a doctor called? Or me? And why the secrecy? Lord help us, digging graves at midnight!"

"You must go back, then." Mother Superior's decisive tone indicated Father Donovan had convinced her of the seriousness of the situation. "Those men deserve our prayers and compassion. And the Last Rites, if nothing else."

"Yes, yes. I quite agree." He skimmed a glance over the group. "Sister Evangeline, you have an understanding of medicine. I'd like you to accompany us. Bring what medical supplies you have."

"Yes, Father." As if he had only suggested a stroll

through the garden instead of an uninvited late-night visit to the notorious penitentiary, the young nun lowered her wimpled head without argument. She was Hannah's age, in her twentieth year, and Hannah marveled at her obedience.

"I'll fetch my prayer book and holy water," he said. "I'll be but a moment."

After he left, Mother Superior turned toward the group of nuns. "We shall return to the chapel to offer more prayers this hour. Sister Mary Margaret, begin the rosary, won't you? I shall join you shortly. Hannah, I'd like a word with you."

Hannah halted in mid-step. Sandaled feet scurried toward the chapel amidst a clatter of rosary beads, leaving her behind and wary of what the abbess might ask of her.

"Sister Evangeline, you'd best fetch a cloak," Mother Superior suggested. "And please fetch an extra one, as well."

"Yes, Mother." The young nun nodded her head and departed toward the sleeping quarters.

In the dimness of the hall, Hannah waited with her gaze to the stone floor.

"Sister Evangeline cannot go alone to the penitentiary, even with Father Donovan as her escort. I would like you to accompany her, Hannah."

Hannah's eyes widened, and her head lifted. "But, Mother—"

"Hear me out, my child." Though she spoke quietly, firmness laced every word. "You have not left the convent since you joined us. This is an opportunity, a test of sorts, to help others in need and to assure us of your calling."

In the low, even voice she had learned to emulate, Hannah dared to protest. "There are other novitiates far more worthy than I to do this kindness at the penitentiary. I—I am not ready."

"There is no other better suited." The abbess hesitated. "Your past has prepared you for this act of mercy. You have been—shall we say—hardened for what you will see there."

"Mother, I seek only to forget."

"You are not here to avoid the world, my child. You are here to embrace it, to pray for others and help them when they cannot help themselves."

Dread draped Hannah like a suffocating blanket. "Please. I ask for only a little more time."

A gentle smile hovered upon Mother Superior's mouth. "You have taken the name of Sister Ariel. 'Lioness of God.' When you speak your final vows, you will no longer be Hannah, but Ariel. A lioness. Strong and proud." The smile deepened, as if she approved of what Hannah must face. "Tonight will be a chance for you to learn if you are worthy of such a beautiful name."

Miserable, Hannah lowered her gaze. "Yes, Mother."

A slender finger tilted her chin up again. "You will be safe with Father Donovan and Sister Evangeline. Try not to worry so. Warden Briggs, for all his sinful ways, will not harm you. He is like the devil who withers in front of Jesus' cross."

The softly spoken words did little to salve Hannah's apprehension. With Father Donovan at her heels, Sister Evangeline hurried toward them and thrust a wool cloak into Hannah's hands. Silently, she slipped into its folds.

"Take the baskets," the abbess urged. "The men will need decent food to eat as well as our prayers."

"Of course," the priest agreed, taking one and handing another to Sister Evangeline. He left the last of them for Hannah. "We will return as soon as we can," he said and hurried outside.

The abbess's head inclined in a deep nod. "God be with you all."

For the briefest of seconds, Hannah met her glance. Beneath the starched wimple, the abbess's smile faded and concern creased her brow. Sister Evangeline stepped out into the night's chill. Hannah swallowed hard, slipped the basket's handle over her arm and followed.

With the clang of the iron gate echoing throughout the hall, Mother Superior clutched her rosary beads and began to pray.

The New Mexico Territorial Prison loomed like a black monster on the horizon. Darkness enshrouded the grim structure; the air hung heavy with the scent of death, and the grisly silence sent shivers of unease down Hannah's spine.

She had not thought she'd be near such a place again in her lifetime, and yet fate had thrown her back when she'd sought only to escape, to leave the memories of a life peppered with evil behind. She did not want this 'test' of her calling. She did not want the uncertainties of the next minute or hour to keep her from the haven she'd needed in recent months. She stared hard at the imposing penitentiary. No, she did not want anything to do with this building or its inhabitants.

Too many times Pa had dragged her with him into

escapades not so different from this one. In the end, she had survived when he had not. It had cost her dearly, and just thinking of what lay ahead clogged her throat with the bitter taste of an ugly premonition.

The carriage drew closer, the wheels growling over the rocky ground in warning of their approach. But it seemed their arrival went undetected. The rig rolled to a stop.

"See them? Over there." Father Donovan pointed to a far corner of the penitentiary grounds. There, on a rise of land, mounds of earth took the shape of newly dug graves. In the meager spray of moonlight, Hannah deciphered an assortment of shovels and spades strewn about, as if the time had not come to put them away, as if they would be needed again soon. She gripped the plain wooden cross hanging from her neck and shuddered.

"The burial place is not easily seen from any road," she murmured.

"Odd the warden would choose such an inconvenient and isolated spot. Don't you think, Father?" Sister Evangeline asked.

"Yes. Definitely so." Abruptly, the priest crossed himself. "May God have mercy on all we find here." He sat up straighter. "Let's hear what the warden has to say about those graves."

Hannah exchanged a troubled glance with Sister Evangeline. She chafed at the risk they were about to take, but the meek obedience Mother Superior had instilled in her forbade the protests she longed to make.

With a slap of the reins, the priest urged the team of horses into a wide circle, and, after a short drive, brought the carriage to a stop at the front entrance of the penitentiary. After setting the brake, he jumped down and offered Hannah his hand. She was grateful; she feared the queasiness in her belly had turned her knees to mush.

After dismounting, Sister Evangeline huddled beside her. "The men harbored here have the blackest of souls, Hannah."

"Yes," she said and tilted her head back to peruse the front of the prison, two stories high, harsh and unyielding. She knew the brand of men locked inside. The swiftness of the knowledge, the clarity of the memory, surprised her. Hannah hooked her arm with Sister Evangeline's and squeezed. "We must have faith."

Father Donovan knocked once, twice. They stood on the top step and waited. After the third knock, the thick door jerked open, and a uniformed guard appeared.

"Who goes there?" he demanded, squinting into the darkness. He lifted the kerosene lamp in his hand higher. A badge emblazoned with the name "Titus" was pinned on his chest. He ran a sharp glance over them.

"Father Donovan, sir. We must speak with the warden. Immediately."

"Briggs? What for?" A jagged scar slashed his cheek. His eyes narrowed in suspicion at the baskets.

"We have gifts for the men. But, more importantly, there's a matter that concerns us."

The guard grunted. His gaze darted behind them, in the direction of the graveyard, then back again.

"He's busy," he snapped and moved to slam the door closed.

In a bold move, the priest's arm shot out and held it open. "We insist."

"Oh, do you now?"

"We'll not leave until we speak with him. Only a few questions, if you please."

"Yeah?" Titus seemed skeptical. "Briggs ain't gonna like bein' interrupted."

"Something is amiss here. An illness?" the priest demanded. "Perhaps it is treatable. We want to help. Nothing more."

The guard glared.

"Do you truly want the deaths of more men on your conscience?" the priest asked, pulling no punches about the penitentiary's secret. "Who knows? Maybe you will be next. Have you thought of that?"

The low-voiced suggestion hit its mark. The guard swore and yanked the door open wider. "He's in the infirmary. If'n Briggs asks, it wasn't me who let you in, y'hear?"

"God bless you." The priest bustled inside. "God bless you, indeed."

Sister Evangeline scuttled in after him. Hannah hurried to follow, but Titus's large hand clasped her elbow, forbidding her to take another step.

"Well, look-ey here," he drawled. "Reckon we ain't never had no Ladies of the Cloth in here before." He raked her with a lecherous glance, his scarred cheek quivering, his words floating toward her on puffs of stale breath. "Hell, we ain't never had no ladies at all."

Hannah's stomach churned. Father Donovan hastily pushed the guard's hand away. "I insist upon respect for the sisters while we are within the confines of this penitentiary. They are here to do God's work. If you feel it necessary to comment, please address me."

Titus chuckled. "Reckon I don't find you as ap-

11

pealin'." But he released Hannah's elbow and stepped back, allowing her to pass.

Sister Evangeline's arm locked with hers. Hannah clung to it tightly and drew in a slow breath.

With a confidence that bespoke his convictions, the priest led the way. Hannah took a measure of comfort in his presence. They were safe enough. Mother Superior had promised, and if there was one thing Hannah had learned in her time at the convent, it was that Mother Superior never lied.

They plunged into the deepest bowels of the penitentiary.

A clinging, choking stench reached them from within a deserted hall, a mixture of sickness and filth and despair, and Hannah fought to keep from gagging. From the depths of the shadows, someone moaned. In others, a man wept. A damp mustiness chilled the air, and Hannah was certain there'd never been a place more miserable than this.

Sister Evangeline kept the front of her cloak pressed to her nose, her gaze darting furtively to the dark corners.

Father Donovan appeared less affected; clearly, he'd known what to expect. His brisk stride slowed.

"Here is where the men sleep," he said quietly, pointing toward the floor. "In cells beneath the ground. One after another. See them? Nothing more than archaic dungeons." He clucked his tongue. "An abomination."

"God have mercy," Hannah murmured.

Keeping her skirts snug about her, she peered downward at an iron grate, two feet square, nestled in the wooden floor. No light shone through the grate, only a dank and wretched darkness, and an eerie silence from within.

"The inmates are made to climb in and out of their cells using portable ladders," Father Donovan continued, his tone restrained. "The guards lower and raise the ladders as they see fit, truly trapping the men at the bottom of these pits."

She scrutinized the opening. "Has the warden no compassion?"

"Very little, Hannah."

"There's no light. No fresh air!"

"The cells are primitive, with packed earth floors and damp walls to let the cold in. They're the warden's version of solitary confinement, an experiment he's—"

"Hey!" A man's shout leapt upward from the grate. A loud clatter, a solid object hurled against the iron, startled Hannah out of her wits.

She jumped back with a squeal. The priest grabbed for her.

"Who's up there? Hey! A woman? Let me outta here, honey!"

Father Donovan dragged Hannah away from the cells. Sister Evangeline fell into step behind them.

"Forgive me," the priest rasped, his hold on Hannah's arm revealing he was as shaken as she. "I should have taken more care. Sweet heaven, let's hope he doesn't incite a riot."

Hannah pressed a hand to her thudding heart and strove to regain her composure.

"The infirmary is just around the corner. We're almost there," he continued and drew a calming breath. "Are you all right, Hannah?" At her nod, he patted her shoulder. "The men can do us no harm while in their cells. Rest assured of that."

"I'm fine, Father. Truly," she said and adjusted her wimple on a wave of dismay. She had acted like a frightened rabbit. Where was her courage?

"Come, then. Let's hope the warden is in a talkative mood."

A woman.

Her voice reached him through the darkness. The silken sound filtered down from the grate over his cell. Drifted over him. Surrounded him.

He strained to hear more. Words of concern, soft, edged in velvet. And then, from the cell next to him, Sol hurling something at the grate, scaring her away.

The silence returned. He sat very still, waiting, his mind working, always working.

Outsiders.

They knew about the graves. That's why they were here.

Sol began the code, the tap of his chains, one link against another, spreading the news of a woman in the house. Down the line of cells, the inmates picked up the rhythm, and the tapping grew louder.

But he didn't take part. Not this time.

He would use her, this woman.

His fingers found the weakened link holding his own length of chains, the one he'd been saving for just this moment. The muscles in his arms tightened, and the link inched apart, the chains gave way, and he was free.

The tapping increased in intensity, a smokescreen for what he was about to do. He crawled to the darkest corner of his cell and clawed at the loose dirt there. He withdrew the pair of broom handles, tied together with strips of cloth, and tested their strength.

He stood and studied the grate above him, knowing the handles would reach, that the chinks he'd made in the earthen walls would provide the toeholds he'd need to climb up.

And out.

The woman.

Hannah.

She was his only chance.

Chapter Two

They stood in front of the infirmary, clearly delineated from the rest of the prison by a wall of bars. Beyond this barricade lay a closed door beneath which a sliver of light shone.

"Normally, these bars are locked to prevent the men from breaking inside to steal the drugs." Father Donovan gave the iron gate in the center a little push, and it inched open. He emitted a soft grunt of amazement. "But tonight, someone has been careless."

He pushed again, widening the opening. The bars groaned on rusty hinges. The creaking sound skidded down Hannah's spine and brought back images of similar bars in nameless jails, of Pa locked inside. . . .

Her heart pattered an uneven beat. She reached out, closing her fingers around the stout iron, cold and unforgiving, just as she remembered. And in that moment, she knew a part of her would never forget.

Never.

She had thought the past buried deep, never to be resurrected again. But here, now, in this awful place, it roared inside her brain with a vengeance.

She shook from the force of the haunting memories. They threatened to overcome her, to drag her down into their sickening, whirling void, but she fought them, fought as she had always done. And this time, as before, she survived.

As if touching a hot poker, she jerked her hand back, curling it into a fist and pressing it against her breast. Slowly, she regained her composure, and awareness returned.

Father Donovan had already entered the infirmary. A glimpse of Sister Evangeline's brown wool habit disappeared inside, too. Hannah hurried to follow, but the sound of clinking chains stopped her cold.

She glanced behind her in alarm. Methodical and demanding, the clinking erupted into a pattern, a code, that only the men understood.

Whatever their secret message, she was certain to be the cause. Her carelessness and curiosity over the cells had alerted them to her presence. Did they think her their salvation?

Glory, never that. Her step quickened to join the others, and she closed the door tightly behind her.

Where the prison's halls had been dim and shadowed, the interior of the infirmary blazed with light. Kerosene lamps graced every available table, their wicks burning to the highest vantage. Hannah blinked in the brilliance.

Six beds crowded the room, each occupied by inmates strapped to the frames by strips of sturdy leather. The men were blindfolded and gagged, their bodies

17

twisting upon the mattresses, their throats emitting primitive grunts. Hannah stared. What illness required them to be treated like this? What crime was so deserving?

A man jotted notations on a pad. The fine fabric of his wool vest and trousers, his spit-shined shoes, and the gleaming gold watch chain hanging from a vest pocket indicated his wealth. He reached for a glass syringe with a long needle and filled it from one of the vials on the tray at his side. His work engrossed him.

In growing horror, Hannah's gaze swept the room. Blood, old and dried and black, spattered a coil of cowhide leather hanging on the wall. Beneath the whip lay a pile of chains—the links heavy, grim—some attached to metal balls, the others to hand or ankle cuffs. A cat o' nine tails straddled the heap.

Another man slouched in a chair tilted on its back legs. He twirled a diamond ring on his finger, then buffed it to a new shine on the cuff of his shirt sleeve. The expensive bauble occupied his full attention; clearly, he didn't care about the atrocities going on around him.

"Warden Briggs!" Father Donovan called out.

Both chair legs returned to the floor with a loud thump. The man bolted to his feet. "What the hell—"

His beady eyes raked sharply over them. A black suit, well-worn and needing a thorough cleaning, stretched across his paunchy frame. His features took on a cunning light, reminding Hannah of a rat caught doing something illicit.

"What is going on here?" the priest demanded.

"How'd you get in?" The warden moved toward

them, dodging the beds in his way, his gaze flicking over the baskets.

"We saw graves outside. Is there sickness?"

"Nothin' we can't handle." A slow, sinister smile spread across his face and revealed yellowed, uneven teeth. He snatched Sister Evangeline's basket and riffled through the contents. "So why don't you just go?"

"Get rid of them, Briggs!"

The warden's head snapped around. "I'm tryin', Fenwick!"

Contempt flitted over the face of the man who held the syringe. Perspiration dotted his brow. His fine cotton shirt was rumpled; the necktie open at his throat. An air of intensity hung about him. Determination. Whatever drove him in his work consumed him.

"We want to help, Warden," Father Donovan said, his frowning glance jumping from one man to the other. "We've brought fresh bread and preserves to share with the prisoners, but we can plainly tell something is wrong here."

"Nothin's wrong, I tell you!" Briggs tossed aside Sister Evangeline's basket. He gave the priest a firm nudge toward the closed door, his smile as false as his words. "Now, I 'preciate what you and these holy sisters are tryin' to do for us, but, you see, we really don't need you."

Father Donovan shook free. "We have no intention of leaving, Warden. All is not right here."

The smile disappeared. "We don't need your help."

"Look at these men. They lie here like animals ready for killing." The priest stepped toward the nearest inmate and deftly removed his blindfold. "What kind of medicine must be administered to a patient under these

19

conditions?" He gave the warden no chance to respond. "Hannah and Sister Evangeline, help me remove their blindfolds!"

They hurried to obey his command.

"Now you wait just a goddam minute!" Briggs sputtered.

"Men are dying. Do you inject them with poison?" the priest demanded.

"Poison?" Fenwick's round face reddened with ire. "A great deal of study has gone into my Solution!"

"I beg your pardon then. Please explain what is going on here."

As if it galled him to account for his actions to the priest, the man holding the syringe stiffened and peered down his long, thin nose. "I am Roger Fenwick. I have developed a revolutionary drug which I call Fenwick's Solution. I'll take the medical world by storm with it, and people will pay me handsomely—"

He halted. The clamor from the underground cells seeped inward, the rhythmic clinking insistent, troublesome.

Unease filtered through Hannah; she exchanged a wary glance with Sister Evangeline.

A murderous expression darkened Briggs's countenance, and he snatched the coiled cat o'nine tails and strode to the door. He bellowed for a guard.

Fenwick swore and lowered the syringe to the wrist of the inmate nearest him, a wiry man missing his teeth. The tip of the needle pricked the skin; a drop of crimson oozed out.

An ugly dread spread through Hannah. The makeshift graveyard flared in her memory, the spades and shovels left behind in readiness for the next round of

20

digging. And she knew, then, that no illness plagued the penitentiary, but, instead, Fenwick's Solution, and that the men housed here, regardless of their crimes, did not deserve this fate.

"Don't!" she gasped. "You mustn't give him the Solution!"

Fenwick paused. His harsh glance lifted to her.

The inmate remained motionless beneath the leather straps holding him, his pleading gaze riveted to Hannah like a lifeline.

"He could die," she accused Fenwick.

"I have adjusted the dosage."

Hannah strove to keep her voice even. "There are graves. You're doing something wrong."

"I'm getting closer. The world will thank me one day." A wildness contorted his features. "Briggs!" he shouted. "Get her away from here!"

In two long strides, the warden reached her. His meaty paws dug into her shoulders and yanked.

"Leave us, woman," he yelled in her ear. "And take your damned friends with you!"

Hannah's instincts took over, and she reacted to a force deep within her, a loathing for Briggs, for the evil and wicked men who'd blackened her past. Her hand delved into her basket and clutched a jar of preserves; her arm swung, and the jar cracked across the warden's jaw. The glass broke, splitting his fleshy skin open. Blood spurted and mixed with the jellied fruit, dropping to the floor in clumps.

Hannah gasped in horror at what she'd done.

His features twisted in a demonic rage, he lunged for her, grabbing her by the arm. His own arm was lifted high, his fist clenched, ready to strike.

21

"Nobody move!"

The door crashed open with such force a hinge wrenched free from the portal. Armed with a long-handled club, an inmate burst into the infirmary. Unshaven, his hair matted with grime, his uniform filthy, he stood with his feet spread, breathing hard. He swung the weapon in a vicious arc.

Fenwick's syringe dropped to the mattress. A scream lodged in Hannah's throat.

"Nobody *move!*" the prisoner roared again.

"Damn you, Landry!" Briggs snarled and released Hannah so roughly she stumbled over her skirt hems. He uncoiled the cat o'nine tails with a lethal snap. "You'll get the hide whipped off your stinkin' bones for this!"

"Shut up, Warden!"

Briggs shook from raw fury. Blood dripping from his jaw, he bettered his grip on the whip, lifted his hand only inches before Landry's club swung and caught him on the side of the head. He yelped and fell back against the floor. The "cat" dropped from his grip.

"Enough of this!" Father Donovan reached for Landry, but the inmate met him with a sweep of his mighty arm, and the priest went flying, landing in a heap on the floor.

"No!" Sister Evangeline rushed forward, her hand extended as if she feared he'd do the priest further harm. His arm swung out again, and she fell over Father Donovan in a tangle of brown wool and rosary beads.

Hannah cried out in dismay, her pulse pounding in terror of this man who was no better than a savage.

"We're okay, Hannah," the priest said, his tone terse,

his hands fighting to free himself from the young nun sprawled over him.

"Fenwick!" Landry snapped. The older man jumped, his skin paling above the starched collar of his shirt. "You make Briggs look like a goddam saint."

Spots of color rose in the man's cheeks. "I beg your pardon!"

Landry's lip curled in a feral sneer. He jabbed the club toward the tray of vials. "Destroy your Solution!"

"What?" He paled again. "You can't mean that! I've worked years on it. I'm on the threshold of success." Fenwick's smooth-skinned hands shook. He ran his tongue along his lower lip. "Look. I'll pay you—"

"Destroy it!"

Landry strode forward and hurled the tray against the wall. Glass vials shattered. Papers flew. Streams of the Solution trailed downward in dark streaks, the clear liquid soaking into the floor and forever smearing the inked notations on the sheets now strewn across the ground.

With an anguished yell, Fenwick lunged for him. Landry slammed the club against the side of Fenwick's face. He screamed and fell back, bounced off the bed behind him and stumbled to the floor. He choked on a sob and curled into a fetal position. His body rocked back and forth. Blood ran from the gash on his mouth.

The inmates squirmed on their beds, their leather straps straining in their quest to be free. All riveted their gazes on Landry, their expressions hopeful, eager.

He ignored them all.

Instead, his dark-eyed gaze found Hannah.

"Come here," he said softly.

She drew back in alarm.

With a shout, Briggs reared up from the floor like a dragon breathing fire and lunged for the bed next to her. His hand closed around the forgotten syringe, the one yet filled with Solution, and before Landry could react, before any of them could, he leapt forward and plunged the needle into Landry's upper arm. His thumb pressed against the syringe's flat top, releasing the liquid into the inmate's body.

Roaring in rage, Landry thrust him aside like rancid meat. His fist clenched and connected with the warden's jaw. Bone hit bone, and Briggs crumpled, out cold.

Landry spat an oath and yanked the needle from his arm. He swore again.

Horror-stricken, Hannah's wide-eyed stare met his. His hand closed around her wrist with a vehement snarl. He jerked her toward him, pressed her back against his chest. His arm folded over her throat.

It seemed he squeezed the very breath from her lungs. The syringe, still a quarter full, hovered only inches from her neck.

"Sweet heaven, don't hurt her," Father Donovan rasped, his features ashen. He struggled to rise.

"Stay where you are!" Landry shouted and backed toward the door, dragging Hannah with him.

"Please! Take me instead!" he pleaded.

A sob rose within Hannah. Sister Evangeline's expression was stricken with despair; her lips moved in frantic prayer.

The club swung in a menacing arc. "Anyone comes after us, she gets injected, too. Hear me?"

And then, too soon, they were out of the infirmary, past the barred wall and in the darkened hall. The stench assailed her nostrils, the clamor from the frenzied code of desperate men all too aware of mutiny pounded in her ears, and she became a part of the awful horror in this penitentiary.

Suddenly, Landry halted and went still. From the shadows loomed the scar-faced Titus. He drew upon them with great, lumbering steps, and Landry heaved the end of the club into the guard's belly. The unsuspecting man doubled over with a grunt and sprawled backwards.

Landry kept moving. Hannah's hand came up and clutched his forearm for balance. Her sandals made poor shoes for running, and it was all she could do to keep them on her feet. Still, he propelled her forward at a rapid pace, his body pushing hers to move faster, faster past the underground cells to the end of the murky hall.

A door blocked their escape. Amazingly, he released her, using both hands to ram the club against the lock. Hannah spun, lifted her skirts to flee, but before she could escape him, he had her in his grip again.

His forearm pressed against her throat; his body pressed her against the wall. The syringe flashed before her, close, appallingly close, and she froze.

"Don't try that again," he hissed. "I'll kill you. I swear it."

His tight grasp allowed her no response. Her heart thudded in her breast. She couldn't breathe.

A rumble of voices reached them from the direction of the infirmary.

"Damn." He stepped back and snared her wrist, jerking her in front of him, pushing her toward the door, its lock now destroyed.

Pam Crooks

He gave the door a swift kick. It crashed open, and they rushed through, leaving the darkness of the penitentiary for the darkness of the night. A sliver of moonlight illuminated the prison grounds, highlighting a courtyard surrounded by plain wooden buildings.

Hannah sucked clean air into her lungs. Landry broke into a run, pulling her behind him, his long legs a full stride ahead of hers. The sandals slipped and slid. Her ankle turned, and she gasped in pain.

They reached a storage building to the left of the courtyard. Landry fell back against it. His muscular forearm encircled her again.

"Please," Hannah said, her chest heaving. "Go without me."

A cynical laugh left him, his breath hot on her cheek. "I don't think so, darlin'." Moonlight glinted on the needle's tip, scant inches from her chin. "You're in this with me to the end."

"I'll only slow you down." She hated the desperation in her tone. "I'll hide here. I won't tell them which way you went. I promise."

"Don't play me for a fool." Menace laced the whispered threat. The syringe dipped closer.

Hannah bit her lip.

He peered around the edge of the building. The courtyard was silent. He turned back to her. "See that rig over there?"

Her glance stretched across a large open area, a rock quarry where the inmates worked, and settled upon the black shape of a carriage, complete with a waiting team of horses.

"Fenwick's," he said. "We're gonna make a run for it."

26

"I can't." A dull ache claimed her ankle. Any minute, the courtyard would fill with angry guards and an even angrier warden. Her sandals were a curse.

"You will."

"Don't make me do this."

"Quit whining."

She clamped her mouth shut. She hated him, and it'd been a very long time since she'd hated anyone.

"Briggs doesn't give a damn about you." His words, cold and unfeeling, locked around her. "It's me he wants. And if you're killed in the chase, you're just one less person to keep him from his blood money. Y'hear me?"

She glared at him.

"Take these off." He bent and ripped off her sandals, one and then the other, and shoved them at her. "You'll run better."

She glanced downward. He wore no shoes, either, only filthy cotton socks. The rocky ground would be torture. Despair washed over her.

"Let's go." He took her wrist again, pulled her with him out of the shadows and into the wide expanse of the deserted quarry. He ran like a man driven by lunacy, with no regard for the pain from stones jutting into the soles of their feet, for the risks they were taking, for the consequences he would pay if they should get caught.

Hannah struggled to keep up. Landry kept her moving from the sheer force of his speed, and it was only because of him they reached the carriage without her falling.

Nestled between a pair of detached buildings used as workshops for the inmates, the rig stood in readiness, ripe for the taking. Landry half-pushed, half-lifted her into the driver's seat.

He heaved himself in next to her, his long body crowding her. She smelled his heat, his sweat, his urgency.

"Take the reins!" he hissed. His chest rose and fell, his breathing hard, labored. Perspiration rolled off his temples.

Fenwick's Solution had begun taking its toll.

A shot rang out. She flinched. The bullet winged by and slammed into the side of the building with a muffled thud.

The team of horses, two fine blacks, lifted their heads and whinnied in alarm.

"Take the reins!" Landry dived for them at the same time she did, his hands closing over hers as she fumbled to unwrap the lines from around the brake. Terror gripped her, a very real fear of getting killed in this terrible place, under these circumstances, and all because of this crazed man.

She wasn't ready to die. Not for him. Glory, she'd come too far for that.

She grasped the reins and slapped the horses' backs. Landry gripped them, too, and the carriage took off hard, fast, tossing her back against the leather seat, knocking her wimple askew.

"Turn 'em!" Landry snarled and jerked the leathers, his fading strength still superior to hers. The rig careened in a tight turn, throwing him into her shoulder, and she braced herself for both of them lest they tumble out the other side.

The pull of the reins strained the muscles in her forearms. If not for Landry, the team would have followed their own lead, and she'd have circled the quarry, blind to the one narrow passageway that would let them out.

From somewhere in the darkness, men yelled. Another shot rang out. And still another.

Hannah's blood ran cold. She feared the bullets that could pelt her body at any moment. The team picked up speed, bolting like twin arrows toward the opening. She hung onto the reins with a death grip, to save her own life and Landry's, and, finally, the carriage hurtled past the penitentiary walls.

They were free. The horses found their stride, their harnesses jangling in the wind, their iron hooves pounding the rough ground in brisk staccato. The dark night surrounded them in all its silence.

Landry loosened his hold on the reins and fell back against the seat. His eyes closed; the strength seemed to ebb from his body. Their escape had cost him.

But not as much as it had Hannah.

Her life had taken a terrible turn. This savage named Landry had stolen everything from her: Sister Evangeline, Father Donovan, her haven in the convent. He'd torn apart her tidy, cloistered world.

Her glance slid toward him. His lean fingers encircled the stout club. His weapon. As terrifying as the syringe. He kept them both in readiness. He kept her, too, at his mercy. Using her as he used his weapons.

Panic rose within her, stifling and suffocating.

She wasn't safe anymore.

Chapter Three

The night sucked them in, swallowed them whole, and Hannah feared she'd never get out again.

The carriage raced deep into New Mexico Territory, so deep she lost her direction, so deep all sense of time and tenuous hope vanished. Her arms grew numb from their tight-fisted grip on the reins, and when she would have pleaded a stop to the wild ride, Landry barked a command to drive the team faster, harder.

The terrain changed, swelled into hills. The rig lurched and stumbled over jutting rocks. Juniper trees sprouted thick and tall, their needle-laden branches gouging the perfectly painted sides of Fenwick's carriage, now sorely abused and covered with dust.

The horses labored in their climb, making their own trail over land not suited for an easy ride. Their sides heaved with the effort, their breathing heavy pants, their hides drenched with sweat.

Somehow, through the canopy of darkness and foliage, they found their way into a small clearing. Froth bubbled from their mouths. Hannah ventured an uneasy glance toward Landry. Forcing the weary animals to go further would kill them.

"Stop here," he ordered.

Relieved, Hannah reined the team to a halt. Their noses lowered to the ground, and for the first time since their frenzied escape from the penitentiary, their harnesses fell silent.

"Get out." Landry's command sounded forced through his clenched teeth. With what looked to be a herculean effort, he pulled himself forward, swung one leg over the side of the rig, and nearly tumbled into a heap in the dirt. He clung to the edge of the seat.

She held her breath. He righted himself, his movements awkward, as if he could hardly will his muscles to work. In the end, he managed it, and leaning heavily against the carriage, he stood.

Hannah stared, her heart beating in trepidation of what he intended. She didn't yet know what he was capable of, only that he was desperate, a madman in the grips of Fenwick's Solution, and she had never been so vulnerable, a defenseless woman alone with him in the middle of nowhere.

Muted hues of moon-silver glimmered downward from the treetops, sheathing him in a faint light. His gaze lowered to his hand, balled tight in a fist. His breathing rasped in the silence, and his fingers loosened, revealing the syringe in his palm.

His glance lifted to hers. Alarm burst within her, a new fear of the awful weapon he used to hold her hostage.

His teeth bared in a snarl, and she drew back, a cry

escaping her. He spun around, away from her, and hurled the syringe into the blackness, freeing himself, freeing her, of all that was left of Fenwick's Solution.

Then, Landry swayed and crumpled to his knees. The club rolled from his grasp, and he retched hard, violently, into the weeds. He groaned and retched again and again.

Hannah's pulse drummed in her ears. Slowly, she slid to the end of the carriage seat and peered over the edge. She steeled herself against his agony.

Whatever his past sins, he paid dearly for them now. He heaved in mighty breaths, as if he feared each one his last. His hands clenched in protest at the indignity which left him helpless.

Helpless.

Hannah slipped to the ground and slid her sandals onto her feet. She took a step back, then another. Lifting her skirt hems high, she pivoted and bolted from the clearing, plunging into the black night made even blacker by the congestion of pine trees and foliage.

Stinging needles plucked at her face and habit. She flung aside the branches in her path. Spikes of pain shot through her tender ankle, but she ignored them, too intent on finding her way down hill after hill, past tree after tree, away from Landry and Fenwick's carriage.

Her lungs burned. She despaired over her troublesome sandals. Where was the path they'd taken, wide enough for the rig to pass through? Renewed panic flared deep within her breast. Nothing seemed familiar.

The toe of her sandal clipped a tree root, and she hurtled to the rocky ground and banged her knee. The air left her lungs with a whoosh.

A sob wrenched from her throat, and she gave in to

a rush of hot tears. She didn't want to be here, didn't want to be lost and frightened. She hadn't wanted to go to the horrible penitentiary in the first place, and if it hadn't been for Mother Superior's test of her calling—

Her tears slowed.

Glory. The test.

She couldn't fathom how or why she had been chosen for a trial of this magnitude. She knew only she must not fail; she must be strong; she must prove she was indeed worthy of the name 'Sister Ariel', and with it, a life of safety and solitude in the convent.

In her self-pity, she'd forgotten about Pa. Her heart ached. He never tolerated self-pity when times were tough, and God knew they'd had *plenty* of tough times. Instead, he'd taught her to think of a better plan.

Using the cuff of her brown wool sleeve, she swiped the last of the tears from her cheeks. She pressed a fervent kiss to the wooden cross about her neck. Her head cleared. She stood, straightened her wimple and brushed at the pine needles clinging to her habit.

A stream gently babbled nearby. She squatted at the edge, dipped her hands into the cold water, and pressed them to her face.

She'd left Landry at his weakest, too weak to be a threat to her now. He wouldn't survive the ravages of Fenwick's Solution much longer.

She'd go back to him. He deserved to die with a degree of dignity, with someone at his side. Afterward, she'd find her way back to the convent. Mother Superior would be frantic with worry.

Bolstered by the plan, Hannah soaked the lower front of her habit in the stream and wrung out the excess water. Holding the wet fabric in her hand lest it drag in the dirt and leaves, she wound her way amongst the juniper trees and climbed the hills again.

She found him much as she'd left him—on the ground in a heap.

The vomiting had stopped, but Landry lay so motionless Hannah feared he'd died already. She approached him slowly, silently, regret building within her that she'd not returned soon enough.

She knelt beside him and detected a slight movement, his back lifting when he took in a breath, and she knew he lived, but just barely.

Still, she delayed touching him, his ruthlessness, his savagery, still too fresh in her memory. She'd not forgotten he threatened to kill her.

But the poison in Fenwick's Solution weakened him. Stole his strength, his power, and for now, at least, he was unable to kill anyone. Including her. Mustering her courage, she grasped his shoulder with both hands and rolled him onto his back.

He groaned, her name slipping from him on a labored breath. Perspiration streamed off his forehead. His eyes remained closed.

"I'm here," she said quietly and pressed the wet portion of her skirt to his cheeks and temples. Heat emanated from him.

He shivered. She worked to cool the fever, running the wool over his face and neck, until she could do little more than wait for his time to come. He moaned and shivered again. She unclasped her cloak and spread it over him, tucking the edges snugly about his long body.

He slept heavily. She rose and tended the horses; afterward, she explored the interior of the carriage and found nothing more than an umbrella, a locked metal box and a thick blanket. She pulled the wrapping around her shoulders and returned to Landry.

Death hovered over him. She sat near him and drew her knees up to her chest. She'd been witness to a man dying only once before in her life, and then, it'd been Pa. The horror of the memory still lingered, the violence, the awful sense of failure she endured when she'd been unable to help him.

And now she couldn't help Landry.

She tilted her head back and gazed up into the black sky. Stars sprinkled the night. The cold air nipped her nose and cheeks; in the distance, a coyote howled. The yipping sound sent quivers of unease down her spine.

Desolation settled over her. She fretted for Father Donovan. For Sister Evangeline. She hoped they'd left the prison by now and were safe back at the convent, that they didn't worry for her overmuch, and that they prayed diligently for her return.

Surely they'd done all those things.

Hannah grasped her rosary beads, seeking the peace she needed, but her own prayers wouldn't come. Not this time. Nothing could give her solace after the horrific events of the night, and she huddled into a tight ball, taking what warmth and comfort she could from the folds of Fenwick's blanket.

"Hannah! Wake up!"

She clawed through the depths of a fitful sleep.

A large hand clasped her shoulder and gave her a rough shake. She made a protesting sound and curled into a tighter ball.

35

Pam Crooks

"Get up. The dogs are coming," Landry said hoarsely.

The events of the past night rushed to her brain. Her eyes flew open.

She scrambled to sit up and blinked at him in the morning sun. Confusion swarmed through her that he still lived when she'd been so sure he'd die.

He tossed aside the cloak and pushed himself to his knees.

"Briggs." He swayed, as if his world was spinning. "He's got the dogs after us."

Only then did she hear the barking, frenzied and thick. A whole pack, it seemed. Her heart lurched.

"Oh, no," she breathed in terror. It was all her fault. She'd tumbled down the hill, then walked back up again. Her scent would lead Briggs right to them.

She swung a horrified glance through the trees. The dogs sounded closer.

"Get up." Landry reached for his club. Beneath several days of dark stubble, his skin was deathly pale. He managed to stand.

"What can we do?" she asked.

"Make a run for it." He took her blanket and cloak and tossed them both in Fenwick's rig.

How could he flee in his condition?

"We can take the carriage," she said quickly.

"There's no time." He unhobbled the horses, slapped each one on the rump. They bolted away.

He was right. It'd take too long to hitch the team; the dense growth of trees would only hinder their escape, and the rig would be an easy target for any animal.

For Briggs.

She hastened to her feet. Landry leaned heavily on the club and gripped her wrist, whether to keep her near or to use her for support, she wasn't sure.

"This way," he said.

They fled up the hill, zigzagged their way from the carriage, dodged the rocks and tree roots and jutting branches. They climbed and climbed, until the thin air stole their breaths, until Landry couldn't go any farther.

He fell against a tree, wrapping an arm around the trunk to hold himself up. Sweat rolled off him, soaking the thin fabric of his prison uniform.

"We'll never make it," he panted.

Hannah fought a wave of panic. Landry was shoeless and weak. He didn't have a chance for escape. The odds were against him.

Against her.

"We can split up," she said. "I'm stronger. I can lead them away from you."

"No." His hard gaze darkened over her. "We're not separating."

"I can delay the warden."

"The dogs are trained to kill. You wouldn't have a chance in hell."

The barking reached them, the frenzied pitch growing in intensity with every heartbeat. She tossed a furtive glance through the maze of junipers below, and there, in the clearing they'd left only moments before, the pack broke through.

Five, maybe six, dogs. Wild. Frantic. Part wolf, part mongrel, pawing the area with great agitation, their noses to the ground, their red-brown bodies taut from the stimulation of the scents she and Landry had left behind.

Hannah stared.

Landry swore.

One dog burst from the pack and loped up the hill toward them. Hannah sucked in a breath. Landry bettered his grip on the club.

"Take your veil off," he ordered and stepped away from the tree.

Hannah hurried to dismantle it, her fingers fumbling in their haste to find the pins holding the chin strap and wimple together. The linen fell away with the brown wool.

The wolf-dog was nearly upon them. Hannah cried out in terror. At the sound of her voice, the animal halted, his slanted, yellow eyes finding them both. With a vicious snarl, he broke into a full run, slashed the distance between them.

Landry was ready for him and swung the club. The beast lunged and caught it between his teeth, his growls raging, the sharp points of his fangs embedded deep into the wood.

Landry gripped the weapon with both hands. The creature swung a sharp-clawed paw and caught Landry's forearm with the swipe. His uniform ripped open, and long rows of bright crimson erupted on his skin.

Hannah's pulse pounded.

"Throw him the veil!" Landry bit out.

She tossed it toward the dog. The fabric fanned out and splayed over him, covering his head and furred body. For an instant, he faltered at the trap.

The club fell from his lethal jaws. He swung his head back and forth amidst a new round of frenzied snarling, his paws working to free himself from the blinding wool.

Landry's fingers snatched hers, and they sprinted toward a wide ribbon of water grooving the land, a feeder from the Pecos River. He pulled her into the stream with him. The cold water swirled around her ankles, her shins. The freezing depths stole her breath.

She stumbled, falling to her knees with a splash. The brown wool soaked up more water, tangled between her legs. He pulled her upright again, and she trudged onward, her skirts heavy and awkward, her ankle aching, her nerves at the breaking point.

"Got to rest," Landry huffed.

He stumbled, too, but caught himself before he fell. She knew sheer adrenaline kept him moving, but he couldn't go on much longer. She feared he'd keel over dead, right here in the water.

A willow tree grew outward from the bank, its roots dangling naked from the earth and hanging into the water. Long branches leaned toward them. Landry grasped the strongest and hooked his arm around it, keeping himself upright.

A man's shout reached them. Landry pulled her with him closer to the muddy bank. Hannah strained to see through the branches.

Their vantage point provided a clear view of the valley below. The wolf-dog freed himself from her veil and yapped and growled at the warden's arrival. Briggs reined his horse to a hard stop, the coiled cat o'nine tails in his hand. The whip cracked across the dog's flanks; he yelped and limped away.

Briggs stared at the ground. Retrieving his rifle from the scabbard, he leaned over the side of the horse and scooped up the length of brown wool from the ground with the barrel. He studied the fabric, shredded beyond repair from the wolf-dog's assault.

Hannah's heart hammered. Briggs stood in the stirrups and twisted about, his gaze probing the hillside, his features harsh even in the distance. Another man rode up beside him.

She recognized Titus, the scar-faced guard from the penitentiary. They spoke together and scanned the area again. The warden pointed toward the stream.

Landry pressed her roughly into the bank and clamped a hand over her mouth, his fierce expression warning complete silence. The horses galloped to the water's edge and halted.

"They're around here somewhere," Briggs said. "They ain't had time to go far."

"The dogs picked up their scents pretty strong. Where do you reckon they'd head for?"

"Damned if I know. Could be anywhere."

"Yeah." Titus swore in annoyance. "Landry's gotta be hurtin' bad by now. He ain't gonna be able to run much longer."

A match struck flint; the smell of sulfur reached Hannah's nostrils.

"Trouble-makin' sonovabitch," Brigg's spat. "No one escapes from my prison and gets away with it."

Hannah shivered at the venom in his tone. A taut savagery radiated from Landry, his hate for Briggs evident.

"No one 'cept that Mexican a few years back," Titus said, exhaling smoke. "That band of his cut him loose, but clean."

Briggs fell silent, as if he just now recalled the incident. " 'Ceptin' him, Landry's the first to escape and by God, he'll be the last."

Leather creaked, protesting Titus's shift in the saddle. "Jesus, you didn't have to shoot that priest and nun dead, Briggs," he said, his tone heavy with reproval, with disgust. "They wasn't doin' nothin' wrong."

. . . shoot that priest and nun dead . . .

Dead. Father Donovan and Sister Evangeline.

The words swam in Hannah's brain, thundered inside her breast.

Dear God.

Her knees buckled in horror. Tears sprang to her eyes, and she sagged against Landry. His grip tightened over her mouth.

"They was tryin' to escape!" Briggs snapped.

"Hell. They was just tryin' to get to their rig. Maybe they was gonna try to help that nun Landry took with him."

"And maybe they was goin' after the sheriff."

Titus grunted. "Maybe."

"They knew too much anyways." The warden's voice turned hard. "Fenwick's newfangled drug was secret. He was goin' to get rich off it when his experimentin' was done. And it'd be *my* ass the prison inspectors would come after for lettin' him do it."

"You wasn't complainin' when he gave you that purse full of gold coin."

"Shut up, Titus." A cigarette stub arced in the air and landed in the water with a tiny plop.

"So now what?"

"So we tell everyone that other nun shot 'em. That she was in cahoots with Landry and helpin' him make his getaway."

41

" 'Cept for Fenwick, ain't no one around to say different."

"She's gonna pay for what she did to me," Briggs said bitterly, reminding Hannah of how she'd hit him with the jar of preserves. "Maybe we'll get lucky, and Landry'll kill her for us."

"Sonovabitch was in for murder. Killin' a nun ain't no different than killin' his brother's wife."

Murder.

Hannah's chest heaved. The nightmare whirled around her.

"We'll stake out the convent in case she goes back." Menace dripped from the warden's tone. "Besides Landry, she's the only one outside the prison who knows about the experimentin'. She'll squeal for sure."

"Yeah."

"Landry ain't going to want to live when I catch up with him," Briggs snarled. "That's for damn sure."

"Unless that poison Fenwick calls his miracle drug got him first."

A faint whinny from horses in the distance followed the grim comment. The men's conversation halted. Saddle leather creaked again.

"There. On the ridge." Titus pointed.

"Fenwick's horses. And no riders. Ain't that strange."

"Anyone with a lick of sense would take them fine animals and hightail it clear into Texas. Landry must be too sick to care."

"Or dead." Briggs scowled.

" 'Cept we ain't found no body."

"Damn it, Titus, I know that!" the warden shouted. "Now you just let me worry about Landry's carcass and you get those dogs together so we can keep movin'!"

"Don't yell at me, Briggs," Titus warned, his tone ominous.

A moment passed, as if the warden strove to control his temper. "Look, Titus, on top of all the other problems he's causin' me, Landry lost me a helluva lot of money when he broke out. No one wants his body found more than me. 'Cept maybe Fenwick. Y'hear?"

"Yeah, I hear you. Just don't yell at me." His boots jabbed the stirrups. "You leavin' the rig behind?"

"If Fenwick wants it, he can get it himself. Let's go."

Bridles jangled, and horse hooves pelted the ground as they descended the hill, the sounds receding into the distance. Landry cautiously released his grip on Hannah's mouth and straightened.

Hannah stared dully through the branches. The cat o'nine tails cracked, and the pack of wolf-dogs dashed ahead of the two men. Soon, they moved out of sight and earshot, and once again, the hills were silent.

"Let's get out of this damned water," Landry muttered. He stepped away from her and sloshed through the stream, his stride heavy, weary.

She held back and fought a wave of hysteria.

"Did you murder your brother's wife?" she demanded.

He turned and faced her. A lock of dark hair had fallen over his forehead. He needed a shave, a hot bath, a fresh change of clothes. He looked every bit a ruthless murderer.

His black eyes glittered over her; his features unfathomable. "She's dead. They said I did it."

"Did you?"

43

A corner of his hard mouth lifted. "Under the circumstances, does it matter?"

"To me it does."

"And if I told you the truth, what would you do then?"

She wanted to scream at him, to pummel her fists against his chest. "I have a right to know."

A muscle moved in his jaw. For a long moment, he didn't speak, as if he delved into the nightmares in his past.

"To hell with my guilt or innocence," he said finally. "I have a score to settle. And I won't die until it's done."

Chapter Four

His resolve chilled her more than the water swirling around her legs. He turned and made his way to the bank. He didn't look to see if she followed.

What score did he have to settle? Would he murder again?

She stabbed a glance downstream. A wild, insane desire to flee him gripped her. She could run after Briggs and Titus and convince them she had nothing to do with Landry's past or future. She could be free of him *now*, this minute.

But she couldn't, of course. Briggs had killed two of the kindest people she'd ever known. He would kill her, too.

And as she stood in the water, a part of her died. The foolish part that had hoped she'd be safe for the rest of her days. In its place, her own past came to life, with all its guilt and dark complexities and the skills Pa had taught her to survive.

Any way she knew how.

The warden had closed off her avenues of escape. Wanted for the deaths of a priest and young nun, she was a woman on the run now, no better than Landry. It was so ridiculous. And unfair. Hot tears of frustration welled in her eyes.

Mother Superior alone knew of Hannah's past, of her crimes. Would she believe Briggs's claim that Hannah partnered with Landry at the penitentiary, that she'd killed to survive?

How could she believe otherwise? Hannah's sins were . . . innumerable. Her past was . . . abominable.

Hannah swallowed hard. She must tell the abbess the truth, that she hurt for the loss of Father Donovan and Sister Evangeline as much as the rest of them. She had to go back to the convent and convince Mother Superior the warden had lied.

But Briggs and Titus would be waiting for her to do just that.

She vowed to find a way. Somehow, she had to prove her innocence. And only one man could help her do it.

Landry.

He hauled himself out of the stream and collapsed onto the ground face down. Resolute, Hannah followed.

She stood over him with her skirts dripping onto the winter grass. She nudged him with the toe of her sandal, then nudged him again, harder.

He rolled over and glowered at her through bloodshot eyes.

"Did you hear what the warden said?" she asked, the words a rasping demand.

His eyes closed again. "I heard him."

"I've done nothing wrong."

He gave no response.

"Do you hear me? Nothing."

Still, he ignored her.

In a fit of pique, she bent over and grasped him by the shirt front. "Damn you! Listen to me!"

His eyes opened. His skin had grown ashen. She released him just before he twisted to his side to retch, his stomach empty but his body still heaving from the devastating drug.

She bit her lip and resisted the sympathy building inside her. When the vomiting ended, he fell heavily back against the ground. Perspiration dampened his hair into ringlets against his forehead. His chest rose and fell in labored breathing.

Hannah stepped to the water's edge and re-soaked her skirt hems. Kneeling beside him, she slipped an arm beneath his dark head.

"Drink, Mr. Landry," she said and squeezed the wool in her palm. The water trickled into his mouth, and he swallowed. The heat of his raging fever touched her skin through the sleeve of her habit.

"You need a doctor," she said and dabbed at his temples with the cool fabric.

His gaze clashed with hers. "No."

"You're very sick. You'll—"

He grasped her wrist hard, his strength still evident despite the drug's effects. "We keep moving. No matter what. Y'hear me?"

"You'll die without help. There's nothing I can do for you."

He released her. "I'll live."

"For what? A life on the run? To forever look over

your shoulder for Briggs and his pack of dogs?"

"I have a score to settle," he said with a growl.

"A score." Her lip curled. "We'll see."

He watched her closely but said nothing. She withdrew her arm and stood.

Hannah perused the distant hills and worked the plan in her brain. She faced him again and took pleasure in looking down at him.

"You need me, Mr. Landry. You've hardly the strength of a newborn pup, but you're hunted by men who will shoot you dead. It's only a matter of time before they find you."

His glazed eyes bored into her. He waited.

"And I need you." It galled her to say the words. "You're the only one who can prove my innocence against the warden's lies."

"So?"

"We make a deal."

"A deal."

"Your life for mine."

His brow arched in wary surprise.

"I'll help you survive, and God willing, you'll settle your score. And you . . ." Her words trailed off.

"What, Hannah? What do you expect of me?" he taunted.

She hadn't thought it'd be so difficult to swallow her pride and rely upon a man of Landry's caliber. But she was desperate, and she had no one else.

"I expect you to return to the convent with me and help me to convince Mother Superior I haven't killed anyone."

His eyes closed. "What if I refuse?"

He was toying with her. She thought of Pa and all she'd learned from him.

"Do not underestimate me, Mr. Landry," she said softly.

He swiveled his harsh gaze over her once more. "Nor you me, Hannah."

A long moment passed between them. She refused to be the first to speak.

"Regardless of what you think, I'm a man of my word," he said finally. "We have a deal."

She kept her relief bottled inside her. "Thank you."

"But if you betray me, you'll pay the price. I swear it."

"I'm no fool, Mr. Landry."

He scowled at that. "And from now on, call me Quinn."

His command took her by surprise. "Under the circumstances, I hardly think it proper to be on a first name basis."

"You heard me."

"I refuse to call you anything else but Landry."

"It's been four years since anyone has used my given name." Bitterness seeped through his proclamation. "Call me Quinn, Hannah."

Her rebellion lingered, but she fought it down. She understood his desire and would do as he asked. But she had a rule of her own.

"My name is Sister Ariel," she said. It didn't matter she'd not quite earned the honor, that she had months of study and prayer and devotion ahead of her when she returned to the convent. After what she'd been through, the issue was moot. "You're not to call *me* anything else. Agreed?"

Pam Crooks

Something flickered within the fever-bright depths of his eyes. Amusement?

"The priest called you Hannah."

"He's—was—my friend. You're not."

"Sister Ariel is a mouthful. I prefer Hannah."

"What you prefer doesn't matter, Mr. Landry."

His head turned. His lids closed. "Are you always so stubborn and narrow-minded, Hannah?"

Irritation shot through her. She'd not exchange another word with him. She pivoted with a flare of her wool skirts. His eyes flew open again.

"Where're you going?" he said with a growl, snatching a fistful of material, halting her.

"To find the horses," she said.

"And then?"

"Re-hitch them to the carriage."

Skepticism flitted over his pale features. "A tough job for a woman by herself."

"I think I can manage easier than you."

His expression darkened, as if the truth in her words reminded him all over again how Fenwick's Solution had plundered his strength, and he resented it more than ever.

"If you try to escape me," he said, the words cold with warning. "I'll find you. And you'd best hope it's me who finds you first. Before Briggs and Titus. Or the wolf-dogs."

She suppressed a shiver, refused to give him the pleasure of knowing she dreaded another encounter with any of them.

"One more thing."

She waited, her back straight, her chin tilted high.

"I'm sorry about your friends." His voice was low,

50

rough. "It was a helluva way for them to die."

Instant tears sprang to her eyes. Her throat clogged with emotion. For their loss. For his unexpected expression of civility. For the genuineness of his sympathy.

She blinked rapidly and made no reply. Abruptly, he released her skirt.

"The horses are at the stream," he said. "They should be easy enough to fetch."

She managed a jerky nod and impatiently swiped at a stubborn tear. She glanced over her shoulder. The animals drank at the water's edge and grazed on the grass lining the bank.

"I'll be back as soon as I can," she said stiffly and headed toward the horses, the absurdity of her reassurance ringing in her ears. She was now captive to her own promise.

By the time Hannah returned to the bank with the carriage properly harnessed and ready for travel, the sun shone warm and bright in the sky. Quinn Landry lay in the same spot she had left him, in an exhausted sleep and oblivious to her arrival. Mindful of her sore ankle, she dismounted from the buggy with care and studied him quietly.

Whatever tasks he performed in the penitentiary had obviously required great strength. His uniform molded to his legs, outlining the corded muscles of his thighs. Though lean and spare, his body showed agility and power—even when ravaged by Fenwick's Solution. Her gaze travelled upward and halted over that part of him which bulged, boldly proclaiming his masculinity.

Her pulse fluttered. It'd been so long since she'd

looked at a man, thought of his privates. She detested the blush this one evoked from her.

She steered her perusal to safer ground—higher ground—skimming over his flat belly and settling on the breadth of his shoulders. Dark hairs curled over the collar of his shirt, hinting at a chest similarly covered. She quickly chased the appealing image from her thoughts.

In rest, his features hinted of a handsome man, an impression shadowed by several days growth of beard and a harshness from his time in the penitentiary. His hand still clutched the club, the other rested palm up in the grass. His fingers curled loosely, relaxed. The gashes on his forearm reared up ugly against his sun-baked skin.

They must pain him. She remembered again the risks he'd taken to deter the raging wolf-dog. Her glance swept the hills for a sign of Briggs—a horse on the horizon, a glint off a rifle barrel—and found nothing. Her instincts told her for now, at least, they were safe.

She sank to the grass beside him. Landry rolled over and moaned. She watched him dubiously, but he made no other sound. His eyes remained closed, and he lay very still. She'd give him a few more minutes to rest.

In the ensuing quiet, she soaked in the sun's warmth and removed her sandals, then rolled down her thick cotton stockings. Her fingers prodded the swelling about her ankle, and she grimaced, but the injury could have been worse. She wiggled her bare toes, reddened but growing warmer, and placed the stockings side by side in the grass with their garters.

A soft breeze tousled the hair at her temples. So odd not to wear a veil, she mused, yet she relished the feel and raked her fingers through the short curls.

Mother Superior herself had chopped off Hannah's long tresses, thick and shining and the color of auburn. If Pa had seen the cutting, he would've been heartbroken. Hannah admitted seeing the heap of strands on the floor all those months ago was difficult. Her hair had been her one concession to vanity.

But she'd adjusted. Wearing a veil and wimple stole away the desire to fuss over its short length. It was ironic that a man like Landry would be the first to see her bareheaded in nearly a year.

Irritation followed the reminder of the abrupt change her life had taken because of him. Along with it, a renewed impatience to take back all she'd worked so hard to attain.

"Quinn," she said and reached over to give him a little shake. "It's time to go."

At her touch, his body jerked and coiled, like a cobra, ready to strike. He turned glazed eyes on her, as if he didn't really see her, as if he still remained in a darker world.

"Quinn, it's only me," she said gently.

At the sound of her voice, a long breath escaped his lungs, an expulsion of the demons lurking inside him. "God, Hannah."

"I'm sorry I startled you."

"I thought—I was sure—"

"It's okay." She didn't know what tortured him, but clearly his life in the penitentiary hadn't been pleasant. Did Briggs haunt him? His own guilty conscience?

Or Fenwick's Solution?

She preferred to think it was the sickness he battled, not the memories of a murderer.

Pam Crooks

"How do you feel?" she asked after a long moment.

"Lousy."

"Is there something I can do?"

He glanced at her, his lids heavy with fatigue.

"My belly's tied in knots. My head's 'bout ready to explode. And I'm on fire from fever. If you can think of somethin', then do it."

Hannah stiffened at his cross response. He hardly deserved her concern.

She remembered seeing a canteen on the floor of the carriage and left him to get it. After a thorough rinse in the stream, she filled the container with clear, cold water and offered him a drink. He sucked the liquid down like a man parched and seemed to feel better for it.

When it appeared he'd not up-end his stomach again, she moved away to refill the canteen, but he caught her bare foot in his grasp. His frowning gaze skimmed over her injured ankle.

"How did this happen?" he asked.

"It's nothing," she answered and tried to wrest her leg from him.

He kept his clasp firm, yet took care not to touch the swelling. "You've sprained it."

"Yes," she agreed and finally pulled free. "At the penitentiary."

"You should have told me."

She rolled her eyes. "After the way you'd treated me?"

He scowled. "I've yet to hurt you."

"But you'd like to, wouldn't you?" One by one, his threats over the past hours marched through her memory.

54

He eyed her, the look of the devil in his eyes. "I don't make a habit of abusing women." He paused, baiting her. "Most of the time."

A vexed huff escaped her. She plucked her sandals and stockings from the grass and pulled them on. "You're a horrid man, Quinn Landry."

"Yeah, well. You'd best get used to it."

Another huff left her, this one less irate. "It seems fate has given me little choice, doesn't it?"

Without waiting to hear another of his mocking taunts, she filled the canteen to the brim, screwed the lid on tight, and turned to find him struggling to stand. He swayed, tried to catch his balance, and she hastened to help him lest he fall. She was of no mind to set a broken bone along with everything else that ailed him.

"I suggest, Mr. Landry, that you go easy until you have your strength back."

He made a sound of impatience. "I have matters to attend to."

His arm hooked around her shoulders. She braced her feet to take his weight, her own arm curling around his waist. His body leaned heavily against hers.

"Did you never learn revenge is a sin?" she demanded, tilting her head back to challenge him. Up close, his unshaven cheeks gave him the look of a pirate, ruthless and dangerous. The stench of the prison lingered on him.

"Revenge is what keeps me alive," he said with a growl.

She clucked her tongue and urged him to the carriage. "It will kill you. And me along with you."

"I aim to see that it doesn't."

He heaved himself into the driver's seat and collapsed against the tufted leather cushion. Hannah crawled up beside him, shook out the blanket and spread it over him. After taking the reins, she paused, the uncertainty of the future looming before her.

She'd become a pawn in Quinn's quest to settle a bitter score, a game piece he used to get what he wanted, uncaring of the cost to her safety or the loss of her refuge at the convent.

But she would see an end to their bargain and survive Mother Superior's test in the process. Her grip tightened on the reins.

"Where are we going?" she asked.

For a long minute, he didn't answer. She sensed he worked through the revenge in his heart, nurtured it, savored it.

"Follow the Pecos River," he said finally. "We're going to Amarillo."

They travelled the rest of the morning and all afternoon, until the air cooled and the horses grew tired, until Hannah's stomach rumbled persistent reminders she'd not eaten all that day and very little the one before.

She tried not to think of the two friends she'd lost in death. Instead she centered her thoughts on Briggs and his determination to hunt Quinn and herself down, and the consequences they'd endure should he find them.

Though the New Mexico Territory numbered few in population, word would spread quickly about the penitentiary breakout and killings. It wouldn't be long before the whole countryside was up in arms looking for them both. Even more worrisome, her wool habit and Quinn's tattered uniform were dead giveaways.

Her glance slid to him. Burrowed under the blanket, his body rocking in time with the carriage, he slept again, trusting her to take him in the direction he bade. He hadn't exchanged a word with her since they left. Hannah was glad for it. Her troublesome thoughts were enough to keep her mind occupied.

She followed a vague northeasterly course, keeping the Pecos River in sight to find her way, as he'd instructed. But with the sun already resting on the horizon, they had to stop. Cold penetrated her clothing. She longed for a blazing fire and a plate full of hot food. And hours and hours of sleep.

She braked the carriage near a thicket dense enough to shelter them from sight, and dismounted. Quinn stirred, opened one eye and frowned down at her.

Hannah's chin lifted. She knew what he was thinking.

"We've travelled enough for one day," she said firmly. "I'm tired. So are the horses."

"A few more hours," he commanded.

"No." Fatigue, sore muscles and a hungry belly spurred her to refuse him. "I'm not getting back in that rig until morning."

"Hannah." The word rumbled in warning.

"Go if you want." She made a shooing motion, her determination solid. "I'll gladly stay behind. And if you'd like, I'll feed and water the team so you can drive them until they drop." She planted her hands on her hips. "It's up to you."

He glared at her through bloodshot eyes. "A little testy, are we?"

"What'll it be, Mr. Landry? Water the horses? Or hobble them?"

"You're a stubborn woman, Hannah."

He made no further argument, and she knew she'd won this round. Keenly aware of his brooding gaze upon her, she set about unharnessing the team. He tossed aside the blanket and moved from his seat. His hands gripped the edge, the knuckles turning white.

"I can tend the horses myself," she said, watching him, her concern growing.

He pulled forward and swung down to the ground, swayed and caught himself.

"I'm not kin to a woman working while I do . . . nothing," he said through clenched teeth.

"It didn't bother you last night when I tended them alone," she pointed out. "Nor this morning when I hitched them to the rig."

As soon as the words were out, she regretted them. She hadn't meant them to sound so cold.

"I'm sorry." Hannah abandoned the harnesses. "You were as sick then as you are now. I don't mind doing the chores." She reached for the blanket. "Come over here and lie down. The grass is soft enough."

"I'm not a suckling babe, Hannah. I'll help, damn it."

He was as mule-headed as Pa had ever been. "All right, then." She handed him two sets of leather hobbles, the swivel chains clinking. "You can put these on them."

His reproving glance revealed he knew she gave him the easy end of the job, but he took them anyway. Yet his fingers fumbled with the buckles. Sweat beaded his brow.

Watching him, Hannah pondered for the hundredth time how much longer he could survive. Murderer or not, he needed something to eat and care far better than she could give him. They had nothing with which to get through the night except for Fenwick's umbrella, his canteen and blanket, and a black metal box.

The box.

She headed for the carriage. Dusk had settled, tossing long shadows into what sunlight remained. Hannah strained to see inside the rig and leaned in as far as she could, one hand groping behind the driver's seat.

She located the box and found it surprisingly heavy. She gave it a hearty shake, heard the rustling of items inside.

A sturdy lock kept her from the contents. She returned to the rig and searched for the key, her fingers skimming over the floor, up the sides, under the seat.

But, of course, she didn't find one. Fenwick wasn't that stupid.

She sat cross-legged on the ground, the box in front of her. It was made of tempered steel, too solid to jimmy apart without the proper tools. She studied the lock and recognized its make. A set of bar-keys wouldn't work, even if she had them.

But a widdy would.

The knowledge came rushing back in a torrent too powerful to stop, memories of skills she'd learned under her father's watchful eye, tricks she'd vowed never to use again.

But tonight, she had to. To survive.

Hannah returned to the carriage again, retrieved Fenwick's umbrella, and opened it. She bent one of the wires, wiggled it back and forth until the metal snapped, then tossed the umbrella aside.

She sat on the ground again and fashioned a loop on

one end of the wire. All she needed next was a length of fine cord.

She hesitated.

The cord stringing her rosary beads would complete the widdy, but to destroy something so sacred to burglarize another's man's belongings. . . .

Mother Superior would be mortified.

But Hannah assured herself if the abbess were cold and hungry and holed up in the middle of New Mexico Territory with an accused murderer, she'd do the same thing. Surely, this was all part of the test? Finding a way to survive?

Hannah removed the rosary from her waist and broke the cord; the beads slid off into a pile in the grass. She formed a tight knot on the unlooped end of the wire. At last, the widdy was finished.

And it was perfect.

Keenly aware of the deepening cold and rapidly fading light, Hannah slid the knotted end into the lock's mortise. Closing her eyes, she worked the tool, allowed a portion of the cord inside. She felt her way and knew just when to pull the cord taut.

The lock snapped open.

She flipped the box lid up and gazed in wonder at the contents inside: a scattering of gold coins and bills; a miniature bottle of whiskey; a pearl-handled derringer; laudanum; a pocket-knife; cheroots; and a box of matches.

Only then, did Hannah remember it was Christmas night.

Fenwick couldn't have given them finer gifts.

Chapter Five

Hell. He'd fallen into blazing hell.

The terrible inferno raged through his gut, tortured him with pain. Tempted him with death.

He wouldn't die. He tried, but death wouldn't come. Then when it did come close, he fought it with all he had left.

He wasn't finished yet.

His belly retched hard from the poison, over and over again. The agony turned him inside out.

The hell went on. On and on. Forever. Until he couldn't take the fires anymore.

She came to him, at last. Just as before. Saving him when he couldn't save himself.

Her voice was soothing velvet. Satin and silk.

Her touch was cool and gentle. Healing and good.

He listened to her voice, swallowed drops from the little brown bottle. He needed her, and she was there. Comforting him, stroking him.

She was his heaven. Without her, he would die in hell.

And then the pain eased and the fires dwindled and he slept at last.

The poison was gone.

She'd saved him. Again.

Quinn's eyes opened.

Sunlight streamed through the leaves in beaming rays. Snippets of blue sky peeked down through the branches, winking at him, inviting him to celebrate the dawning of the new day.

He lay on his back without moving. A gray-tailed mockingbird chirped a noisy song above him, the tune lively and gay. Quinn waited for the hell to return.

Nothing happened. The drug had run its course.

He drew in a breath and relished the triumph. He expelled the air in his lungs with a grateful sigh.

He'd survived Fenwick's Solution. He'd survived when others had not.

The knowledge humbled him. Invigorated him. For the first time in four long, hard years, he was free.

Free.

He turned his head. Hannah filled his vision. She'd fallen asleep in a sitting position with her knees drawn up to her chest, her head resting on her crossed arms, her wool cloak tight around her.

She was like a brown bird wrapped in all that wool. No bigger than a sparrow. She'd been up most of the night. Because of him, she was exhausted.

Quinn sat up. He took her shoulders, laid her in his place, then covered her with the blanket.

She didn't stir. Long, red tinted lashes rested on her

cheeks. Her skin showed a hint of freckles, the texture smooth. Like satin. His gaze lingered over her mouth.

Hannah, alias Sister Ariel. His suspicions took root. Who was she?

She'd opened the black box with the ease of an experienced thief. Her skill both surprised and troubled him.

He owed his life to this woman, whoever she was. A nun with the talents of a common criminal.

His glance took in the campfire and the crude spit she'd erected. She shot a rabbit with Fenwick's derringer and roasted the thing over the fire.

She, too, was a survivor.

He added more wood to the campfire embers, stoked them until they gave way to flames. The heat would keep her sleeping a little longer.

He headed for the river. The morning air curled around him, seeped through the thin fabric of his prison uniform and chilled his skin. After a night ravaged by fever, he welcomed the cold, filled his lungs with its bite.

Kneeling at the bank, he bent over the water, washed his face and rinsed his mouth. The sun shimmered over him, and he stared at his reflection.

His hair had grown long and shaggy, a tangled mass dirtied from sweat and squalor. A beard roughened his cheeks. His bones were too prominent, his eyes too bitter, his mouth too hard.

Loathing filled him at what he'd become. A wild animal bred beneath Warden Frank Briggs's brutal hand.

A savage.

Christ. He had to rid himself of the horrors of the past, shed the filth and smells layering his body and mind. He peeled off his shirt, shucked his pants, yanked off both socks and plunged full length into the river.

The cold stole his breath, and he came up for air with a loud whoop. Blood pumped through his veins, and he gloried in the rush. He dove in again, swam and scrubbed and emerged from the river clean and refreshed.

Gooseflesh raised on his wet, naked skin. His uniform was nothing more than a pile of tattered rags, and he eyed them with fierce disgust. The cold forced him to put them on again.

He returned to camp and warmed himself by the fire. Hannah still slept, snuggled in the folds of her cloak and his blanket. They draped her small form, outlining the curve of her shoulders, her hips, and an unexpected surge of lust went through him.

He swore softly and banked his desire. She was a nun, after all, and he never claimed to be a heathen. He would use her in other ways. Too bad bedding her wasn't one of them.

Fenwick's horses were hobbled at the edge of camp. He went to them, his glance grazing the midnight black hides, the strong backs, the powerful hindquarters. Quinn's admiration flared. Their bloodlines were impeccable. For all his faults, Fenwick had fine taste in carriage horses.

Quinn ran his hand down the sleek neck of one of the geldings. The animal's earthy smell, his heat and vitality filled Quinn with the yearning to ride again.

It'd been four years since he had a horse beneath him. Four years since Elliott took everything that ever mattered to him. His stallion. His ranch.

His son.

He swallowed down bile from the bitter memory and unhobbled the gelding, then bridled him. The drug had weakened Quinn's muscles, and it took several attempts to hoist himself on the horse's back without a saddle or stirrups.

Once astride, he took the reins and left the camp again. He took his time, relearning the skill, testing himself. The walk lengthened to an easy canter, then a gallop, and Quinn pressed his knees against the animal's belly. He felt the gelding's powerful muscles move beneath him, and he urged the magnificent creature even faster.

He reveled in the power. The speed. He leaned forward, molded his body to the horse's. Wind whipped his face, tore at his hair, and an exultant yell escaped him.

He rejoiced in the freedom. Beautiful, reckless, glorious freedom.

He reined his mount into a wide turn back to camp and glimpsed Hannah searching for him. He raced toward her, the horse's iron hooves throwing back clumps of dirt in their wake.

She spied him and froze. He drew closer, and she quickly stepped back, as if she feared he'd run her over.

"Quinn?" she gasped. "What are you *doing?*"

He pulled on the reins and brought the gelding back to a walk.

"Riding."

She gaped at him, her hazel-green eyes as big as saucers. "Why?"

"Because I felt like it." He moved the gelding in a slow circle around her.

She turned with him, keeping him in her sight. "The fever has addled your brain."

"No." He shook his head with a rueful smile.

"You're still very sick. You must get down from there."

"No," he said again. To both of her statements.

"Quinn, please." She reached a slender arm toward him, and the horse stopped. "I'll help you."

"I feel fine, Hannah. The drug is gone."

She stared at him as if he'd taken on a severe case of dementia. "How can you be sure?"

"Because I feel good."

She pursed her lips and pulled her hand back. "So you just decided to go on a pleasure ride."

"Yes."

"Your hair is wet. I suppose you bathed, too?"

He nodded, watching her.

"In the river. And now you'll catch your death from pneumonia." She sounded exasperated with him.

"You thought I'd deserted you, didn't you?"

A moment passed. Her chin lifted to a defiant tilt. "It crossed my mind."

"And then I wouldn't keep my end of our deal."

"Men who murder think nothing of promises, Mr. Landry. Why would you be any different?"

His mood began to sour. "You'll just have to trust me, won't you?"

"Trust you? I don't think that will ever be possible."

He matched her glare with one of his own. "I don't give a damn whether you trust me or not," he said. "Just don't forget you need me. I'm the only one who knows you didn't kill those two people."

Her mouth tightened. Quinn sensed it vexed her

deeply to have the disadvantage. "I'm well aware of that."

"Ironic, isn't it?" he taunted.

Her ire was a tangible thing, but she kept it locked inside her. A credit to the holy nuns, he thought none too charitably. She'd primed him for a healthy argument and then refused to oblige him.

"You're a fugitive, Hannah. Hunted, just like me." His words were flat, cold. "Like it or not, we're stuck with each other."

She paled, but said nothing more and headed back toward camp, leaving him filled with resentment that she'd managed to ruin a perfectly good morning.

Quinn sprawled in the carriage driver's seat and propped a foot on the front edge of the rig. He clasped the reins in one hand and a cheroot in the other.

He inhaled the expensive tobacco and held the smoke in his lungs before exhaling slowly. He savored the sweet taste. Not only did Fenwick have a liking for quality horseflesh, he spared no expense in his cigars.

Quinn glanced over at Hannah. She huddled on the far end of the seat and stared at the sparse countryside, spotted with mesquite and winter grass and the occasional prairie dog. Her concerted effort to ignore him caused him a twinge of annoyance.

The black metal box sat between them, its lid open to the valuables inside. He was glad she'd discovered them. Simple items, crucial to their survival. What would they have done without the matches? The derringer? Or the laudanum?

His pondering gaze settled on her once again. He took a lazy drag on the cheroot.

"Do they teach you thievery at the convent, Hannah?" he asked softly.

His question clearly startled her. Her glance bounced from him, to the box, and back at him again. The color drained from her cheeks.

"Of course not," she said.

"Then who taught you how to throw the lock?"

She speared him with a cool gaze. "It is of no concern to you."

He grunted and considered the burning end of the cheroot. "You sacrificed your rosary to make the widdy. Not many nuns would do that to something they considered sacred."

"Under the circumstances, it was necessary. I don't regret doing it." Her expression turned challenging. "What do you know of widdies?"

"Very little." His eyes connected with hers. "Except that only a master thief would know how to make one, then use it with skill."

"But you recognized mine." She arched a delicate brow. "Perhaps you are a thief, too? As well as a murderer?"

"Ah, Hannah." She'd strung her words with barbed wire; Quinn leaned back in the seat and enjoyed their sting. "You give me too much credit. I only learned of them during my time in the Big House."

"Really?" Her tone indicated she was skeptical. "What else did you learn?"

Quinn fell silent. He wouldn't tell her how he'd been schooled in the ways of the lowlifes he'd lived with for four years, the liars, drunks and cheats, the rapists and perverts. He wouldn't tell of the times he'd been accosted in the privy, of how he fought back with all he possessed, even though it cost him ten lashes from the "cat" and thirty days in the Hole with no light and only stale bread to eat and dirty potato water to drink.

He wouldn't tell her. He suspected she knew of those things already.

"Never mind what I've learned," he said finally. "But understand one thing. I lived in hell through all of it. And I don't know which hell was worse. My time in prison or Fenwick's Solution."

For a moment, she said nothing. Quinn sensed her pity and hated it.

"It's over now," she murmured.

"Yes."

"You're not sick anymore."

"No."

"And you're free."

"Yes."

"Then let's go back to the convent, Quinn. Now."

He glanced at her sharply. "No."

She leaned toward him, her features intense. "You don't need me. Not like before. Take me there, and we'll talk to Mother Superior. Convince her of my innocence, and you can be on your way. You'll never see me again."

His eyes narrowed.

"You're a fool to think I'd even consider it," he said with a growl.

She emitted a cry of frustration. "You had no right to kidnap me. We were only there to help—"

"To my good fortune."

"—and you *stole* me as if I were a tin of beans on the grocer's shelf."

"That's right. I did. Because I had to. Because I'd be dead by now if I didn't."

"I don't want to be here with you," she whispered.

He steeled himself against the shimmer of her tears, of the brutal honesty in her words.

"Well, I reckon I don't much like being here myself, Hannah. But I am. Same as you. Whether either one of us deserves it." He took an impatient pull on the cheroot and flung it aside. Her anguish touched a raw nerve inside him. "Briggs would've shot you, too, if I hadn't taken you. You knew too much. We all did."

"There's always the chance we might have made it," she said, persistent.

"No chance, Hannah. Not a one in hell."

She turned away from him, her jaw set.

"Briggs is waiting for you to go back to the convent," Quinn said after a long moment. "You know that."

She faced him again. "Yes. And he's waiting for your body to show up somewhere, too. It won't take long for him to realize you're still alive, and he'll track you again."

This time, Quinn fell silent. She seemed to know how the warden's brain worked.

"We'll be in Texas in a few days." He scanned the New Mexico Territory horizon with a narrowed eye. "And Amarillo shortly thereafter. When my business is complete, we'll take a stage back to the convent."

She let out a skeptical huff.

"You don't believe me," he said and reached for another cheroot from the leather case on the seat.

"No."

"I've never lied to you."

"You'll say anything to shut me up. Deal or no deal."

He plucked a wooden match from its gold-plated case. "Think what you want, Hannah."

With a flick of his thumbnail, the match hissed and flared. Quinn touched the flame to the end of the cheroot. He drew inward, then exhaled a swift puff of blue-gray smoke.

Movement on the horizon stopped him cold. Riders appeared in front of them. An entire band of Mexican bandeleros, riding hard, fast. And heading right toward them.

"Shit," Quinn muttered.

Hannah's gaze followed his into the distance. She sucked in a breath. "Oh, glory."

"Here." He rustled through the black box and pressed Fenwick's knife into her hand. "Hide this somewhere where you can get to it quick if you have to. And keep your cloak tight about you."

He took the derringer and slipped it into the waistband of his uniform; his senses prepared for what lay ahead.

"What do you think they'll do?" Hannah asked, her voice not quite steady. She pulled the hood of her cloak over her head.

"I don't know." Quinn knew her fear, tasted it as if it were his own. He gripped her chin, forced her to face him. "Not a word from you. Hear me? Let me do the talking."

"There's money in the box," she said, hope evident in her voice. "Maybe that's all they want."

"Not enough there to make them rich." He released her, then closed the lid to the box. The lock snapped into place, and he slid the box beneath the seat.

The band thundered closer. Sunlight glinted off their

71

ammunition belts, the thick leather slung over their shoulders and heavily laden with rows of gleaming bullets. Conchos jangled from their horses's harnesses. Rifles filled their scabbards.

Quinn braked the carriage to a stop. He lifted the cheroot to his lips and took a long drag.

He hoped it wouldn't be his last.

Chapter Six

The rifles cocked simultaneously. The riders fanned out into a semicircle in front of the carriage. Eight of them. With sombreros on their heads and moustaches over their lips and the clear message that Fenwick's rig wasn't going anywhere.

Quinn's gaze locked with one of the bandelero's. The leader. Quinn gauged his age to be near thirty, close to his own. Lean and straight-backed, he sat in the saddle with arrogance, as if he knew his power and reveled in it. The kind of man who could treat another with honor or plunge a knife in his back.

He kept his beaded sombrero low over his eyes. Unlike the others, he wore no moustache; his skin was smooth, his features almost delicate. He wore a brightly striped serape over his shoulders, and the wrap hid any hint of his build, but the legs hugging the palomino's belly were slim; the boots in the stirrups sheathed small feet.

The Mexican returned his rifle to its scabbard and nudged his horse into a lazy walk around the carriage. He took his time, letting his men wait, letting them all wait. His admiring gaze stroked each side of the rig from top to bottom, front to back.

He took his place in the semicircle and leaned on the saddle horn. Beneath the sombrero's brim, the dark eyes fastened onto Quinn, raked him with an insolent glance.

Quinn inhaled from the cheroot, exhaled slow and easy. The silence stretched his nerves taut. He bided his time, endured every slow-moving second until the Mexican made the first move.

The bandelero dragged his attention from Quinn to Hannah. He stared hard at her, pinning her with unyielding scrutiny. She endured the stare, not flinching, not uttering a sound.

Finally, the Mexican inclined his head, as if he approved of what he saw.

"Buenos dias," he said, his voice a low rasp, his smile but a shadow beneath the sombrero's broad brim.

"Buenos dias," Hannah replied coolly.

"Step down where I can see you better." He pulled a revolver from his holster, bettered his grip over the trigger. He gestured toward Quinn. "Both of you."

Quinn flicked the ashes from the smouldering cheroot and chanced a look at Hannah. From the recesses of her hood, her slender throat moved, but she gave no other sign of her alarm. He eased from the driver's seat to the ground, and she followed.

"Julio!" the leader said. "Search the carriage."

One of the men rode forward. He sat heavy in the saddle, his frame paunchy, his arms and thighs thick.

74

He climbed into the rig and yanked at Fenwick's blanket, threw the canteen to the ground, then the broken umbrella. He paused at the leather cigar case Quinn had inadvertently left open on the seat.

A broad smile erupted. He snatched up the case and held it up for his fellow bandeleros to see.

"Ee-yah!" he cried out. "We will enjoy these, no?"

He stuffed a cheroot between his teeth before tossing what was left to the others. Someone produced a match, and one by one, they lit up, grunting their delight between puffs. The last man in the line tossed aside the empty case.

Quinn grimaced at the loss. Julio remounted and took new notice of Hannah. He leaned toward her, made a lewd gesture, called out something in Mex that drew the band's loud, appreciative laughter. Clearly, he lusted for her. Quinn's belly tightened.

The leader barked a terse command, and the men quieted. He indicated Hannah with his revolver.

"Your name," he ordered.

Her chin tilted a fraction higher.

"Hannah," she said smoothly. "Hannah Landry."

Landry? Quinn speared her with a sharp glance.

"Don't, Hannah," he warned.

The revolver swung toward him, and he bit back further protest. He wanted to throttle her for assuming control of their predicament, for forcing her own plan on the Mexican leader, conning him with her lie, as if Quinn had evaporated into thin air.

"The gringo's name," the leader demanded, his attention on Hannah again.

"He is my husband. Quinn Landry."

She looked at him, then. Cool as ice. Quinn narrowed an eye, a mute promise he'd retaliate for her impertinence later.

"Senor and Senora Landry. A pleasure." The leader inclined his head in a show of mocking courtesy and indicated the fleshy Mexican at his left who had stolen the cheroots. "My cousin, Julio Cortez," he murmured and motioned toward a gray-haired man of slight build on his right. "Ramon Huerta, my father-in-law." Another shadow of a smile appeared. "And you may simply call me . . . Huerta. That is enough for you to know now."

The Mexican was toying with them. The knowledge slashed through Quinn, convincing him there was far more lurking behind the bandelero's taunting smile than he allowed them to see.

"Tell me, Hannah. Your husband wears a prison uniform. Why?"

Hannah met the bandelero's gaze. Her fingers lifted to the clasp on her cloak. Her hood fell back, and she pulled the garment from her shoulders.

"Por Dios!" the leader exclaimed.

Rumbles of surprise went up among the men. They recognized the plain wooden cross around her neck and the drab shape of her brown habit signifying her as a Lady of the Cloth.

"I escaped the penitentiary," Quinn said, refusing to be silent any longer, bristling that Hannah had neither kept her cloak about her or her mouth shut as he'd instructed. "Two days ago. She—"

"Frank Briggs's penitentiary?" The bandelero exchanged a swift glance with Ramon.

"Yes." Quinn's brow furrowed.

"Do you know him?" Hannah asked, wary.

Huerta's arrogant mouth twisted, and he spat on the ground as if he couldn't stand to have the taste of the warden's name on his tongue. "Si. I know him. We all do."

Ramon considered Quinn.

"The escape was not easy, eh?" he said.

Quinn met his scrutiny squarely. "No."

"And now you run for your lives."

"Yes."

"In those clothes?" Suspicion mingled with skepticism.

"We had no choice," Quinn grated.

"A nun's habit is unusual." The leader studied Hannah. "Why did you choose to dress this way?"

"My attire allowed me to enter the penitentiary without harm," she said, her tone steady.

"A clever disguise." The ghostly smile appeared beneath the sombrero again, once more approving. "Si. Clever."

Hannah's lips curved. "Matters at the penitentiary had grown quite out of my control. I fear my 'clever disguise' had little to do with the final events of the night."

He shrugged. "Yet because of you, your husband escaped."

"Yes," she said.

He sat back in the saddle, accepting her confidence game.

"She is a brave woman," he said to Quinn. "You are fortunate to have her as a partner. And a wife."

"It seems I am," Quinn said roughly.

"The land is not kind when a man runs with little

77

but the clothes on his back. Perhaps we can strike a bargain."

Quinn frowned, tense again. "A bargain?"

"We will talk over a bottle of tequila."

"I don't want your generosity, senor."

"I give it gladly."

"We must keep moving. Briggs gives us a hard chase."

Huerta's shadowed features grew harsh. "I insist, gringo."

He snapped a command to his men. With a jangle of conchos and harnesses, two riders assumed positions on either side of the rig. Another pair took up the rear.

The revolver jerked toward Quinn.

"We are ready to ride, gringo," he ordered. "Get in the carriage with your wife."

Quinn remained unmoving, his hard gaze riveted to the leader while he flicked yet another admiring glance over Fenwick's carriage. Hannah pulled the cloak over her shoulders and the hood over her head, shielding herself from the band.

She turned toward him. Quinn pulled his gaze from the Mexican and held hers instead.

"He wants the rig," he said in a low voice.

"Are you sure?"

"He did everything but drool on it."

"The rig is *ours*."

Another time, he might have been amused at her reasoning. The carriage was no more theirs than the Mexican's. After all, they'd stolen it from Fenwick.

"Senor Landry!" The leader's tone rasped with impatience.

Quinn nudged Hannah firmly toward the buggy, but

she stood her ground, spearing him with a damning glance.

"You should have listened to me," she said under her breath. "We could be on our way back to the convent by now."

"The band will buy us some time. The warden won't look for us in an outlaw hideout." He spoke roughly.

"What's worse, Quinn?" she challenged. "Recapture by Frank Briggs? Or being prisoners of a renegade outlaw band?"

Not waiting for his answer, she strode away from him, her pique obvious. He doubted she cared if he followed or not.

He chafed with irritation. At her logic, at her displeasure, at the frustrating delay in his return to Amarillo.

And to lose the carriage in the process. . . .

He breathed a silent curse.

Immersed in his troubled thoughts, he'd forgotten his cheroot, now burned down to a stub of ashes. A waste of a damned good cigar—his last one.

And he cursed that, too.

They stopped to camp for the night along a stream that flowed east from the Pecos. Dusk had fallen, and the horses labored under the weight of their riders. A stand of cypress trees offered seclusion, and at Huerta's direction, the men began to dismount.

Quinn looped the reins around the carriage brake and ran an uneasy eye over the fierce-looking band. Hannah sensed the tension in him, though he'd not spoken to her since they'd been taken captive.

Conversation would have been difficult if he'd tried.

The riders positioned on each side of the rig had stayed within arm's reach. They would have heard every word. She was convinced Quinn's silence had been safer.

Suddenly, Julio Cortez appeared from around the far side of the carriage.

"Get down, gringo!" he ordered.

He leaned forward from the saddle and jammed his rifle barrel into Quinn's ribs, then grasped his shoulder and yanked him from the carriage seat. Quinn scrambled to keep his balance and hit the dirt hard.

Hannah cried out and reached for him. Cortez lunged for her next, dragging her by her arm to his side of the rig.

"Leave her alone, Cortez," Quinn yelled.

Cortez ignored him and yanked hard on her elbow. No match to his superior strength, she tumbled from the seat like a rag doll, sprawling to the ground with a soft thud. Every bone in her body rattled from the fall.

Quinn leapt toward him. With all the savagery he'd shown in the penitentiary, he tore Cortez from his horse and hurled his fist into the fleshy jowl. Cortez's head snapped back and blood burst from his lip. He fell backwards in a heap.

Quinn went for him a second time. Hannah's heart jumped to her throat.

"No, Quinn!" she gasped, hastening to her feet.

A rifle shot exploded in the air. Quinn clutched the front of Cortez's vest and hauled him up by his ammunition belts.

"Senor Landry! Julio! Enough!" Huerta commanded in a harsh rasp, charging toward them from astride the palomino.

Quinn yanked Cortez higher so that the bandalero was inches from his face.

"Don't touch her again," he grated through clenched teeth.

Two of Huerta's men pried him from Cortez. This time, Quinn didn't resist, and relief flooded through Hannah. Glory, he couldn't fight a firing squad.

Loathing burned in Cortez's eyes, and he leapt toward them again. Clearly, he intended to finish what Quinn had started.

Ramon stopped Cortez with a shove to his burly chest.

"Julio!" he barked. "Leave the gringos alone!"

Huerta slid from his horse before the animal thundered to a stop. His hand lashed out and struck Cortez against the cheek. The bandelero gasped and sucked in a breath.

"*I* am in command here, Julio. When I tell you to stop, you will listen!" Huerta said with a hiss.

"I must end the fight he started!" Cortez shot back.

"He protects his woman! Tomas would have done the same!"

"You defend the gringo before you defend me!" Cortez could hardly contain his outrage. "Me! Your flesh and blood!"

Huerta's lip curled with disgust. "Stop your whining, you fool! Now go! Unload the pack horses before I am forced to tell Tomas of your tantrums!"

Cortez quivered and didn't move.

"*Vamos!*" Huerta snapped.

His chest heaved. "Si. I will obey, but I will not *forget.*"

He glared at Quinn with blistering hate before pressing the cuff of his sleeve to his bleeding mouth and storming off.

"And you, Senor Landry! Give me your gun."

Quinn's nostrils flared, and he snatched at the derringer still tucked in the waistband of his pants. His features hard, he handed over the weapon.

Huerta slipped the gun beneath his serape. "Your horses are tired. Take care of them!"

A long second passed, as if Quinn debated obeying the order. Finally, he swung his glance toward Hannah.

"You okay?" he demanded.

"Yes," she said, managing a jerky nod.

"Don't wander off. I want you where I can see you," he ordered, the words clipped.

She nodded again and swallowed.

He hurled a harsh look toward Huerta, but said nothing more. He hurled another toward Cortez's retreating form, then began unharnessing the team of black geldings.

The Mexican leader watched him work. He gestured toward Ramon, and his fury appeared to dissipate.

"Find him some clothes," he said. "Those prison rags are not fit to be worn."

"And they make us remember too much, eh?" the older man said softly.

"Si. Too much."

"I will post guards around the camp. Two hour shifts."

"Gracias. That will be good."

Ramon squeezed Huerta's shoulder and left. Huerta kept his back to Hannah and angled his head, the broad sombrero brim casting his face into deep shadow.

"My men are exhausted and hungry. Perhaps, Hannah, you can find us wood to build a fire for our supper, eh?"

His voice had gentled to a near whisper. The impatience in him had disappeared, too. The cold, stark command that seemed to infiltrate his every word had mellowed to civilized courtesy.

"Yes," Hannah murmured.

Huerta nodded and strode away to tend his own horse.

She stared after him, and a sudden shiver went through her. From the power he wielded over the bandeleros. Over Quinn and herself. From Julio's rage. From the deadly certainty that escaping the band would be practically impossible.

But mostly from Huerta himself, whose face he would not let her see, whose real voice he would not let her hear.

Night had fallen. Quinn found Hannah near the stream, perched on a rock, her habit and cloak gathered close about her.

A big, cheerful moon beamed over the water, illuminating the shape of her. She stared into the sky, studded with stars and glittering like sugar crystals tossed onto black cloth.

The aroma of roasting chilies hung in the air. One of the bandeleros stirred beans in a cast iron pot; another clattered tin plates and cups; still another stoked the fire until it roared and snapped.

Hannah seemed oblivious to the activity around her. Detached. As if she couldn't bring herself to become a part of it.

Pebbles crunched beneath Quinn's bootsoles as he

drew closer, and Hannah's head swiveled toward him in alarm.

"It's only me, Hannah," he said.

Eyes wide, she dragged her gaze down the length of him and back up. Ramon had supplied him with clean clothes and plenty of soap. Her jaw lagged open. "Quinn?"

He wasn't surprised she hardly recognized him. Hell, he hardly recognized himself.

"Amazing what a razor can do, isn't it?" With the crook of his finger, he nudged her jaw closed again.

"You—you're so different."

He'd not worn a hat since Briggs had taken his Stetson away four years ago and thrown him into prison. Nor had he felt the denim of well-worn Levis encasing his thighs, or a knit undershirt warming his back, or a decent cotton shirt covering his shoulders and arms.

It felt good to be wearing them now. Damned good.

"I'll never wear a prison uniform again," he said with a determined nod. "I'll die first."

She made a sound of sympathy, of understanding.

"Ramon was generous. You're fortunate he found you something to wear," she said.

"Yes." He considered her a moment. "Too bad he had nothing for you."

She turned away. "My habit suits me."

Quinn's mouth thinned in silent disagreement. He found himself wondering what she'd look like in satin and lace, with fine kid-leather boots on her feet, gloves on her hands, jewels about her neck. He imagined her with ribbons in her hair, a parasol twirling against her shoulder.

And cursed himself for it.

She preferred to look like a brown sparrow in all that wool. A shame. A living shame.

He reached inside his shirt pocket for the cigarette Ramon had given him and scraped a match tip with his thumb nail.

"So you want to pretend we're married." He touched the flame to the tobacco.

"Hush," she said. "Someone could be listening."

No one was. He'd counted sombreroed heads, found every bandelero where he was supposed to be before he came to her.

"Huerta will be furious when he learns the truth." He put the cigarette to his lips.

"Don't say anything, and he won't."

He inhaled deeply, held the smoke in his lungs before exhaling, savoring the taste of it.

"Men like Huerta have a twisted code of honor that'll allow for killing a man for his money, but not for a lie they believed in front of their men," he said. "We'll pay the price if he finds out."

She sighed. "I know." She fingered the wooden cross hanging from her neck. "Pretending you were my husband wasn't very clever, I'm afraid. It was all I could think of at the time."

In spite of everything, his mouth softened. "Mother Superior wouldn't approve."

A sound of dismay slipped from her. "I don't want to think of it."

He'd meant to tease her, but she'd taken his comment with utmost seriousness.

"You're trying not to get killed," he said, squinting an eye over the darkened ribbon of water. "She isn't. Don't fret over it."

"Please don't make light of my sin, Quinn. I'm quite aware of the consequences and will confess it at my first opportunity."

"I wouldn't bother, if I were you."

"But you're not me, are you?"

"It's called survival, Hannah. You're feeling guilty for something you had to do. You lied to save yourself. And me." He slid another cautious glance toward the outlaws. "We'll do it your way. We'll make the marriage thing work. At least if they think you're my wife, Huerta's men will think twice about their lust for you."

"Cortez. . . ." She hesitated. Then, she reached out and took his hand in hers, held the knuckles to the moonlight.

"You should not have hit him," she said quietly, her thumb brushing over the tiny cuts on his skin. "He hates you more than ever now."

Quinn grunted. "Stay away from him."

"Yes." She nodded for emphasis, the promise easy to give.

"Use the knife if you have to."

She drew in a breath and nodded again. "Glory. I hope I won't."

It'd been a long time since a woman touched him, and this one distracted him from the conversation at hand, from the seriousness of it, and kept him absorbed with the feel of her skin skimming lightly across his.

A little thing, her thumb upon his knuckles. But it disconcerted the hell out of him. He pulled away.

"I expect you to sleep with me," he said roughly. "Like a good wife should."

"What?" A gasp of horror followed the word.

"Strictly platonic." He fought a nip of impatience

that she'd misinterpreted his intent. She was a nun, for godsake. "Do what wives do. But don't go getting all uppity and prim about it. Loosen up a little. This was your idea, after all."

She stiffened. "Of course. I understand."

"Play the con game, and you'll be safe."

Her gaze was direct. Unwavering.

"It's what I want more than anything," she said firmly. "To be safe. I'll do whatever I must."

It surprised him she agreed to his demands so readily. He brought the cigarette stub to his lips and took a final drag. With his thumb and forefinger, he sent it arcing into the water.

The old suspicions about her crept into his brain. A nun who lied with the skillful ease of a con artist, then agreed to sleep with him at night. One who could throw locks with tools she'd fashioned with next to nothing.

Maybe she wasn't a nun. Maybe she'd lied about that, too.

But she'd been at the penitentiary with the priest the night of Quinn's escape. Quinn had seen Father Donovan there before, performing his works of mercy, and knew he was legitimate. The cleric would not have brought her if she hadn't been from the convent.

Quinn fought his suspicions down. He had to trust Hannah. And Hannah had to trust him.

Over her head, he studied the bandeleros, sitting around the campfire with their tortillas and plates of chilies and beans.

All of them, except Huerta. He kept himself separate from his men. Quinn sensed an air of expectancy about him. A tautness. He paced, a restless mountain cat primed for a hunt. His sharp gaze continually probed the darkness beyond the camp.

Huerta was expecting something. Someone.

Quinn took Hannah's elbow and pulled her from her perch on the rock. If there was going to be trouble, he had to get closer, to anticipate it, to ready himself and Hannah before it hit.

Suddenly, one of the guards yelled out in Mex. The men jumped to their feet. Water splashed—horses crossing the stream in haste. Amidst the thunderous pounding of hooves, a trio of riders roared into the camp and came to an abrupt stop.

Huerta cried out. He threw off his beaded sombrero, letting it fall back on its strings against his serape. Long, obsidian tresses cascaded from beneath its crown and splayed over his shoulders, and he ran toward one of them, his arms outstretched.

Hannah gasped in shock. Quinn stood stock still. And stared.

Christ.

Huerta was a woman.

Chapter Seven

"Tomas!"

Her face alight with pleasure, she squealed his name with none of the rasp Hannah heard her speak before. The tall, lean Mexican barely had time to remove his ammunition belt before he took her against him. They kissed with passion, their mouths hungry, their tongues searching, and both oblivious to the group who waited around them.

Stunned, Hannah watched. Huerta cared for this man. Deeply. Like one whose lover fills a need in her, clear to her soul.

Hannah's mind struggled to make the switch, to think of Huerta as a woman when she'd been so convincing as a man, a dangerous leader who wielded power over an entire band of outlaws.

Over Quinn and herself.

Why had the Mexican woman been compelled to hide her gender? Why had her men played along?

Pam Crooks

Their kiss ended at last, and the others pressed closer, jeering good-naturedly, welcoming the tall Mexican into their midst. Clearly, they knew one another, and Hannah guessed they were members of the same band, now reunited and complete.

For the moment, it seemed she and Quinn had been forgotten. In the next, the Mexican glanced up and found them.

His broad smile faltered. Suspicion glinted in his black eyes, and he pushed the men aside, allowing himself a closer look.

"Mi querida," he said, wary. "We have guests?"

"Si." Huerta swept her arm outward, a mocking gesture. "Quinn and Hannah Landry. They have joined us just this afternoon. And look, my love. They have a most beautiful carriage."

He glanced in the direction she indicated. Fenwick's rig sat beyond the camp, its gleaming sides faintly touched by firelight. Even in the distance, Hannah admitted the carriage looked stately and elegant.

"Beautiful," he said, obviously struck by the sight of it. "Very beautiful."

The pair exchanged a look, and Hannah knew Quinn had been right. Huerta wanted the rig for herself.

"Por Dios!" With a sudden smile that would be disarming if it could be trusted, the bandelero swept the sombrero from his head. "Forgive me. I have not introduced myself. My name is Tomas Huerta. I am Sophia's husband."

"Husband?" His own smile mocking, Quinn inclined his head and turned to Sophia. "You were quite successful in making us think you were not . . . of the fairer sex."

90

She clucked her tongue in feigned regret. "You must accept my apologies for misleading you. Perhaps you would not have taken me as seriously if you had known I was a woman, eh?"

Quinn lifted a shoulder. "Eight rifle barrels will make a man think whatever you want him to think."

"Si, Senor Landry. My intent, of course."

"We were outnumbered four to one," Hannah said coolly. "Man or woman, you had us at your mercy. As you still do."

Dark heads swung to her in unison.

"My husband is a great leader to his men, Hannah. He has done wonderful things for our people," Sophia replied, all signs of pleasure from his arrival gone. She spoke with intensity, but, strangely enough, without animosity. "When he cannot be with us, I have learned to take his place. My authority equals his. His men know they must obey me or pay the consequences."

An image of Julio Cortez flashed into Hannah's memory, of his bitter resentment and hate for Quinn, of how Sophia had been forced to intervene to end their fight.

She'd almost failed. Cortez easily doubled her weight. He'd vowed vengeance against Quinn, showed lust for Hannah.

Would he obey Sophia next time? Or Tomas? Would he obey anyone?

Hannah found him in the throng of outlaws, his expression brooding, sullen, as if her challenge to Sophia reminded him, too, of the scathing reprimand the bandelero's leader had given him. Beneath his thick, coarse eyebrows, his eyes burned with the promise of retaliation.

Pam Crooks

A shiver slithered along Hannah's spine. Julio Cortez would not forget.

Sophia turned to her husband, stroked his cheek.

"You must be hungry," she said. "Come. Sit by the fire and eat."

"Did you bring us tequila?" someone demanded.

"You promised, Tomas!" another said.

Beneath the thin line of his moustache, his white teeth gleamed against his bronzed skin.

"Our raids have been successful," he declared proudly. "Si. I have tequila and more!"

A roar went up amongst the men. Tomas retrieved bottles of liquor and pouches of tobacco from bulging saddlebags and tossed them into the group where they were snatched greedily and plundered with masculine fervor.

The tequila flowed freely. The outlaws' boisterous laughter abounded while Tomas and the two men accompanying him consumed the meal with relish.

Sophia snuggled next to him. She appeared relaxed, as if Tomas's presence shifted the burden of responsibility from her shoulders to his. Her high cheekbones and dark skin were like that of the other outlaws, and her obsidian eyes sparkled in amusement as Tomas regaled them with stories of his time away from them.

Nearly a month, Hannah surmised, listening while she toyed with the food on her own plate. He had just returned from Mexico where he'd shared the spoils of his thievery with his people, starving peasants much in need of the cattle he'd rustled and the money he'd stolen from landowners too wealthy to know any of it was gone.

His contempt for the rich had garnered him the re-

92

spect of the poor. His ruthless exploits kept him constantly running from the law, from the men and rules he had no intention of obeying.

With his meal finished, Tomas's glance settled, at last, on Quinn. The bandelero leaned back against a tree stump and lifted a bottle of tequila to his lips. He studied Quinn over the flickering campfire light.

"Sophia tells me you broke out of the Big House. That Frank Briggs hunts you and Hannah," he said, the words strung with grim curiosity.

"Yes," said Quinn.

"I, too, spent time in the very same prison. If not for Sophia and Julio and a few of my best men, I would have died there."

Hannah's surprise equaled Quinn's. This was the Mexican who escaped Frank Briggs's prison, the only man to accomplish the feat besides Quinn. She assumed Sophia had been involved. She marvelled at the woman's courage.

"You were fortunate," Quinn said.

"Si, but you were, too, no?"

Quinn grunted, agreeing. "There were drug experiments. We were used like dogs."

"And Briggs did not care because he was paid well for your trouble." Tomas spoke with snarled conviction.

"Very well. By a man named Fenwick. Roger Fenwick."

The Mexican appeared to commit the name to memory. "The rich gringo used the inmates to test his drug, eh?"

Quinn gave a callous shrug. "He had nothing to lose. They were sent there to die for their crimes."

"And what crime did *you* commit, Senor Landry?"

A hush fell over the bandeleros. Only the crackle of the fire broke the silence. Hannah held her breath, knowing the answer and dreading it.

"I was convicted of murder," he said.

Low rumbles of reaction went through the men, waves of admiration, as if he were more like them than they first realized. Queasiness stirred in her belly.

"And the Senora. Hannah. She helped you escape."

"She saved me from certain death."

Tomas took another swig of tequila. "There is talk she killed a nun and a priest afterward." He held the bottle up to the fire, studying its contents with grim intensity. "The talk spreads quickly in the Territory."

Hannah's head came up. "I've killed no one!"

"Por Dios! A nun and priest?" Sophia appeared astounded.

"Briggs wants me recaptured," snapped Quinn. "He'll use Hannah to do it."

Sharp and assessing, Tomas's black eyes bored into her. "She is hunted by the law."

"Maybe with a price on her head, eh?" Julio Cortez said, his eyes glittering with anticipation.

"The warden is lying. He's conspiring with his guard to see us dead." Desperation crept into Hannah's words. She rose. "I've killed no one. They were my friends."

"Hannah," Quinn said, rising, too, reaching for her, but she evaded his grasp.

"Maybe she works for Briggs, Tomas." Cortez taunted. "He uses her to find you. See?" Cortez's grimy paw flicked her wool cloak open. "She wears a nun's habit. She is in disguise for Briggs."

"What?" Hannah choked on the word and slapped his hand away.

"Shut up, you sonovabitch!" Quinn spat.

The bandelero leader's eyes flitted over the plain cross about her neck and the drab brown fabric. His features registered surprise, then renewed suspicion.

The outlaws began to stand, one by one. Tomas did the same, his booted feet spread, his expression contemptuous.

"Briggs pretended to be my friend once," he said. "He promised me many head of cattle for my people. He told me to meet him in a special place to get them. When I go, the Federales are waiting for me." His lip curled. "He has no cattle, and soon they throw me in his prison." His hard gaze raked over Quinn and Hannah. "He tricked me with his disguise as an old farmer who has sympathies for my people when in fact he feels only hate." His mouth curved in cold humor. "So you can see why I do not like disguises."

"I wear no disguise," Hannah said slowly, succinctly.

"Maybe she plans it that Briggs will meet her soon," Cortez said, relentless in his quest to incriminate her. "She will lead him right to us."

"No." Hannah fought to stay cool, to keep her panic from showing. "No. You're wrong."

"Or maybe she is really a nun," Tomas said, as if thinking aloud.

Sophia threw her hands up in exasperation.

"Maybe, maybe, maybe," she mocked, glaring at Tomas, then Cortez. "Your minds go crazy with 'maybe.' " She strode over and thumped Cortez on his paunchy belly. "What do you want of Senor Landry, Julio? Proof of Hannah's virgin blood that they are married?"

Hannah yelped in dismay. In humiliation. She refused to listen to these people, these renegade outlaws with their dreadful implications, speaking as if they were her judge and jury.

They had no right. Not when they'd committed enough crimes amongst them to warrant their own judge and jury.

She spun on her heel. She had to flee them. To flee Quinn.

Especially Quinn.

But his hand snaked out and snared her wrist in an iron grip.

"Yes, she wears a nun's habit," he said, his voice low, so low he injected venom into each syllable. "But beneath it, she is a woman. My woman. And I won't have her shamed by your accusations."

Cortez's expression turned thunderous. Suspicion lingered in Tomas's features.

"She is mine." Quinn's voice rasped from the depth of his rage. "Look at her. All of you."

He lifted her arm high about her head, firmly, and twirled her. Presented them her back, her side, her front. So there would be no question.

She was his. Untouchable. By any of them.

Hannah's eyes closed tightly.

He stopped turning her. Her eyes opened again.

His gaze smouldered, stroked her with its growing heat. Her mind emptied. She thought only of the role they played. Of the deal they'd made. She thought nothing of brown habits and a convent that seemed forever unreachable.

She thought of Quinn, the man.

He filled her senses. She knew his intent, even before

his head lowered, and his jaw nuzzled her temple.

"You mustn't do this," she whispered.

"Convince them, Hannah," he murmured. "Make them believe."

His chin brushed her cheek, then lowered to her jaw. She waited for what would come next, the anticipation building within her with every frenzied beat of her heart.

At last, warm and firm, his mouth slid over hers. She trembled, and his muscle-thewed arm slid about her waist, pulling her closer. She needed him to hold her, for her legs seemed to sift away beneath her like fine sand, and she feared she'd swoon into a heap on the ground. Her fists balled the cotton fabric of his shirt. Her arms folded against the hard wall of his chest.

Hannah had long ago buried her desire for a man's kiss. She did not need his embrace and strength and power, but Quinn resurrected that need with a vengeance. He devastated her will to resist. He made her forget the lies they'd fabricated.

Too soon, before she could even think it, he lifted his mouth and eased away. Hannah's lashes fluttered, and she struggled with the onslaught of reality.

Quinn's gaze swept the bandeleros. His eyes, moments ago blazing with fire, turned gun-metal cold.

"I, alone, know of her innocence," he said roughly. "Do not speak of her guilt again."

Hannah's breath jammed in her throat. The kiss had been only a ruse to prove a point, a concession to Tomas's and Cortez's accusations.

She knew it, of course. Quinn had told her so.

Still, the kiss meant nothing to him when it had

rocked the very foundation of all the womanly yearnings she refused to feel.

Until now.

Hannah pushed away from him. Before she could humiliate herself further, she pivoted to flee him. To flee them all.

But Sophia stepped in front of her and prevented it. Her scathing glance scorched each of her men.

"Senor Landry would not dare to kiss a Lady of the Cloth with the passion he uses to kiss Hannah, eh?" She snapped the challenge. For a miniscule second, Hannah detected the glint of respect in her features.

And then it was gone. Her expression turned harsh once more.

"Do not accuse her again. Or I shall help Senor Landry make you regret it." She searched out one bandelero in particular. "Julio! Do you hear me?"

Cortez bared his teeth and narrowed his eyes. His jowls quivered with suppressed rage.

He stared long and hard at Hannah. "Si, Sophia. I hear you."

He'd done a lot of stupid things in his life. Kissing a nun had never been one of them.

Quinn delayed going to her and kept to the shadows of the cypress trees. Once again, Hannah sought solace in the night and perched on the rock along the stream, huddled in the folds of her cloak. He guessed she prayed, or meditated, or did whatever it was a troubled Lady of the Cloth did to seek peace.

Huerta and Cortez had shot accusations at her in rapid-fire succession. Frank Briggs's intent to pin the deaths of the priest and nun on her left her scared and panicked.

Condemned.

Christ. She deserved none of it.

Her anguish had torn at him. He wanted only to comfort her. Protect her. The kiss had just happened, a desperate means to convince the others to leave her alone. The instinct to hold her in his arms had been too quick, too strong, to deny.

He rubbed a hand along his jaw. The memory of her mouth moving tentatively, shyly, beneath his stirred a heat within him that would only burn them both. Even now, just thinking of it . . .

He swore again, softly. He'd been too long without female company. As soon as they got to Amarillo, he'd find a willing woman and end the celibacy Briggs—and a murder conviction—had inflicted upon him. Until then, he had to keep thinking of Hannah as a nun. And not as a woman.

He moved toward her.

Hannah heard the crunch of his bootsoles and knew he'd come to make amends.

She didn't turn to him. She didn't have to. She knew the exact moment when he stopped behind her; she could gauge the precise distance that separated their bodies. Even through the layers of her habit and cloak, in the chill of the late night air, she could feel his warmth. His strength.

She tilted her head back and gazed up into the stars. They made a canopy of serenity, she thought. A solitude she'd not found anywhere else on earth.

Except in the Daughters of Perpetual Glory convent.

"They'd be in the chapel saying the Night Prayers of

the Divine Office about now," she said quietly. She turned to him, then. "The nuns, you know."

"Would they?" he murmured.

She nodded and pursed her mouth. "Afterward, they'd get ready for bed. Lights out by nine o'clock, then up again at midnight to start the series all over again. Prayer after prayer. Six times a day. Day in and day out."

It hadn't taken long to fall into the sisters' routine. The rituals never changed. Hannah found them strange at first but soon learned to take comfort in them.

To find peace.

She'd lost that peace. Quinn had stolen it. The bandeleros had stolen it. The whole world had stolen it, kept her from the serenity she relished. And needed.

He removed the Stetson, ran his fingers through the thickness of his dark hair. "Look, Hannah. About tonight."

"Quinn, don't say anything."

"I have to."

"I know why you did it. Kissed me, I mean."

"Do you?"

She nodded, somber. "It's all part of the con game."

Glory, she knew about con games. Her childhood had been spent mastering them all, training to be a con artist. Pa had seen to that. No matter what it cost her.

"Hell, it's more than a game," he said, the denial rough. "I put you on display in front of everyone. I took the husband-wife thing too far."

"You made the game believable. Nothing more."

"Hannah . . ."

She heard his frustration. His guilt.

"My name is Hannah Benning." Her hands were

100

clasped tight in her lap. "Ironic, isn't it? To have kissed me like you did and not even know my last name."

His gaze touched her. "You refused to tell me."

She recalled the morning before when they'd hidden from Briggs and Titus in the cold stream. She'd been determined to keep him at a safe and proper distance.

"I wanted you to think I was a real nun," she said, the admission soft. Bemused.

A moment passed. "Aren't you?"

She sighed. "I'm a novitiate, Quinn. The first stage in becoming a nun. I've taken temporary vows. I have much studying ahead of me before I profess the final ones."

"Temporary?" He hung on the word.

"But vows, nonetheless," she said evenly. "When I return to the convent, I'll resume my studies in earnest."

He crooked a finger beneath her chin. Gently, incredibly so, he turned her to face him.

"Why are you telling me all this?" he asked.

Their eyes met. She hadn't thought he could be so gentle when she'd seen him so savage.

"I'm not sure," she said. "Maybe . . ."

"Maybe what, Hannah?"

"Maybe I'm starting to trust you."

A slow smile softened the hard line of his mouth. "Well, I'll be damned." The smile widened into a crooked little curve. "Mind if I swear in front of you?"

She clucked her tongue in exasperation. "You've not been concerned with it before. Why start now?"

He chuckled, the first from him since he'd taken her captive.

"I've heard some oaths that would drop the leaves

101

off the trees," she admitted. "I'm ashamed to say I've used them myself a time or two. When I've been deeply vexed."

"Really. We'll have to swap sometime."

She sniffed, resisting his teasing. "I think not. Most of them were positively disgusting."

"Somehow, I can't see you doing anything that wasn't pure and right."

Pure? Her soul was anything but that. And right? Glory, she'd done so many wrong things in her life.

"Don't put me on a pedestal, Quinn," she sighed. "I'll only fall off."

He seemed about to reply, but a sound behind them snatched his attention.

"Someone's coming," he said in a low voice.

Hannah stabbed a glance into the darkness. Through a slight parting of the trees, she discerned two shapes. They seemed unaware of Quinn and Hannah's presence.

"Tomas and Sophia," he said.

"Thank goodness." Relief swept through her that it'd not been a wild animal. Or Julio Cortez.

"They're slipping away to find a little romance together," he said.

She peered at him doubtfully.

"They're entitled, you know. They've been apart a long time." Again, the hard line of his mouth softened. "And they're married."

Indignation rippled through her. "I may have chosen a life in a convent, Quinn, but I'm not ignorant of the desires of the flesh between a man and a woman."

"It's good you're not."

She blinked up at him, at the abrasiveness of his

comment. The darkness hid his expression.

"Are you ready to turn in?" he asked curtly. "The Huertas want to leave at dawn."

His sudden impatience, the swift way he changed the subject, threw her off guard.

"No," she said, her defenses rising. "I'd like a little more time to myself."

"The rest of the band has fallen asleep. You're alone, except for the Huertas and the posted guards. Don't be too long."

"I won't."

He hesitated, as if he was reluctant to leave her, but the camp was within easy sight and earshot. In the end, he touched a finger to the brim of his Stetson and left.

Hannah watched him go, her gaze lingering upon his lean form longer than was necessary. A vague dismay left her feeling unsettled. Out of sorts.

She saw him differently now that he'd kissed her. He seemed more manly somehow. More attractive. Stronger and more powerful.

Her heart did a funny, unexpected flip.

Hannah closed her eyes tightly to shut out his image. She delved into her memories, instead, for a glimpse of the convent, of candles and incense and rosary beads, of chants and prayers and Latin hymns, of the simple chapel and the stark, narrow confines of the cubicle she called her bedroom.

It proved difficult. Appallingly so.

She blamed her failure on the night cold seeping into her toes and fingertips and gave up. Slipping from the rock, she pulled her cloak tighter and started for camp.

A woman's throaty moan stopped her. Hardly thinking, Hannah darted a glance into the trees and found the silhouetted shapes of Tomas and Sophia standing together.

A twinkling moonbeam revealed their nakedness, and in the few seconds before Tomas wrapped his wife snugly into the folds of his blanket, sheltering her from the cold, Hannah glimpsed the slim and definite curves of the other woman's body.

Hannah's mouth parted in surprise.

Sophia Huerta was pregnant.

Chapter Eight

They broke camp at dawn and rode long and hard into the New Mexico Territory's hill country. Hour after hour, they travelled at a grueling pace, stopping only to rest the horses while eating a light meal of dry tortillas and tasteless beans at midday. Then, before Hannah's aching muscles could quiver a protest, they mounted up and rode out again.

Why not, she thought on a surge of weary peevishness. Tomas and Sophia rode in comfort in Fenwick's rig while she and Quinn rode on the backs of their horses and choked on the dust raised by the carriage wheels.

She immediately recited a prayer of contrition. In her expectant condition, Sophia deserved the carriage far more than she did.

Hannah had been unable to find a moment to tell Quinn of her discovery. He appeared unaware of the pregnancy, as did the rest of the band. Indeed, Sophia's serape kept the swell of her belly well hidden, and it was little wonder she wanted the rig. Before long, the babe in her womb would prevent her from riding astride with the ease and ferocity of her men.

With each hour that crawled by, Hannah's patience wore thinner. She wanted only to go to Amarillo, to see Quinn settle his score. And then to return to the convent.

She *didn't* want to go to an outlaw hideout in the middle of nowhere.

But she swallowed down the frustration as penance for her past sins, and, more importantly, as one more step she must endure to pass the test of her calling.

Quinn rode straight, even relaxed, in the saddle, the brim of his Stetson pulled low over his forehead, the reins laced loosely through his lean fingers. *He* endured the journey with the stamina of a seasoned rider. His dark eyes continually skimmed the horizon, the men, the carriage in front of them. And sometimes, his eyes skimmed over her.

Somehow, she always knew when they did. Her blood hummed a little faster in her veins. Did he need to assure himself she was still safe beside him? Or did he worry for her comfort?

She schooled her features to show none of her petulance or fatigue. Keep a poker face, Pa always said. She was determined no one would know of her discomforts, not even Quinn.

The terrain grew rocky, and the horses labored to climb the hills, their hooves striking the hard ground like hammers on flint. The band, with Fenwick's carriage in the lead, squeezed through the mouth of a pass leading into a secluded valley, shadowed heavily by the setting sun.

Tomas and Sophia signaled them to stop. Hannah realized they'd reached their destination at last.

Her gaze made a slow, apprehensive sweep of their surroundings. The bandeleros' hideout had once been a tiny community, it seemed, a handful of weather-worn cabins constructed of adobe and rough-hewn logs, tin roofs and boarded up windows. A mining town gone bust.

Beyond the forlorn structures stood, remarkably, a mission church, its yard well-tended, the adobe recently painted. As if too proud to be reduced to ruin, the church had been blessed with loving care. Yet if a priest remained in residence, he was nowhere to be found.

Her gaze clung to the little sanctuary. She longed for time inside, to sit in the cool solitude and enjoy its peace. But she quelled the desire and exchanged a wary glance with Quinn.

"Now what?" she asked quietly.

He, too, swept the hideout with a grim once-over.

"Guess we'll find out soon enough," he answered.

All about them, the bandeleros began to dismount, their faces split in wide grins beneath their thick moustaches, their relief at having finally reached the end of their journey evident. The Huertas dismounted, too. Tomas barked orders to his men, sending them scattering in all directions to obey.

The bandeleros seemed at ease here, and Hannah guessed this was a refuge they used often. A home, of sorts. A protective haven.

Quinn draped his reins over the saddle horn and swung free of his mount. He strode over to Hannah and studied her from beneath the brim of the Stetson.

She peered down at him and didn't move. She couldn't help the tug of a frown on her lips.

His brow lifted at it. "You going to sit there all night, woman?"

Hannah refrained from confessing she feared she couldn't move for the stiffness of her muscles and the numbness in her behind. Drawing a determined breath, she slid free of a stirrup and maneuvered from the saddle, only to tumble ungracefully to the ground.

Quinn instinctively grabbed for her. She reached for him in turn and clutched the hard breadth of his shoulders for support.

Her legs wobbled. A faint grimace touched her mouth.

"You okay?" he asked, the words husky with concern. His hands gripped her hips. She could feel the strength in them. The warmth.

"I've not ridden astride in a long while. I'll be fine in a minute or two. Truly." Embarrassed at her lack of tenacity, she could lift her eyes no higher than his top shirt button.

Tomas and Sophia approached. Quinn turned toward them but kept a hand securely upon her hip, as if he expected her knees to buckle again at any moment.

He met Sophia's obsidian gaze. His glare blamed her for Hannah's discomfort.

"Yesterday, you spoke of a bargain between us, Sophia," he said without greeting. He indicated Fenwick's carriage with a terse gesture. "You claimed our rig. What will you give in return?"

Her stern expression gave way to amusement.

"We give you clothes on your back. Food in your

belly. And protection from Frank Briggs," she said. "Is that not fair enough in exchange for your beautiful carriage?"

"He'll search long and hard for us," Quinn said. "I told you we have to keep moving."

Her smile disappeared. "I have not yet decided when you will leave."

"There's nothing for us here," he said, his tone sharp. "We'll only bring you trouble."

"That is for us to decide. You could be valuable to us."

Quinn's eyes narrowed. "Valuable?"

Tomas crossed his arms over the gunbelts upon his chest. "You are tall and strong, Senor Landry. You ride a horse as if you were born to it." A smile lurked under the thin line of his moustache; clearly, he enjoyed the battle Quinn fought with his wife. "I would guess you can drive cattle, brand them, work a herd?"

"I could manage," he scowled.

"And your lovely wife could cook and clean?"

"She's no one's servant," Quinn snapped.

"But to save her life, she could be, eh?" Sophia asked.

Cooking and cleaning. To save her life?

It was too easy. There was more to the Huertas's bargain. There had to be.

Hannah puzzled over it, but Pa had taught her to be patient, and Mother Superior stressed humility. Until the time came, she'd combine the two virtues and learn the Huertas's covert plan before they could put it into place.

In the meantime, sweeping floors and stirring pots over a fire wouldn't be so terrible.

"Quinn." Hannah turned to him in a silent plea to accept the terms of their so-called bargain, at least for now. Refusing would only destroy any chance of possible escape. "I'll do what they want. We both will."

His gaze slammed into hers. She longed to assure him their time here amongst the outlaws would not be long.

She made that pledge, deep inside.

Finally, he nodded, and his grim gaze found Sophia's once more.

"My wife"—his tone caressed the words in mocking challenge—"needs a long, hot bath. She'll need some decent food to eat, too, and a real bed to sleep in."

If Sophia disapproved of the demands he placed on her, twisting the terms of their bargain to suit his desires, she didn't show it.

"I would like that as well, Senor Landry," she said and smiled faintly.

"Our bargain is settled, then." Tomas suddenly clapped his hands in a show of courtesy that might or might not have been genuine. Hannah couldn't decide. "Miguel! Miguel, where are you?"

At his shout, an ancient little Mexican appeared in the doorway of the largest of the cabins, an apron tied around his spare waist. His delight in seeing the leaders of his people was evident, and Tomas and Sophia embraced him briefly.

"Heat plenty of water, Miguel. Sophia and the gringa want a bath," Tomas said.

"Si, Tomas." Miguel bobbed his graying head, and he eyed Hannah with undisguised curiosity before flashing her a snaggle-toothed smile and hurrying away.

Tomas turned to Sophia. "Give them Julio's room,

mi querida. He can sleep with the horses."

"Of course, Tomas."

Quinn frowned. "We don't want Cortez's room."

"You are our guests," he said simply. "The horses will not mind him with them." He gripped Quinn's shoulder, urging him forward. "Come. We will allow our wives some time to themselves, eh?"

"No," Quinn said. "I'll stay with Hannah."

"The senora will be safe," Tomas said firmly. "She will be with Sophia. No harm will come to her."

The Mexican's patience was not to be tested, and Hannah feared the consequences should Quinn push him to his limits. She turned to Quinn, her gaze lifting to his.

"I'll be fine," she murmured. "Don't worry."

She knew the inward battle he fought. She sensed it in the hard line of his jaw, in the unyielding set of his mouth.

"Hannah . . ." Her name trailed off his tongue in frustrated protest.

"Please. Don't worry," she said again and took a small step back from him. "Go."

His hand fell away from her hip. "I'll see you later, then. Soon."

She nodded with a jerky movement. She clung to his low-voiced promise and watched him leave. A vague feeling of loss, of being all alone, crept over her. She swallowed it down.

"Come, Hannah," Sophia said. "I will show you into our grand hacienda."

Her rueful expression revealed the mockery of her words. She strode ahead of Hannah, the hems of her serape brushing against the knees of her snug-fitting pants with each long, confident stride.

Hannah tried not to think of Quinn and followed more slowly, her tight muscles loosening with each step. She cautiously entered the cabin, which, in its early days, might have been a stagecoach station large enough to put up boarders for a night or two.

Sophia halted in the main room, furnished with little more than a table and chairs and a bright woven rug. A fire crackled in the fireplace. The scent of spices and meat simmering on a stove hung in the air.

She swept off her beaded sombrero and tossed it onto the table top. With swift and dexterous fingers, she unplaited the midnight black braid hanging down her back and shook her hair free.

She continued through the room and into a narrow hall.

"Here is where you and Senor Landry will stay." She opened a door and stepped aside. "Tomas and I will be across from you."

"There's no need to give us Cortez's room," Hannah said, reiterating Quinn's words, as wary of the repercussions as he. "We can stay somewhere else."

Sophia shrugged. "It is Tomas's wish. Do not worry about Julio."

She returned to the main room and paused at the cast iron stove. Using a towel to protect her hand, she lifted the lid to the big pot and inspected its contents.

"Miguel has prepared jerky and rice soup, my favorite." She smiled, her delight rare and unfettered. She bent over the pot and inhaled approvingly of the aromas wafting upward, then set the lid back onto the pot.

Suddenly, she paled. The towel dropped, and she

clutched her stomach. She moaned and swayed.

Alarmed, Hannah rushed to her side. "Sophia, what is it?"

"Por Dios! I think I'm going to be sick."

"Sit," Hannah said and pushed her into the nearest chair. "Put your head between your knees. It'll help."

Amazingly, Sophia obeyed and doubled over, her long, silken hair falling over her head and pooling on the floor.

Hannah removed the wool cloak from her shoulders and laid it aside. The first time she'd seen Sophia Huerta, she'd been a fierce outlaw leading an entire band of lawless men, determined to steal Fenwick's rig for herself and taking Quinn and Hannah captive in the process.

Now, the tiny innocent within her belly toppled her into the ageless role of motherhood and burdened her with the miseries of morning sickness.

Hannah found a clean cloth and dipped it into a basin of cool water.

"Feeling better?" she asked.

"Si. Some." Sophia's voice sounded muffled.

"I'll help you to bed. Perhaps you should nap."

"No." Sophia sat up again, groaned, and leaned back against the chair. Her eyes closed. "I am fine."

Her sun-bronzed skin remained ashen. Hannah touched her cheek and noted the clamminess of it.

"When will the baby come?" she asked softly.

Sophia's eyes flew open. "You know of my baby?"

Hannah met her gaze. "Yes."

Sophia's mouth pursed, as if she puzzled over Hannah's discovery and her own failure to prevent it. Pensive, she rubbed her abdomen. "He will come in the spring."

Soon, Hannah thought. Very soon. She pressed the damp cloth to Sophia's forehead and smoothed away her hair. She thought of the years she'd lived with Pa, impressionable years when she'd longed for the normal life of a young girl growing into womanhood.

She'd never wanted a life running from the law.

"The baby will change everything, Sophia. You must realize that," she said.

The black eyes flashed with a touch of anger.

"Of course, I do. Every day, I think of it." She struggled to remove her serape, and Hannah helped her. "See?" Sophia patted her belly, too rounded to hide much longer. "I think of him always, and when he kicks inside me, I want to weep with happiness."

Her words touched Hannah's heart. This woman, harsh and unyielding when she was with her men, possessed all the tender feelings of any expectant mother.

"Twelve years, we try, Tomas and I," Sophia said. "We wanted a baby, and I was sure I was barren. When I realized God had given me His gift, I fell to my knees in thanks."

"But you spend your life always on the move," Hannah challenged. "Is that how you want to raise your child?"

"Por Dios. No."

"You waited so long. Think of the risks. He is an innocent. He will be defenseless against lawmen who chase you and Tomas."

Sophia leaned forward, her vexation returning the color to her cheeks.

"Do you think I do not worry about all these things?"

she demanded. "Do you think I do not want a real home? And land? And chickens and cows and pigs? Por Dios! I want them more than anything! And Tomas has promised me they will be mine!"

"When, Sophia?" Hannah persisted, skeptical.

Glory, how many times had she heard those same words from Pa? Promise after promise made but never kept.

Until it had been too late.

"For a long time, we have saved our pesos, Hannah." Sophia sat back, calmer. "Tomas has enough cattle now to start his own herd. It is time to find us a real home. Far away from here. We are ready now."

Hannah eyed her dubiously. "To be respectable citizens?"

Sophia hesitated. "Si."

"Just like that." She snapped her fingers.

Impatience darkened Sophia's features. "Si."

"And lawmen will never chase you again."

"Si." Sophia's toe tapped on the floor. All signs of her nausea seemed to have passed. "Except for one."

Hannah stilled. She could think of no other. "Frank Briggs?"

"*Bastardo!*" Sophia spat. "He, alone, haunts Tomas. Too long!"

Only then did the ragged pieces begin to fit—the bargain Sophia had been quick to suggest earlier. And enforce.

"You're using us, aren't you?" Hannah said, her eyes widening in shock. "To get even with him!"

Sophia stood abruptly and flung her hands upward. "Pah! I talk too much."

115

"How will you use us?" Hannah demanded. "What will you force us to do?"

Sophia turned, took a step toward her bedroom. Clearly, she had no intent of answering.

In a burst of temper, Hannah snatched Sophia's arm and spun her around.

"Tell me the terms of the bargain!" she commanded hoarsely.

Sparks of fury shot from the obsidian depths of Sophia's eyes. For a moment, she said nothing but glared at Hannah as hotly as Hannah glared at her.

In the next, the fury began to cool. The tension eased from her.

"We wait," she said simply.

Hannah blinked in a struggle to comprehend. "What?"

"We will see what the warden will do to recapture you and Senor Landry."

"And you expect us to—to just sit around here until he *finds* us?" Hannah gaped at her.

A smile curved Sophia's lips. "It is a little more complicated than that, Hannah."

Hannah opened her mouth to argue, to demand more information, but clamped it shut again. Sophia was too shrewd to reveal her plan until she was ready.

Hannah thought of the deal she'd made with Quinn. She thought of the peace she'd left behind in Mother Superior's convent.

And she thought Sophia Huerta was a fool.

She and Quinn would wait, Hannah knew. They had no choice but to comply with the terms of the Huertas's bargain.

But in the end, Hannah and Quinn would be the victors. The con game would be theirs. Hannah swore it. It was the next step on her long journey back to the security of the convent.

Sophia strode toward the hallway leading to her bedroom. She paused and glanced at the damp cloth she held in her hand. Her gaze lifted and found Hannah's.

"I have known of the child I carry for more than six months," she said softly. "In all that time, I could not tell my men of it. They would not give me sympathy when my stomach was twisted inside out with the morning sickness. Nor would I want them to." Her expression turned wry. "They would not obey orders from a woman in such a delicate condition, eh?"

Hannah said nothing. But she understood.

"Except for Tomas, only you, Hannah, have showed me kindness." She stood straighter, her chin hiked up a notch, as if the admission did not come easy. "Gracias. I will not forget."

Hannah could hardly wait to climb into the tub of bath water sitting in the middle of Julio Cortez's little room.

Sophia had gifted her with privacy. Four walls and a roof proved to be a privilege Hannah hadn't realized she missed. She hung her cloak on a peg behind the door and lighted a lantern. Then, for the first time since she'd left the convent, she took off her habit.

Wearing only her chemise, she contemplated the brown garment with a twinge of regret. She had no need of it now. Not with the role she must play as Quinn's wife, and she hoped Mother Superior would understand.

Hannah folded the habit with care, making sure her rosary beads, wooden cross and the widdy were all safely esconced in a pocket. She tucked her stockings and sandals inside and tied it into a neat bundle with the narrow length of rope she used for her belt. Finally, before she could change her mind, she stashed it all under Cortez's bed, well out of sight.

Sophia had been generous in lending her clothes and toiletries—a clean chemise, skirt and blouse, soap, a hairbrush, delicate combs to slide into her hair. She had even changed Cortez's sheets and brought extra blankets to ward off the night's chill.

An impeccable hostess, Sophia Huerta. If Hannah hadn't seen the change in the woman herself, she'd never have believed it.

Hannah removed her chemise and stepped into the tub. The deliciously warm water tingled over her bare skin, and she sank into the depths with a sigh of delight.

Within minutes, she scrubbed away the smells of campfire smoke, saddle leather and horse from her body. She washed trail dust from her hair and soaked the soreness from her limbs. Afterward, luxuriating in the feel of being clean again, she eased back against the side of the tub. A wonderful lethargy spread through her, and her eyes closed.

She didn't know how long she dozed, only that the water lapping against her breasts had turned cold, and gooseflesh had raised on her skin. Something awakened her—a sound in the hall outside the room, she realized—and her gaze instinctively darted to the door.

The knob turned, and Quinn stepped inside.

Chapter Nine

Hannah yelped and lunged for the towel lying next to the tub. She pressed the fabric to her bosom.

Quinn closed the door. His gaze drifted over her. Heat flickered in his dark eyes, a banked heat smouldering to life.

"I knocked," he drawled. "You didn't answer."

"I—I fell asleep."

"I see that."

He set a bowl brimming with jerky and rice on the rickety dresser and approached the tub.

Hannah squeezed her knees together.

"Quinn, please. I'm not dressed," she said, floundering with an acute sense of vulnerability she'd never experienced before.

"I see that, too."

"Get out. Now." She strove to put firmness into the command.

He ignored her.

"Stand up," he said.

Her imagination went wild at what he intended, at what the hidden side to his savagery might do.

"*Not* until you get out," she said.

"Your lips are blue with cold." He reached for one of the blankets Sophia had left and shook free its folds. "Now, stand up."

She eyed the blanket, then eyed him. "Why?"

"Because your towel is soaked through, that's why."

Indeed, most of it had fallen into the water in her haste to cover herself. She bit her lip.

He gripped the edge of the blanket with both hands and spread his arms wide, holding it high. "C'mon, Hannah."

She hesitated. Then, assuring herself he had only her best interests in mind after all, she rose slowly, her fingers keeping the towel plastered against the front of her body.

He swept the blanket snugly about her shoulders and lifted her from the tub. Bath water streamed down her legs and pooled at their feet.

She tilted her head back and studied him. A day's growth of stubble roughened his cheeks. Mingled smells of leather and smoke assailed her, the masculine scent of him she'd come to recognize.

Their gazes met. Deep and dark, like rich sable, his eyes locked with hers. They held her entranced.

"When you didn't show up for supper, I got worried," he murmured.

"I'm sorry." The words drifted between them on a husky whisper. "I lost track of time, I guess."

His hands slid from her shoulders down her arms and back up again. Warming her. Drying her.

"Sophia said you were taking your bath. I waited awhile, then decided to come after you."

"I'm fine. You needn't have worried."

The beginnings of a frown turned those sable depths stormy.

"There's plenty to worry about around here," he said. "You're at the top of the list." He released her. "I don't like it when I can't see you. Anything could happen when I'm not around."

Beneath the blanket, Hannah's spine straightened. She could take care of herself. Pa—and the men he'd chosen as his friends—had seen to that.

Yet she remembered the dismay she'd felt when Quinn left with Tomas shortly after their arrival into the bandeleros's hideout. The dismay of being on her own. Without him.

The reality of their situation left Hannah all too aware of her nakedness beneath the blanket. She clutched it tighter.

Quinn went to the window, lifted aside the plain curtain with a lean finger and directed his attention to the night outside. She suspected it was his way of giving her privacy without leaving the room.

"How was your time with Sophia?" he asked.

Hannah reached for the clean chemise. "I discovered she was human."

Quinn grunted, clearly skeptical. She dropped the blanket and towel with one hand and shimmied into her chemise with the other.

"She's going to have a baby," Hannah added.

"A baby?" He shot a surprised glance toward the closed door, as if to see for himself.

"She'll make a good mother, I think." Hannah put

on a white cotton blouse, embroidered around the neckline with bright, dainty flowers. "She already loves the child. Very much."

"No one knows?"

Hannah shook her head. "Except for Tomas. And us."

He digested the news. "Poor kid will cut his teeth on rifle cartridges and learn to crawl on the back of a horse."

Hannah's lips twitched. "Hardly."

"You have to admit the Huertas aren't society's version of perfect parents."

"Yes, but Sophia is ready to settle down." She pulled a deep green skirt over her head, adjusted its fullness around her waist. The fabric had been rendered supple from many launderings and weighed far less than the heavy wool she was accustomed to. "She said as much."

"Neither she nor Tomas will do anything until this so-called bargain with us is settled."

"Ah, yes. The bargain. They want Briggs."

His gaze shot to hers.

"She said that, too," Hannah murmured.

"Tomas escaped from Briggs's prison and is afraid he'll be recaptured. They think we'll lead Briggs to them? So they can get rid of him?"

Hannah marvelled at his perception. "Very good, Mr. Landry."

"Christ," he breathed, turning back to the window. "I can't wait to get out of here."

"Just play the confidence game, and we will."

His dark head swiveled to her once more. He made a dark-lashed examination of her, the intensity of it leaving her feeling naked again.

"And that means no more nun, doesn't it?" he purred.

She stilled. "Yes."

The curtain fell back into place. He stepped toward her, his presence overpowering in the little room. He circled her, studying the skirt and blouse as if he could see right through them.

As if he liked what he saw.

Hannah didn't move. Her heart thumped within her breast. Suddenly, she wanted her habit back. She felt far safer in the thick, drab fabric that hid the shape of her body, whose coarse threads reminded her of the life she'd chosen and the peace she sought.

He trailed a lazy finger along the scooped neckline.

"Embroidered flowers become you, Hannah. Brown wool doesn't," he said softly.

"Quinn, don't."

"How long has it been since you've worn ordinary clothes?"

Her eyes flashed in defiance. "A year. Since the first day I entered the convent."

"Tsk. Tsk. Too bad."

She pressed her lips together.

"You're a fetching woman, Hannah Benning. Do you know that?"

"Vanity has never been one of my strong suits," she retorted.

"I'll bet it hasn't." He reached for a mirror, cracked in one corner. "Look at yourself."

"I don't want to." She angled her head away, refused to admit to him mirrors were forbidden at the convent for the selfish and vain thoughts they fostered.

Or that she was gripped by a raw fear of what she

might see, the changes that had occurred over the past twelve months.

Or that were occurring now. This minute. Without her brown wool habit.

"Look." Determined, he gripped her chin.

Because he would allow nothing else, she reluctantly obeyed.

"Do you see?" he asked, stepping behind her, staring into the mirror with her.

The top of her head reached his chin. The expanse of his chest enveloped the slender span of her shoulders. The column of her throat, the pale color of her skin, contrasted with the sun-browned maleness of his.

His hand lifted, and he gently speared his fingers into the damp curls along her nape.

"Your hair is silky," he said. "Smooth like satin. The way a man likes a woman's hair to be."

"It's too short," she protested, in spite of everything.

"When it feels like this, he doesn't care how long it is. Or how short."

She held her breath, not wanting to be affected by his compliment. He shifted the mirror's position, letting her see the swell of her breasts below the blouse's neckline. The white cotton tapered downward, where its hem disappeared into the waistband of her skirt. The green fabric lay against her flat belly and hugged the curve of her hips, then finally ended at her bare ankles.

"I'd warrant a good many women would love to have what you hide away in that habit of yours, Hannah."

She glanced away. "I made the decision a long time ago. It's the right one for me."

"Is it?"

She refused to look at him. "Yes. Of course."

"Damned if the whole male race would disagree."

She clucked her tongue and eyed him dubiously. "You exaggerate, Quinn Landry."

"I speak the truth."

His head lowered, as if he was drawn to the fresh, soapy scent of her. She held herself straight, afraid to touch him, afraid to let him touch her.

"This con game of ours," he said, his breath warm against her neck, "is going to be hell."

Her startled gaze flew to his, and she twisted away from him.

"Our con game will save our lives," she said, the words unsteady.

He straightened and returned the mirror to the dresser top with an impatient toss. "We'll survive by our wits. Nothing more."

"And afterward, we'll go back to our former lives and never see each other again."

His gaze slammed into hers.

"Yeah. That's right. We will." He thrust the bowl of soup toward her. "Eat your supper before it gets cold."

He strode toward the door and jerked it open.

"Where are you going?" she asked before she could stop herself.

"For a swim."

"A swim?" She gaped at him. "The water will be freezing."

"Damn right it will."

The door slammed behind him. Hannah winced.

His sudden change in mood left her pensive. Balancing the bowl in her hand, she picked up the mirror and studied her reflection.

She'd nearly succumbed to Quinn's flattery and her

Pam Crooks

own feminine desire to believe him. A dangerous mix, she thought, on the heels of panic. The mistake could prove disastrous and send her tumbling from the course she'd chosen for her life.

Hannah vowed to be stronger next time. More focused. She wouldn't let Quinn and his potent manliness distract her from shunning the ways of the world.

Yet her fingers lifted to the curls at her neck. She touched one, stroked the feel of it, just as he'd done a few moments ago.

Hannah let out a troubled breath. Mother Superior had taught her many things at the convent, all different from what she'd learned from Pa.

And neither of them had taught her how to feel like a woman.

The bandeleros allowed Quinn a quick dip in the valley's spring, though one of the guards kept in clear sight through the duration. The water chilled his body, but had little effect on cooling his blood.

He blamed Hannah for it. Hell, she could wear sackcloth and ashes and still stir his lust.

He lingered outside smoking a cigarette for as long as he dared. He didn't want to leave her alone anymore than he already had. The hideout had grown quiet; most of the men had turned in for the night. Tomas and Sophia had gone to bed long ago, trusting the guards posted about the place to watch over Hannah and himself, to see that they didn't escape.

Snuffing the cigarette, Quinn finally entered the quiet cabin and paused outside the closed door to their room. A sliver of light shone along the floor and indicated Hannah had not yet gone to sleep. A part of him wished she had. It would be easier that way.

He pushed open the door and strode inside, his glance sweeping the room. Her supper bowl was gone. The empty bathtub sat in a corner, the wet towel hung over the edge to dry. On the dresser lay the skirt and blouse with its embroidered flowers, folded neatly in readiness for the next day.

He found her in bed, lying on her side, turned away from him. At his entrance, she scurried to a sitting position and pulled the bed covers up to her neck.

"Oh!" she said, her voice soft in the low glow from the lantern. She held the sheets in a death grip. "You startled me."

"Sorry." He shut the door, slipped the latch into place. "I wasn't sure you'd still be up."

She nodded, a jerky movement. She was as tense as he. "I was just lying here. Thinking. That's all."

He ran his fingers through his wet hair. Fatigue had begun to set in.

"You could have used the tub, Quinn. Miguel would have heated more water—"

"If I'd wanted the tub, I'd have arranged for it."

"But you could catch pneumonia out there." She frowned, her brows puckered in concern.

He shucked his shirt and tossed it over her blouse and skirt. The sight struck him, the intimacy of having his clothes draped with hers.

"I'm never sick, Hannah. Fenwick's Solution excepted."

A vision of what she wore beneath the bedcovers flared in his brain. The chemise, thin against her bare skin. . . .

He scowled and pulled off his boots and dropped

127

them to the floor. His socks followed. He strode to the empty side of the bed.

Hannah watched him, her expression like a doe staring at the wrong end of a shotgun, and Quinn knew what she was thinking.

He pulled back the covers and loosened the top button of his Levis. He reached for the second, and Hannah let out a squeak. She leapt off the mattress, taking half the covers with her.

Her throat moved in a hard swallow. "I've been thinking how we can do this."

"Do what?" he asked, letting her squirm.

"Pass the night." She swallowed again. "Together."

A brow arched. "And?"

She ran her tongue around her top lip. "I thought, perhaps, you could take the floor. I'd share the blankets, of course, and—"

"I think, perhaps, you thought wrong." He set his hands on his hips. "Do you know how long it's been since I slept in a real bed, woman?" He growled the challenge. "With a pillow and clean sheets and a decent roof over my head?"

She paled.

"Tonight, I will."

Panic flitted over her features; he could almost see her mind scrambling to come up with a logical solution.

"And I'm not kin to a lady sleeping on a cold, hard floor, either," he continued. "Unless, of course, she insists." He paused, letting the words sink in. "You decide, Hannah."

Her gaze darted downward to the floor's rough wooden slats and back up to him. "This—this whole thing is ridiculous. It's not proper."

"You've spent the last several nights with me. Why is tonight any different?"

"It just is. We're here in this little room together and you're—you're—"

"Lusting for you?" he demanded softly. "Yeah, I admit it. If I thought you looked fetching in Sophia's clothes, you're doubly so wearing next to nothing now."

She emitted a shocked gasp and struggled to keep the bulky bedcovers in front of her. Her efforts pulled the hem of her chemise higher over her knee and teased him with the view of a well-shaped leg.

"How dare you insinuate I'm trying to seduce you!" she said, aghast.

"I insinuate nothing of the sort," he refuted. "You seduce without realizing it."

Spots of color blossomed in her cheeks. "Then I apologize."

"Don't." His scowl deepened. "I give you my word I won't ravish you. I prefer my women willing. Believe me."

Clearly, she didn't. She clutched the bedcovers tighter. Moments passed.

"Hannah," he rumbled in warning.

"All right, then." Her hazel-green eyes snapped a warning of her own. "I'll share the bed with you. But I swear I'll hold you to your promise. If you touch me"— she yanked one of the blankets free and tossed it at him—"my knife will swing. And you'll have no need of a woman ever again."

The vehemence of her threat stunned him. The violence of it. Maybe she wasn't as innocent as he'd thought.

"Do I make myself clear, Mr. Landry?"

A lazy smile of admiration curved his mouth. "Quite clear, Miss Benning."

Her movements sharp, she swaddled herself from ankle to neck in the blanket, using the fabric as a shield against him, preventing any chance their bodies might come in contact during the night.

She blew out the lantern and flopped on the mattress in a huff, presenting him with her back and heaving a provoked sigh.

Not sure if he should be annoyed or amused, Quinn spread the blanket over his side of the bed. He removed his Levis and climbed in next to her.

But sleep eluded him. He stared at the dark ceiling, then at the shadowed shapes scattered about the room. His head turned upon the pillow, and he studied Hannah, the gently curved silhouette of her head, her shoulders and the womanly flare of her hips.

Hannah Benning. A beguiling mix of innocence and mystery. She intrigued him. And he wanted her more than he should. A yearning, he suspected, that went beyond four years of celibacy in Frank Briggs's penitentiary.

He pitched forward into the darkness, falling end over end into an abysmal hole. The blackness swallowed him. Terrified him.

He landed in the most wretched bowels of the earth. Forever lost. Forgotten.

He would die here.

Screams of terror filled his lungs and lodged in his throat. Choking him. Tearing him apart.

The stench of excrement filled his nostrils. Vomit and

sweat. Evil and pain. Sickness and death.

Everywhere.

He couldn't breathe.

His fingers clawed the damp walls, slimy and slick from the blood of men before him.

Dead. All of them, dead.

The chains weighted him down, the links cold, solid. Iron shackles bound his wrists and ankles.

He'd never escape. Ever.

Heavy breathing, hoarse with rage, filled his ears, prickled the hair on his neck. Panic surged through him.

He was going to die.

A reptile's beady red eyes appeared in the darkness. The demon slithered closer. Hissing and snapping. Its breath was fetid. Greed oozed from grimy pores. It reared up, a whip clutched in sharp claws.

The cat o' nine tails cracked across his chest, tearing him open. Blood spurted. The whip lashed out, again and again. The pain staggered him.

His heart labored to keep him breathing, to keep him alive, but the darkness kept pulling him under.

He didn't want to die.

But the whip was raised one more time. . . .

Quinn awakened with a jolt.

His pulse thundered against his temples. A cold sweat dampened his forehead.

He pressed his palms to his eyes and tried to shut out the horrors, but they stayed to haunt him. The scars on his back ached, a tribute to the vivid nightmare. A violent shudder racked his body. He sucked in a breath and opened his eyes again.

Pam Crooks

The nightmare became less vivid. His heart rate slowed, beat by beat. The pain eased. Reality returned, and relief flowed like soothing waters through him.

His gaze swept the darkness, and he recognized the peace it brought. He embraced the night. Never again would he take it for granted.

Over the years, he'd lived through one hell after another. And if not for Hannah . . .

His head swiveled, and he found her beside him. She slept deeply, one arm curled above her head, her face angled away from him. A slender leg had found its way free of her blanket, the chemise's hem hiked to mid-thigh.

If not for Hannah, he'd be dead.

She'd saved him from the nightmare, and gratitude flooded him in a rush. The depth of it moved him.

In blissful sleep, she seemed vulnerable and helpless, incapable of the strength she'd shown again and again. A fierce possessiveness went through him.

He raised up on an elbow and grasped the edge of her blanket, tugging it up to cover her against the room's chill.

She sighed. In a shift of womanly arms and legs, she rolled toward him and snuggled against his chest.

He stilled.

Her threat marched through his memory. He'd given his word not to touch her.

But he hadn't expected this.

The clean scent of soap lingered in her silken curls. The warmth of her body ebbed into his, and the embers in his loins flared hot.

A roaring need convinced him he could take her now.

132

He could join his body with hers and sate this lust plaguing him.

But the civilized side held back. And he cursed himself a fool for being so damned noble.

He arranged the bedcovers over them both, slipped his arm beneath her and fitted her comfortably against his shoulder.

He dipped his chin against the satiny wisps at her temple. She calmed him, gave him new strength.

Quinn closed his eyes again. And slept.

Chapter Ten

Hannah awoke the next morning to find Quinn already gone.

She rose, washed and dressed, telling herself all the while she didn't need to see him to start the day, that if he declined to wake her and let her know he was leaving, or that he preferred not to tell her where he'd be or what he'd be doing, then that was certainly fine with her.

But throughout the day as she helped Miguel serve the noon meal and, later, begin preparations for supper, her gaze strayed often to the window in search of him.

Sophia explained that Tomas had ordered Quinn to assist him and several of his men in rounding up mustangs wintering in a nearby canyon. Hannah knew Quinn had no choice in the matter. Tomas was determined to keep him in close range as part of his intent to flush out Frank Briggs.

Hannah, in turn, had been relegated to kitchen chores. She clung to the virtues of humility and obedience, and she swallowed down the urge to refuse her assigned duties. If nothing else, the menial tasks helped pass the time until Quinn returned.

Thus, she spent the day in a low-roofed cabin that had once been a saloon in the little mining town and was now used by the bandeleros as their cantina, a glorified chow hall and the hideout's gathering place. The men took their meals there, and later at night, Hannah guessed, their tequila, as well.

Miguel proved to be an affable companion. He worked hard for the Huertas, appeared loyal and trustworthy. Sophia respected him; indeed, she treated him as she would a revered family member. He was patient with Hannah, kind and good-natured. She found his snaggle-toothed smile endearing, and of all the fierce, ruthless men in the place, she was convinced she was safest with him.

"Senora, listen." Miguel's knife paused over the potato he was peeling. His graying head cocked. "Tomas returns with his wild horses."

Hannah glanced up from her own bowl of potatoes. She, too, heard them before she saw them, the low drone from the clomp of their hooves on the hard, packed earth. The rumble grew louder, intensifying as the animals drew closer.

Suddenly, a small herd of about a dozen mustangs thundered past the cantina, churning up dust and pebbles and rattling the window glass.

"Your husband rides with them," Miguel said, indicating one of the men flanking the horses.

Hannah's gaze found Quinn, his eyes squinted

against the dust and sun, his shirt billowing over his back and shoulders in the wind. He held a coiled rope in his hand; his expression revealed his concentration in guiding the powerful mustangs to the corral.

She marvelled at his ease in the saddle, his expertise with the powerful animals.

"You would like to watch him awhile, eh?" asked Miguel knowingly.

Her heart gave an involuntary lurch at the opportunity. "Well, yes, but—"

Miguel waved a thin arm toward the direction of the door. "Go, Senora. Sophia will not mind if you leave for a little while. Go."

Her heart pounded a little harder in anticipation. "Thank you, Miguel."

She left the cantina and strode toward the pole fence surrounding the corral. Lifting the hem of her dark green skirt, she climbed up to sit on the top rail and searched for Quinn amongst the sea of constantly moving horses.

The mustangs were breathtaking in their wildness. Plucked from their freedom by Tomas Huerta, they fought against their captors at every turn. The men worked diligently to guide them inside the fence, but the animals pranced and reared, their nervous whinnies high-pitched and combative.

One of them, a *gruello* stallion with black mane, tail and feet broke from the herd and headed toward a space between the riders. Hannah frowned at the opening. It shouldn't have been there.

If the leader broke free, she knew in growing trepidation, the rest of the herd would try to follow. Tomas, at the entrance to the corral, shouted and waved his arm frantically to the flank riders.

Quinn twisted in the saddle and spied the bolting stallion. He yelled and spurred his own mount after him. Keeping a firm grip on the reins with a gloved hand, he swung his lariat high over his head. The loop whirled in continuous motion, widening steadily as the slipknot slid down the length of hemp.

Hannah gripped the rail, her nerves humming with tension. If the lariat missed its mark, Quinn would have no time to tighten the loop and start over. The stallion would be long gone. And victorious.

Quinn took aim. For a heart-stopping second, the rope spun in mid-air; in the next, it dropped like a noose over the blue-gray neck. Quinn jerked hard, his bootheels dug into the stirrups, and his horse braced its legs to keep the line tight.

The *gruello* reared, screamed and fought. Quinn held the line, his muscles bunching with the effort as he dodged the flailing forelegs and battled the horse into submission.

After what seemed an eternity, the stallion's cries subsided, and he gave up the fight. He stood wary, yet docile, nickering low in his throat. Quinn reached over and stroked the glistening neck, then gathered up the lariat's slack. He turned the *gruello* and trotted toward the corral.

Hannah pressed her fingers to her mouth, holding her elation in. His skill stunned her. Exhilarated her.

"He's good, senora. Very good."

Hannah turned at the smooth-voiced comment. Sophia draped her arms over the top rail and watched the herd part like peasants for their king. The *gruello* entered the corral, his arrogant head held high in defeat.

"Yes," Hannah said softly, her gaze on Quinn again.

With the herd captured and secure within the pole fence, the men dismounted with broad grins beneath their moustaches. They gathered around Quinn, their admiration obvious.

Watching Quinn in his victory, Hannah realized how little she knew about him. He'd been accused of murdering his brother's wife. Glory, he was capable of it. She'd seen the violence in him at the penitentiary the night he escaped. He'd been brimming with rage, had acted the savage from a festering desperation and hate.

And yet . . .

And yet she'd seen the civilized side to him, too. He hadn't abused her when there'd been every chance. Instead, he'd seen to it she was warm and dry, with food in her belly and clean clothes on her back. He'd kept her as safe as he could with the turn their lives had taken.

The towering walls around her heart weakened, softening her initial impression of him. Something in his past had shaped him to the man he was, had hinted at honor, had honed his skills as a horseman.

And had branded him a man accused of murder.

But was he truly guilty of it?

He spied her from across the corral. Their gazes connected for a single charged moment before he left the group of bandeleros. He removed the Stetson and batted it against his thigh, loosening the dust that had collected along the brim.

"Bravo, Senor Landry," Sophia called out. "You have made Tomas very happy just now."

His dark glance lighted on her. "It would've been a

helluva shame to let that horse go, Sophia."

Her reply dimmed in Hannah's ears. Quinn returned the hat to his head as he drew closer to the fence, then reached up to clasp her waist and swing her down to the ground.

She clutched his shoulders in surprise, found his muscles solid beneath her palms. Her body leaned into his to keep her balance.

"You've roped horses before," she said breathlessly, quietly, steadying herself against him.

"A few times."

Her brows raised at his flippant reply. She knew his mastery over the animals went far beyond that, but with Sophia near, she said nothing more.

Quinn hooked his arm lazily over her shoulder. His intent, certainly, was to play the part of an attentive husband, yet Hannah stood rigid beneath the weight of it, for she found the gesture unnecessarily possessive. Far too bold.

And much too pleasing.

"Something went wrong with the *gruello* stallion, Senor Landry," Sophia said. "What happened?"

He shrugged. "One of the riders was out of position when the horse bolted," he said, accusing no one.

But Tomas spoke heatedly with Julio Cortez. The leader's hand slashed through the air in his outrage. Cortez accepted the tongue-lashing, but his fleshy cheeks quivered with the effort of holding back his excuses.

Sophia's scrutiny slashed across her cousin.

"Julio!" she said with a snarl in disgust. "His carelessness almost cost Tomas the entire herd."

139

"Everything happened fast," Quinn said. "Any of us could have slipped up."

Sophia didn't seem to hear. The dangerous thrust of her jaw indicated she longed to give Cortez a thrashing of her own.

At Tomas's terse gesture, Cortez stalked away from the corral, hurling Quinn an ugly glare as he passed.

Tomas joined them and slipped a hand to Sophia's waist, pulling her close. She gazed up at him, and her expression mellowed.

"Tomas will use the wild mustangs to start a herd for us. They will be broken to saddle, then sold to horse traders for a handsome price," she said.

"Senor Landry has proven his skill with horses. Perhaps he will help us tame them, eh, Sophia?" Flashing her a conspiratorial smile, his fury with Cortez seemed to dissipate at the prospect.

"I don't intend to stick around long enough, Huerta," Quinn said evenly. "You'll have to find someone else to break them."

The bandelero laughed heartily. He clearly took no offense at Quinn's blunt refusal. "The gringo speaks his mind. He is not afraid of us." Though he spoke to his wife, his attention settled on Quinn, and his mirth faded. "If the herd had escaped, we might never have found them again. Gracias, senor."

Quinn lifted a shoulder in a dismissive gesture. "Might have to call the favor back on you sometime, Tomas."

A guarded light stole into the black eyes. The Mexican made no promises.

"You have worked hard all day, *mi querido,*" Sophia said, touching her husband's cheek. "You must be hungry. Hannah, surely supper is ready by now. Miguel will need your help in serving the men."

Hannah stiffened at her condescending manner, and she strove for the humility she needed to obey the order without complaint.

"I'll walk her back," Quinn said, his shadowed expression daring the Huertas to deny him.

But Tomas merely nodded. "We will join you soon."

Quinn directed her from the corral, his arm still looped around her.

"Everything go okay today?" he asked.

"Well enough." She shrugged. "Under the circumstances."

"We left early this morning. Before dawn." He regarded her with a trace of amusement. "You were sleeping pretty sound. I didn't want to wake you."

She remembered her chagrin at discovering him gone, at not knowing where he was or when he'd return. Was she getting too accustomed to being with him?

Was she liking it too much?

"You're not beholden to me for your every action, Quinn," she said, fearing the truth of her thoughts and rebelling against it. "Leastways, not until we're riding toward Amarillo again."

"Not beholden to you?" His arm slid from her shoulders. He halted and turned her around to face him. An impending storm brewed in his dark eyes. "We're beholden to each other, Hannah. I kept telling myself you were safe with Sophia, that Cortez was with me and couldn't harm you. But that didn't stop me from worrying about you all day."

And she'd worried about him. Minute after minute. Hour after hour.

"I'll survive, with or without you," she declared, needing to hear herself say it. To believe it.

"Don't quarrel with me, Hannah." The roughly spoken words coaxed for a truce between them. "I don't have much time with you—"

Before she could puzzle over his statement, his head lifted.

"Ssh." Quinn touched a finger to his mouth and pulled her into the deepening shade of a grove of cottonwood trees. His glance narrowed on the lean-to stable located a short distance beyond the cantina.

Julio Cortez withdrew a bottle of tequila from inside his coat. He halted, swayed, and pressed the bottle to his mouth. Liquid dribbled down his unshaven chin, and he dragged his sleeve across his lips to wipe it away.

Beside the stable, Tomas had parked Fenwick's carriage for safekeeping. Cortez attempted to climb into the rig, but his foot slipped, and he fell between the driver's seat and the floor, wedged like a pig in a poke. He wriggled his paunchy frame free and staggered back to the ground.

He held the black metal box in his hand. A swift list of its contents formed in Hannah's brain.

"Our money," she whispered and took an involuntary step forward.

"Let it go," Quinn said, holding her back.

But she couldn't let it go so easily, not when the coins and bills Fenwick had left behind would help them get to Amarillo.

And help her return to the convent.

142

Cortez fumbled with the lock, but it refused to yield. He went back to the stable and came out with a crowbar in his big hand. He worked the tool on the lock, his sun-brown face twisted from the difficulty of the job.

Finally, the lid popped open. Muttering an exclamation in Mex, the outlaw snatched the flask of whiskey inside and held it up to the sun, as if to convince himself its contents were real. He stuffed the bottle inside his coat with the tequila and did the same with the gold-plated box of matches. Picking up the laudanum, he squinted at the tiny letters on the label with an uncomprehending expression and flung the container to the ground.

"Ee-yah!" he cried.

Hannah knew he had, at last, discovered the money. He groped inside the box, then tossed it aside with one hand while he gripped the bills and coins in the other. Her heart plummeted.

He began to count the loot, his attention absorbed with stuffing the coins and bills into a small drawstring pouch before tucking it away in his coat.

Quinn stepped from the trees, his hand low on Hannah's spine.

"He's heading toward the cantina," he muttered, watching Cortez shuffle away. "Let's get you back to the kitchen before Huerta sends the entire band out looking for us."

Hannah's gaze remained riveted to the empty black box. They'd been wise not to confront Cortez over its contents. She'd long ago learned there was nothing worse than a liquored up outlaw with money hiding in his pocket.

But Hannah couldn't forget it. She couldn't survive

143

being meek and obedient, as Quinn expected, as Mother Superior had so often encouraged. Not now, amongst these ruthless men who took what they wanted at their whim. And even if Quinn could find his way amongst them, thinking little of the loot Cortez had stolen, Hannah was different.

She wanted the money back. Every cent.

Revolvers and rifles, ammunition belts and Bowie knives heaped a table just inside the door. Enough for a whole army, it seemed. Huerta had demanded all weaponry be deposited there during the meal, a celebration of the successful roundup of the mustangs and the impending birth of his child.

With Hannah's help, Miguel prepared huge portions of roasted chilies, wild turkey and fried potatoes, tortillas and refried beans. Tequila flowed freely. The outlaws' boisterous laughter abounded while they consumed his fare with relish.

Afterward, Hannah gathered their empty plates while the men leaned back in their chairs to enjoy a leisurely smoke. She carried the dishes back to the kitchen for washing, dumping the final load into a tub of soapy water.

She blew out a tense breath and tucked a curl behind her ear. Her gaze slid to Quinn, seated near the front of the cantina. She'd not yet taken the time to eat her own meal, and she longed to take her place beside him at the table he shared with Tomas, Sophia and Ramon.

But there would be time to eat later. She had another purpose in mind. And the time had come to see it through.

Cortez sulked in a shadowed corner of the cantina.

He slathered a tortilla with the last of the beans on his plate. Hannah took the coffee pot from the stove burner and went to him.

His bloodshot eyes followed her approach. He stuffed the chunk of tortilla into his mouth, chewed slowly and swallowed.

"I'll take your plate to the kitchen for you, Julio," Hannah said. The bandelero made her flesh crawl. She strove to keep her tone even. Pleasant.

He pushed it toward her.

"Coffee?" She indicated the pot in her hand.

"Senor Landry does not appreciate you for saving his life," he said in a slurred voice.

Hannah schooled her features to hide a flicker of alarm.

"Why do you say that?" she asked and poured the hot brew into his cup.

"He ignores you. He thinks only of his place of honor with Sophia and Tomas."

"Really?"

Quinn's gaze had hardly left her throughout the meal. He'd discreetly voiced his concern, his desire to have her stop working and eat with him.

It had been Hannah's decision to refuse, to bide her time until now. This moment.

"Si. He does not act like a loving husband." Cortez's lip curled. "He does not make you act like a loving wife."

The blood faltered in her veins. She feared he saw through their sham of a marriage. Equally troubling, she suspected Quinn had taken Cortez's exalted place with the Huertas, that Cortez's negligence in herding the mustangs had cost him the privilege.

145

That Cortez was jealous. Deep in his gut.

Hannah kept her expression cool. "It's true. My husband has had little time for me of late." She lowered her lashes, baiting him further. "Perhaps you know how it is when a wife wants her husband's attention?"

The fat mouth curved. From under the table, his beefy hand found her knee and slid slowly up her thigh.

"Si, Senora. I do," he murmured.

It took every inch of Hannah's willpower not to shrink back, to keep the con game going.

To win at it.

"Senor Landry is a fool." Cortez rose drunkenly from his chair, his grimy hand finding her waist and gripping hard. Her fingers tightened over the coffee pot's handle. "We shall teach him a lesson, eh, Senora? You and me."

He reeked of stale tequila, of last night's garlic, of horses and manure and his own unwashed body. He flung an arm around her and yanked her against him.

Hannah fought to quell the nausea roiling in her stomach. She squirmed against him, angling her face sharply to avoid his wet lips on hers.

Panic bubbled inside her. This, *this*, was the evil she'd wanted to escape in her past, men like Cortez whose hearts were as black as their souls, who'd forced her to flee to the sanctuary of Mother Superior's convent to be rid of them forever.

She'd underestimated Cortez's strength and her vulnerability in his grizzly-bear grasp. The coffee pot clattered to the floor, splattered her skirt and his pant legs with hot liquid. She slipped her hands between them, pushed against his burly chest with all the strength she owned.

She must have screamed in the struggle. In the far reaches of her consciousness, she heard chair legs scraping and men shouting. Cortez persisted, ignoring them all in his lurid intent to sink his teeth into her skin and rake his tongue over her flesh.

Desperation drove Hannah to the knife she kept at her waist, the one Quinn had given her to protect herself. Her fingers clutched the handle, and she swung out. The blade sliced across the fleshy cheek, and a stream of bright crimson appeared.

Only then, did Cortez release her. He howled in surprise, in pain, and lunged for Hannah again, but this time, a blurred maze of moustached faces and muscular bodies appeared in her vision, keeping him away.

Hannah choked on a sob and dropped the bloody knife to the floor. She turned and fled from the cantina.

The door to their room had no sooner slammed shut when Quinn flung it open again.

"Hannah. Christ, Hannah, are you hurt?" he demanded hoarsely.

He found her hunched over in the darkened room, her arms crossed over her breasts. She heaved in long, ragged breaths.

"Hannah, sweetheart." The sight of her cut through him. He reached for her, bundled her against him, tight to the wall of his chest.

She trembled violently. He closed his eyes, fed the rage inside him.

"Cortez won't get near you again. I swear it." Raw and jagged, the words tore from his throat. Her body was stiff, her arms huddled between them, her forehead pressed to the hollow of his neck. "I should have been more careful. I should have watched him closer. Damn him to hell."

His hands slid along her spine, stroked her, soothed her. Whispering her name over and over, he gave her time to compose herself while he brought his own thundering pulse under control.

She shifted beneath his embrace and rested her cheek on his shoulder with a quavering sigh.

"I could kill him, Hannah." Savage images of what might have been tortured him, stirred the fear and fury brewing within him. If she'd been alone, if he hadn't been there to rip Cortez from her. . . .

"No, Quinn." She made a sound of despair and pushed away from him.

"He'll pay for this."

"It—it wasn't his fault. Not entirely." She sat wearily on the bed, the mattress sagging a bit with her weight.

"I saw him groping you. He would have raped you if he had the chance."

She speared an unsteady hand through the auburn curls at her temple. "I provoked him."

Quinn's glance sharpened over her. "Provoked him?"

"For this." Sighing again, she tossed a small object toward him. Quinn snared it from mid-air and stared at the drawstring pouch in his palm.

"Fenwick's money," he said, stunned.

"Yes."

"Cortez kept it stashed inside his coat. How the hell did you get it?"

"I picked his pocket. Obviously." Her tone carried no triumph, only a grim and miserable resignation.

"You picked his pockets for this?" He gaped at her. "You're a damned fool, y'know that?"

"Maybe." Her eyes lifted to the ceiling, as if she sought forgiveness from her Maker. "I told myself I'd never steal again. I *vowed* it. But there was no other way."

All the old suspicions about her flooded back, real and more intense than ever. They shoved aside his anger with Cortez. Suddenly impatient with her, with himself for being duped by her skill, he yanked a match from the dresser and lit the lantern. A muted glow bathed the room. He turned back to her, setting his hands on his hips.

"You've got some explaining to do, woman," he said, his low voice ominous in the scattered shadows.

"Yes," she said simply.

"Who are you?" he demanded. "Is your name really Hannah Benning?"

"Yes. And I never lied to you about being a novitiate in the convent. It's all true."

"You know how to make widdies and throw locks."

"Yes." Her glance never wavered.

"What else can you do?"

A long moment passed. Her reluctance to reply was obvious.

"I can blow a bank safe," she said at last, her mouth pursed into a remorseful pout. "I can sneak-thieve by day or housebreak by night. I can make my own skeleton keys or bar-keys. And I can engrave my own counterfeit plates." Her chin tilted a notch, as if she relived her entire past in these few minutes. "But I swear I'll never pass boodle again. Ever."

Quinn's jaw dropped. His brain fought to comprehend all she told him.

"Now you know," she said, not looking at him.

"You're lying."

From the pocket of her skirt, she pulled out Fenwick's flask of whiskey, stolen from Cortez, too. "Would you like a drink? It might help you get over the shock of what I've just told you."

She spoke with utmost seriousness. He snatched the bottle with a muttered oath, took a swig and decided she was telling the truth.

"So who taught you the tricks?" he demanded.

"My father."

"Your father."

"James Peter Benning. Master con artist." She swallowed. "He was the best."

"Was?"

She stared down at her hands and nodded. "About a year ago, he was killed. Hung by an angry mob when he tried to pass counterfeit bills in their town. They didn't appreciate him cheating them."

"And the law failed to protect him?"

She made a bitter sound of contempt. "The marshal's father-in-law was the town's wealthiest banker. He was the only lawman and was conveniently detained with another matter during the lynching. He arrived after it was over. Pa never had a chance."

Quinn let out a long breath.

"Hannah, I'm sorry." He hunkered down in front of her. He meant it. Had justice been served in his part of Texas, he never would have lived the nightmare of four years in Briggs's penitentiary.

"I'm sorry, too."

Intrigued, wanting to hear more, he straightened and took another drink of whiskey, this one more thoughtful.

"Tell me about your mother," he said.

Again, her expression revealed her journey into her past.

"She died when I was twelve. She was beautiful and respectable and thoroughly in love with my father. But she couldn't abide his ways. I lived with her until she passed on. The day we buried her, my father came for me. We were together until he—he died."

Her proud gaze rested on Quinn. "In spite of what you must think, I hated the life Pa led. Yes, I was his accomplice in many of his crimes, but only to make sure he'd be safe. I was as good as he was. Maybe better. I figured, between the two of us, we wouldn't get caught. And if we did, we'd still be together."

"You never spent time in the cooler?" Quinn asked, his heart melting for her.

She shook her head. "Never. Sometimes, when I think about it, I'm amazed I didn't. I should have." She drew a shaky breath. "I deserved to."

Quinn reserved judgement. After all, he'd be the last man to qualify for sainthood.

"After your father died," he prodded. "What happened then?"

"That's when I fled to the convent. For the first time since my mother died, I felt safe. I had peace. I'd reconciled my past sins. And Pa's. Or at least I was still trying."

"Until the night you came to the penitentiary."

"Yes."

A corner of his mouth lifted. "And then all hell broke loose."

Hers softened in gentle amusement. "Yes."

"And I'm to blame."

"No." She shook her head for emphasis. "It's all part of the test, Quinn. That's why I wanted the money Cortez took from us. To make sure I can go back to the convent and show Mother Superior I made it through."

She fascinated him. In spite of her past, or because of it, she was like no other woman he'd ever known.

He extended his hand toward her. After a brief hesitation, she took it and he pulled her toward him.

"You shouldn't have picked Cortez's pocket for a few dollars," he said quietly. "It was too dangerous."

Her lashes lowered. "My father taught me how to watch out for myself. To survive. Even the best laid plans go awry sometimes. I learned to always have a better one."

She made him ache for all she'd gone through, for what she'd lost in her life.

And for what lay ahead. . . .

"Hannah," he whispered. He bent a finger beneath her chin and tilted it higher.

Her gaze settled on his mouth, and his head lowered to hers. Their lips touched, a tentative joining, chaste but daring. Forbidden. Still, their mouths clung and trembled, one moment stretching into another, and yet another. And still another.

A slow fire ignited inside Quinn. He thought of the bed behind them, of the long night to come. He thought of the warmth of her skin and the soft curves of her body and the pleasure they could bring him.

And digging deep, hard, for the integrity within him, he drew back.

Hannah's lashes fluttered open. There was so much he wanted to say, but couldn't.

"Tomorrow, Julio will have discovered his money missing," she said softly. "He'll know I stole it."

The words destroyed the intimacy of their kiss and shattered his lusty musings. He resisted a scowl. "Julio will be gone tomorrow. So will I."

She drew back to look up at him. "Gone? Where?"

"Tomas has several small herds of rustled cattle around here somewhere," he said, stepping away from her. He raked a hand through his hair and fought to cool his blood. "We'll be riding out first thing in the morning to round them up. We'll be gone five, six days. Maybe more."

"Five or six days!" Hannah's eyes widened.

He turned back toward her. "Tomas is working to build a herd of his own, just as he's doing with the mustangs. I wish I could bring you with me."

"Why can't you?"

"Because it's hard work. You're not suited for it."

"But nearly a week, Quinn!"

He steeled himself against the lament in her tone.

"A long time. Hell, I know." He set his jaw. "Cortez is coming with us, but Miguel will stay behind with you and Sophia. She's tough as nails, and she's got enough firepower around here to start her own revolution. You'll be as safe here as anywhere, Hannah."

She peered at him, a hint of a pout in her features, but made no further argument.

They both knew he had no choice but to ride with Tomas. It was all part of the confidence game; it would be easier to escape the bandeleros once they regarded him as one of them. It was imperative he and Hannah gain their trust.

But Quinn couldn't help thinking of Cortez and how he'd retaliate against Hannah when they returned, or of Frank Briggs, still out in the New Mexico Territory hunting for them. Quinn was gambling the warden was nowhere close, that he wouldn't think to search for them in an outlaws' hideaway.

He hated the thought of leaving Hannah.

Suddenly, five or six days seemed a lifetime.

Chapter Eleven

"Have you ever felt a baby kick, Hannah?" Sophia asked. "In the womb, I mean."

Nearly a week later, Hannah's pestle hovered above the stone mortar she was using to grind dried corn.

"No," she said, taken aback. "I've never had a baby."

Sophia sat on a wooden chair, her feet propped on another in front of her. She no longer wore slim-fitting pants and her serape, but instead a loose blouse and skirt. Her midnight black hair tumbled across her shoulders and down her back.

Sitting there, she looked like any other Mexican woman—albeit one who was particularly striking in her beauty and awed by the wonder of impending motherhood.

Sophia waved a hand impatiently. "Si, I know that. But a baby's kick—" She made a tsking sound. "Come here. Feel."

They'd been working the entire morning in the can-

Pam Crooks

tina's kitchen, making stacks and stacks of tortillas and grinding what seemed to be bushels of corn. Fatigue had settled over Sophia, and she'd needed to rest. Hannah welcomed the opportunity to put down the pestle and join her.

Sophia tightened the cotton fabric of her blouse over her rounded belly. "See? He is a busy little man today."

To Hannah's amazement, the other woman's stomach moved here and there as the baby stretched and jabbed his mother while he wriggled inside her.

"Now, feel." Sophia took Hannah's hand and laid it against her abdomen. Hannah breathed a soft exclamation at the miniature bumps against her palm.

"Is he not wonderful? And feel how firm it is here." She pressed Hannah's hand to a spot at her side. "His head, I think."

Hannah clucked her tongue. "He will be as hardheaded as Tomas, I think."

"Si. You are right." A rare sparkle of amusement danced in her eyes.

The past days had brought a change between them. A budding friendship formed by the absence of Quinn and Tomas and a lessening of the need for Sophia to exert her authority over the men her husband had left behind.

And over Hannah.

They had only each other. Two women in a hideout tucked away in the vast Territory. It was only natural, Hannah supposed, they would turn to each other for companionship.

"Senor Landry had been in prison a long time. Four years before you helped him escape, eh?" Sophia mused.

"Yes," Hannah said.

"Did you miss not having a child to love and care for while he was gone?"

The question startled Hannah. She picked up the pestle and began grinding corn again. "I—I don't know. I mean, it's quite complicated between us."

Sophia's shrewd gaze seemed to miss nothing. Hannah was determined not to give away the con game she and Quinn had devised.

"Now that he is out of prison, it is time to make a home with him. Perhaps with a baby or two, eh? Like me and Tomas."

Hannah hesitated. "There are obstacles, Sophia. They're too difficult to explain."

"Frank Briggs?" Sophia's face hinted at the harshness Hannah would always associate with her. "Si. He is an obstacle, but not for long. Tomas and Senor Landry will see to that. As will you and I. He will not have a chance against all of us."

Her resolve left Hannah's blood cold. Glory, she never wanted to see Frank Briggs again.

"I'm almost done with the corn," she said, seeking refuge in a change of topic. "Is there any more?"

"No. That is the last of it. And I can hardly wait for my siesta." She straightened in her chair and arched her back. "Will you clean up without me?"

Once, Sophia would have issued a command. Now, she made a request, and Hannah could hardly refuse her.

"Of course. It'll give me something to do while you're resting."

In a show of sentiment she'd not exhibited before, Sophia squeezed Hannah's hand. "Gracias."

The gesture touched Hannah, in spite of the power Sophia wielded over her. After she'd gone to her room, Hannah finished the tortillas and covered the tall stacks with a clean towel. She drained the large kettle of beans Miguel had soaked overnight, added fresh water and put the pot on to simmer while she washed the table and dishes and swept the floor.

With the chores finally done, the afternoon loomed before her. She strolled outside to escape the silence of the cabin and perched on the front step, drawing her knees up.

After the warmth in the kitchen, the crisp air cooled her cheeks, filled her lungs with an invigorating bite. The sun winked on the tin roofs of the adobe structures clustered together in the valley, and the wind stirred up whirls of fine dust on this secluded land long ignored until the Huertas claimed it.

A melancholy mood descended upon Hannah. She found a security of sorts from the seclusion, a security not unlike what she'd cherished in the Daughters of Perpetual Glory convent. With most of the men gone, no one wandered about. And perhaps, more importantly, no one from the outside world wandered in.

She was free to roam, she supposed. Had Sophia not trusted her in that, she would never have taken her siesta.

Sophia. Hannah hadn't thought it possible to become friends with her, however fragile that friendship might be. Sophia spoke openly, honestly, the animosity and arrogance she had once demonstrated notably absent.

It is time to make a home with him. Perhaps with a baby or two, eh? Like me and Tomas.

158

The words returned to swirl in Hannah's head.

Making a home with Quinn.

Making love.

Making babies.

Sophia's advice tweaked her with an unexpected sense of loss. Her home would always be behind the cinderblock walls of the convent. She would never make love. She would never have a child of her own to suckle at her breast.

Hannah pressed her fingers to her mouth. Why was she thinking of such things?

She hadn't been troubled by them in the convent. A life of prayer and meditation had suited her. Mother Superior and the nuns had given her peace and love, and that had been enough.

Until now.

Until Quinn.

Everything was changing. *She* was changing.

The mirror's reflection showed a different person, one no longer draped in brown wool, no longer meek and obedient.

The abbess wouldn't recognize her anymore, Hannah thought miserably. Hannah hardly recognized herself.

Needing to vanquish the somberness of her musings, Hannah rose abruptly and strode past the cabin, the cantina and the corrals. She saw no one, only Miguel behind the cantina, seated in a chair, basking in the sun, his sombrero over his eyes.

She could escape.

Her step faltered at the realization. She could take a horse from the corral and leave the hideout. No one would discover her gone until she was out of the valley and on her way to freedom.

Freedom?

She had no freedom. She was held captive by Frank Briggs's lies, his accusations of the murders of Father Donovan and Sister Evangeline.

She heaved a mighty sigh. No, she couldn't leave without Quinn. She needed him to testify to her innocence.

But even as her gaze swept across the horizon in yet another search for him, deep in her heart she knew she was beginning to need him as more than just a witness to help refute the charges against her.

Quinn rode into the Mexicans's hideout flanked by Tomas and Ramon. The rest of the men were scattered loosely behind them. The late afternoon sun shone bright in the sky, and he squinted beneath the Stetson brim, his glance making a slow sweep of the land before him. Countless hours in the saddle, of roping stubborn cattle on too little sleep in a too harsh land, wearied his body, but his blood thrummed with energy in his veins.

Hannah.

He saw no sign of her, though none of them made any pretense of riding in quietly. Surely she would have heard them, but only Miguel stirred, straightening from his chair behind the cantina and pushing his sombrero up from his face. He offered them a toothy grin and a hearty wave.

Quinn dismounted at the corral, his glance straying often to the cabin. Hannah's absence unnerved him. Even Sophia had not appeared to give her usual loving greetings to her husband.

"Perhaps our wives take their siestas, eh?" Tomas asked, seeming to sense his unease.

Quinn made no reply. He'd never known Hannah to nap, would not have expected her to pamper herself with the luxury of it. Still, he'd been gone a long time.

Anything could have changed.

Hannah could have changed.

He frowned.

"I will check the cabin for them," Tomas said, already heading in that direction. "If they are not there, we will hunt for them."

Quinn nodded. His growing trepidation seemed to filter over to the bandelero, and Tomas's steps quickened. Once again, Quinn's sharp glance raked the premises.

He searched for some sign of Hannah. Of Sophia. Of something amiss that might hint of trouble.

"Miguel would not be so cheerful if something had gone wrong," Ramon said knowingly, watching him. "I am sure the senoras are fine. Who would find them out here?"

Quinn grunted. Anything was possible. And obviously Miguel had been napping himself. Quinn placed little credence on the Mexican's ability to keep the women safe.

Tomas called out, and he appeared at the door, his arm around his sleepy wife. Obviously, Sophia had been taking her siesta, as Tomas suggested. Trouble had evaded her.

But where was Hannah?

Quinn moved away from the corral, his steps lengthening with every stride. He refused to believe she'd left

Pam Crooks

without him, that she'd broken their deal.

God help him if she had.

He found her, at last, behind the church picking wild-flowers.

The sight of her slowed the pounding of his pulse, eased the coiled tension in his muscles. He swore from the relief.

Picking wildflowers.

Quinn moved closer, his bootsoles crunching over clumps of hard dirt. He halted, set his hands on his hips.

"I've been looking for you," he said without greeting. "I couldn't find you anywhere."

Her head came up. Clearly, he'd startled her.

"I thought you'd escaped," he added roughly.

She straightened, clutching the bouquet to her bosom.

"No," she said. "Not without you."

It had occurred to her, then. She'd thought about escaping. About leaving him.

The knowledge forced a shudder through him.

She would've faced countless perils alone out in the Territory. Wild animals. Cold and hunger.

Briggs. Titus. Fenwick.

Damn.

Grimly, he strode beyond the church, sighted Tomas and Ramon near the cantina. He waved his Stetson, signalling them he'd found her. Tomas nodded, lifted his hand in answer. The men relaxed and went their separate ways.

"My chores were done." Defensiveness tilted Han-

Hannah's Vow

nah's chin to a defiant angle. "Sophia was napping. I decided to go for a walk."

"I reckon you're entitled, Hannah," he said, returning to her.

"They why are you angry with me?"

"I told you. I thought you'd escaped."

What would he have done? After so many days apart from her, counting the minutes until he'd return, trusting she'd be there . . . only to have her gone?

He would've charged after her. Flung over every stone, peered around every tree, climbed every mountain and delved into every canyon until he found her.

She was getting to him. Deep inside. The certainty had grown stronger each day he was gone, haunted him each waking moment. Those hazel-green eyes and shiny curls, wispy about her face. And that voice of hers, all silky and soft, like velvet.

It had been easier before, when she was trussed up in her nun's habit. A little brown sparrow. Untouchable.

But she was different now. Fetching. Pure woman. He saw what the drab wool had always hidden— rounded breasts that jiggled enticingly inside her cotton blouse, a waist slender enough to fit the span of his hands. And a body that loved to snuggle with his at night.

Hell.

He groped in his shirt pocket and retrieved a rolled cigarette and match.

That's when he missed her the most. At night.

"Did you get Tomas's cattle?" she asked, tentative, wary of him, as if she did not yet trust his mood.

"Yes. We herded them in a pasture just north of here.

We made good time, considering they were scattered in the brush and didn't want to come out." He touched the burning flame to the end of the cigarette, blew the match out, tossed it aside.

She cocked her head, considering him. "You've herded cattle before, then. As well as roped horses."

He nodded, thinking of how little she knew about him. "Before my arrest, I had a spread of my own outside of Amarillo. Kept some cattle and horses there."

"And after your arrest?"

"I lost everything."

A frown tugged at the delicate arch of her brows. He knew the questions she longed to ask, the answers he wasn't ready to give.

She'd learn them soon enough—after he took his revenge for Elliott's betrayal. She'd know every sordid detail.

Quinn swept the hate for his brother aside. He eased onto a stone bench situated in the church garden and stretched out his legs, crossing them at the ankles. Bringing the cigarette to his lips for a lazy drag, his gaze glided up the length of her, then back down again.

"You're a skinny little one, y'know that?" he murmured, exhaling gray swirls of smoke. She looked small enough to blow away in the wind. "Didn't they feed you in that convent of yours?"

Her eyes met his. "Of course they did. But the nuns—we—don't concern ourselves with food. Fasting is good for the soul."

He grunted, reserving judgment. He'd done enough fasting of his own during his time in prison. And it did damned little for his own soul. "When we get to Amarillo, I'll see that you get plenty of steak and potatoes."

Her mouth pursed. "During my time with the nuns, I never ate meat. We had simple meals—mostly fish, fruits and vegetables. And pecans." She grimaced. "Lots of pecans."

The plain life she'd chosen left Quinn pensive. Bemused. She paid a helluva price for the peace she craved.

Clearly, she'd found it with the nuns. He envied her that peace; he'd been eaten up with rage and vengeance for so long serenity seemed an impossibility to him.

Hannah bent over a wild columbine plant to pluck a stem full of its red and yellow flowers. Quinn's gaze lingered over the intriguing curve of her backside.

She straightened and furrowed her brows in exasperation.

"You've been frowning ever since you found me. How long are you going to be mad at me?" she demanded. "I did nothing wrong."

"I'm not mad."

"You're staring, too. Like I'm a—a whore or something."

His brow raised. Her perception amused him. "What do you know of whores? Or the way a man looks at one?"

She faced him, the flower still in her fingers. "I've been friends with a few."

"I find that hard to believe."

"I'm telling you the truth." She considered him coolly. "Perhaps you knew a few, too?"

"A few." His brain filed through the ladies of the evening who'd pleasured him over the years. Before Briggs. Before four years of hell.

He could use one now, he thought. Another female who would take his mind off Hannah.

"When I was with Pa, whores were often the only friends I had," she said, adding the stem to the rest of the bouquet. She bent to pick another. "When we were in Denver, Mattie Silks was so very gracious. My father enjoyed her girls, but they were quite expensive." Her lips curved as she dipped into her memories. "I met Squirrel-Tooth Alice when we stayed in Dodge City. She was petite and pretty and lots of fun. She taught me a lot."

"What could a woman like her teach you?"

Her glance skittered away. "Feminine things."

"Like what?"

"What a man liked. What he didn't. Womanly wiles. That sort of thing."

"Womanly wiles." He regarded her.

She regarded him back. Her lips moved into an impish grin, and she slipped the flower stem between her teeth. She stood a little taller and strolled through the garden toward the church. Her hips swayed in an exaggerated imitation of a strumpet, and Quinn's eyes narrowed. She stopped, cocked her hip, batted her lashes in blatant, outrageous invitation.

He tossed aside the cigarette, rose from the bench and started for her.

She saw him coming and pulled the flower from her teeth.

"You're frowning again." A giggle bubbled in her throat. "Quinn, I'm sorry."

"No, you're not."

"Yes, I am." She backed up a step, then another.

He kept her going until she couldn't go any further,

until he'd forced her to the wall of the church. "You were flirting with me."

"Yes. I mean, no." More laughter threatened to spill, but she clamped her mouth shut and tried to hold it in.

Quinn braced his hands on either side of her head, trapping her between his body and the adobe. "I'm not a young boy ignorant of a woman's power over him, Hannah," he said in a low voice. "Play with me, and my blood runs hot."

Her merriment wavered. A hiccup escaped. She stood very still.

"I can take you right now, you know." His voice rumbled. "Here. Against the church. And you wouldn't be able to stop me."

"But you won't."

"How can you be so cocksure?"

"Because you gave me your word." Bold challenge darkened the hazel-green depths of her eyes, no longer mischievous and playful. "And I'm trusting you to keep it."

She made a tough case. He fought to keep from giving her the win.

"Today," he grunted and eased away. "We'll see about tomorrow."

Her mouth softened. When he would've left her, her hand touched his chest, keeping him there.

"I've never done any of the things Alice told me about," she said. "I want you to know that."

He listened, absorbed her every word.

"I'm not like her. Or Mattie, or anyone else."

He waited, letting her convince him.

"I have principles. Morals. In spite of everything else

I might have learned." Her gaze roamed his face, as if his impression of her mattered.

He'd known few as fascinating. Hannah Benning, who could blow a bank safe or pray vespers at midnight, had stolen his heart.

Completely.

Guilelessly.

"*Buenos dias*!"

The cautious voice of a Franciscan priest rounding the corner of the church carrying a bucket of feed diverted Quinn's thoughts. He stepped back from her.

"*Buenos dias*, Father," Hannah said and smiled, a slight pink tinging her cheeks.

The priest drew closer, set the bucket down and extended his hand to Quinn. "I am Padre Ignacio Reyes. And you are?"

He made no attempt to introduce himself to Hannah; Quinn guessed the two had already made their acquaintance in his absence.

"Quinn Landry." He took the hand in a brief clasp.

"Ah. Senor Landry!" Slender beneath his robes, he stood as tall as Hannah and appeared to be only a few years older. "Hannah has spoken of you."

"Good things, I hope," he said and wondered how much of the truth of their circumstances she'd revealed.

"Of course, of course." The priest's kind glance touched on her briefly. "You see, I travel to the missions in my district. I only returned to this church a couple of days ago." The priest gestured toward the cantina. "You have come back with Tomas, then?" He waited expectantly, his dark brows raised.

"Yes," Quinn said. "A short time ago."

"Padre Reyes understands we are visiting the Huertas," Hannah said, her gaze steady. "And that we will be leaving soon."

"It is a shame, I think," the cleric said. "Sophia has enjoyed having Hannah as her friend."

"We've stayed only long enough to help Tomas herd his horses and cattle," Quinn said firmly and paused. "You've known the Huertas a long time?"

"Si. A long time. Sophia is my cousin."

Quinn's brow raised in surprise.

"I have little control over their . . . activities," Padre Reyes said sadly. "I can only pray they will abandon their lawlessness and live a respectable life." He shrugged. "God loves sinners, too. What can I say? I do what I can for them. Tomas and Sophia must do the rest."

The spicy aroma of roasting meat drifted from the direction of the cantina. The priest bent and picked up the bucket again.

"It is getting time for supper, eh? I am pleased to meet you, Senor Landry." He inclined his head graciously. "God be with you, Senorita." He blessed them and departed.

"We'd best be getting back, too," Hannah said, watching him go, as if she found him out of place here amongst the outlaws. "Miguel will be wondering where I'm at."

Quinn placed a hand to the small of her back, nudging her forward.

"The padre called you 'Senorita,' " he said. "You didn't tell him we were married?"

"No." She gave him a rueful look. "Conning the Huertas with the lie is one thing. Conning a Man of the Cloth is quite another."

Pam Crooks

"I see," Quinn said drily.

She sighed, the sound troubled. "Padre Reyes doesn't concern me as much as Julio. He suspects the truth, I think."

An image of the burly outlaw, his bitterness and hate, loomed in Quinn's mind. Cortez had kept his distance the past week, but his resentment had been a palpable thing.

They walked slowly back to the cantina, the rocks and gramma grass crunching beneath their feet. Hannah cradled the early blooming flowers in the crook of her arm, and at the cantina's door, she halted.

"The wild columbine will look festive on the tables," she said. "I had hoped—I intended them to cheer the cantina as a welcome of sorts for you." She peered up at him. Then, her hand lifted, and she slid her palm to his cheek. "I missed you, Quinn. I'm glad you're back."

As if she feared she'd revealed too much, that she touched him too freely, she pulled her hand back and disappeared inside the cabin.

The feel of her lingered on his skin. He tucked the softly spoken words into his memory, into his heart, and wondered how in hell he'd ever be able to give her back to Mother Superior.

Chapter Twelve

The next day, the door swung shut behind Hannah and muffled the raucous laughter and male conversation inside the cantina. She blinked from the brilliance of the afternoon sun and hefted an enamel tub onto her hip, then headed toward the water pump.

None of the bandeleros ambled about the old mining town, not with dinner just served and sitting in their stomachs. After the successful roundup of the rustled cattle yesterday, Tomas had given them the day to celebrate and be lazy.

Hannah was glad to be free of them, of their noise and smells and close proximity, if only for the short time it took to fill the tub. She was tired of cooking their food and washing their dishes, of sweeping the floors clean of the dirt from their boots.

And she'd had enough of the virtues of humility and obedience, no matter what Mother Superior said. Ever since Quinn's return, restlessness and impatience had eaten away at her. Their con game had played itself out.

Hannah set the tub on the ground and positioned it beneath the spigot. She'd sensed the same restlessness in Quinn, a raw tension that hinted at his urgency to return to Amarillo.

His need of it.

Hannah knew she and Quinn had to form a new plan. No more fake marriage. No more being held captive by the Huertas. It was time to move on. Their way.

She lifted the pump handle, pushed it down again, and repeated the process. Clear, cold water flowed into the tub. The splash and splatter against the enamel almost drowned out the sound of approaching horses.

Almost. Hannah's head lifted, and her heart dropped to her toes.

Warden Frank Briggs reined his big buckskin mount to a halt near the pump. Roger Fenwick and Titus followed suit.

Hannah had no thought of the guards who should have been keeping watch or of Quinn, in the cantina and unaware of their arrival.

She thought only that Frank Briggs would recognize her, and that, after everything she'd endured, after all she and Quinn had done to prevent it, she'd been caught.

They'd *both* been caught.

Briggs reached for his canteen and unscrewed the lid. His beady eyes flicked over her, and he thrust the flask toward the pump.

"Fill it for me, honey. I've been dry all day," he said.

Fenwick reached for his canteen, too. The sun and wind had reddened his face, and dust coated his expensive suit. He ran a finger along the collar of his cotton shirt.

"Where the hell are we?" he demanded. "This godforsaken country goes on forever."

Hannah let out a slow breath.

They hadn't recognized her after all. They knew her only as a nun in her wool habit, with its veil and wimple that circled her face and hid her hair. They didn't know her without it.

The knowledge, the relief of it, halted her panic. She fought to keep her hand steady as she reached for Briggs's canteen.

"This is an old mining town," she said to Fenwick, aware Briggs kept his gaze upon her while she dipped his flask under the running water. "The silver didn't pan out. Most folks left a long time ago."

Water dribbled up and over from the inside; she put the lid back on and handed it to Briggs.

"Plenty of horses in that corral over there," he drawled.

An ugly, jagged wound snaked across his jaw, put there by the jar of preserves she'd hurled against him. Hannah took satisfaction from it.

"I said 'most folks.' Not all of them."

His shrewd, calculating eyes never left her. She reached for Fenwick's canteen.

"We'd never have found this place if not for the smoke from the chimney," Fenwick said. "Reckon you don't get many visitors."

"No," she murmured, hoping, *praying*, they'd ignore the aroma of roasted chilies and beans from the cantina, that they'd not demand a meal from her. "Very few."

"I'd reckon a pretty woman like you would get mighty lonely out here," Briggs purred.

Her gaze lifted and met his. She refused to let him think she was lonely and defenseless, that she didn't hold a power of her own over him.

"I have all the company I need," she said. "A rider, certainly, for each horse in that corral."

"That so?" He leaned forward and crossed his wrists over his saddle horn. His lips pulled back over yellowed teeth in a sardonic smile. "One of them horses wouldn't belong to a prisoner of mine, would it?"

"We're looking for an escaped murderer. Name's Quinn Landry. A nun, too, he's taken hostage," Fenwick clarified briskly. He took his canteen from Hannah without a word of thanks. "Leastways, she was dressed as one."

"I would certainly have noticed if such a pair had arrived," she murmured.

"Got reward money for 'em," Titus piped up and tossed her his canteen as well. Only quick reflexes allowed her to catch it. "One thousand dollars."

"A thousand dollars!" she gasped before she could stop herself.

"Yep. Each."

Only then did Hannah notice the satchel tied to Fenwick's horse, the holsters around the men's waists, the rifles in their scabbards. Horror lay heavy in her belly.

"The woman with Landry is a killer, too. As mean and dangerous as he is. We want 'em both," Briggs said. "Dead or alive."

Her horror twisted into contempt for the vicious lies he had spread about her throughout the Territory, for

Hannah's Vow

the outrageous price he had put on her head when she was innocent of all he declared.

But she schooled her features to reveal nothing.

"I'll keep that in mind," she said demurely and handed the full canteen back to Titus.

"You do that, honey." Briggs's tone turned coaxing. "Remember. Cold, hard cash. A woman who knew their whereabouts could buy herself a lot of nice things with that kind of money."

Hating him, Hannah smiled and nodded.

He kicked the buckskin into a trot and headed north toward the pass leading out of the hideout. Fenwick and Titus followed, neither giving Hannah a backward glance.

She watched them go. The warden held his paunchy frame alert in the saddle. His beady eyes swept the tin and adobe buildings, the mission church, the weatherbeaten stable. . . .

Glory. Fenwick's rig was parked there.

Her heart thundered in her breast, but if Briggs saw the carriage, he gave no indication. The buckskin never slowed its stride.

But Hannah didn't trust him. Not for a single instant.

"Damn! Damn! Damn!" She whirled, swearing freely, her vexation overruling any sense of guilt from the words. She ran toward the cantina and burst inside. "Quinn! It's Briggs!"

His conversation with Tomas halted. He yanked his gaze to her.

"He was just here," she said. "With Fenwick and Titus."

Quinn leapt from his chair and grasped her by the shoulders.

175

"Here?" he demanded. "Just now?"

"They just wandered in, I think. I filled their canteens and—and—"

"Christ." His glance darted toward the window, to the receding figures heading deeper into the hills, and his body tautened at the sight. "What did they say?"

"They're looking for us, and they've got a bounty on our heads. Quinn, it's two thousand dollars!"

Sophia strode over, her skirt hems swaying about her ankles. "Por Dios! Two thousand? They must be lying."

"I saw the satchel of money," Hannah said. "The three of them are well-armed."

"This is our hideout." Sophia leveled her with an intense gaze. "We are at risk, too. Do you think he recognized you? Do you think he suspects that you and Quinn are hiding with us?"

"I'm almost certain he saw the carriage parked near the stable. If he did, he would have to know Quinn and I are here."

"The carriage." Sophia took a breath, and her features grew troubled.

"The reward is a fortune, Sophia." Julio Cortez slurred the words from a back table, his big hand clutched around the neck of a tequila bottle. "Give Landry and his woman to Briggs, then you and Tomas can buy the land you dream of."

Sophia appeared taken aback at the plan; Tomas discarded it.

"You can say such things, Julio, because *you* did not spend time in his filthy prison. Nor did you escape it." Tomas's lip curled. "Frank Briggs will recapture me, too, if I let him. Will you spend the reward money, then?"

At the taunt, Julio reddened with rage. "You will regret not listening to me, Tomas. Too many times, you mock me. No more!"

He stood, knocking his chair back with the suddenness of it, and stormed from the cantina, taking the tequila with him.

Tomas moved to follow, but Sophia held him back.

"Let him go, *mi querido*. He will only find some place to pout. He will be sorry for his actions tomorrow."

Quinn grasped the leader's arm.

"We've met the terms of our bargain, Tomas." His harsh glance included Sophia. "You used us to lead Briggs to you. Settle your revenge with him as you choose, but Hannah and I are leaving."

"No." Tomas's black eyes held a dangerous gleam.

"Briggs is heading north toward the pass. Hannah and I will leave from the south."

Abruptly, the staccato of hoofbeats on the road outside the cantina's window snagged their tense glances. Julio Cortez rode by at breakneck speed, heading toward the mouth of the pass.

Toward Briggs.

Tomas's expression turned murderous at the betrayal.

"Por Dios! We must stop him, Tomas!" Sophia cried.

"I'm going after him," Quinn said. "Hannah, stay here." He jabbed a finger at Tomas. "No one follows me, you hear? I can track him easier by myself."

And before Hannah could mouth a protest, he sprinted out the cantina toward the corral.

She could lose him. The thought, the dread, seared Hannah's brain. She bolted out the door after him, despite the Huertas's shouts and attempts to stop her.

"I'm coming with you, Quinn," she called, reaching the corral only moments after he did.

"Like hell you are," he said with a growl and snatched the reins to a saddled horse.

"You got me into this mess when you took me hostage. I aim to see that you get me out." She took the reins to a second horse, lifted a foot into the stirrup and climbed up.

"I don't want you hurt." Impatience hissed through his teeth. He stepped toward her, as if he intended to pull her bodily from the saddle.

"And I don't want you hurt, either." She evaded his grasp with more luck than skill. "We have to get to Cortez before he gets to Briggs. We'll do it together. You want to go back to Amarillo, don't you?"

"Damn it, Hannah!" He shot a glance toward the Mexican, hardly discernible in the distance. "Hell. I don't have time to argue with you." He swung onto his horse. "You stay right beside me, understand?"

Briggs was as shrewd and ruthless as any of the inmates in his prison. Cortez was driven by jealousy and fury. Hannah had no intention of leaving Quinn's side to face either of them alone.

Quinn kicked his mount into a run. Heart pounding, Hannah did the same, her eyes on the narrow pass ahead.

It didn't surprise him they'd come after him.

It *did* surprise him to see only one.

Briggs peered through the shrubs hiding him from view. He studied the stocky Mexican as his horse wound its way over the rocky trail, the sole passage through the range of tree-covered hills. He studied the conchos and leather tooling on the saddle, trimmed in inlaid silver. And he studied the bullet-laden ammunition belt crossed over the burly chest.

An outlaw, just like he figured.

The secluded valley was a perfect hiding place. He'd seen all the fine horses in that corral, and if there was a rider for each one, like the woman said, then the renegade band was formidable. He'd seen Fenwick's rig, too, and guessed Landry had to be among them.

Unless Fenwick's Solution had gotten to him first.

Either way, the outlaws laid claim to the rig somehow and Briggs surmised they'd know about Landry and the nun—whether they were dead or alive.

And where they could be found.

He signalled sharply, and Fenwick took up position on one side of the pass; Titus, the other.

They waited.

The Mexican appeared. Three rifles cocked. Briggs burst from the bushes.

"Get your hands up!" he roared. "Try anything stupid, and you're a dead man!"

The outlaw hesitated. His bloodshot eyes darted all around him, but he obeyed, lifting his arms slowly into the air.

"Take off your gunbelt and throw it to the ground, real careful-like. Your ammunition belt, too." He complied, and Briggs nodded. "Now, pull that rifle from its scabbard and drop it." That done, Briggs gestured toward the ground with his weapon. "All right, then. Get down from that horse, and don't do nothin' fancy."

Saddle leather creaked. The Mexican eased his bulk from his mount and kept his hands raised.

"Take off that there sombrero. I want to see your ugly

face. Titus, search him! Make sure he don't have no more guns inside his coat."

Keeping his weapon level with one hand, Titus searched the outlaw with the other. He found nothing more than a half-empty bottle of tequila, which he promptly uncorked and brought to his lips.

The Mexican tossed back his sombrero on its chin cord. Briggs stared at him, at the slash running across his cheek.

The wound wasn't much different than his own. Same side of the face, same angle of assault, as if their attackers had been of equal height. . . .

The nun.

"She knifed you, didn't she?" he demanded, stunned, thinking of the night Landry escaped. Her eyes had been hazel green. . . .

Like the woman at the pump.

Angered that she'd duped him, that he hadn't seen beyond the wimple and veil and recognized her, he swore vehemently.

"Senora Landry?" The Mexican spat the name. "Si, she knifed me."

Briggs's eyes closed to near slits. "What're you talkin' about? She ain't married to Landry."

"He calls her his wife," the Mexican sneered.

"It's a lie."

"He's alive then," Fenwick said, stepping closer, his features rapt. Excited.

The Mexican angled his dark head toward him. "Alive. Si. Unfortunately."

Briggs caught the unmistakeable hate in the words.

"Well, I'll be damned," Titus said. "They were in the valley the whole time. Right under our noses."

"Shut up, Titus!" Briggs snapped. "Don't you think I'm just figurin' that out?"

The guard clamped his mouth shut and glared at him, but said nothing more.

Briggs turned back to the Mexican.

"What's your name?" he demanded.

"Julio Cortez."

"Who're you holin' up with?"

For a moment, Cortez didn't answer.

Fenwick jabbed him in the gut with his rifle.

"Answer the question, Mr. Cortez," he ordered. "We don't have all day."

Cortez wetted his bottom lip with his tongue. "Tomas Huerta."

Huerta. The name rocked Briggs. The Mexican who'd escaped the prison a few years back. The only man to do so besides Landry. His brain fought to make the connection, to figure out how the two men knew each other. Were they working together?

He stepped closer to Cortez.

"You know who I am, don't you?" he asked softly. "Or else you wouldn't have followed us all the way through that pass. You took a helluva chance, y'know that?"

"I knew what I was doing," Cortez said.

"What do you want from us?"

Again, he delayed answering, as if in his eleventh hour he questioned the wisdom of his intentions.

Stupid Mexican.

It was too late to question anything. Especially with Landry and Huerta within reach.

"Reckon he's got a hankerin' for that reward money, Fenwick?" he drawled.

Fenwick shrugged. "Could be."

"Or maybe he's got a hankerin' for Landry's woman." He chuckled at the thought, at the wickedness of it.

"Pah!" The taunt raised Cortez's rage. He touched the wound on his cheek. "The bitch! She cuts me. She robs me. She deserves to die, like Landry."

"My thinkin' exactly."

"I come out here to tell you they are down there." He pointed a grimy finger toward the valley. "I did not want you to ride away without them."

Briggs was skeptical, but he let the Mexican talk.

"I will help you capture Landry and Hannah. On one condition."

He eyed the outlaw with disdain. Who the hell did he think he was, makin' his own rules?

"What condition?" he demanded.

"Tomas goes free," Cortez said.

A snort erupted from him. "And if I refuse?"

"He will fight you." Cortez's thick moustache quivered in defiance. "His men are loyal. They will die for him!"

Watching him coldly, Briggs stroked the rifle's trigger with his thumb. "Would you die for him, Cortez?"

The outlaw stiffened, his cheeks purpling. "Do not underestimate Tomas and Sophia."

"Sophia?"

"Tomas's wife. My cousin."

Hell. Blood ran thick. Briggs took in the information. Her presence could make things interesting.

And complicated.

A plan bloomed in his mind. He glanced at Titus and Fenwick, including them in his decision.

"We'll move into the valley at midnight," he said. "Cortez will be our ticket in."

The Mexican's head jerked. "No."

"I'm sayin' you will!" Briggs snapped.

"I told you about Landry." Cortez took a step backward. "I will do no more for you."

Briggs's pulse quickened with merciless resolve.

"I have the Federales comin'," he lied. "They'll be here in a few hours. We'll charge the place. You won't get arrested if you get us Landry."

"Federales?" Panic leapt onto Cortez's face. He shook his head vehemently, turned, and with surprising agility, leapt into the saddle to flee.

Before he could take the reins, before his heels even kicked the horse's flanks, Briggs pulled the rifle's trigger.

Cortez lurched. A crimson stain spread across his back. He slumped forward, then sideways, and landed with a dull thud into the dirt.

Fenwick cursed.

"Gawd, Warden!" Titus choked, gaping at the lifeless heap. "What'd you go and shoot him for?"

Briggs flicked an impassive glance over the outlaw, thrust a boot toe into his fleshy ribs and flipped him over.

"How do I know he wasn't workin' with Landry, settin' me up for an ambush?" He cast a heavy-lidded glance toward the pass, half-imagining Landry, Huerta and his band of renegade outlaws storming through it.

The tinny taste of dread coated his tongue. He snatched the heavily laden ammunition and gun belts from the ground, tossed them to Fenwick and Titus, and kept the rifle for himself.

"Strap those belts to your person," he ordered them. He peered into the sky, into the sun that would set soon. "I have a feelin' you're gonna need 'em."

The single gunshot echoed through the valley. Quinn grimaced as Cortez fell from his horse. He curled his fingers around Hannah's forearm, pulling her with him as they shimmied on their bellies through the thicket of scrub to get a closer look.

Cortez was dead.

They were too late. The Mexican had gotten to Briggs before Quinn could stop him. And then, Briggs had gotten to Cortez.

Shit.

Quinn rolled to his back, made a quick study of the rough terrain, knew the steep, rock-strewn hills and tangled brush surrounding them would make reaching the warden damned near impossible.

The only way to get to him was the pass—a single trail leading from the valley to the other side, hardly wide enough to allow horse and rider three abreast.

Briggs knew it. The pass was his advantage, the ace up his sleeve, and he'd be waiting to play the card.

If Quinn had been alone, he might have attempted to shoot his way through with more guts than brains and waylay all three of them.

But he couldn't. Not with Hannah along.

Cortez had done a helluva lot of damage running to Briggs. The warden knew of their presence in the Huertas' hideout. The hunt, the cold-blooded pursuit to recapture them, would intensify a hundredfold.

Quinn needed more time, a diversion, to stall Briggs. He had to escape with Hannah without the warden breathing hot and ruthless down their necks. He had to get back to Amarillo.

He had to. For Hannah's sake. For his own.

The mood in the cantina was grim.

Rifles and carbines, oiled and fully loaded, lay on every table top. Bowie knives gleamed. Ammunition belts were stocked with bullets and slung over the shoulders of every man present.

Quinn's nerves hummed with tension. Dusk had already fallen. Nightfall would settle upon them within minutes.

Anytime after that, Briggs could make his move.

Quinn's brisk announcement of Cortez's death had unleashed Tomas's rage and Sophia's grief-stricken dismay. At her command, the bandeleros erupted into action, pulling provisions from the shelves and packing them into saddlebags, rolling blankets into bedrolls and readying their weaponry. In an amazingly short period of time, the Mexicans were prepared to vacate the hideout.

But not before they confronted Frank Briggs.

"I do not believe the warden is working with the Federales," Sophia said stubbornly, oblivious to the frenzied activity around her. Her haughty features showed the strain of her cousin's betrayal and the impending risks of a shoot-out with Briggs, the anguish of the blood that would spill.

"It is what he claims," Tomas said simply, buckling a holster around his hips. "Senor Landry heard him say it."

"If it is true, Tomas, then how can we fight them?

The Federales will outnumber us. We will not have a chance with all of them."

"What choice do we have?"

"We can leave. Now. We will wait for another time to kill Briggs, a time when we are sure he works alone." Her voice carried a thread of pleading.

Quinn agreed with Sophia. Briggs had stumbled into the hideout by accident, but what measures he would use against them, Quinn couldn't be sure.

"For all we know, he's sent Titus or Fenwick for reinforcements," Quinn said. "We can't assume it's the three of them against all of us. And we can't assume he'll strike at midnight."

"Which is why we must act quickly." Tomas glanced upward as Ramon entered the cantina, a wooden box in his arms. "Put it down by my rifle, Padre," he said, indicating a table next to him. "I will secure the black powder to the saddle myself."

Hannah's head came up. She stopped wrapping tortillas in a towel.

"What is this about black powder?" she demanded.

Sophia strode over to the box, lifted the lid and peered at the powder-filled paper cartridges inside. She shuddered and let the lid drop back into place. "They fascinate Tomas. Por Dios, they scare me."

"When I find them abandoned in the old mine last spring, Tomas is happy," Ramon said. "He knows the cartridges are dangerous, but he knows, also, they are a valuable weapon." His somber gaze settled on his son. Clearly, he shared the sentiment.

Hannah went to the box. She took a cartridge, its fuse dangling like a rattail, and rested it in her palm. She held the explosive with reverance, with respect.

But without fear.

"What the hell do you intend to do with them, Tomas?" Quinn demanded.

"There is nothing better to stop Frank Briggs from capturing us."

"How? By blowing him and the other two to bits?"

"Si. If I must."

"Then you'll have the damned Federales on our asses for sure." Impatience, fierce disagreement with the idea, soared through Quinn.

"There is no other way," Tomas shot back.

"Yes," Hannah said firmly. "There is."

The cantina fell silent. Sombreroed heads turned toward her.

She strode forward. "The only way Briggs can reach us is by way of the pass. We can use the black powder to blow it shut."

"Blowing up a mountain pass is a helluva lot different than blowing a bank safe, Hannah," Quinn grated.

She faced him. "Only because the bank safe is smaller. The premise is the same."

"No," he said, shaking his head for emphasis. "Absolutely not."

"The plan is brilliant!" Sophia's eyes shone with excitement, as if Quinn had never spoken. "You will do this for us?"

"Yes." Hannah nodded once.

"No, she won't," Quinn said firmly.

"I've used powder before. It's a good plan, Quinn."

"Si." Tomas stroked the thin line of his moustache, his dark-skinned features intent. "A good plan. If the pass is closed, Briggs must circle from the north and reach us from the south. A day's hard ride, at least."

"By the time he comes, we will be long gone." Ramon beamed.

"It is decided, then." Tomas reached for the box on the table.

"No!" Quinn's roar shook the rafters.

Tomas spun toward him. "Your wife helps to save our lives, gringo! Yours, too, and her own."

"She is not my wife." Quinn spat the truth through his teeth. "I took her hostage the night I escaped from prison. She is innocent of anything I have ever done, and *I do not want her involved in this.*"

Hannah froze at his blurted revelation.

Sophia gasped in shock. A tumultuous shadow crossed her expression.

"Not your wife, senor?" She repeated his words with deceptive softness. "You have lied to us, then. And we all believed you."

Tomas threw his hands up in masculine exasperation and scooped the wooden box into his arms. "Por Dios, Sophia! What does it matter who she is? We do not have time to discuss it!"

With a few long strides, he left the cantina. Ramon followed, and the room emptied of the remaining bandeleros.

"Quinn, please." Hannah stood before him, her gaze peering up into his. She spoke his name like a lover in the night, coaxing him to see her point of view. "I know what I'm doing. I wouldn't have suggested blowing the pass shut if I didn't think I could do it. Or that it'd work."

"It's dangerous, Hannah. You could be killed."

He thought of all that could go wrong, of the innumerable factors beyond their control. And he thought of her in her brown habit, protected behind the cinderblock walls of the convent.

It was where she belonged. Safe among the sisters. Not blowing up a mountain pass in the middle of the night.

"I want you with me, of course." She touched his cheek, trailed her fingertips down to his jaw, conning him to her way of thinking. "You'll be right there at my side."

His defenses crumpled beneath the effect of her touch.

"Damned right, I will," he muttered, agreeing to her plan and hardly realizing it. "Someone's got to keep you from blowing your fool head off."

A light smile touched her lips, victorious in its guile. "Afterward, we'll head for Amarillo. We'll ride all night."

"Yes." He was powerless to resist her con game, to make his own rules when she was so adept at winning with hers.

She stepped back. The smile, the persuasiveness, faded from her face. In their stead, a serious acceptance of what lay ahead.

"I'll meet you at the corral in a few minutes," she said. "There are some things I must do before we go."

He nodded, watching her leave, and encountered Sophia's dark stare upon him, reproving and cunning in its intensity.

She'd not left with the others, and her stare troubled him. But before he could question her, she pivoted and was gone.

Chapter Thirteen

It seemed to Hannah a lifetime had passed since she'd crawled on her belly through the brush to spy on Frank Briggs.

In actuality, it had only been a few hours. Long enough for the sun to disappear and drape a heavy blanket of darkness over the Territory. And long enough for the warden, his guard and Roger Fenwick to lay out their plan of action.

Neither she nor Quinn nor Tomas had any idea what that plan was. They were too far away to hear what the three men were saying, but Hannah knew that whatever they discussed over a scant campfire engrossed them, that they were armed to the teeth, and that they listened and watched the mouth of the pass with arduous diligence.

She expected little else. She signalled to Quinn and Tomas, and they half-scooted, half-slid down the steep hill, staying under the protective cover of the shrubs.

"Give me the black powder, Tomas," she ordered in a whisper.

He delved into the wooden box, retrieved fourteen cartridges, and handed them to her. Hannah gave eight to Quinn and stuffed the remaining six inside her coat. She reached for a spool wound with jute.

The Mexican leader glanced over his shoulder and into the valley. "Sophia and the others are already at the church. Padre Reyes prays with them that this will work and we will escape tonight."

"It'll work," she said crisply.

Hannah intended to say a string of her own prayers when this was over. Prayers of thanksgiving and forgiveness. For now, though, the job ahead claimed all her attention. Resolutely, she cut a length of fuse from the spool.

"We will be waiting at the bottom of the hill." Tension shimmered from Tomas. "Work quickly, Hannah. The fuses will not burn long." With that, he disappeared into the darkness.

Quinn set a tin can of mud beside her.

"You sure you know what you're doing?" he said with a growl.

"You forget I was taught by the best," she answered and stuffed the jute into her pocket.

"I've got to be crazy to let you go through with this."

"Briggs has forced us into it. We have no choice." She reached for the tin of mud, tucked the can into the crook of her elbow and rose.

He rose with her. When she would have ascended the hill, he grasped her by the elbow and halted her.

"Hannah," he said roughly.

She strained to see him, to define his shadowed features in the darkness of the night. She knew his worry, his concern, felt it as her own.

"If something goes wrong, if you're killed—" he said, the words terse.

Her fingers lifted to his mouth, pressed gently to their grim line.

"We cannot think of it," she whispered.

"I can think of nothing else, damn it."

She winced at the ferocity in his tone. "If we survive this, Quinn, I'll never touch black powder again. I swear it." Guiltily, the avowals from her past returned, promises she'd made never to do the con games and illicit tricks her father had instilled in her. She dismissed the guilt, as she'd done so many times of late. "But tonight, I have to. You know that."

Precious seconds ticked by. She sensed his inward battle, his struggle to accept her assurances.

On a muttered oath, he turned her to the steep wall of the hill she planned to blow apart.

"Tell me what I need to do," he said.

The powder cartridges were left over from the mining heyday of drilling and blasting. Hannah was certain they'd rip through the dirt and rock like it was butter.

She understood explosives, thanks to Pa. Together, they'd opened numerous iron bank safes, using a sophisticated air pump to insert sticks of dynamite into the crevices around the door.

Now, she and Quinn scraped holes into the packed earth, aided only by the blade of Fenwick's knife.

She had no time to think of the irony of it. They worked quickly, quietly, arranging three narrow cavities, spaced several feet apart, into a crude triangle, then making four more at the outside top, sides and bottom.

She reached into her coat pocket, withdrew three cartridges and wedged them into the holes of the triangle, the fuses hanging like tails on rats. Quinn did the same with four of his. Hannah secured the cartridges in their holes with mud.

They repeated the process on the opposite hill. Hannah stepped back and pulled the length of jute from inside her coat. She listened for Frank Briggs, for some sign they'd aroused his suspicions, but the night was still. The air carried no sound.

Her heart thundered within her breast. The time had come.

"Ready?" Quinn asked.

She drew in a breath. "Ready."

He struck a match. The twisted strands of jute surrounded a core of powder. A layer of twine, then another of waterproof tape, covered the jute. Hannah dipped one end into the flame, and the powder sparked and spit.

Back at the camp, she had timed the burning of several of the fuses she'd removed from the cartridges and knew each one burned at a uniform rate. She painstakingly figured the amount of jute she'd need and just how long it would be before it reached the black powder and exploded.

Hannah put her thumb and forefinger on the estimated length. That little spot would save her life—and Quinn's.

Careful to light them in sequence, the center cartridges first, then the outside ones, Hannah hastily touched the dangling fuses with the hissing jute. After counting seven, she scrambled to the adjacent hill and started all over again.

The tiny flame gobbled up the spitter fuse. The heat grew stronger against her fingertip.

"Hurry, Hannah." Quinn kept his eye on the rapidly descending flame.

Only moments from now, the first cartridge would explode.

Only a few more fuses left.

She forced herself to keep her hand steady, to keep the red glow true. She prayed none of the fuses would fizzle out, or worse, burn too fast and detonate too quickly.

The heat singed her finger, and she lit the last one.

Quinn pulled her from the wall of the hill with such force she dropped the spent fuse and fell into him. They lost their footing and hurtled to the steep ground, their bodies rolling and rolling over the jutting rocks and spiny brush.

BOOM!

The earth rattled and shook.

BOOM!

Quinn grabbed Hannah and . . .

BOOM!

. . . shielded her with the breadth of his body.

BOOM! BOOM! BOOM!

The cartridges discharged with deafening force, hurling a shower of debris over them.

Seven. Eight. Nine.

Hannah hung on to Quinn and kept counting.

Ten. Eleven. Twelve.

It seemed the earth would split in two. He held her tighter.

Thirteen. Fourteen.

And, then . . . nothing.

His head lifted; she twisted beneath him to stare at the narrow trail.

It was gone.

The trail was totally, blissfully gone.

The acrid smell of black powder lay heavy in the air. A fog of dust and debris stung Hannah's eyes and wrenched a cough from her throat. She scuttled out from beneath Quinn.

The explosions had blasted huge cavities into the jagged mountainside and dumped the rubble into the pass.

Filling it. Destroying it.

Elation swelled inside Hannah. She turned to Quinn and flung her arms about his neck.

"We did it!" she cried. "We did it!"

He laughed, a deep-throated sound rich from victory. He clasped her to him, lifted her high and swung her around.

"*You* did it!" he said. "Damn, woman, you're amazing!"

Horses' hooves intruded into their celebration. Smiling broadly, his teeth gleaming against his skin and the dark night, Tomas waved his sombrero in joyous greeting. Ramon rode with him, the reins to a pair of horses, Fenwick's fine-blooded geldings, in his hand.

"Frank Briggs has received the surprise of his life tonight, eh?" Tomas asked.

Quinn grinned. "One that knocked him clear back on his ass."

"We must hurry to the church," Ramon said. He tossed a glance toward the battered mountainside, as if he expected the warden and his two cohorts to burst through any minute.

"Si," Tomas conceded. "Sophia will want to know we are all safe."

The church had been their agreed-upon meeting place. If the black powder explosions proved successful, it would be the church from which the bandeleros—and Quinn and Hannah—would part company. If the explosions failed, Sophia planned to order her men into a decisive, albeit bloody, confrontation with the warden.

Hannah couldn't wait to get there, not to have Padre Reyes pray over them in thanks, but to collect their few provisions and ride with Quinn from the Huertas's hideout.

To leave the New Mexico Territory.

To head for Amarillo. At last.

Hardly realizing her plans didn't include thoughts of the convent, Hannah accepted the set of reins Ramon offered her, his expression filled with a new respect. Quinn mounted, too. She followed his gaze as he stole a final look toward the demolished pass.

It was dark, imposing.

And silent.

The mission church held a regal position overlooking the town ruins. A plain white cross hung above the doors. Above that, a statue of St. Francis of Assisi nestled inside a niche carved into the adobe. Still another cross perched on the uppermost point of the roof.

A faint light spilled out from the narrow windows. Miguel watched for them between rough-hewn double doors. At the sight of the four riders, two of whom yipped elatedly in Mex, he rushed forward, a lantern in his hand.

"We are victorious, Miguel!" Tomas exclaimed, sliding from the saddle before his horse came to a full stop. "We have shown Frank Briggs we are smarter than he is."

"Si, Tomas." Miguel's face creased with a snaggletooth grin. "My ears are still ringing."

"Where is Sophia?"

"Inside, waiting and praying."

Tomas pushed back his sombrero and strode into the vestibule, his bootsoles clomping against the scarred wooden floor. Inside, two more smiling bandeleros spread wide the doors leading into the main body of the church.

Ramon dismounted and indicated Quinn and Hannah should follow him.

Impatience cut through Quinn. He didn't want the delay. Amarillo called to him too loudly to tarry now, when the terms of their bargain with the Huertas had been met.

He glanced at Hannah. "For whatever reason they want us here, it'd best not take long."

She nodded, a slight frown puckering her brows, and dismounted. Quinn took her elbow, and they entered the church. Sophia knelt at a front pew, her obsidian head bowed, but at her husband's arrival, she rose quickly and embraced him. They spoke together, their tones hushed, then turned to wait for Quinn and Hannah to join them.

With all the solemnity of a congregation preparing for Mass to begin, the rest of the Huertas' men waited, too, their dark, moustached faces impassive.

197

Hannah's step faltered. Suspicion curled through Quinn. Ramon prodded them forward until they reached the end of the aisle.

A bright-striped *robozo* hugged Sophia's shoulders. Her long braid hung over one shoulder, its end brushing the swell of her belly.

"You have used the black powder to close the pass," she said quietly. "This you do for us."

"And for ourselves," Quinn said. He had no need of her gratitude. "Briggs chases us, too."

"Si. Of course, I know that. But blowing the pass was dangerous. You could have been killed."

Quinn said nothing, his silence his agreement.

"You have given us valuable time to make an escape. Por Dios, even if it is only a single day, it is time we would not have had if the warden attacked us with the Federales at his side." Her solemn gaze settled on Hannah. "It is a great skill you have with the black powder, Hannah."

Like Quinn, she made no reply, but her scrutiny swept the gathering of the bandeleros, the altar, the closed door of the sacristy.

Sophia's presence dominated the little church. Regal and haughty, she held the attention of everyone present.

"You lied to us, Senor Landry, when you called Hannah your wife."

Every muscle, every sense, every instinct in his body leapt inside him.

"A man fights to survive any way he can. My concern was for Hannah." He inclined his head, the gesture mocking. Careless. "My apologies if we've offended you."

Join the Historical Romance Book Club and GET 4 FREE* BOOKS NOW!

A $23.96 Value!

Yes! I want to subscribe to the Historical Romance Book Club.

Please send me my **4 FREE* BOOKS.** I have enclosed $2.00 for shipping/handling. Each month I'll receive the four newest Historical Romance selections to preview for 10 days. If I decide to keep them, I will pay the Special Members Only discounted price of just $4.24 each, a total of $16.96, plus $2.00 shipping/handling ($23.55 US in Canada). This is a **SAVINGS OF AT LEAST $5.00** off the bookstore price. There is no minimum number of books I must buy, and I may cancel the program at any time. In any case, the **4 FREE* BOOKS** are mine to keep.

*In Canada, add $5.00 shipping/handling per order for the first shipment. For all future shipments to Canada, the cost of membership is $23.55 US, which includes shipping and handling. (All payments must be made in US dollars.)

NAME: _____

ADDRESS: _____

CITY: _____ **STATE:** _____

COUNTRY: _____ **ZIP:** _____

TELEPHONE: _____

E-MAIL: _____

SIGNATURE: _____

If under 18, Parent or Guardian must sign. Terms, prices, and conditions subject to change. Subscription subject to acceptance. Dorchester Publishing reserves the right to reject any order or cancel any subscription.

Hannah's Vow

"Do not apologize." She shrugged. "It does not matter. I would have done the same." She considered him coolly. "I think, in truth, you would like to be married to her, eh?"

Behind her, Miguel lit candles on the plain altar, one by one.

Quinn's breath hitched. Her statement, its intent, stunned him.

Hannah's glance jerked from Miguel to her. "Sophia, it cannot be."

"I have the power to do many things, Hannah."

"You don't understand." A faint panic, stronger with every word she spoke, filled Hannah's voice.

"I understand the worry and the longing in your eyes when Senor Landry is not with you," the Mexican woman said simply. "I see how you look at him when he is." Her dark head swiveled to Quinn. "And I see the passion in Senor Landry when he kisses you to prove to us you are his."

Hannah's fingers flew to her mouth in shocked reaction. Quinn's narrowed gaze slammed into Sophia's.

"You twist the terms of our bargain," he said. "You make new rules to replace the old ones."

"I give you a gift. Nothing more."

"A gift!" Hannah exclaimed.

"For all you have done to help us escape Frank Briggs." Her full mouth curved. "And because I think it is what you want, deep in your heart."

"We want nothing more than to leave this place," Hannah said. "To leave all of you."

Sophia inclined her head slightly, as if she understood Hannah's protests but had no intention of heeding them.

Pam Crooks

"Long ago, I learned to know what is best for my husband and my men. I make decisions for their welfare. I do the same for you."

Quinn's mind worked through their options.

The consequences of refusing.

The benefits of agreeing.

His heart thundered inside him. Every pulsating beat intensified an unexpected appeal at the prospect of being married to Hannah, if only for a short time.

The tension dwindled from him.

"This is the last condition of our agreement, Sophia," he said. "We go through with this, then we leave. No holds barred."

She exchanged a glance with Tomas. "We lose valuable time talking. Si. We agree."

Eyes wide, Hannah spun toward him, giving the Huertas her back in an attempt for privacy.

"Quinn." She swallowed. "I can't go through with this. I've taken vows."

"Temporary vows."

"The padre will make me say different ones."

"He's performing a wedding ceremony, Hannah." Annoyance flicked through him that she'd not grasped the opportunity as quickly as he did. He refrained from swearing while on the holy altar. "Would you rather he say your eulogy instead?"

She paled. And swallowed again.

Quinn wanted to take her into his arms, assure her they were doing the right thing, coax her into yet another con game to save their lives.

To make their escape.

But her troubled expression told him she realized all that.

200

She tilted her head back and studied him, as if to assure herself he truly meant to go through with Sophia's plan.

That he wanted to be married to her.

She must have read the smouldering truth in his eyes, in the words he couldn't say here and now.

"We have no choice, do we?" she whispered.

"No," he said.

Her lashes lowered, accepting that truth, and she faced Sophia again.

"You win, of course," she said. "Though I fear you make a mockery of a blessed institution, Quinn and I will allow you to marry us."

Sophia nodded, her expression satisfied. "It pleases me you accept my gift without too much resistance."

She retrieved a bouquet of wild columbine from the seat of her pew and pressed it into Hannah's hands, then slipped a ring into Quinn's palm.

Her dark eyes lifted, met his. "The day will come when Hannah cannot bear to remove this from her finger. I am certain of it."

Before Quinn could reply, she took Tomas's arm and sat with him in the pew.

Quinn's fist closed over the narrow gold band that would bind Hannah to him, keeping it safe, secure, until it was time to slide it onto her finger.

Silence fell over the church.

The door to the sacristy opened.

And Padre Reyes stepped out. . . .

Warden Frank Briggs groaned.

His body felt kicked and trampled, like he'd been run over by a damned herd of buffalo.

He opened his eyes. He blinked at the darkness. At the eerie quiet surrounding him.

Dust coated the back of his throat. A coughing spasm wracked him. Only then, did he remember.

Explosions. *Hundreds* of them.

His brain relived the deafening noise, the feel of his body being thrown back and pummeled by flying debris, his head hitting the hard, rocky ground, knocking him unconscious.

He sat up, his body and battered muscles protesting. Instinctively, he searched for Titus and Fenwick.

They lay scattered in the dirt, out cold. Just as he'd been.

Only red-orange embers remained in the campfire, its flames doused by the onslaught of dust and rocks.

He couldn't find the horses. Hell, he couldn't hear a single nicker. They'd probably hightailed it clear to Mexico by now.

An unfettered rage built up inside him.

Landry and the woman. They were responsible.

The pass.

He spun around, gaped at the mountainous wall of earth before him.

It was gone.

The realization stunned him.

He trembled from the fury. They'd pay with their lives for this.

They'd pay.

He staggered to his feet, swayed from a spell of dizziness and forced it down.

"Titus! Fenwick! Get your sorry asses up and

movin!" he barked and landed a rough nudge into each man's ribs. They groaned and stirred.

His head cleared, little by little. Raw, jagged determination overrode everything but revenge.

By God, they'd pay.

Chapter Fourteen

After running the horses hard all night and most of the morning, Quinn allowed them to make their way into the canyon at their own pace.

They moved deep into the steep-sided valley. The canyon walls stretched a good sixty feet above them. A mossy curtain of ivy clung to the rock, slick from the seep of water that gathered and pooled into the creek flowing along the canyon floor. Ahead of them, a ridge of bare sandstone jutted outward, shielding anyone taking shelter beneath it from the glare of the sun or the breezes swirling off the mesa.

Quinn reined his horse to a stop and waited for Hannah to draw up even with him. She tilted her head back and ran her gaze over the cliffs. A frown tugged at her mouth.

Quinn leaned forward on the saddle horn.

"Briggs won't find us here, Hannah," he said quietly. "No one followed us. I'd have known if they did."

"Yes," she murmured, pondering the rushing creek, the narrow trail skirting the edge. "I'd have known, too."

He dismounted. She followed, moving slowly, stiffly, as if every muscle in her body ached.

"Here." He untied their bedroll and tossed it to her. "We can bed down over there." He gestured toward the sandstone shelf and the shade it offered. "I'll tend the horses."

Casting their supplies aside, he pulled off both saddles and bridles. Hannah gathered fallen pine needles and cottonwood leaves to cushion the hard earth, then spread one of the blankets over the neat pile. Afterward, she collected fallen branches for firewood.

"You want something to eat?" he asked, watching her while he brushed down the geldings.

She shook her head. "I'm too tired to be hungry."

The admission touched off a spark of guilt in Quinn. He was responsible for her fatigue, for keeping her going—*both* of them going—at a relentless pace since leaving the Huertas' camp.

He left the horses and went to her. She needed matches to start a fire; he delved into his shirt pocket and took out a few.

Kneeling on the ground, she arranged the wood into a heap. He extended his hand, the matches in his palm. She reached for them. His hand slid over hers, and he pulled her to her feet.

He didn't let go. The gold wedding band turned easily on her finger. Pensive, Quinn rubbed his thumb against the shiny surface.

The ceremony had lasted no more than ten minutes. After Padre Reyes had closed his prayer book, blessed them, and wished them well, the bandeleros mounted up and rode out of the hideout. Tomas and Sophia, in Fenwick's rig, led the group south, Quinn and Hannah headed east.

"What have we done, Hannah?" he murmured.

A hint of a smile, tremulous and rueful, formed on her mouth. She, too, studied the ring and all its implications.

"We did what we had to do to survive, Quinn. Sophia was determined to see her plan through, no matter what it cost us."

He studied her and wondered what was in her heart when he was only just beginning to discover what was in his.

He crooked a finger beneath her chin, tilted it up an inch, coaxed her to look at him.

"Was it such a terrible cost?" he asked.

She exhaled a breath, soft and confused.

"I think of things now that I refused to let myself think of before. Earthly things that are forbidden in the convent."

"Earthly things?" He gave her time to sort her tumultuous thoughts, to give him her honesty.

"Every woman thinks of having a man in her life. Getting married. Birthing children. I suspect Mother Superior thought of them, too, in her younger days." She pulled her hand from Quinn's, hugged her arms close about her. She turned and stared into the rushing creek. "I was determined not to think of them. Ever. Now, this marriage of ours brings them all back again."

The revelation ended on a note of bitterness. Of frustration.

"I never intended for it to happen," Quinn said, frowning. "If I'd have known—"

She whirled, facing him again. "When? The night you escaped from prison?" She shook her head, dismissed his clumsy attempt at apology. "You were desperate, then. Just as we were both desperate last night to leave the Huertas for good. We did what we had to do."

"I won't force myself on you," he said. "I won't touch you unless you want me to. We'll get an annulment—"

The rest of the sentence stuck in his throat.

"—in Amarillo." She finished the sentence for him and made a disparaging sound. "Glory. Sometimes, I think we'll never get there. And when we do . . ."

The words trailed off. Quinn reached for her, his need to comfort, to assure and protect her, overriding his promise not to touch her against her will.

She let him draw her closer. Surprisingly, a shimmer of tears shown in her eyes. After all they had been through he'd never seen her on the verge of crying.

The sight nearly buckled his resolve not to haul her against him and soothe her anguish with the heat of his mouth. He wanted to kiss away the worry that haunted her, to infuse her with the strength of his body.

His fingertip blotted a drop of moisture at the corner of her eye.

"So many times, Hannah, when I was locked in my cell, shackled in chains, cold, hungry, out of hope, I'd think of"—he hesitated before baring his soul, laying it naked it before her—"I'd think of having a woman like you waiting for me when I found my way out. It kept me sane. It kept me living."

She didn't move, didn't speak, as if her every breath hinged on the words he needed to say.

"You saved me from a life in hell, y'know that? Over and over again. You're the one good thing that has happened to me the last four years. A gift, like Sophia says. Rare and beautiful."

"Oh, Quinn," she whispered.

It'd not been his intent to invoke her pity, to woo or sway her, and when she raised up on tiptoe and pressed her mouth to his, she took him by surprise.

The kiss was brief, asking no more than what she gave, but his fingers dallied over her skin, trailed down the slender line of her throat, and curled around the back of her neck. His thumb rested over her pulse, felt it falter, then lurch and pound inside her.

He suspected she was more affected by him than she wanted to be. The knowledge pleased him. Humbled him. His thumb glided under her chin, up and over the soft curve and onto her mouth, skimming its shape, one side and then the other and back again.

He expected her to pull away. Maybe she should, to stop them both. He wanted to hear her scold him, to remind him he had no place in her life.

Her gaze lifted to his, and she did none of those things. He read the uncertainty in her eyes. The hesitancy. He knew the war she fought inside herself.

"A gift, Hannah," he said simply. "My gift."

Her gaze lowered, fastened on his mouth, and it seemed she forgot to breathe.

She was vulnerable. As vulnerable as he was. Quinn's fingers tightened on the back of her neck anyway, and drew her toward him. Her face lifted to meet him, and giving her no more chances, his lips commanded hers.

He fought hard to contain the sudden surge of hunger she invoked in him, to keep the promise he'd made to her only a few minutes ago. He thought he'd drown in the softness of her mouth, was certain his bones would melt from the feel of her lips moving tentatively beneath his. His blood warmed and simmered. His manhood stirred with want. And need.

His head angled, and his mouth opened over hers. He slid his tongue over her lower lip, wetting it, stroking it, and repeated the seduction with her upper one. She moaned and parted for him, and he plunged inside, ever hungry to taste her, to know the intimacy of her. Her tongue met his, shy, demure, and guileless in its proclamation that she'd never kissed a man the way she kissed him now.

It was nearly his undoing. He shuddered and dragged his mouth off hers to seek his control in the soft curve of her neck.

"Hannah," he breathed. "God, Hannah."

His plea rasped in the air between them, the yearning so blatant she could have no question of his desire for her. She was his wife, vowed to him in the night. He ached to claim her, here, now, with the creek gurgling past them, with the birds singing in the trees, and the sun beaming down on their bodies.

Her hand splayed over his chest, as if she explored the breadth of him, the tightening of his muscles, the heat of his skin beneath his shirt. She breathed his name, the barest hint of a whisper, and his mouth caught hers again.

He kissed her hard this time. Showed her no mercy.

He cupped the back of her head, keeping her lips to his, allowing her no resistance. His hand found the curve of her waist and swept upward to fill his palm with the delicious weight of her breast, and her nipple pebbled. She molded to him, every soft, supple, sweet part of her.

He groaned, low in his throat, at the sensation. At how she made him feel, and of all she made him want—

Hannah ended the kiss with a gasp. She pushed against his chest, wrenched from his embrace with a half-sob. She trembled, sucked in a breath, strove for the composure Quinn should never have taken away from her in the first place.

Knowing he'd gone too far, he grasped her shoulders, but she shrugged him away.

"Everything is happening so quickly. My life is—is changing. I can hardly think straight. I need time, Quinn, to absorb it all."

She hurried from him, abandoning the firewood she'd intended to light. She crawled onto the blanket and curled into a tight ball.

Quinn refused to feel remorse for wanting her, not when he knew she wanted him just as much. He only regretted pushing her to that realization when she wasn't ready. She had a helluva lot more at stake than he did.

He noticed the matches in the dirt. He lit one, touched the flame to the pile of firewood and watched it roar to life, then he finished up the chores. Afterward, he tethered the horses to a young box elder and left them to graze.

He went back to Hannah, his bootsoles noisy on the rough ground, and hunkered beside her.

She'd fallen into an exhausted sleep. Her shoulders lifted, then lowered with every deep, even breath she took. She looked deceptively fragile burrowed in her brown cloak. A little sparrow that would crush too easily if she wasn't handled with care.

But God, she was strong. She knew how to roll with the punches. To survive when the chips were down. She had spirit. Guts. She was more woman than any other he'd ever known.

Raw emotion swelled within him. The empty cavern of his chest opened wide, and she tumbled inside, wrapped around his heart and found her place within him.

Hannah. His wife.

And he'd fallen in love with her.

He resisted the impossibleness of it and vowed Frank Briggs would never take her from him. Nor would Elliott.

Especially Elliott.

A more formidable enemy lay in Mother Superior and her convent. Quinn knew Hannah would keep her end of their deal, that she would not return to the abbess until they reached Amarillo and righted his troubled affairs with Elliott. Then, she would want to return to the convent, to leave him. Quinn did not relish the thought. He knew he would fight to keep her.

He reached out and gently took her limp hand into his. Again, his thumb stroked the gold wedding band in a slow caress.

No, he wasn't a man kin to giving up easily what was his. And she was *his* wife. His love.

A second blanket lay near the fire, and he spread the warm covering over her. The desolate solitude in the

211

canyon assured him again of their safety and that he could afford a few hours of sleep.

He tossed aside his Stetson and combed his fingers through his hair. He lifted the blanket, stretched out beside her and winced at the protests his own tired muscles made. Shifting to his side, he slid his arm around her waist and pulled her close.

Their supper passed with few words spoken between them.

Hannah had risen before Quinn and slipped away to bathe quickly in the cold creek. She was only too glad to shed the old coat and man's pants Sophia had found for her to wear to blow up the pass. She washed the dust and black powder from her skin and donned the embroidered blouse and green skirt. Afterward, she caught a few fish on a crude pole and line—another survival skill she'd learned from her father.

By then, Quinn had awakened, and he cooked the fish to perfection, hot and flaky and satisfying to their empty bellies. Yet the tension between them stretched their nerves taut, left Hannah flustered and aching for the fulfillment he could give, but which she could not accept.

Throughout the meal, his gaze had been bold upon her. She sensed his coiled restraint and was grateful, for she didn't think she'd be able to resist him if he took her in his arms again.

She suppressed a sigh of longing—of confusion and unsettled emotions. Quinn rocked her well-laid plans and left them teetering. He made her forget the vows she'd made to Mother Superior, the precious words she'd clung to for months, ensuring her a world of safety and peace of mind.

Instead, she could only think of the newest set of vows, the ones she'd spoken with him at her side.

Marriage.

Her husband.

Through the fringe of her lashes, Hannah peered at him while he buried the trouts' entrails to prevent any animals from prowling their camp. He made a fine specimen of a man—tall and strong and a little bit dangerous. But she felt safe with him. Protected.

And desired.

Her perusal lowered and settled on his hands while he pressed down the dirt over the hole he'd made. She knew the strength in those hands. The gentleness of which they were capable. And she knew how they felt on her body when they touched her face or caressed her skin or took the fullness of her breast within their tender hold.

Her heart fluttered. She'd had so little experience with men, had despised and kept her distance from those with whom Pa had associated. Her life with him had prevented her from ever being courted.

Or seduced.

Quinn looked up at her, then, and found her staring. Embarrassed, Hannah tore her gaze away and vigorously rinsed the last of their utensils in the creek. He straightened to his full height and approached her.

She stood quickly, pressing the wet dishes to her bosom, forgetting to dry them first with Sophia's towel.

"A fog's rolling in," he said. "We'll have to spend the night here."

She glanced upward. A vaporous cloud had de-

213

scended from the heavens and covered the moonlit sky with a cataract of mist. Travelling the narrow trails before the fog lifted would be treacherous.

"All right," she said softly.

"Might as well turn in and get a little more sleep. I want to leave at first light."

She nodded, and he bent and hefted one of the saddles to his shoulder. Hannah sensed his brooding gaze following her movements as she tidied up the camp, gathered more wood and piled it near the fire. By the time she had stoked the flames to a robust roar, he'd pulled the blanket over him, leaving half for her. Their saddles lay side by side to pillow their heads. She lifted the blanket and settled in next to him.

She couldn't help thinking of her old room in the convent with its tiny cot and crackly straw mattress that itched and poked in her sleep, or how alone she felt there.

Her pensive sigh rang loud in the fog-shrouded silence. She'd been so sure she'd found her calling at the convent. Now, that life seemed far away, and she rarely thought about it anymore.

Instead, she thought of being with Quinn, of sleeping next to him, of going to Amarillo with him.

What waited for them there?

"If you've got something on your mind, Hannah, just say it," Quinn said. He raised up on an elbow. "I want no barriers between us."

She hesitated.

"But if you're angry because I kissed you," he went on, his expression grim in the campfire's golden light, "don't expect me to apologize."

His declaration, stubborn and emphatic, touched her heart.

She shook her head. "That's not it at all."

She didn't blame him for the kiss, not when she'd melted from the mastery of it, had savored and relished every moment of his mouth moving against hers.

"What then?" He captured her fingers and twined them with his, holding them against his chest. "You've been ignoring me all night."

"No." She spoke the denial softly. "I haven't been ignoring you."

He wanted a response from her. Would he think her too bold to delve into his past to soothe the uncertainties of her future? Would she be too selfish to want to know the things about him—about Amarillo—he kept shuttered inside?

She met his gaze. He waited for her to ask those questions, didn't he? It seemed important to him to clear the air between them.

"I was just thinking. About your life in Amarillo," she said finally.

"What about it?"

"You told me once you had a brother. Does he live there?"

He appeared taken aback. Then he shifted, sliding his arm beneath her shoulders and fitting her against his side. She didn't resist. Glory, she liked the position, having found herself in it more than once when she'd awakened from a night in bed with him.

"Yes, my brother lives there," he said quietly, adjusting the blanket over her. "His name is Elliott."

"Elliott." She pondered the name and lay her hand

215

over his flat belly. "Do you have other family? Parents? Sisters?"

"None. Except for a son."

"A son!" Aghast, she sprang back.

"Whoa. Take it easy." He pulled her back against him. "Manny wasn't mine by birth. His mother, Rosa, was the daughter of an old foreman who worked my ranch, and Manny was the product of a good roll in the hay she had with one of the cowhands. He took off before he knew Manny had been conceived. Rosa never saw him again."

"Did you marry her?"

"No." He brushed the curls from Hannah's temple. The smouldering depths of his eyes revealed an earnestness that held her riveted. "You, Mrs. Landry, are my first and only wife."

"But how could you claim her son as yours? Did you live with her?"

Hannah was insistent to know about this woman named Rosa, about the place she'd held in his life.

"I took Manny in when he was only two. Rosa had been killed in a freak accident—thrown from a horse, though she was an expert rider. She had Manny with her that day and somehow he managed to survive."

Hannah peered up at him. The campfire cast Quinn's face into a sharp contrast of shadows and flickering light, and showed him reliving the darker side of his past.

" 'Somehow'?" she asked.

"Rosa loved that boy. He was all she lived for. She would have tried to save him when the horse reared, even if it cost her her own life."

She considered that. "What do you think really happened?"

He shrugged. "I think she tossed him off the horse to keep him from being trampled. We found her with her skull kicked in, but Manny had hardly a scratch. Except—"

He halted.

Hannah held her breath.

"Except he had a bruise on the side of his head. And a small bump. Nothing to worry about. Or so we thought. Out of respect for Rosa, I took Manny in to raise as my own. Shortly after, he began to have seizures. Violent ones. I brought him to the best doctor in Amarillo, and he treated him with Triple Bromide Elixir, the best medicine available for seizures. He was content and healthy when I was arrested."

Arrested.

The image destroyed what would have been a happy ending to Quinn's story. Hannah sat up, hugged her knees to her chest.

Perhaps now was the moment of reckoning—that point in time when all her fears and trepidations of the ruthlessly savage side of him would be put to rest.

Or resurrected.

He sat up, too, his expression grim and showing no remorse.

"I was arrested for killing my sister-in-law, Hannah. Elliott's wife." His voice was devoid of emotion.

Her eyes closed. She swallowed.

"They found her in my hotel room. Naked in my bed."

A chill cloaked her spine. She strove to keep her voice even. "Were you in bed with her?"

217

"Yes."

"Naked?"

"Yes."

She released a shaky breath. "Glory."

"It didn't matter I didn't have a drop of her blood on me, that they found no weapon, though she'd been brutally beaten. And raped."

Hannah pressed her fingers to her mouth in horror.

He scowled at her reaction. "*I* didn't rape her, damn it. I had no designs on her. She was my brother's wife, for godssake."

"But you were together. In bed."

"Yes." He breathed an oath. "Hell. I don't know how she got there. Elliott claimed I was stinking drunk and managed to convince everyone else I was, too. The bedclothes reeked of whiskey. An empty bottle was on the floor, but I had only a few drinks that night. I swear it. Next thing I knew, I was in chains and in a wagon headed for New Mexico Territory."

His words swam in her head. "Do you think Elliott framed you?"

"I know he did. I just can't prove it."

"Oh, Quinn."

Hannah's temples began a slow, throbbing ache.

He was capable of it all, she thought dully. Hate. Violence. Rage for those who wronged him. She'd seen it for herself at the penitentiary, when he used her to make his escape.

"Now you know the score I have to settle," he said, the set of his jaw resolute. He gripped her chin, forced her to look at him. "I wanted you to hear the truth from me. I want you to believe me."

Intense and desperate, his gaze probed her features

in the firelight. He searched for her faith in him, and he found her doubts instead, clear as rain on her face.

He swore and released her.

"Somehow, Mrs. Landry, I thought you'd be different from the rest of them," he said softly. "Damned if I wasn't wrong about you."

She recoiled from the bite in his words, felt the hurting sting of tears in her eyes.

"We'll be in Amarillo by the end of the week." His tone clipped the air between them. "Elliott will be thrilled to meet you."

He twisted away from her and lay on his side, presenting her with his broad back and giving the blanket a fierce jerk.

Hannah blinked furiously. She didn't want to meet Elliott. And she didn't want Quinn angry with her.

His disappointment in her left her feeling cold. Bereft. And strangely haunted by a pathetic longing to have him make everything right again, to return to the way things had been when he'd kissed her that afternoon.

Chapter Fifteen

In the days following, their lives fell into a grueling routine that included far more time spent riding in the saddle than it did resting in their bedroll. Their food supply had dwindled, but Quinn had seen to it they filled their bellies with rabbit, squirrel, and whatever fish they could catch along the way. Hannah never went to sleep hungry, and if she did, she was too exhausted to notice.

Quinn's stamina amazed her. There never seemed to be enough daylight hours to suit him. He was tireless, a man possessed by inner demons compelling him to return home and right the wrongs dealt to him. She could only shudder at what means he would use to satisfy his need for revenge, for she had long ago learned he would be a formidable enemy. She hoped Elliott was prepared for the battle.

Even if his brother dominated his thoughts, though, Quinn hadn't forgotten Frank Briggs. Beneath the low slouch of his hat brim, his dark eyes continually swept the New Mexico Territory, then the sprawling lands of the state of Texas, for signs of their pursuers. His constant vigilance eased Hannah's worries, and she grew confident the warden and his cohorts had not yet picked up their trail.

From the edges of her brown wool hood, Hannah slid her gaze toward Quinn. He rode slightly ahead of her, his back straight in the saddle, the reins laced loosely through his fingers. His foot rested casually in the stirrup, and his lean body flowed with the motion of the horse, as if he'd spent much of his life on the back of one.

Coiled power, she thought. He emanated it.

Violence, too. Just beneath the surface.

Had he really killed Elliott's wife?

A thousand times, Hannah asked herself the question. If he was guilty, then why hadn't he violated *her?* Glory, he'd had plenty of chances. And it had seemed so important to him that she believe in his innocence. In fact, she was sure he remained offended by her doubts.

Unexpectedly, Quinn drew in his mount near a stand of pinon pine and juniper trees, and Hannah scrambled back to reality. They'd halted on the rise of a hill. At her questioning glance, he pointed to the small ranch sprawled below them.

A cabin, built from logs and adobe, dominated the spread. Near it stood a corral, a crude shed and a few head of livestock left to graze on the winter grass.

A woman hung laundry while two small children toddled close by. Smoke curled from the cabin's chimney, and Hannah detected the faint aroma of fresh-baked bread lingering in the air.

Quinn crossed his wrists over the saddle horn.

"Reckon my belly could stand for some of that grub she's cookin' up," he said. "How about yours?"

"Yes," Hannah murmured, keenly aware neither of them had had breakfast that morning. "Do you suppose she has any to spare? They look as poor as church mice."

"I won't take food out of her babies's mouths." He regarded her. "It's only right we pay her."

Up to now, Quinn had skirted every town in their path to Amarillo, had taken every back road to avoid detection. This woman and her children were the first of humankind they'd seen since leaving Huerta's camp.

There'd been no need to dip into Fenwick's money, carefully sewn in Hannah's cloak hem. She remembered her intent to use it for a stagecoach ticket back to the convent.

But she stifled her selfishness. Her conscience would not allow accepting food from the young family without payment.

"Of course," she said. "I'll give you the money."

Quinn dismounted, and when Hannah would have done the same, he reached upward, clasping her waist between the folds of her cloak. She accepted his assistance—though she was quite capable of climbing down from the horse herself—and after she was safely settled upon the ground, his hands remained.

She lifted her head, and her gaze met his.

He released her, then, but not before Hannah glimpsed the heat in his eyes, a blatant yearning that still ran strong within him. Hannah stepped back and fumbled with the clasp at her throat.

It pleased her, that yearning.

"It'll only take me a moment to undo the hem," she said softly. She removed her cloak, sat cross-legged on the thick grass and plucked at the threads lining the edge of the cloak. The fabric fell free, and the pouch with the bills and coins tumbled out.

"How much is there?" he asked, hunkering down in front of her.

"Eight dollars and twenty-one cents."

He slid the coins around her palm with his index finger, more in thoughtful consideration than to check her arithmetic.

"It's not much," he said.

It seemed a small fortune to Hannah, who'd had no dealings with money since she entered the convent.

"But there's enough to buy our food?"

His shoulder lifted. "For now."

"Take it," she said, thrusting their limited wealth toward him. "Use what you need to pay the lady."

He tossed her an amused glance, as if he knew how she'd zealously guarded the treasure until now. Finally, he stuffed the money into his shirt pocket.

"Stay here." He straightened. "We'll raise less suspicion if it's only me she sees."

Hannah nodded in agreement. Giving her a brief wave, he mounted and left. She rolled to her stomach, cupped her chin in her hands, and watched him ride down the hill.

Several scrawny chickens clucked and scattered in protest as he drew closer to the woman. She straightened, slowly, warily, from her basket of laundry.

Her children, two little girls, ran behind her skirts. Quinn spoke, and the woman seemed to relax, eventually nodding her head and indicating the well located a few yards away. Hannah guessed she offered him a cool drink. After a moment, the woman entered the cabin, her daughters tagging close behind.

Quinn dismounted and looked in Hannah's direction. Though she doubted he could see her, he tipped his hat in a disarming gesture that told her he was thinking of her, that he knew she watched him, and that he knew she'd be waiting for him when he returned.

Her cheeks warmed. He had the ability to fluster her, even this far away.

He strode toward the well and filled their canteen. While screwing the lid back on, the oldest of the two girls emerged from the cabin and approached him shyly. She clutched a rag doll in her hand.

Seeing her, Quinn squatted down to her level. He spoke to her, and Hannah found herself holding her breath, wondering what he said. The child held the doll out to him, and Quinn took it gently, placing it to his shoulder as if it were a real baby, and patted its back.

Hannah's heart melted.

The troublesome doubts that lingered over his guilt or innocence wavered inside her. She had seen his savagery, his strength, his protectiveness. She had tasted his kisses and craved his warmth. But this humble and tender side, the one that invoked the trust of a child, revealed with sudden clarity what her stubborn judgment up to now had refused to acknowledge.

He hadn't killed his sister-in-law. He was innocent of the charges brought against him. Had it been the guilt from her own past that blinded her to the truth about him for so long?

The child's little sister toddled from the cabin, her own doll in tow. Quinn put this one to his other shoulder and repeated their game of pretend, to the girls' delight.

And in that moment, Hannah realized she had fallen in love.

He brought back fried chicken, pickled tomatoes, thick slices of warm bread dripping in butter, and several apples for dessert.

Hannah couldn't remember the last time she'd eaten so well. Quinn lamented his over-stuffed belly and dozed against the tree trunk, his Stetson covering his face.

She let him sleep. Amarillo could wait.

He'd paid the woman well for her generosity, and she'd been clearly grateful for the money. She would always think of him as a drifter down on his luck, and if she knew he was a convicted murderer . . .

Hannah grimaced. The poor woman would have been terrified.

It would be a curse Quinn would live with for the rest of his life, Hannah knew. That same curse had followed Pa, though his crimes were not of violence but of cheating and thievery. No matter how hard she'd tried to reform him, his past had always haunted him.

As it did her. Hannah had a string of her own crimes with which she had to live.

Difference was, Pa was dead, and she wasn't. And where she had fled to the convent to escape her sins, Quinn boldly returned to his past to confront his.

Pam Crooks

An intriguing man, her husband. No wonder she loved him so.

Impulsively, she knelt beside him, lifted his hat and dropped a kiss to his forehead.

"Hey." He roused and reached for her, but she sashayed away, and he missed grabbing her skirt by inches. "What was that for?"

"For being so sweet to those little girls. For caring about them and their mother." She tossed the Stetson back onto his head.

He grunted and pulled it off again. "And that's all I get for my trouble? A tiny kiss?"

"Be glad for it, Mr. Landry. I'm not prone to kissing men at will." She peeped at him through her lashes. "Especially one convicted of murder."

"Hell." He frowned. "Don't I know it."

She laughed softly and tilted her face to the sun to soak in its warmth. Her arms lifted, and she stretched up on her tiptoes and tried to reach the sky.

"It'll be spring soon. I can hardly wait," she declared.

"Well, it's still winter in Amarillo. Things could get damned chilling when I meet Elliott." He stood up, flexed the muscles in his back. "We'll be there in a few hours time."

Dismay replaced her exuberance. She went still.

"I didn't realize we were so close," she said. "I'm—I'm a mess."

She ran her fingers through her tousled curls. They'd left the Huertas's camp with next to nothing. At the time, food and bedding had been most important. Now, Hannah would have bargained her soul for a bar of soap and a fresh change of clothes.

Quinn picked up her cloak, its hem trailing since she

226

didn't have a needle and thread to repair it. He draped the garment around her shoulders.

"The last time I saw Elliott, I was in chains and stripped of my innocence and dignity. He'd taken away everything I ever worked for. I had nothing left." He lifted her hood over her head. "I'm going to get it all back again, Hannah. When I meet Elliott again, it'll be on my terms. And you can be damned sure when he sees me, I won't be covered in a week's worth of trail dust and wearing someone else's clothes." His gaze roamed over her face. "Nor will you."

She held that gaze without wavering. "I believe you."

A moment passed. Her words, the implication in them, seemed to stun him. "Just what is it that you believe about me, Mrs. Landry?"

His voice sounded husky. As if he was afraid to breathe.

Or to hope.

"I believe you didn't kill Elliott's wife. I was wrong to think you did. At least later, after I'd gotten to know you."

He sucked a slow breath inward. And waited.

"Your brother has done a horrible injustice against you, Quinn. Before I go back to the convent, I want— I'll do what I can to help you prove your innocence."

"Do you know how long I've wanted your trust, Hannah?"

Regret that she'd not discovered her love for him sooner coursed through her. The simple trust that went with it was priceless. "Yes."

"Elliott is dangerous. I won't put you in any situation with him where you'll be hurt."

She believed Quinn about that, too. A sudden wave

of apprehension flared within her. "I'll be meeting him soon, then. And your friends?"

"You're my wife," he said, as if that was all the answer she needed.

It wasn't. She knew so little about him and the life he'd led, the people with whom he associated and what they were about.

More apprehensive than ever, she glanced away.

"You're a beautiful woman, Hannah. I'm proud to have you with me."

"I know nothing of being a wife and how to act as one. I've never been schooled in social niceties. Well, my mother taught me some, but I was so young then—"

He halted her babbling by covering her lips with his, and her worries floated away on a sigh.

"Hush," he breathed into her mouth. "Just keep on trusting me, darlin', and you'll be fine. We both will." He drew back, his dark eyes smouldering into hers. "Okay?"

She nodded, though she wasn't as sure as she led him to believe.

"Let's go, then." He nudged her toward the gelding and hefted her up. "I've got a strong hankering for a shave and a long, hot bath."

There was a time in Quinn's life when he thought he'd never again see this particular landscape, and the reality of it clogged his throat with raw emotion.

Amarillo. Vibrant and alive in the grand state of Texas.

Jesus. It felt good to feast his eyes on the place.

In the time he'd been gone, the town's boundaries

had widened in all four directions, and his chest swelled with pride and amazement.

From their vantage point on a knoll along the outskirts, he recalled when Amarillo wasn't much more than a cowtown. They'd gone to school here, he and Elliott, until their mother died and their father, T. J. Landry, bought into one of the fastest-growing ranches in Potter County. Over the years, his father had assumed ownership, changed the brand to Star L, and when he died, left the entire outfit to Quinn.

From the time he was a lowly cowhand still wet behind the ears until he became the owner of a quarter-million acre spead, Quinn had worked hard to build a name for himself amongst his fellow cattlemen. The citizens of Amarillo loved and respected him. Life had been full and rich and good.

Until that fateful day when he'd been yanked from his bed, convicted, and dragged across the state line. An ugly, festering sore on the town's butt. Disowned and dishonored.

Now, the thought of going back, of walking amongst honest citizenry, eating and drinking and talking with them, unnerved him. He'd been locked up in a dark, foul-smelling cell for so damned long.

What if he had forever lost the man he had been?

"Scary, isn't it?" Hannah asked quietly.

He clawed through his grim thoughts and focused his gaze on her.

"Yeah," he said roughly, surprised she knew what he'd been thinking. "It is."

"It's been a long time for me, too. The convent hid me away from polite society. I worry that I have forgotten what it is like." She settled those velvety hazel-green eyes on him. "To be a normal woman, I mean."

He was responsible for pulling her out of her safe world and thrusting her into the uncertainties of his.

Was he no better than Elliott?

The thought disgusted him. Quinn reached over and took her hand in silent apology, then pressed a kiss to the smooth skin over her knuckle.

A touch of pink covered her cheeks, but she didn't pull away.

"Whenever Pa and I were on the run," she continued, "we'd end up in a strange town, and I was always terrified someone would recognize us, and we'd be thrown in jail for his latest crime." Her mouth softened in a rueful smile. "Or mine."

Slow and assessing, her gaze swept the horizon, broken by assorted rooftops and chimneys along the skyline.

"We were recognized only once. Later that night, they lynched him." A faint sheen of tears shone in her eyes, but she blinked them away and drew in a breath. "That won't happen to you, will it, Quinn?"

He'd be a bald-faced liar if he told her he'd never thought of it or that it wasn't possible. They both knew it was.

He gave her hand a reassuring squeeze.

"Hell, darlin'. You're takin' all the fun out of my homecoming. Let's just ride in and see what happens, shall we?"

She nodded. He released her, and she took the reins. Quinn pulled his Stetson's brim low over his eyes, and they entered the town limits at an unhurried pace.

They rode onto Third Street. Men, women and children hustled along boardwalks far more crowded than

Quinn remembered. The pungency of warm horseflesh and manure, the taste of dust on his tongue, the clatter of bells and shouting voices and barking dogs were all familiar. Suddenly, it was as if he'd never lived the nightmare, as if he'd left Amarillo only yesterday.

Damn, it was good to be back.

"Ever been in Amarillo before, Mrs. Landry?" he asked over the clamor of wagons and buggies.

"Never." She appeared fascinated by the variety of falsefront businesses and brick buildings. "Been to Austin once, though."

"A fair city, Austin. Been there many times myself."

They turned the corner onto Polk Street.

"Ah. The Amarillo Hotel." He took in the sight of it, braced himself for the memories it evoked. "The finest place in town for a man to get a good night's rest."

"Really," she murmured, tilting her head back to scan the two levels of the sprawling structure. "I'm impressed."

He dismounted and tied the gelding to one of the dozen hitching posts. After assisting Hannah down, he secured her horse next to his.

She studied him, her expression somber with unanswered questions.

He went to her, rested his hands easily on her hips. She was less skittish these days, allowing him to touch her more often. He wondered at her thoughts. Did she still think him capable of murder?

"I was staying here the night Sarah, my sister-in-law, was killed," he said. "They always kept a room ready for me when I could get away from the ranch." A corner of his mouth lifted. "My home away from home."

"Oh." She sent an uncertain glance toward the double doors, inset with beveled glass. "And you want to go back? Now?"

"I have to, Hannah."

She pursed her mouth and appeared doubtful. He slid his hand to the small of her waist and guided her up the stairs.

Pushing through the doors, Quinn inhaled the scents he'd always associated with the hotel and had never forgotten—linseed oil and beeswax, expensive cigars, imported whiskey. And money. Lots of it.

The Amarillo spared no expense in the upkeep of its lobby, smoking and billiards rooms, and especially not in the sleeping rooms for its guests. Everything was as he remembered. Every polished, velvet-draped, Oriental-rugs-and-furnishings-from-London inch of it.

But, hell . . . the lavishness still stunned him.

It was all so different from his filthy prison cell. The comparison forced him to appreciate the beauty. The privilege. And he'd taken it all for granted once, when he'd been a cocky cowboy still sowing his oats, and even later, as a wealthy cattleman.

"Can I help you?"

The hotel clerk's cool question tugged at Quinn's attention, and he urged Hannah into the deserted lobby. From behind his gleaming, tidy counter, the man, in his early forties, eyed him with haughty disdain.

Quinn didn't recognize him. He'd expected to find someone else at the counter, one of the hotel's most loyal servants who always saw to it that Quinn's every need had been met.

"Is Humphrey here?" he asked.

"Humphrey?" The man appeared taken aback.

"Why, no. He has not been with us for quite some time now."

A loss, Quinn thought. For himself *and* the hotel.

"I need a room, then. The best you've got," he said.

A thick eyebrow rose. The clerk's gaze dragged over Quinn's dust-covered clothes, seemed to note the growth of beard on his face, then flitted dismissingly over Hannah.

Neither of them looked as if they owned a pot to piss in, Quinn thought with some amusement.

Which they didn't.

Not yet, anyway.

The man sniffed. "Our *best* room comes with a price, I'm afraid. Do you have means, sir?"

"Charge it to my brother's account," he said. "Elliott Landry, from the Star L ranch."

The clerk's expression remained impassive. "Is your brother aware of the charges, sir?"

"I'll tell him." Annoyance flickered through Quinn. "Just as soon as I see him."

The clerk appeared skeptical. "I'm sorry. Until I receive agreement from your, er, brother that all fees will be settled, I cannot give you a room. You understand, certainly."

"Give him what he wants, Wesley. He'll make good on the bill. I'll see to it."

Quinn turned slowly at the sound of her voice.

A woman, dressed in a plain black dress and starched white apron and cap, stood at the foot of the staircase leading to the second floor rooms. She gripped a cloth and a bottle of linseed oil in her hand.

Loretta Carter had worked at the Amarillo Hotel for the past five years. She'd been a prostitute before that, and Quinn had been one of her regulars, more out of friendship than lust.

He'd been the one to persuade Loretta to leave her madam and lead a respectable life, had even gone as far as finding her employment at the Amarillo. She'd taken pride in her job, had worked hard at it, and was newly married at the time of his arrest.

"Is it really you, Quinn Landry?" she asked, her voice hardly above a whisper. She'd gone pale. Hauntingly so.

He grinned in genuine pleasure and held out his arms. She dropped her cloth and bottle of oil and ran to him, clinging tight as he whirled her around in a full circle, forcing Hannah to move quickly aside lest she get in their way.

"Lord, I thought I'd never see you again!" She kissed him full on the mouth. "Oh, *Quinn!*"

She hugged him again, hard.

"It's good to see you, too." He set her from him gently. Firmly. "I want you to meet my wife, Loretta. This is Hannah."

"Your *wife?*" She gaped at Hannah, her jaw lagging. Tears shown in her eyes, threatening to snake down her cheeks. She was visibly shaken not only at seeing Quinn again, but at meeting his wife, as well. "But, how—when?"

"I'll explain later." He wasn't eager to tell his story in front of the staring hotel clerk. "Hannah, this is Loretta Carter."

"I'm sorry. You must forgive me." Loretta took Hannah's hand before Hannah could say a word. "Quinn and I go way back." She gaped at him. "I—I haven't seen him since—since—"

"Before my arrest."

"Yes," she whispered. A shudder took her.

Hannah appeared uncertain at his relationship with this new woman, and he twined his fingers through hers in silent assurance. Her clasp tightened, and he thought she moved a little closer to him.

"Let's put them in the front suite, Wesley," Loretta said firmly, turning to the clerk. "I've just aired the rooms this morning. They'll be clean and fresh."

"But—" he sputtered.

"Just give me the key." She slid the guest book toward Hannah, along with a pen. "They'll pay the bill. I promise."

Quinn crossed his arms over his chest and let Loretta take care of the matter. Hannah took the proferred writing utensil and prepared to register them. The tip hovered over the paper, and after a moment's hesitation, she wrote their name on the proper line.

Mr. and Mrs. Quinn Landry. Amarillo, Texas.

He liked the looks of it, scrawled in her neat, precise handwriting. Seeing the words written in black and white made their marriage even more real.

Evidently, Hannah thought so, too. She refused to look at him.

"Come on, you two." Loretta hastened toward the stairs with their room key in her hand. She retrieved the cloth and polishing oil as she made her way to the second floor.

Quinn and Hannah followed, leaving the hotel clerk frowning after them.

Chapter Sixteen

Loretta led them up a winding flight of stairs and turned into a wide hall. A skylight brightened the area and allowed hotel guests to appreciate the mica satin wallpaper and the thick carpet in deep hues of green, gold and blue.

But Quinn hardly noticed. A powerful sense of déjà vu gripped him.

He halted in mid-stride. His gaze fastened on the door they'd just passed, its front inscribed with the numbers 201 in shining brass.

His old room.

The one in which Sarah had died.

His mind reverted to a blinding flash of the past, of this hallway, of Elliott and someone else dragging him from his bed. He'd been dazed, his brain sluggish and drugged, but he'd fought back.

His gaze leapt to the mahogany pedestal at the end of the hall. A lush fern used to sit on its marble top.

He remembered kicking out, knocking it over. He remembered hearing the planter break and seeing dirt scatter.

A philodendron sat on the marble now, its foliage green and profuse. The fern was gone, as if that night had never happened.

"Do you want to go inside?" Loretta asked, her tone solemn.

He stared at the numbers again.

"No," he said, the memories heavy on his shoulders, so heavy he feared he'd crumple beneath their weight.

Room 201 had haunted him when he'd been in the depths of despair, chained in his prison cell and hanging on to his sanity by his teeth. He'd vowed to hunt down its secrets, to throw open wide the truth of what had really happened the night Sarah was killed.

Seeing the room, reliving the horrors, wouldn't bring her back.

"Quinn?" Hannah's soft voice drew him. She touched his shoulder and moved closer. "This is where it happened, isn't it?"

"Yes," he whispered.

An involuntary shudder wracked him. She murmured his name again and wound her arms around him. He closed his eyes and held her tight.

"They burned the mattress and all the bedding after your arrest." Loretta's voice sounded far away. "There was so much blood. That room is evil. I've never set foot in there since."

He wanted to go on holding Hannah, but he knew Loretta waited with respectful patience, and he reluctantly ended the embrace. Loretta followed them inside the suite and closed the door firmly behind her.

She had Mexican blood, but her predominantly Anglo heritage presented her with light skin. Black eyes and hair, combined with exquisitely carved features, had formed Loretta into an exotic beauty. Her years as a prostitute had toughened her to the ways of the world, and there was little that shocked her.

Sarah's death seemed to be one of the exceptions.

"How did you get here, Quinn?" she asked quietly. "They said you were dead. That you'd died in prison."

"They?"

"Everyone. It was the talk of Amarillo. Even the newspapers picked up on it."

His brow rose in thinly veiled contempt. "Then maybe they should check their facts before they print them. I'm alive, though there were days when I'd wished I wasn't."

"You escaped?"

"Yes. From the New Mexico Territorial Penitentiary."

Tears welled all over again, formed dark pools in her eyes. "They took you out of the state. God, Quinn. The New Mexico prison is known for its—" She halted, her features pained. "How did you ever survive it?"

"By the hide on my sorry ass, that's how." He glanced at Hannah. She'd removed her cloak and stood hugging the tattered thing to her bosom. "And with the help of my wife."

Loretta sniffled and swiped at the tears. "I should have done more for you."

Quinn took off his Stetson and tossed it on the bed. "There's nothing you could have done."

She bit her lip. She'd yet to move from the door.

"Is there anything I can do now?" she asked. "Just name it."

He leaned back against a washstand with shiny tiles. "As a matter of fact, there is."

"I'll do it."

Her willingness surprised him. And satisfied him.

"For one thing, don't say a word to anyone that I'm here. I'll meet with the necessary people as I see fit. The news will spread soon enough."

"And Elliott?"

"Elliott." He paused, thought of the revenge that had kept him alive. "I'll meet with him when I'm ready."

She nodded. And seemed to understand.

"Draw a bath for Hannah. See that she has everything she wants. She'll need clothes, too. From the skin out."

Loretta wiped at the last of the tears. "My shift here is over. I'll take her shopping."

"No. I don't want her to leave this room until I return." He appealed to Hannah, though his decision was firm. "Okay?"

"A long soak in a hot bath would be heavenly," Hannah said wistfully. "But, Quinn, you're being far too forward in asking Loretta to buy—"

"I don't mind, truly," Loretta broke in. She gave Hannah a womanly perusal, and Quinn could tell it was favorable. "You'll be easy to buy for. If you trust my tastes?"

"If Quinn trusts you, then I do, too."

"Charge the bills to the ranch account, Loretta. Does Collette still have her dress shop?"

"Yes. She's recently gotten some lovely gowns in from New York."

"Good. She'll honor the charge."

"Anything else?"

"That's it."

She prepared to leave, but hesitated. "Elliott no longer comes to the hotel. Not like he used to. He stays mostly on the ranch, and when he does come to town, he's with"—she halted, as if she'd divulged too much—"Well, it seems he's fallen into a bad crowd."

Quinn pondered the news. Elliott's absence explained why the hotel clerk didn't recognize the Landry name or its outfit.

"Thanks for telling me, Loretta. I owe you."

"No." She spoke the word almost sharply. "You owe me nothing."

"We appreciate all you're doing to help us out," Hannah added.

"It's no trouble." She unlatched the door. "I'll have your bath drawn immediately, Hannah."

"Hey, Loretta?" Quinn called, just as she was leaving. "You look good. Life's been treating you pretty fair?"

She smiled, but was still pale, still shaken by his return. "Yes. I have a baby. A girl."

"Congratulations." He knew she'd always wanted a family. Respectability. A decent job. He was happy for her.

Questions about Manny skittered across his mind, but he refrained from asking them. She seemed in a hurry, and she still had shopping to do for Hannah. He didn't want to keep her from her baby any longer than he had to.

After she left, he found Hannah admiring the brocaded panel on a Japanese screen situated near the dressing table. She turned wide eyes on him.

"Everything in this hotel is so lovely, Quinn. And expensive." Her expression turned worried. "I don't think Elliott will be happy you're making him pay for this."

"Every dime Elliott has is one he's stolen from me. He can afford it. The Landry coffers are full." He frowned. "Leastways, they used to be."

She appeared doubtful. "I can't imagine anyone having money like this. The Landrys or otherwise."

He grunted. She had a lot to learn.

"You were bossy with Loretta," she observed.

His mouth curved. "Was I?"

"But I think she'd have given you all of Texas if you asked her for it." She trailed her finger along the polished bedside table top. Her mouth hinted at a pout. He wondered if she was jealous.

"We've been friends a long time," he said.

"I noticed."

He let her stew on it. A little jealousy could be a good thing.

She cocked her head. "Where will you be while I have my bath?"

"Getting that shave I've been hankering for. And a haircut. And a new suit."

"Will Elliott pay for all that, too?"

He grinned. "Yes."

The worry in her expression returned.

She halted at the bed, a massive four-poster affair with too many pillows and ruffles to make a man comfortable.

But, then, if he were in it with Hannah, he wouldn't care. Or even notice.

Pam Crooks

And he'd be damned comfortable.

His loins stirred; his yearning for her fired up again.

"I'd best be going," he said, moving toward her despite his words to the contrary.

"When will you return?"

She backed into the mattress. With him at the front of her, she had nowhere to go.

But down.

The yearning flamed higher.

"I'll be back at four," he murmured.

"Okay." She held herself very still, and her gaze had dropped to his mouth. He remembered what had happened the last time she'd looked at him that way. "Four o'clock."

Her voice sounded husky. Breathless.

"Stay here," he said, his head lowering a little. "Don't let anyone in."

"I won't."

He lowered even more. "No one except Loretta."

"Loretta."

She was whispering now. And trembling. And she kept looking at his mouth.

"Keep the door locked." He was almost there, could already feel the softness of her luscious lips moving under his.

"I will." She swallowed. Her eyelids drifted shut. Her chin tilted up just enough to meet him.

"I'll lock it now, darlin'." A plea had crept into his voice. A pitiful, pathetic plea from a man aching to make love to his wife. "I don't have to get that shave—"

A knock sounded on the door.

"Hannah? This is Loretta. Your bath is ready."

Quinn swore and drew back.

242

Hannah's Vow

Hannah emitted a tiny squeak and twisted from him like a delicate butterfly evading the net.

He raked a hand through his hair. The door opened, and Loretta, smiling, stepped in.

He snatched his Stetson from the bed.

"Four o'clock," he snapped to Hannah. "And not a minute later."

With that, he strode through the door and left both women gaping after him.

How in blazes was he supposed to keep his hands off her when she looked so damned beautiful?

Quinn kept asking himself that question as they walked down Polk Street. She sorely tested his restraint, fouled his mood, distracted him from his well-laid plans, and made him want to bed her right here on the boardwalk.

"Just look at us, Quinn." From the crook of his elbow, Hannah's gloved fingers tugged him to a stop. "The change in us is so . . . amazing."

They paused in front of the large glass window of a millinery shop and stared at their reflections.

He grunted his agreement. They were a couple who turned heads and drew admiring glances—brought them attention he'd rather not have.

Not yet, anyway.

The top of her head reached his shoulder, but her new hat, adorned with satin ribbons, flowers and a froth of feathers, made her appear taller. The edge of an Ottoman mantle brushed the flare of her hips and matched the striped silk of her gown, rich with the jewel tones of sapphire blue and emerald green.

Loretta couldn't have picked a finer gown for Han-

243

nah. Its hues embellished the color of her eyes, accented her skin; and the cut of the dress fit her body to perfection.

Nothing could have made Hannah prettier—unless she was wearing nothing at all. Desire flickered anew within him.

Her fingers slid beneath the lapel of his jacket, tracing its shape, then smoothed it flat again.

"Have I told you how handsome you are, Mr. Landry?" she asked. "Black broadcloth suits and string ties become you."

"I'm glad you think so," he said gruffly.

He pulled her away from the window. She peered up at him and quickened her pace to match his.

"You're cross with me," she said. "Why?"

"If I thought you'd be agreeable to all I'm thinking, I'd tell you. Since you won't be, there's no point in discussing it."

"Agreeable?" She appeared perplexed by his sour mood. "I don't know what you're talking about. And if this has something to do with Loretta spending a sinful amount of money on my clothes—"

"It doesn't," he said. "I gave Loretta full rein to outfit you with all you needed. She did a damned fine job of it."

"You are far too loose with Elliott's money," she sniffed.

"*My* money," he said, annoyed. "And get used to it. I'll be spending more on you in the future."

She clamped her mouth shut, her disapproval obvious.

He steered her around the corner, down one more block and across the street to a white frame building with clapboard siding. By the time they climbed the porch steps, Hannah's breathing revealed her exertions to keep up.

She held back just long enough to read the sign hanging from little hooks next to the door—*Joseph Daniel Hartman, Attorney-at-Law*—before Quinn opened it and nudged her inside.

Quinn felt some of his tension ease as he stepped into his old friend's office.

Jody. Thank God he was still here.

Jody's longtime secretary sat at the desk Quinn doubted had ever been used by anyone else. Bernard made notations in a ledger, his hawk-like nose bent to the paper, his plain gray suit hanging, as ever, on his gaunt frame.

Quinn pulled his Stetson lower over his forehead. He had no intention of explaining his presence to the crotchety old man, not before he'd explained it to Jody first.

"Is Mr. Hartman in?" he asked, his tone crisp. Impatient to see his boyhood friend, Quinn kept walking toward his office.

"Yes, sir." Bernard didn't look up, his concentration snared on the last flourish of the word he was writing. "But he's not to be disturbed."

Quinn grasped the doorknob and turned. Before Bernard could push back his chair and protest, Quinn ushered Hannah inside, following close behind and latching the door after himself.

"What is it, Bernard?" Engrossed in work of his own, Jody's blond head lifted with obvious irritation. He aimed his pen toward the inkwell.

And froze.

"Jesus." The blood drained from his face. He blinked at Quinn once, twice.

The pen slipped from his fingers and upset the inkwell. Ink spread in a dark pool over the paper he'd been working on. Jody swore. Viciously. He bolted to his feet and reached for more paper to dab up the mess, grabbed the nearest pile and plopped the entire sheaf on top to stop the flow.

He stared at Quinn again, his jaw agape.

"Hope you didn't ruin anything important," Quinn drawled.

The door burst open.

"Mr. Hartman, I'm sorry. This gentleman had no right to simply *barge* in here—"

Jody scrambled from around his desk and grabbed the older man's shoulders.

"Never mind, Bernard. I'll talk to him," he said shoving him out the door and slamming it shut. On an afterthought, he opened it again. "And I do *not* want to be disturbed. In fact, Bernard, take the rest of the afternoon off. I won't be needing you any longer. Lock the office up when you leave. That's a good boy. I'll see you in the morning."

He slammed the door shut a second time, grabbed a nearby chair and wedged it beneath the doorknob.

He whirled, his gaze fastening on Quinn.

"Christ. I thought you were dead," he choked.

The last four years fell away then, and they clasped each other in a tight embrace. Emotion pushed up into Quinn's throat, and he swallowed hard to contain it.

After long moments, they separated.

"You have a helluva lot of explaining to do, Landry," Jody said roughly. He'd lost none of his handsome looks nor his lean, muscular build and sharp, assessing eyes. "You lousy sonovabitch. And it better be a damned good story to make up for what you put me through."

"Watch your language, Jody. There's a woman present."

Jody pivoted, his surprise at seeing Hannah obvious. He'd been so engrossed in Quinn he hadn't noticed her until now.

A slow smile curved his lips. "Well, well, well. Who do we have here?"

Jody always had a weakness for beautiful women. Quinn scowled at his appreciation of this one. "She's my wife."

"You're lying." He moved to Hannah, took her hand and kissed it, gallant as ever. "Tell me he's lying, sweetheart."

She smiled, charmed. "It's true."

She'd removed her gloves, Quinn noticed. Jody's gaze dropped to the gold band she wore, and he sighed dramatically.

"Damn." A reckless grin chased his disappointment. "But if you ever need a divorce, I *am* a lawyer, you know."

Quinn rolled his eyes.

"Oh, my." She appeared taken aback at the offer. "I—I'll keep that in mind."

"Please do." His tawny eyes remained riveted on her like a smitten calf. "Do you have a name, pretty lady?"

"Of course." She withdrew her hand and smiled. "It's Hannah. And I assume you are—"

He bowed low, then straightened. "Joseph Daniel Hartman. Joe D. Jody." He grinned wide. "Get it?"

Her laughter tinkled in the room. "Very clever."

"I have Elliott to thank for the appellation. He's two years older than Quinn and me and ever since we were mere tots, he considered himself superior. Never liked my name, and so he simply changed it. Unfortunately, it stuck." He grew serious. "Speaking of Elliott—" He halted, glanced at Quinn. "Would either of you like a drink? Whiskey? Brandy?"

"Whiskey, thanks," Quinn said, removing his new black felt Stetson and setting it on the corner of the desk.

"Brandy, please," Hannah said.

"Good enough. Have a seat, and I'll be right with you."

Quinn pulled a pair of tapestry-covered arm chairs forward and arranged them in front of Jody's desk. He held one out for Hannah, and after she settled in, he couldn't resist stealing a quick kiss.

"No smooching between you two lovebirds," Jody scolded, handing them each a crystal glass of their preferences.

Hannah's cheeks pinkened from her fluster. Quinn frowned.

Lovebirds? Hardly.

He took the whiskey and threw back a healthy swallow. After sitting in the chair next to Hannah, he took another and relished the burn sliding down his throat.

"It's been a long time since I've had a drink this good." He swirled the amber liquid, watched it spin against the crystal. "A helluva long time."

From across his desk, Jody fastened his grim attention onto Quinn. And waited.

Quinn's eyes lifted. "I thought you'd come for me, Jody. I counted on you."

Slowly, Jody leaned forward.

"What?" he gasped.

"Of everyone—every damned friend, acquaintance, and business associate I'd ever known, of all of them, I thought you'd be the one to bail me out."

"Of prison? Jesus!" Jody exploded. "I tried! Don't you *dare* think I didn't!"

Quinn remained unmoved.

"I was in Chicago for my cousin's wedding, remember? I was gone two weeks. When I came back, Sarah had been dead and buried, you'd been tried, convicted and shipped out to God knew where."

Yes, Quinn thought. It had happened that fast.

Within hours.

"Elliott left right after you did. Took off to Mexico. To grieve, he said." Jody sneered. "To grieve and spend Star L money on cheap tequila and even cheaper women, that's what he did."

Suddenly, he jumped up and strode to a wooden cabinet. Flinging open the doors, he withdrew a sheaf of papers.

"I wrote letters," he said, tossing a copy of one on the desk. "Dozens of them." He tossed another and another toward Quinn. "I wrote every goddamned jail in this state trying to find out where they'd taken you. The authorities all claimed you'd never been sent to them."

Quinn didn't glance at the letters. He didn't have to. Jody had never lied to him.

Jody halted, his eyes narrowing. "Where *did* they send you?"

"New Mexico. To the territorial prison there."

"New Mex—" His cheeks paled, then flamed with fury. "I *went* there!"

"You *what?*" Quinn demanded, stunned.

Jody began to pace in agitation. "I took Bernard with me. If you want proof, just ask him. The New Mexico Territorial is the closest prison outside of Texas state lines. It was a wild shot. They never should have hauled you out of Texas, but I was checking every angle. Damn, damn, damn!"

Quinn leaned forward. "When did you go?"

"About five months after your arrest. It took that long to hear back from—"

"And what happened when you got there? Who did you talk to?"

Jody raked a hand through his hair and started pacing again. "Some guard answered our knock. I demanded to talk to the warden, to ask him some questions. He finally met with us. His name was"—he squeezed his eyes closed, remembering—"Frank Briggs. Warden Frank Briggs."

Quinn swore.

Hannah's fingers flew to her mouth in dismay.

Jody's gaze darted between the two of them. "He denied ever hearing of you. But you were there the whole time, weren't you?"

Grimly, Quinn nodded.

"I tried to get past the warden's office to check out the prison for myself, but the place was crawling with guards. A scar-faced one ended up throwing us out."

Quinn exchanged a glance with Hannah.

"Titus," he murmured.

"Yes," she said softly. "Titus."

Hannah's Vow

Quinn finished off his whiskey in one gulp.

"It gave me the willies to be there," Jody said, his tone horror-stricken. "The conditions were despicable, the people were appalling, and the *smells* . . ." His pity clearly ran deep. "I was there only a few hours, and I had nightmares afterward. God, Quinn. You were there for four *years*."

"Yeah, well. I lived to tell about it. That's the main thing, isn't it?" He rose, went to the liquor cabinet and refilled his glass.

Jody sat back down in his chair. He steepled his fingers, and Quinn knew his lawyer's mind, with all its analytical brilliance, worked like crazy.

"How did you figure into all this, pretty lady?" he asked finally.

Her mouth curved. "In my husband's desperation to escape the penitentiary, he took me hostage. Quite against my will, I might add."

"Hostage!" Jody exclaimed, his brows arched high. He emitted a burst of quick laughter. "Brazen and downright ruthless!" He stared at her. "But what were you *doing* there?"

"I am—was—a novitiate at the convent located a few miles from the penitentiary. We went there to bring holiday baskets for the inmates, but also because graves were being dug, and Father Donovan was quite concerned—"

"Wait a minute. Whoa." Jody rubbed his forehead. "You're a nun?"

"A novitiate," Hannah corrected patiently.

"She took *temporary* vows," Quinn added.

Jody stared at him in disbelief. "You stole a *nun*, and then you *married* her?" He threw back his head and laughed heartily. "That is too rich. Too *rich*."

"And just what is so funny?" Quinn demanded.

"Half of the women in Amarillo were panting after you because you were the most eligible bachelor in the state, and then you're convicted of murder and come back married to a nun!"

"Ours was not a normal courtship," Hannah said hastily.

"And if you'd quit snickering long enough to hear the whole story, you'd know the truth of it." Quinn scowled.

"Sorry." Jody hid his broad smile behind his hand. "I'll listen. I promise. Go on."

They told him everything: Roger Fenwick's drug experiments; Frank Briggs's plan to blame Hannah for Sister Evangeline and Father Donovan's deaths; Hannah and Quinn's capture by Sophia Huerta; blowing up the pass; their marriage; and all the details connecting these events.

By the time they finished, darkness had fallen and all traces of Jody's humor had disappeared.

He sighed heavily. "And now you're both running for your lives. What a mess."

"It's a mess all right," Quinn agreed.

"Damn Elliott to hell for putting you through this," said Jody, his features suddenly harsh. "He denied ever knowing where you were. He completely disowned you." His fist pounded the desk top. "We'll find a way to make things right again. I swear it. If it's the last thing I do."

But at the moment, Quinn thought on a wave of weariness, none of them had an idea how.

Hannah leaned forward. "Loretta said the newspapers picked up Quinn's story."

Jody frowned. "Loretta. Carter? You've seen her?"

Quinn nodded. "At the Amarillo Hotel. She wrangled a room for us there."

"How was she?" he asked.

"Glad to see me. Fell all over herself trying to help me."

"I'm not surprised. She took the news of your death hard. She always thought the world of you, Quinn. It meant a lot to her that you rescued her from the whorehouse." He paused. "Her husband had to have her committed for a spell after Sarah died. She had to be sedated, then had a relapse when the newspapers claimed you were dead."

Quinn pondered that. Loretta had been a friend, but her grief ran unusually deep.

Jody strode to the cabinet, removed a faintly yellowed bundle of newsprint. "You can read the stories yourself."

Quinn read the headline shouting out from the top of the pile.

Prominent Cattleman Dies in Prison.

His brows furrowed. "If no one knew where I was, then how did the papers know I was dead?"

Jody leaned forward, his features intense. "Elliott. Who else? He's the only one that article quotes. And they printed it because Elliott Landry of the prestigious Star L outfit would not lie!" he said with a snarl. "Or so they think."

Hannah sighed. "I've got a headache."

"All right. Let's call it a night." Quinn admitted to a pounding in his own temples. He set aside his empty

Pam Crooks

whiskey glass and reached for the Stetson.

Jody walked them to the door and sheepishly removed the chair wedged beneath the knob.

Quinn extended his hand. "I can't thank you enough, my friend. For trying so hard. And for not asking if I was guilty."

Jody's mouth pursed ruefully. "If I thought you were, I'd clamp the chains back on you myself. I was as close to Sarah as you were."

They made their good-byes. On an afterthought, Quinn turned back to him.

"I almost forgot. How's Manny doing?"

Jody blanched; his throat bobbed in a hard swallow. "Didn't Loretta tell you?"

Quinn stilled. Dread crawled up his spine. "Tell me what?"

"Manny died. Less than a month after your arrest."

Chapter Seventeen

She hurt for him.

The pain in Hannah's heart was separate from the one in her head. Words failed her. She clung to Quinn's arm, offering him comfort when she had nothing else to give.

They walked silently from Jody's office back down Polk Street toward the hotel. The crisp night air nipped at Hannah's nose and swept through her lungs, chilling her to the bone.

Much as Jody's revelation had done.

A different clerk had assumed duty in the hotel's lobby, a young man in his early twenties. Hannah requested he send a light meal up to their suite. Having none of the haughty airs that Wesley possessed, the clerk agreed and hastened to place their order in the hotel's kitchen.

Hannah and Quinn climbed the flight of stairs. Once inside their room, he flipped the switch to the electric chandelier hanging from the high ceiling. The glass globes shed a subdued light in the room. He strode toward the window, opened it wide, and leaned on the sill to stare somberly at the Amarillo streets below.

Hannah bit her lip. He still hadn't spoken.

She set the bundle of newspapers she'd brought from Jody's office on the writing table. Crossing the room to the floral-painted wardrobe, she removed her new mantle and hat and put them inside one of the drawers, then set her gloves and crotcheted handbag on top of them. Carefully, she closed the drawer again.

She cast a worried glance at him.

A short rap on the door indicated their supper had arrived. Hannah wheeled the cart in herself and positioned it next to the fireplace. She set a highly polished round table with plates and silverware, wine glasses and linen napkins. Finally, she lit a single candle and put it in the middle of the arrangement.

She waited. He made no attempt to join her.

Her ache intensified for what he was going through.

"Quinn?" she said. "I'm sorry about Manny."

His hands clenched over the window sill.

"He was only a little boy." His voice rasped the words. "He died before his time."

"Yes."

From the tintype Jody had showed her, Manny had been a captivating child with big round eyes and thick hair falling to his eyebrows. His dimpled smile had stolen her heart; she understood why Quinn wanted him as his own.

He had died from a violent epileptic seizure, Jody had said. Puzzling, since he'd been provided with the best of medicines, had been healthy until Quinn's arrest.

What had gone wrong?

"I'll kill Elliott for this," Quinn threatened, pushing away from the sill. "With me gone, Manny was his responsibility."

Hannah didn't move, didn't speak. He needed time to vent his grief.

"He would have been seven now. Going to school, riding a horse on his own, doing chores." Quinn yanked off his string tie and dropped it on the shelf over the washstand. "I'd have given him a pony and shown him how to take care of it. I would have taught him about cows and bulls and planting cotton and hay."

"Yes," she said.

He would have done all those things.

He turned both faucets on in the lavatory, let the water run into the porcelain basin, shut them off again. His fingers worked the buttons of his shirt.

"He was so damned smart. Curious about everything. He would have been good for the Star L. Hell, he was good for me. And now I'll never see him again."

Tears welled in her eyes, for all Quinn was going through, for all he'd been denied.

He jerked his shirt out from the waistband of his pants, shucked free of it and hurled the garment aside. He turned from her, bent over the basin, and pressed a wet washcloth to his face.

A lattice work of ugly scars criss-crossed his back. Up to now, he'd spared her the sight; she realized she'd only ever seen his chest without a shirt, never his back.

Hannah sucked in a breath. "Oh, my God."

Her grief over Manny's death was buried by the onslaught of this new pain. The scars tore at her, just as the whip had torn across his skin. She went to him, pressed her cheek against his warm shoulder.

He stilled.

"Who did this to you?" She lifted her head again, choking on the sob rushing to her throat. "It was Briggs, wasn't it? Briggs did this to you."

The cat o'nine tails. She remembered seeing it that night in the penitentiary.

How much pain did one man have to endure? How much agony and horror?

He must have felt so alone. Abandoned. He must have despaired from the hopelessness of it all.

Her eyes closed, and she was tortured by a vision of that whip being raised again and again over his naked back, of him shackled in some dark, foul-smelling place, unable to fight back. She heard his screams, smelled the sick scent of his blood pouring in rivulets across his body.

The pain would have been staggering. The tears flowed unchecked down her cheeks. She touched her lips to one scar, then another. Some had long since healed, others only recently. Her open palms glided across the breadth of taut muscles, wanting to take the terrible scars away, knowing she couldn't, knowing no one could, and still she went on kissing and stroking to ease away his hurt.

"Hannah, Hannah."

His whispers reached her through the sobs wrenching from her throat, and he turned her firmly, pulling her from his back and crushing her to his front.

She moved with him, circled her arms around his neck. The tears wouldn't stop, and she cried for him. For Manny. For Sarah and Jody and Loretta and for all the injustices for which Elliott might have been responsible, and for those he wasn't.

"I love you, Quinn. I love you. I love you."

He trembled. His mouth closed over hers ruthlessly, and she met his savagery with her own. Emotions ran high, strong, deep. Her lips opened. She had to taste him, feel his vibrance and his heat. His tongue delved inward to curl and chase and mate with hers.

She moaned. It wasn't enough. Their mouths couldn't satisfy the yearning to give herself to him, to console and love him as completely as possible, to give him all he deserved.

And wanted.

His fingers pulled at the tiny buttons at her neck, and she helped him finish the row. Her dress fell open, and his mouth dragged across her cheek to press fevered kisses along the curve of her neck and the base of her throat, his hands clutching upward at the countless yards of fabric draping over her hips.

One long, sinewy arm wound around her waist, holding her as they tumbled to the floor. Her hands plucked at the buttons on his pants, brushed them aside with frantic impatience, and bared him in all his pulsing, hot masculinity.

Their breathing quickened, grew ragged and frenzied. He rose above her, swept aside her chemise, and her thighs widened to take him. His mouth plundered hers, kissing without mercy, without tenderness, and she reveled in this primitive side to him.

But it still wasn't enough. She wanted more, needed it, and her fingers gripped his buttocks, pulling him deep inside her. She gasped at the parting of the virginal barrier, at his continued thrusts, at this fierce interlocking of their bodies. Her hips lifted, her back arched. He drove into her with unrestrained passion, sent her catapulting into the throes of sensation and pleasure, and she cried out as wave after wave of sweet release rocked through her.

He held her there on the pinnacle of ecstasy, let her savor it, holding back his own, and then, with one last shuddering thrust, he took her completely, claiming her in blatant, fervid possession.

Their loving ended as wildly as it began. Quinn lowered himself slowly, gently, on top of her, as if every quivering muscle had lost its strength, and he couldn't separate himself from her. As if he wanted to stay joined forever.

She lay limp beneath the warm weight of his body. She'd never known such exhaustion, such utter fulfillment such as Quinn had just given her, and she closed her eyes.

Her tears were gone now, her sorrow calmed. The scars on his back would not be forgotten, but she would always love him more for them. For what he'd endured.

Their pulses, once thundering, slowed by degrees. Finally, Quinn groaned in male satisfaction and rolled off of her, sweeping her on top of him with a rustle of silk and petticoats.

"A hundred times I've thought of making love to you," he murmured into her hair. "But not once did I think it'd be when we were both still dressed."

Her mouth formed a sleepy smile against his chest. In the next moment, her eyes flew open.

"My new gown!" she said. "We're wrinkling it." Thinking of the expense and waste if it was ruined, she tugged and smoothed the hopelessly twisted garment.

"Just take it off," Quinn said, amused. "Then come back and lie with me some more."

She wriggled off him, caught a glimpse in the mirror of them with their clothes half on, half off their bodies but their shoes still firmly on their feet, and she couldn't help laughing. Shifting to all fours, she bent down and touched her mouth to his.

"I'm shameless with you," she breathed.

"We've done nothing to be ashamed of." He curled his hand around the back of her neck and thrilled her with a languid kiss. "Don't ever think we did."

After long moments of kissing him back, she drew away.

"No," she murmured, thinking of the awful scars. "It was fitting and right."

His dark eyes smouldered, and he released her, his gaze hot upon her while she removed the dress and fussed over it, finally deciding the gown needed only a good pressing to restore it. She folded the petticoats and her delicate stockings in a drawer, all the while admiring their fine quality and her good fortune to own them.

She took so long Quinn eventually tired of waiting for her and got up from the floor. He stripped, wrapped a thick towel around his lean hips, and finished washing at the basin. Afterward, he padded over to the round table to investigate the supper she had readied for them.

By the time he poured them both a glass of wine, Hannah had washed, too, and donned a lace-trimmed wrapper. Acutely aware she wore nothing beneath, and feeling wickedly feminine for it, she accepted the glass he offered.

"Any regrets?" he asked quietly.

She sipped the burgundy before answering. She remembered his promise to give her an annulment after his business had been completed in Amarillo.

Now, everything had changed.

Regrets?

"No," she said to him. "None."

Not at the moment. Perhaps in the morning. Or next week. Or even next month.

But not now. Returning to the convent was the farthest thing on her mind. Making love to Quinn, and righting his life, took precedence.

"Manny is happy, you know," she said, trailing a fingertip round and round Quinn's dark nipple. "He's with his mama. The way he should be."

"Yes," he murmured, as if he'd not thought of it that way. "Maybe it was best he died while I was in prison. The separation has made his death . . ." He hesitated.

"Easier," she finished, understanding.

"Yes. Easier. But if I didn't have you, Hannah—" He halted again, his features intense. Grim. "If I didn't have you, I'd go stark, raving mad."

"I'm here, my love. And if I weren't—" she cocked her head mischievously—"you'd have Jody."

"Jody." He made a sound of exasperation. "Not the same. Not at all."

She laughed softly. "I like him. And Loretta, too."

"Good people. Both of them." He set his empty glass down on the table. "I have lots of friends I want you to meet. I know it doesn't seem like there's many of them around, but there are. And they'll be smitten by you from the minute they first lay eyes on you."

He took her glass from her, though she'd not yet

finished the wine. He slowly pulled the top ribbon of her wrapper loose.

"I fell in love with you the minute I heard your voice coming through the grate over my cell. You were a piece of heaven sent down to save me." He undid one button, two, three.

Her heart stepped up its beat. "You didn't act like I was a piece of heaven. I was afraid of you. You threatened to kill me."

He grimaced. "I went half-crazy in the prison. And I was scared. I needed you to rescue me. And you did."

Only a few buttons held the robe together. He didn't bother with them, but gently pushed the fabric off her shoulders, first one, then the other. The garment drifted to a heap at her feet, and she stood naked before him.

"You gave me no choice." Her voice turned shaky, husky.

"Best decision I ever made." His hands circled her neck, his thumbs lazily coursing down her throat. His fingers spread and his palms flattened as they continued their sensual, unhurried descent onto her breasts.

And lingered there. He caressed the rounded flesh, the pads of his thumbs stroking her nipples until they hardened to pebbles. No other man had ever touched her in such a way.

Her knees quivered at the pleasure, and she sighed with the longing building up inside her.

"I love you, Hannah Landry. I love you for saving me from Fenwick's Solution, and I love you for all you've given me tonight."

He pulled at the towel, and it dropped onto the wrapper. His manly virility, blatant in its desire for her, stole her breath away.

Slowly, his arms circled around her back, and he drew her to him. Her breasts pressed against the hard wall of his chest, skin against warm skin, and she closed her eyes, revelling in the feel of their intimate, tender embrace.

"You'll always be mine," he murmured against her temple. "I'll never allow anyone—or anything—to take you away from me."

She drew back, touched a finger to his lips.

"Don't speak of it," she murmured, for she knew his words were true. He wouldn't let her go easily, no matter what the circumstances, and the thought of ever leaving him pierced her heart.

There would never be another man. No matter what the future held. The knowledge rendered her love for him priceless, and she raised up on tiptoe for his kiss, needing his assurance that it would always be like this between them. He responded without question, his lips warm and full and lazy in their seduction.

"I'm feeling shameless again," she whispered, nuzzling his chin, his jaw.

"I love it when you're shameless."

He drew back, hooked his arm behind her knees and scooped her into his arms. He carried her to the bed, the thick coverlet and ruffled pillows already thrown aside.

He laid her on the mattress and stretched his lean, sinewy length next to her. There was not a bit of un-needed flesh on him. Every inch was man and muscle, and she delighted in looking at him.

"You're easy on the eyes, husband of mine. So handsome and strong and manly." She skimmed his torso with the palms of her hands. "All the women in this state will be jealous of me for having married you."

"Hardly." His low chuckle surrounded her. "And you're wrong. It's the men in this state who will be jealous of *me*. Jody's only the first."

"Jody?" Her mouth curved at the comment, at how he interpreted his old friend's outrageous flirting. "It's you I want, Quinn. No one else."

She locked her arms around his neck and kissed him long and tenderly. She cherished this time, these moments, with him. They'd opened themselves to each other without holding back, given freely of their bodies and souls.

The kiss ended, and Quinn's burgeoning desire for her made her shiver in longing for the excitement that lay ahead.

"I love you, Hannah," he said.

"Then love me now, my darling. The whole night long."

He groaned and traced the swirl of her ear with his tongue, nipped her lobe gently with his teeth. He moved lower, licking the sensitive skin along her neck and shoulder.

Awash in the delicious sensations intensifying inside her, she drew in a breath. Slowly. Her eyes closed, and she allowed herself to *feel,* to savor all the wonderful, erotic things he did to her, privileges a wife gave her husband.

Privileges she'd never enjoy if she still lived in the convent.

The truth of it only made her want him more, and her knees parted, accepting the shift of his weight over her, cradling him against the juncture of her thighs. He took her breasts into his hands and massaged their fullness, the nipples already hard and inviting beneath his touch.

He took one into his mouth, and she moaned at this new pleasure. Her fingers delved into his hair, holding him to her as his tongue swept over its sensitive peak again and again, leaving her hungry for more. He did the same to the other, and her hips began to move as she climbed higher and higher, the pressure inside her building and building.

"Quinn, please," she breathed.

"Not yet, darlin'," he whispered. "Soon."

He stroked her breasts, his fingers masterful in their arousal. His head lowered to dip his tongue into her navel, to whirl across the soft skin of her belly.

And the sweet pressure climbed even higher.

He kissed the inside of her thighs. His touches grew bolder, his intent doubly so. He enslaved her with his caresses.

Hannah thought she'd die from the want of him. He parted her feminine folds with his tongue. Squirrel-Tooth Alice had told her of this, of how a man kissed and licked the most private parts of a woman to give her pleasure, and back then, Hannah had doubted.

Not now. Not with Quinn.

She drew in a ragged breath at the beauty of what he made her feel. Wet and hot, his tongue stroked her until she couldn't hold back any longer, until the crescendo within her built until it couldn't build any more.

And the sensations exploded. Again and again and again.

He rose and slid himself into her, riding the waves with her, keeping them coming. The bed rocked with the rhythm of their arching bodies, the walls held in their exultant cries, until spent, exhausted, they tumbled from their glorious heights and settled peacefully back down to earth.

Stunned at the intensity of what had happened between them, Hannah lay motionless beneath him for long moments. Then, she drew in a breath and blew it back out again.

"*Glo*-ry!" she said.

He laughed, a low rumble of delight in his chest, and hugging her fiercely, he rolled with her across the mattress, switching their positions.

"We are *good* together, woman!" he exclaimed, his breathing showing the rigors of their lovemaking.

She laughed, too, and remembered his foul mood earlier this evening before they'd gone to visit Jody.

"Is this why you were cross with me tonight? Because you wanted to make love to me?" she asked softly, wiser now.

"It was." His arms tightened around her in a brief squeeze. "I'd wanted you for so damned long. I couldn't have you, not until you were ready, and I was feeling mighty frustrated."

"Was it worth the wait?"

"You know it was. Better than my lustiest dreams."

Pleased he thought so, she stacked her hands on his chest and rested her chin on top. "But you deserve all the credit. I didn't do much to pleasure you in turn."

He blinked up at her in disbelief. "What are you talking about?"

She shrugged and thought of how she'd done little more than lie back and let him work his magic on her.

"I fear there are drawbacks to a man taking a virgin

as his wife," she sighed, being honest with him. "She has no experience to bring with her."

She knew he was trying not to laugh. "Did I look like I wasn't enjoying myself?"

"Well, no."

"A man takes pleasure while giving it. Did you think of that?"

"No, but—"

"And I'm glad you've not been with anyone else before me. Anything you learn about pleasuring me I want to come from me."

Her mouth pursed. "But—"

"But what?"

"I just think—" She halted and sighed again. "I want to know how to please you, that's all."

"After what just happened between us? Not once, but twice? Jesus." He seemed incredulous. "Listen to me." He tilted her chin up, and she met his gaze. "Maybe it takes a stint in hell for a man to value what he's got when he has it. He learns not to take anything—or anyone—for granted again." He rubbed her spine in long, languid strokes. "Having you naked in my arms, in my bed, makes me want you all over again. You're a hot-blooded woman, Hannah. Before the night is through, I'll wager you'll teach *me* a thing or two."

She laughed softly. "The bet's on."

He smiled, reckless and disarming. She loved it when he smiled.

"All right, then." His hands settled on her bare buttocks. "Are you hungry?"

She eyed him coyly. "For food? Or you?"

"Food now. Me later."

He rolled her back onto the mattress and followed the command with a soul-destroying kiss.

And later, again and again, she obeyed that command.

In perfect order.

Chapter Eighteen

A knock on the door pulled Quinn sharply awake.

His gaze swept the darkened room, focused on the elegant furnishings, the dishes, the empty wine bottle on the low-lying table.

And Hannah, soft and luscious, snuggled against him.

The knock sounded again.

"Hey, Quinn. It's me, Jody. You two up yet?"

Quinn eased away from her and slid out of bed. He reached for his pants.

Hannah stirred. "Is someone at the door?"

Her voice sounded thick with sleep, though she'd had precious little of it. She rolled to her back and slid her fingers through her hair, tousled from the pillow. From him.

Remembering their fiery lovemaking enflamed his loins. She'd given him all he could handle. And then some.

"Yes. It's Jody," he said, fastening the last of the buttons on his pants. He reached for a fresh shirt with one hand, her wrapper with the other.

"It's early. Why would he be here?" With bedcovers rustling, she scrambled to sit up. The sheet slipped, presenting him with a delectable glimpse of high, rounded breasts. She yanked it back up again.

He debated a quick fondle of their fullness, even a suckle or two, then reluctantly thought better of it. He'd kept Jody waiting long enough.

"We'll find out. Here's your robe," he said, tossing it to her.

She snatched the wrapper, hurried her arms into it. By the time she'd fastened the thing clear up to her neck, he'd unlocked the door, and Jody strode in, pushing a metal cart.

"It's about time you two lovebirds woke up," he declared cheerily. "Do you know how late it is?"

"No," Quinn murmured, eyeing the coffee pot on the cart.

"After ten. And the day's a-wastin'!" He parted the chenille curtains, raised the damask shade beneath. Sunshine flowed into the room. He grinned. "I brought breakfast."

"Thanks," Quinn said and went for the pot.

"Good morning, pretty lady." Jody leaned across the mattress to give Hannah a brotherly peck on the cheek. "You're looking exceptionally lovely this morning. Did he keep you up half the night?"

She blushed and drew her sheet-covered knees up to her chest. "He did."

He clucked his tongue in mock disgust. "A rutting stag, that's what he is."

271

Pam Crooks

"Shut up, Jody. You're embarrassing her." Quinn handed Hannah a cup of steaming coffee and winked at her.

The blush deepened, but she smiled at both of them. "He didn't rut by himself, Mr. Hartman. I gave him a good chase, I assure you."

Jody threw his head back and laughed heartily. Hannah slipped from the bed, taking the cup with her. She gave Quinn an affectionate pat to his bare belly on her way to the floral-painted wardrobe. Beneath the thin fabric of her wrapper, her firm buttocks swayed just enough to keep him staring.

Jody sighed dramatically.

"I could hate you for having her all to yourself, you know," he said, his voice low so Hannah wouldn't hear. "She's a gem."

Quinn sipped pensively from the cup. "I know. It scares me sometimes." Without elaborating, he changed the subject. "What brings you here this morning?"

"We have work to do, that's what."

Quinn nodded in agreement and wheeled the breakfast cart into the adjoining sitting room to give Hannah her privacy. "I've got questions that need answers. I hope you'll have them for me."

He laid out the dishes in preparation for their breakfast. Jody opened the curtains in this room, as he'd done in the main one. Brilliant daylight beamed inward. "Ask away. We'll plan out a strategy, and—"

He halted abruptly. The color flowed from his face, leaving him ghostly white. "Christ, Quinn. Your back."

Quinn straightened, wishing he'd put his shirt on

272

sooner. He feared Jody would be sick all over the thick Oriental carpet.

"What else did they do to you?" Jody's features twisted in a rare fury. He grasped Quinn's shoulder, forced him to turn around. His gaze lighted on the faint scars around his wrists. "The shackles." Jody shook his head in disgust and indicated Quinn's forearm. "What about these?"

"A wolf-dog," Quinn said and donned the shirt, hating Jody's pity, but touched by it. "Those days are gone, Jody. I won't relive them again."

"I'll make sure you won't!" he exploded. "Damn Elliott."

"We'll damn him when we're sure he's guilty," Quinn said firmly. "Before I see him, I want cold, hard evidence to throw in his face. I want the truth."

"Quinn?"

At the sound of Hannah's voice, they both turned. She entered the sitting room wearing a day dress of navy blue sateen, with prim white collar and cuffs. She'd combed her short curls and smelled delectably of rose-scented soap.

His heart filled, just looking at her.

"Will you help me?" she asked. "I can't reach the buttons."

She turned her back and presented him with a row of dainty pearl ones, left unfastened halfway down her spine. He hooked them easily and thought how adept he'd become at fastening—and unfastening—her clothing. He dropped a warm kiss to her nape after he finished.

"Ah. The picture of domesticity," Jody purred, watching them. "Pouring coffee. Setting breakfast. Buttoning buttons. You're mellowing, old man."

Quinn heard the envy in his friend's teasing. "Prison will do that to you. That, and having a beautiful wife in your bed."

Hannah tossed him a loving glance and took the chair he offered her. She began spooning hot scrambled eggs and crisp strips of bacon onto their plates.

"What's this talk between you two of evidence?" she asked. "Against Elliott?"

Jody's questioning gaze darted to Quinn, as if unsure she should be included in the matter, which could turn ugly before it was finished.

"She's as much a part of this as I am," Quinn said. "I've got no secrets from her."

Jody accepted his decision with a brief nod. "To answer your question, Hannah, yes. If we're to prepare a case against Elliott, we must have strong evidence to present to a judge and jury."

A case against Elliott.

Quinn had planned his revenge for a long time, but hearing Jody speak of it, to sit with him and plan its execution, left Quinn with a gnawing, sick feeling in the pit of his gut.

Elliott was, after all, his brother.

They were only two years apart, and Elliott was the older. Their mother had dressed them in matching knee-pants, and they'd grown up with many of the same friends, had learned to shoot and ride and brand calves together under their father's keen eye. But something had happened in their later years. Elliott had changed. Drastically.

And Quinn had paid the price for it.

The knowledge strengthened his will to see through his revenge, to fine-tune it to perfection.

"Loretta mentioned Elliott had fallen in with some bad friends," he said, slathering a roll with strawberry jam. "Who are they?"

"Actually, he has very few friends," Jody said. "Only a couple I'm aware of. All of Amarillo was shocked by your arrest, by Elliott's handling of Sarah's death and all. He made some enemies because of it. Anyway," he said around a bite of bacon, "his cronies are James Steadman, a local newspaper reporter, and Stephen Larson, a physician."

"Odd choices for a cattleman," Quinn said, frowning. "Is Larson any relation to Dr. George Larson?"

The elder had been Manny's doctor, and Quinn had complete faith in him.

"Yes. His youngest son. Stephen spent most of his time in boarding schools and then medical school. Which is why we never knew him. George died, by the way. About a year ago. Went peacefully in his sleep."

The news speared Quinn with regret. The old doctor had been a friend. "Tell me more about Stephen."

"He's a spoiled bastard. A daddy's boy. George let him into his medical practice with an eye toward retirement. Word is Stephen has lost many of his father's longtime patients."

"Why? Through death? Or dislike?"

"Both, I think. Stephen doesn't have the bedside manner his father was known for. And he leans toward radical medicine. Quackery. Never the tried and true methods George used. Damned if I'll ever go to him with influenza."

Quinn pondered Jody's comments. Bedside manner

had always been George's strength. He truly cared for his patients, and his treatments had been effective. Manny was proof of it. George's death was a loss to the medical profession. To him.

"And then there's James Steadman." Jody's handsome features showed his disdain. "God's gift to the newspaper business."

Hannah frowned. "He wrote the articles about Quinn's arrest and supposed death in the *Amarillo Champion*. I remember seeing his byline on each of them."

"You noticed, eh? Funny. No one else seemed to think that odd. By the time I made the connection, it was too late. All the other big city papers had picked up the stories."

Quinn's eye narrowed. "Why is it I'd never heard of Steadman before my arrest? Is he young, too? Like Stephen Larson?"

"No. He was a washed up reporter from the East who'd spent long years chasing fires, writing obituaries and boring society pieces. Until he pulled up stakes, moved out here, and your story came along, that is. It was a real gold mine for him."

"He wanted to make a name for himself," Hannah mused thoughtfully.

"And he did. Hell, he didn't care if the stories were true. He just wrote them."

"The way Elliott told him to," Quinn said.

"Precisely." Jody grimaced. "Everyone believed him when he wrote you were dead. Myself included, eventually."

Quinn pondered Jody's information, sorting through all he'd learned.

"How do you know about these two men?" he asked.

"Oh, ye of little faith." Jody grinned. "I hired a private investigator to check them out. A friend of mine from Chicago."

"Really."

"His report is filed away safely in my office."

"Good. Very good."

"And you know what else? I think it's mighty strange Sarah happened to die and you happened to be arrested when I happened to be in Chicago. I rarely travel. Too tied down to my law practice. My cousin's wedding was the first time I'd left Amarillo in a long time. Hell, years."

"And Elliott knew you were leaving?" Hannah asked.

"Damn right he did."

"Sounds like a frame job to me." She cast Quinn a sympathetic glance.

"A suspicious set of happenings," Quinn agreed darkly. "Elliott knew Jody would defend me to the letter of the law."

"And beyond," Jody added.

They fell silent, and Quinn wrangled with every word of the discussion to come up with a motive, a logical explanation why Elliott would go to such lengths to see him thrown in prison.

And die there.

Suddenly restless, he pushed away from the table and began to pace the sitting room. The motive was elusive—they were a long way from finding the proof they needed to see through Quinn's revenge.

"Based on Jody's investigation, we have a rough idea of what happened after my arrest," he said, thinking out loud. "Steadman did his part by convincing everyone I was dead. We don't know why he'd bother. Or how Stephen Larson fits in." Quinn braced both hands on the table top. He leaned forward, intense. "But we still don't know what really happened the night Sarah was killed."

"I know what happened, Quinn. I was there. I saw everything."

At the sound of Loretta's voice behind him, he whirled.

Hannah's eyes widened.

Jody choked on his coffee, spewing most of it back into his cup.

Dressed in her maid's uniform, Loretta Carter stood trembling in the archway dividing the sitting room from the main quarters of the suite. Her nervous gaze bounced from each of them before settling back onto Quinn.

"What did you say?" he demanded hoarsely.

"I was there. I talked to Sarah only moments before she was killed."

Waves of shock rolled through him. He recovered slowly. "You'd damn well better tell us about it, Loretta."

She nodded jerkily.

He'd never seen her so agitated. Indicating the chair he'd just vacated, he urged her to sit.

"Would you like some coffee?" Hannah asked softly. "Might help calm you some."

"No, but thanks for offering." She lowered her eyelashes. "Forgive me for eavesdropping. I came up to see if there was anything you needed. I knocked, but no one answered. I just walked in."

"Under the circumstances, I'm glad you did," Quinn said roughly.

"So talk, Loretta." Jody bent forward, a you'd-better-tell-the-truth-or-else lawyer look on his face. "We're listening."

She drew in a long breath.

"I was working late that night," she began, twisting a lace handkerchief. "There was a cattlemen's meeting here at the hotel. We were full and very busy."

"Yes," Quinn said, remembering. "The association's annual meeting."

"That's right. You were staying in your usual room. Sarah and Elliott had theirs downstairs. I was just coming back from bringing fresh towels to one of the other guests when I ran into her outside your room. She was crying, obviously upset about something."

Loretta smoothed her starched apron over her lap.

"She was always polite to me and all, considering my past. I had a lot of work to do, but I told her I'd listen if she needed to talk. We went into a maid's closet for privacy, and—and she said in case something ever happened to her, that someone needed to know the whole story. The truth."

"The truth? About what?" Quinn demanded.

"She and Elliott were having problems, for one."

He rubbed his chin. "Yes. For quite some time."

Sarah had wanted a child, he recalled, and Elliott refused. Hell, he would have made a lousy father. Just as he made a lousy husband.

And brother.

"She was going to ask for a divorce that night. That's why she was pacing outside your room. She was waiting for you, Quinn. She was going to tell you first, before she told Elliott."

A pang of regret shot through Quinn. Sarah had confided in him often. It would be just like her to come to him with her decision.

If only he'd been able to talk to her . . .

"Sarah was afraid of Elliott," Loretta continued. "He was terribly jealous of you, Quinn, because T. J. left you the Star L. He never forgave you for that."

Elliott had been furious after the reading of their father's will. For years, Quinn had struggled to make things right between them, to ease that fury and resentment, but as the eldest son, Elliott believed the Star L should have been his birthright. Though Quinn did his best to include him in ranch decisions, Elliott remained bitter.

Bitter enough to hurl him into a nightmare in prison.

"Sarah said he was plotting against you, Quinn. She didn't know the details, but he was working with someone else, and—"

"Who?" demanded Jody.

"She didn't say. I didn't ask."

"Go on," Quinn said, frowning.

"About then, someone came down the hall. From the closet, we couldn't tell who it was, but it looked like you, Quinn. Sarah went rushing out."

"And it wasn't me."

"No," she whispered. She dabbed at a tear trickling from the corner of her eye. "It was Elliott. He'd been drinking. He had a key to your room, I guess, and when he saw Sarah, he yelled at her, accused her of having an affair with you. Then he slapped her, and—and pulled her into your room with him."

She sniffled, heaved in a breath, and continued.

"I heard awful sounds coming from inside, and I knew he was beating her. I got so scared." She covered her face with her hands. "Oh, God." She fought a sob. "I should have done something. I should have burst into that room and stopped him, but I was so *scared.*"

Quinn's blood ran cold. "What did you do then?"

"I went to find Humphrey. I trusted him. He'd know what to do. By the time we ran back up there, the room was quiet again. Humphrey opened the door, real slow-like, and peeked inside." Loretta hiccuped. "I couldn't see much, but I could see the blood on the bed, and Sarah didn't have her dress on anymore, and then Humphrey started breathing funny, wheezing a little, you know, and I got even more scared. He told me to go get the sheriff, and I started to, I swear I did, but someone was coming up the stairs and I hid in the closet again. *God! I was such a coward!*"

Dead silence followed her vehement words.

"I watched through a crack in the door. Two men I didn't recognize were helping you up the stairs. I've seen enough drunk people in my day to know you weren't drunk that night. You'd been drugged with something, and you were trying to stand, but your legs wouldn't let you."

"Quinn?" Jody's low voice drew his attention from Loretta. "What do you remember?"

He rubbed his hand over his eyes. "Very little at that point. I'd had a few drinks, but—" he pursed his lips "—the drinks I *did* have were always brought to me by the same waitress, even though there were several of them serving us that night. I remember thinking she must have singled me out because she was sweet on me."

"Probably working for Elliott," Jody said.

Quinn nodded in agreement. "Keep on with your story, Loretta."

"By now, Humphrey was having trouble breathing, and he kept clutching his chest and leaning on the wall. The men were real nervous seeing him there, and one of them pushed him into your room, saying something about letting Elliott take care of him."

Tears streamed down her face, her damp handkerchief having little effect at drying them.

"He had a stroke," Loretta said, her voice hardly above a whisper. "He collapsed into a coma in your room and died the next day. I never spoke to him again."

Brows furrowed, Jody crossed his arms over his chest.

"The newspaper claimed Humphrey had been the first one to discover you and Sarah together in bed, and that he was so horrified from the killing, his heart couldn't handle it. No one questioned the story. He was old. In his late sixties." Jody shrugged. "Hell, it was believable. Until now, *I* believed it."

Quinn's mouth twisted from the irony. Besides Loretta and the two men, and of course Elliott, Humphrey would have been the only one to know of Quinn's innocence.

"Did you ever go for the sheriff, Loretta?" he asked quietly.

"I was going to, I swear it. When I thought it was safe to come out of my hiding place, I hurried down the stairs. Then Elliott came tearing down behind me, covered in blood and yelling that you'd killed Sarah. God, he ran right *past* me!"

Loretta burst into tears again.

"I tried to deny it, but no one would listen. It was chaos, Quinn. Pure *chaos!* Everyone running and screaming. No one would *listen* to me. And why should they? I was a nobody, a—a whore-turned-hotel maid. How dare I dispute the high and mighty Elliott Landry from the powerful Star L ranch, with all its money and millions of acres! God, he was so convincing!"

Hurt and disgusted, she swiped her handkerchief across her nose.

"It would have been my word against his. Don't you see?" Clearly desperate for Quinn to believe her, she took his hand tightly into hers. "Because of you, I had a new life here at the hotel. I was happy, happier than I'd ever been. I had Billy and a home, and I knew, I *knew,* Elliott would take it all away from me."

Gall burned in Quinn's stomach. Elliott would have done exactly that. He would have used every weapon to destroy her.

Loretta released his hand with a despairing sigh.

"Everything happened so quickly after that. Elliott and some of the men dragged you from the room and down the stairs and into jail. I ran then. I ran all the way home. I was so scared. I didn't know what else to do."

"Have you told anyone else what happened that night?" he asked.

She shook her head. "No one. Not even Billy."

She'd lived her own nightmare. She'd suffered as much as he, Quinn realized.

Pam Crooks

Hannah knelt beside her, pressed a cool cloth to Loretta's cheeks.

"It took courage for you to tell us this now," she said. "Thank you. Quinn deserved to know the truth."

"Is there anything else you haven't told us?" Jody asked.

"No, I've told you everything."

"Will you testify in court, if it should come to that?"

"Yes. *Yes!*" she said fiercely. "It's the least I can do."

Jody nodded. "I'll hold you to it, then."

She looked him square in the eye. "I want you to."

Loretta rose, her lids puffy, her nose red, but seeming to feel better for the confession.

"I have to get back to my job. But there's one more thing I want to add." She turned to Quinn. "I wronged you terribly, after all you'd done for me. If you could find it in your heart to forgive me . . ."

The words trailed off, as if she knew she hoped for the impossible.

Quinn thought about hating her for what she'd failed to do.

He thought about denying her absolution, of prolonging the hell she'd lived. After all, he'd lived his own nightmare, far more horrific than hers.

He thought about all those things. But if he allowed her to continue to suffer, he'd be no better than Elliott.

He took her into his arms, then, and held her for a long moment before releasing her.

"We survived, Loretta. Four years later, we can talk about it. Reckon we should be grateful and see that it doesn't happen again. For either of us."

She leaned toward him, kissed both of his cheeks.

"I'm not worthy of your forgiveness, but I thank you for it. From the bottom of my heart."

Drawing back, she turned to Hannah and clasped her hand warmly. "You're fortunate to have him."

"I know," Hannah said. "Very fortunate."

Loretta's gaze found Jody's. "I'll do anything to bring Elliott to justice. You know that now, don't you?"

"Yes," he said. "I'll be in touch."

"Please do."

Raising her hand in a wave, she hurried from the room to return to her duties. She latched the door firmly behind her and left the three of them silent and pensive in her wake.

Finally, Jody whistled, long and low. "Helluva story, wasn't it?"

"But it's still her word against Elliott's. After all this time, how can we possibly get evidence against him?" Hannah asked, sighing.

Quinn's mind groped hard to dissect that fateful night, to search out every loose end they might have missed.

"I want to see the coroner's report," he said suddenly. "George Larson had the job then. Maybe there's something in his notes we could use."

"And how the hell do you expect to see his report?" Jody demanded.

"I'll insist on seeing it. Or you can."

"Whoa. Slow down." Jody held up his hand. "Have you forgotten you're a fugitive, Landry? A convicted murderer on the loose! They'd string you from the nearest rafter so fast your teeth would sing."

"Damn." That detail *had* escaped him.

"You go strolling around town demanding to see

285

four-year-old reports, and you're digging your own grave. And why would *I* stir things up after all this time? Hell, Stephen Larson would know something was brewing. You think he'll give up those notes without a fight?"

"All right, all right. There's got to be a different way, then."

"You took enough of a risk walking to my office in broad daylight yesterday. And registering in this damned hotel under your real name! And yes, I checked."

"I won't hide under a rock, Jody. Not anymore."

"It'd be best if you did. Thank God, no one has recognized you yet."

"Yet," Hannah added somberly.

Clearly, she dreaded the moment when his arrival in Amarillo spread like wildfire through the citizenry. The local lawmen.

Elliott.

All the more reason to have his evidence gathered and ready. Soon.

He had to see that report, Quinn thought. Any way he could.

It came to him, then. Clear as a bell on a mission church.

His gaze found Hannah. She paled.

Jody watched the exchange, his puzzlement evident.

"How can *she* help you?" he demanded.

Quinn flashed him an impatient glance. "She's a con artist. She can throw locks and blow bank safes and pick pockets. And she's damned good at it."

At the revelation, Hannah rose and left the sitting room.

Jody's jaw dropped. "She's *what?* You said she was a nun!"

"A novitiate," he corrected in a rough voice. "And she's not one anymore. She's married to me now. Different vows."

He strode into the main room of their suite. She stood at the window, her arms crossed tightly over her bosom.

"Hannah. Just get us into Larson's office. We'll find his notes, then get out again. It'll be an easy job for you."

She rolled her eyes. "Easy. And what if we get caught?"

"We won't. You're too good to let us."

She bit her lip. "I vowed never to sneak-thieve again."

"Please." He lowered his head and touched his mouth and tongue to hers, his coaxing blatant and sincere.

Slowly, his head lifted.

"Some vows are made to be broken," he said and grinned.

"Glory. When I think of all I've broken of late. . . ." A reluctant smile curved her lips, and she stroked his cheek. "Yes, my love. I'll break into Larson's office for you."

Chapter Nineteen

Larson's Drug Store sat on a corner lot one block off of Third Street and four more from the hotel. While she sat on a parkbench across the street sucking on a licorice stick, Hannah studied the building's location, noted the six-foot high picket fence squaring the back and side yards, and the second-story level.

A nuisance, that second story.

"He sleeps there, you know," Jody commented, inhaling leisurely from a cheroot. "Same as his old man did. Stephen never married, so he'd be up there alone. Far as I know, anyway."

"A problem, darlin'?" Quinn asked, rolling his cheroot between his fingertips.

"Not if he's a heavy sleeper," she replied and took another lick of licorice.

Tall windows graced the front of the store, and from their vantage point in the park, Hannah could see the merchandise lining the long counters and shelves reaching to the ceiling. Larson did a fair business in his store, filling his own prescriptions, selling patent medicines, soaps and sundries.

And licorice sticks.

He'd taken Hannah's money with a nod and no idea she'd return tonight in search of evidence against him.

That was the beauty of thievery, Pa always said. They never knew.

Larson kept his doctor's office in the back. Hannah's slow, sweeping glance had taken everything in—his desk, the oil lamp on top, the drawers of files, the leather-bound medical books on one wall. The examination table, pill press, amputation kit. The location of the back door, the key in the lock. Stairs. Windows. Shades.

She'd noted them all, just as Pa had taught her.

Satisfied, Hannah rose. All that remained were tools to purchase and fashion to suit her needs. "Ready, gentlemen? The hardware store is our next stop. I need a few supplies for this evening."

"Will our plan work?" Quinn asked, pulling his Stetson lower and hooking her arm with his.

"It will. Nicely, I think." She popped the last of the candy into her mouth.

"And it's as dangerous as standing bare-assed in a snake pit." Jody glowered. "I'll be glad when it's done."

Understanding his concern, Hannah slipped her other arm in his. "This heist should be easy enough. I've done worse."

"I've seen her work, Jody," Quinn said. "She's been schooled by the best. I wouldn't have asked her if I wasn't convinced she could do it."

"There are risks." Jody frowned. "But if anyone can

do it, I guess James Peter Benning's daughter can."

Hannah exchanged an amused glance with Quinn. Her father's reputation as a master con artist had been more widespread than she'd realized. Jody had recognized the name immediately, was shocked to learn he was her father. His shock had given way to grudging admiration and reluctant agreement to the night's illicit activities.

All in Quinn's interest, of course.

Still, he was right. There would be risks. And Hannah's belly bunched in apprehension at the thought of all that could go wrong.

But nothing would. She wouldn't let it. She had to do this for Quinn, to prove his innocence.

Elliott must be brought to justice.

At midnight, Quinn and Hannah prowled through the deserted streets with the stealth of two cats on the hunt.

Dressed in black woolen shirts, pants and felt-soled slippers, they clung to the shadows and hurried to the park across from Larson's Drug Store.

Jody stepped out from the second tree on the left, third row back, their agreed-upon meeting place.

"Lights have been out for over an hour," he said without greeting. "He's alone. No dog in the back. The store is as quiet as a morgue."

"Good." Hannah was glad Jody had volunteered for the stake-out. His assurances eased her trepidation. She glanced at Quinn. "Ready, then?"

"I've been ready for four years, darlin'," he drawled. "Let's do it."

With Jody following, they skulked to the alley behind

Larson's store and pressed back against the fence. The slats reached to the top of Quinn's head.

"You're turning me into a damned shyster, Hannah," Jody grumbled, pulling his collar up against the cold.

"Exciting, isn't it?"

She yanked at the drawstring on her black flannel bag. Delving inside, she removed a ball of strong twine and briskly tied the end to Quinn's wrist.

"Give this a good pull to alert us to anyone coming," she said to Jody, handing him the ball. "The night is still. Sound will carry easily."

"Just make it quick. I can feel my hair turning gray already."

She closed the bag again and turned to Quinn. "Okay. Heft me up."

He complied, lifting her easily toward the top of the fence, her buttocks firmly planted into the palms of his hands until she scrambled over the top. Within moments, he joined her, his movements as noiseless as hers.

"Did I ever tell you you're a skinny chit?" he asked under his breath.

Her mouth twitched. "Yes. Hush."

She sprinted across the yard to the back of the store. Her hand closed over the door knob.

It didn't yield, but she didn't expect it to. She dipped into the black bag a second time and retrieved a pair of fine nippers, slipped the nose into the keyhole and turned the inside key. The door opened with ease, and she removed the tool, dropping it safely back into the bag.

She drew in a slow, careful breath.

The first step in was always the worst, when she

made that initial furtive search into the haunting stillness of a room, never knowing exactly what waited for her.

When she was at the greatest risk of detection.

Yet Pa had thrilled at it, had gone back again and again in his years of thievery to relive the rush of excitement from the possibility of getting caught.

Hannah only tasted raw tension. But everything seemed as it had been that afternoon. She felt better hearing the silence and was convinced the doctor's room was empty. She took confidence in being safe, in knowing just what to do.

And why they were here.

Once inside the office, she pulled the shades over the two windows while Quinn lighted the oil lamp on Larson's desk, keeping the flame low. Silence was imperative. She was grateful for their woolen clothing, which didn't rustle as starched cotton or something firmer would have, and for their soft slippers. She didn't even dare a squeak of shoe leather.

Hannah stepped to a wooden cabinet labeled "Coroner Reports" and found the drawers immovable. Producing a bureau pick, she slipped one end in the lock, worked the wire, and pulled it out again. The drawer slid open.

She fixed her concentration on the papers filed inside. They were arranged by year, and within those, by case. Her fingers crawled to the back of the drawer and latched onto a file labeled "Landry, Sarah."

Triumphant, she pulled it out.

A sound from above raised the hairs on the back of her neck. She stared at the ceiling and listened.

Snoring. Stephen Larson slept directly over them, and she trembled in relief.

A good thing, his snoring.

Acutely aware he could awaken at any moment, she opened the file. Quinn moved closer and read with her:

Victim died from severe trauma to head, consistent with repeated blows from blunt instrument, possibly a man's fist. . . .

They skimmed the entire report but found nothing different from what Loretta had told them. Fighting disappointment, Hannah returned the file to the drawer.

"Damn," Quinn muttered, obviously as disappointed as she.

"Perhaps Doctor Larson was careless in his record keeping," she said and bit her lip at the thought.

"I've never known a man more precise than he was," Quinn said, shaking his head in disagreement. "He always took copious notes."

Hannah searched her brain for different angles.

"Maybe he filed you under 'Quinn Landry' instead of 'Landry, Quinn,' " she said, but already her searching fingers failed to find such a heading. Her disappointment deepened. "Is there another name he might have used?"

Quinn's features furrowed in thought. "Well, it's a long shot, but check the H's for 'Hombre.' "

She blinked at him in dubious surprise.

"It's a nickname from when I was a kid. It means 'tough man' in Spanish. He always teased me with it, even when I got older." Quinn peered over her shoulder as she searched.

Again, she found nothing.

"Okay." Nonplussed, he moved away toward another cabinet. "Let's check the patient files. Maybe he hid the evidence there, away from the regular coroner reports."

Hannah followed and produced her bureau pick again; within moments, the second drawer opened. Her fingers moved quickly to the 'H's', and with a soft cry of delight, she withdrew the file and opened it.

No scratches, cuts or bruises were visible on the accused's knuckles, hands or elsewhere....

The words leapt up from the paper.

... his naked body was clean of blood or other markings.

And more.

Accused plainly smelled of imbibed liquor. However, his condition resembled bromism, a semi-imbecile condition with slurred speech and drooling mouth....

"Bromism?" Quinn whispered, clearly stunned.

"Didn't you say Manny had been given Triple Bromide Elixir for his epilepsy?" she asked, her tone hushed.

"Yes."

Quinn continued reading, his attention too absorbed to elaborate.

These findings suggest that the accused was drugged with around 60–125 grains of bromide ... rather than advanced drunkenness as reported....

"It's all here," he breathed. "Christ. Everything."

He stuffed the entire sheaf of papers into Hannah's black flannel bag. Like a man possessed, he strode past the bottles of female remedies, stomach bitters and cod liver oil, stopped at the bookcase and strained to read their titles in the dim light.

"Find me Manny's file," he ordered.

Larson's snoring continued above them. Hannah hastened back to the drawer. By the time she found the little boy's records, Quinn held two leather-bound books in his hand.

In the largest, *Epilepsy and Other Chronic Convulsive Diseases*, by a physician named W. R. Growers, Quinn studied a chart of dosages.

"Five to ten grains per day is recommended," he said, his low voice grim. "It says sixty to one-hundred twenty-five grains would lead to bromism."

Appalled, Hannah's eyes met his.

Quinn had been given twelve times the recommended dosage of bromide the night Sarah had been killed.

Dear God.

He went on to skim the index of the other book, *Epilepsy, A Report*, by Hughlings Jackson of the National Hospital for the Paralyzed and Epileptic, England, 1870. He began reading about the use of bromides. She peered over his shoulder and read with him:

When bromides are withdrawn, seizures become even more severe. . . .

The author went on to warn:

Bromides must not be withdrawn abruptly, but by a gradual reduction in dosage. . . .

Hannah's glance met Quinn's. Had Manny been allowed to die by violent seizures because his medicine had been stopped?

George Larson had been meticulous in his record-keeping. He'd prescribed the recommended five to ten grains of Triple Bromide Elixir for Manny, and Quinn had seen to it the child had been given the medicine daily, and that the prescription had been refilled at regular intervals.

After Quinn's arrest, the entries stopped.

Suddenly, the string on Quinn's arm went taut, and his arm flew outward. The books almost toppled to the floor.

Hannah's heart jumped to her throat. The string jerked again and again.

Someone was coming.

Lightning quick, she doused the lamp. Quinn slid Manny's file and both books into the flannel bag.

Hannah closed the file drawer, heard the low click of the lock. Quinn raised both window shades.

The bell at the front of the store tolled loudly.

"Hey, Doc? Doc! The baby's comin'! My wife needs you." The front door shook frantically. "Hey, Doc. Wake up!"

The snoring ceased.

Hannah's swift glance revealed the office was exactly as they'd found it, shy only a few key pieces of evidence Stephen Larson would never miss.

Until it was too late.

She slipped out the door with Quinn and pulled it firmly shut behind them. She slid the nippers in the hole, turned the key, and locked the door again.

A light in the second-story bedroom went on.

But by then, Quinn and Hannah had safely scaled the fence to freedom.

A light morning breeze fluttered the gossamer feathers on Hannah's hat. She wore the striped silk dress again, Quinn's favorite of the two Loretta had chosen for her.

A teasing light glinted from her hazel eyes.

"You're sure you don't want to come back tonight? I can blow the bank safe, you know. We can take all the Star L money you want."

Quinn smiled down at her.

"After last night, woman, I'm convinced there's not a better thief than you in the entire country. James Peter Benning would have been proud." He peered at the front door of the Bank of Amarillo, and his smile faded. "But we're going to withdraw the money legitimately. Just like any ordinary citizen."

She cocked her head. "You're not an ordinary citizen, Quinn. You're on the run from the law. You could be arrested before you get a single dime."

"It's a chance I'll have to take."

She curled her gloved fingers into the crook of his elbow.

"Yes," she murmured. "I suppose it is."

They walked slowly toward the front door.

"If anything goes wrong, run to Jody's office. He'll know what to do, just like we discussed. Remember how to get there from here?"

She nodded.

"Word will spread like a match to dry tinder that I'm back. Different than when we registered at the hotel." His mouth softened. "And you know what?"

"What?" she asked.

"No matter what happens, I love you. More than anything. Don't ever forget that."

"You're scaring me, Quinn." Hannah tugged him to a stop, her features intense. "If they try to arrest you, I'll tell them everything. About Elliott, I mean."

"Leave that to Jody. He's got all the evidence locked

297

away in his office. I don't want you involved."

"I'm already involved. I have been, from the moment I first set eyes on you."

Her loyalty stirred the blood in his loins. He crooked a finger beneath her chin and tilted her head back for a languid kiss.

"I love you." He said it again, as if those very words could protect them both. "If we were in bed, I'd show you just how much."

A disappointed sigh left her. "I wish we were there. Everything is so perfect then."

"I know, darlin'."

But to make their lives truly perfect, he had to right the wrongs of the past. Finding evidence with which to prove his innocence, as they'd done the night before, had been the first step. Announcing his presence in Amarillo by visiting the financial institution responsible for the Star L accounts was the second. Gently, he nudged Hannah inside the bank.

Little had changed in the years since he last walked across the floor tiles. The air smelled of old ledgers and new ones, of ink and money and lingering cigarette smoke. The teller windows, three of them, were in the same place. The bank officers were there, too, just as he remembered, tucked away in desks arranged behind a low railing, its spindles and gate richly varnished.

The lobby was filled with patrons intent on their business, and no one seemed to notice their arrival. Quinn and Hannah approached the railing.

"May I help you, sir?" asked one of the officers, a man in his twenties.

"Is John Mahoney in?"

"Mr. Mahoney is preparing year-end reports and is

not to be disturbed. Is there something I can help you with?"

As president of the bank, John Mahoney enjoyed the privacy of his own office. Quinn's gaze shot to the closed door, and annoyance rippled through him. He braced both hands on the officer's paper-strewn desk.

"Disturb him anyway," Quinn said. He was of no mind to wait on the man, not after four years.

And not because of a few lousy reports.

The bank employee stiffened. "I'm afraid that's not possible."

"Damned if it isn't. Tell him Quinn Landry is here to see him." A feral smile curved his mouth. "I'll warrant he'll see me then."

"Landry?" He frowned, and Quinn knew the moment he recognized the name. His smooth-shaven cheeks paled. "From the Star L outfit?"

"None other."

The officer scrambled from his chair, as if he feared Quinn would shoot him on the spot.

"I'll—I'll tell him, sir. Just a moment. Sir."

Quinn straightened from the desk, and Hannah turned toward him in discreet amusement.

"Your reputation precedes you, Mr. Landry," she said under her breath. "Of a sudden, he seems quite eager to please you."

"Reckon there's advantages to being accused of murder," he replied drily.

Over her head, he encountered another man's startled gaze upon them, a gentleman dressed in a derby and a deep green herringbone suit. He stood in line at the teller's window, close enough to hear Quinn's conversation with the bank officer.

Pam Crooks

"Do you know him?" Hannah asked quietly, unduly intent on brushing imaginary bits of lint from the front of Quinn's jacket.

"No," he said and dismissed him. The Star L ranch was known throughout the state of Texas; the Landry name equally so.

Mahoney's office door burst open.

"Quinn? My God." John Mahoney stood in the portal and appeared stricken with shock, as if he'd just witnessed a ghost raising from the dead.

In a way, Quinn thought grimly, he had.

"Come in," Mahoney urged.

Quinn slipped his hand to the small of Hannah's back and ushered her ahead of him into the office. Mahoney shut the door.

"You're out of prison." He indicated two chairs positioned in front of his broad, polished desk. "What happened?"

"I escaped. By the skin on my ass."

The banker showed little surprise at Quinn's words, as if he knew there could be no other way to account for Quinn's presence. He eased into his stuffed-leather chair, his expression serious. He'd changed little over the years. Life behind a desk kept his hands smooth and his belly paunchy, but he was as shrewd as ever.

Quinn could see it in his eyes, in the piercing way he studied them both.

"This is Hannah, John. My wife."

Brows salted with gray shot up. "And you got married, too?"

"Much has changed since they hauled me off in chains."

"I can see that." He acknowledged Hannah with a

300

cool nod, his suspicion of her part in Quinn's criminal past evident. He steepled his fingers. "Does Elliott know you're back?"

"No." Quinn regarded him steadily. "I had business to tend to first. I'll see him soon."

"He'll be . . . surprised."

"So far, everyone else has been, too."

Those shrewd eyes bored into him. "Have you reconciled yourself to the law yet?"

"That will come in due time," Quinn said smoothly.

"Until then?"

John Mahoney never minced words. He dealt with facts in black and white, like the numbers he wrote in his ledgers every day. Quinn had always admired him for the trait, had long trusted him with the Star L accounts because of it.

Quinn leaned forward.

"I need to get my ranch back," he said.

"That may prove difficult." Mahoney's gaze was unyielding.

"Why?"

"Elliott has assumed control of the Star L."

"The ranch is mine. T. J. willed it to me."

"You were convicted of a heinous crime and punished for it. We received word you had died."

"From who?"

"It was in all the papers."

"Damn the papers." Irritation festered inside Quinn. "I didn't die, and I was sent to prison for a crime I didn't commit. That ranch should never have fallen into Elliott's hands."

"Unfortunately, it did. We had no other recourse, under the circumstances."

"Circumstances," Quinn said with a snarl. "I've had four years of my life stolen away. I'll never get them back again, but I sure as hell will get the Star L."

Mahoney's mouth thinned. "Elliott will fight you."

"He can fight my lawyers and the entire judicial system in this state."

"It may well come to that."

Quinn seethed. At Mahoney. At the truth in his words.

Hannah placed a calming hand on his arm.

"Certainly you understand my husband's situation, Mr. Mahoney," she said in her velvet voice. "He's merely trying to get his affairs in order. He has a right to resume his life as it was before—before it changed."

"Yes," the banker said, frowning. "But first you must have the law behind you." He glanced at Quinn. "Set up a meeting with Elliott. Perhaps a compromise can be reached until you are officially aquitted."

Quinn snorted.

"I'll attend on your behalf," Mahoney added.

"I don't want a compromise." Quinn scowled. "I want the Star L. All of it."

Mahoney hesitated. "The finances are not as strong as they were under your ownership. Of course, we want to see the ranch profitable again, and if you would simply discuss the matter with Elliott—"

Unease filtered through Quinn. "Let me see the ledgers, John."

"I don't believe Elliott would agree."

Quinn gritted his teeth. "The ledgers, damn it!"

Mahoney remained immovable. "Until I speak with Elliott, I'm afraid—"

"*Mr.* Mahoney." Hannah's no-nonsense tone snatched their attention. "If you choose to refuse him the information he's asking to see, there are other avenues we can pursue to get it." She looked him square in the eye. "Not all of them lawful."

The gray-streaked brows shot up.

"Are you threatening me, Mrs. Landry?" he demanded.

"Yes, I am." Softening, she bestowed him with a demure smile. "As you can see, my husband is determined to regain ownership of the Star L. Once that is accomplished, I'll insist he take his business to one of your competitors if you neglect to cooperate with him now."

He sputtered at her impudence. Grudging admiration eased the tension in Quinn. She knew how to hit a banker where it hurt most.

"I'll return with the ranch accounts," he said finally.

He left the office and entered a short hall, at the end of which stood a mammoth safe of heavy steel, its doors wide open. Hannah strained to see inside.

Quinn's mouth curved. "Another mark, darlin'?"

"Yes," she purred. "If it's necessary. A thief must always be prepared, you know."

She settled back in her chair, and Mahoney reentered the room. He displayed the ledgers for Quinn's scrutiny, beginning with the month of his arrest.

Quinn scanned the voucher entries.

"As you can see, the Star L remained self-sufficient for a period of time after Elliott took over. But it didn't last long," Mahoney said.

The numbers trailed down the page, payments for feed, veterinary supplies, lumber. Normal expenses. Quinn frowned at one, a sizable amount wired to a hacienda in Mexico. Another, higher still, for attorney's fees. The totals wrung a low whistle from between his teeth. He turned the page, read two more entries and went cold.

Elliott had ordered two drafts made out to James Steadman and Stephen Larson, each for exhorbitant amounts.

Hannah drew in a slow breath.

"What were these for, John?" Quinn asked. "Why would Elliott pay these men this much money?"

"A small fortune, isn't it?" Mahoney grimaced. "I don't know for sure. It wasn't my place to ask, and Elliott certainly didn't volunteer his reasons. But my suspicions were aroused, I assure you."

A sickening feeling spread inside Quinn.

"He seemed to have a run of bad luck after that," the banker explained. "A prize bull took sick and died. We had a couple of harsh winters, and he developed an interest in the poker table. . . ."

Mahoney's words droned inside Quinn's head. The balances spiraled downward, page after page. In a span of four years, Elliott had managed to squander a majority of the Star L assets.

Assets that had taken T. J.—and Quinn—a generation to build.

Quinn snapped the ledgers closed. He'd seen enough.

"Have you advised Elliott about this?" he demanded. "Christ, he's damn near run the well dry."

Mahoney appeared offended. "Of course I've advised him. Elliott is quite aware of the Star L's affairs. The ranch is still solvent, I assure you. But it's not as stable as it once was."

Quinn rose and took Hannah's elbow. Rage kindled inside him, flamed higher with every word the banker spoke.

He had to see Elliott.

"There'll be a few bills coming in," he said, yanking the office door open and hustling Hannah out. "From the hotel, clothing stores and such. See that they're paid."

"As a show of my faith in you, I will." Mahoney answered, ever the practical businessman.

Quinn strode past the cluster of desks, his fury growing with each step. Mahoney hastened to keep up.

"I don't want Elliott to get another dime. Not one."

He'd raised the interest of the other bank officers, of the gentleman in the deep green suit now sitting at a bench along the spindled railing.

"I understand your concerns, but how could I possibly enforce your request if Elliott should come to me?"

Quinn spun and clutched the front of the banker's shirt.

"You're working for me now, that's how. Elliott is no longer entitled to *any* Star L money. Hear me?"

Mahoney held himself stiffly against Quinn's temper. His throat bobbed. "You're making a scene."

He didn't care. He had a point to make. "The ranch is mine. Elliott will learn that soon enough."

The graying head nodded. "We want the same thing."

Quinn released him. "We're in agreement?"

"Yes. *Quite* in agreement."

Rapt silence had fallen over the bank's lobby and the curious patrons who filled it. Quinn's sharp gaze swept them all, a dark challenge to anyone who dared to defy his command.

To defy *him*.

A movement in the corner of his eye jerked his attention, a flash of green near the door. He stabbed a glance at the bench along the railing.

It was empty.

Obviously, the man had overheard the entire conversation. Had he fled to someone who would use the information against Quinn?

The law?

He bolted after the man, saw him dash across the street at a full run, and disappear into the crowd.

Quinn halted on the boardwalk and swore at the thought of being arrested again. Not now. Not when he was just about to confront Elliott.

John Mahoney joined him on the boardwalk, Hannah following close behind. She slipped her hand into Quinn's.

"Who was he, John?" Quinn asked, holding on to her tight.

The shrewd eyes glared into the crowd. Quinn sensed the banker's keen disapproval.

"It was Steadman," he answered. "Mr. James Steadman."

Chapter Twenty

The Star L ranch sprawled over the Texas horizon, a monstrous parcel of land that had been a part of Quinn for most of his life. With a slow, sweeping glance, he drank in the harshness and the beauty, the twisting ravines and jutting buttes, the thorny mesquite and swaying winter grass.

He drank and drank. Sweet Jesus. He thought he'd never see it again.

"Is it all yours?" Hannah asked, eyes agog.

"Ours, dear wife. It's all ours."

He squinted against the setting sun. He'd taken the Star L with its privileges and challenges in stride once. A lifetime ago. Now, it pleased him to have Hannah to share them with.

"Where are the boundaries?" she asked. "The land seems to go on forever."

"It does." Her awe touched him. Had he ever thought of the Star L the way she thought of it now? "I can't show you the boundaries in a day, Hannah. I'd have to use a map."

"Glory, glory."

He slapped the reins, and the team of black geldings lurched forward. He'd rented a buggy and harnessed Fenwick's horses for the trip out. Now, they were almost there.

Home.

A thousand times, he had dreamed of this ride. Of this moment. Of this road leading to the two-story frame ranch house, with his big, warm bed and clean clothes and a pantry stocked to overflowing with food.

He dreamed of the welcome they'd give him, too. The entire Star L outfit gathered to cheer him on his return. They'd thump him on the back and tell him how much they missed him and how he'd been wronged. They'd give him a cold beer and an expensive cigar, and they'd celebrate until dawn.

Now, it was enough he had only Hannah beside him. She graced him with a new beginning.

He pulled into the yard and expected to see Elliott with a posse of lawmen waiting to arrest him, to shatter the dreams all over again. He braked the rig and saw no one.

"He's not here," Hannah said, bemused.

Quinn's glance swept the empty ranch yard. He could be anywhere. The Star L was massive. It wouldn't be unlikely for Elliott and the Star L outfit to be out on the range with the cattle.

Inwardly, he was torn between relief at the delayed confrontation—and disappointment at not seeing it through now.

Dismounting, he reached for Hannah and helped her

down. Quinn wanted to hold her for awhile before they went inside. She gave him power. Control. She helped him keep his troubles in perspective.

But he refrained. Elliott was nowhere to be found, and she seemed entranced with the house, the wide porch curving along the front and around to the side, the ornate gingerbread trim gracing the eaves, the tall windows with their glass panes trimmed in blue.

"It's so big," she murmured, tilting her head back to peruse the second level. "I can't imagine anyone owning something like this."

The size was formidable, he supposed. A tribute to the ranch's success. He'd never thought about it much, but after what he'd lived in the past four years, well, the place was a castle.

"Better get used to the idea, Mrs. Landry," he said with a slow smile. "Come on. I'll show you the inside."

She handed him the black flannel bag he'd entrusted to her care during the ride out, along with another in leather, filled with his own money withdrawn from the bank. He intended to keep them both in the hidden safe in his office until he met with Elliott. Elliott didn't know about the additional safe and would have no idea what was stored there.

They climbed the stairs in silence. Quinn ran a critical eye over the steps, discerned a board or two that needed replacing and noticed that the slat siding could use a fresh coat of paint. Even the lawn needed more care. He frowned. Elliott had been lax in the maintenance.

The interior of the house suggested the same. The rooms needed airing; clutter was everywhere. The wooden floors, once shining from polish, were dull and dirty. The furniture showed layers of dust. Soot and ashes covered the fireplace.

"Never been one for housework myself," he scowled in annoyance, eyeing a dead plant on its wrought-iron stand. "We always had a housekeeper who came in and cleaned for us."

"Looks like she quit," Hannah observed drily and absently righted a picture hanging askew on its wire.

"If T. J. could see this, he'd throw Elliott out on his ass," Quinn said. "He never tolerated laziness." He hissed out a breath through his teeth. "Sorry, darlin'. I wish the place was in better shape for you."

She made a soft clucking sound and went to him, curling her arms around his waist.

"Don't apologize to me, Quinn. It's not your fault. Besides, there's nothing here a little soap and water won't cure."

Reaching up, she touched her mouth to his in a brief kiss of reassurance. But retaining hold of the black flannel bag and the leather money pouch in one hand, Quinn slid the other along her spine, pressed her tightly against him and lengthened the kiss.

"I'm glad you're here," he whispered and nibbled the curve of her jaw. "And I'm glad you like the house, mess and all."

"Mmmm. I do. Know what?" Her tongue trailed seductively along his throat, drawing a ragged breath from him.

"Tell me."

"I want to see the bedrooms next. *Your* bedroom."

His pulse leapt, and the blood warmed in his veins. For the moment, he was glad Elliott was gone. He chuckled and stole another kiss before reluctantly drawing back.

"You're insatiable, Mrs. Landry. I'm hard-pressed to keep you satisfied these days."

Her sultry laugh curled around him, seducing him. "And you, Mr. Landry, run a mean race. Every woman should have a man like you in her bed."

His loins stirred hot. He threaded his fingers through hers and pulled her with him toward the office.

"I have to put these bags in the safe before we go up," he said, maneuvering the knob and pushing the door open with his hip.

"Be quick about it, then. I have this wild need to strip naked and—"

She saw Elliott before he did.

The glint off the revolver told Quinn he was there, sitting in the darkened office at the mammoth desk once used by their father. Elliott had been waiting for them, he realized. Just as Quinn had waited to confront him for four long years.

The time to settle their score had come.

"Get out of here, Hannah," he said roughly, never taking his eyes off Elliott and the weapon he wielded. "Wait outside until I come for you."

"No." Elliott cocked the hammer, the sound lethal in the stillness of the office. "I want to see her."

Quinn's fingers tightened reflexively over Hannah's. "This has nothing to do with her. Let her go."

"Open the drapes, Hannah. That's what he called you, wasn't it? Hannah?"

A tremble went through her. "Yes."

The revolver jerked toward the window. "Open the drapes. Like I told you."

Pam Crooks

Elliott had never been a patient man. Quinn gestured to Hannah to obey, hating it when her hand left his, that he could no longer protect her with the shield of his body.

A dusky light spread inward with the parting of the heavy fabric, and Quinn studied his brother. A shock of unruly hair had fallen over his forehead. He needed a shave, clean clothes. The collar of his rumpled shirt hung open at the throat; his tie slung forgotten around his neck. A bottle of Cyrus Noble Whiskey sat in front of him. Its contents were nearly gone.

Elliott had always been fastidious about his appearance. And he could never hold his liquor.

His heavy-lidded gaze dragged over Hannah, from the feathers on her hat down to the toes of her kid-leather shoes and back up again.

He turned to Quinn.

"I heard you had a woman with you. You married to her?" he drawled.

"Yes," Quinn said, and knew James Steadman had not been gone long from the house.

"You work fast. Go into prison a condemned man. Escape. Come back married. Christ." He tossed back the last of the whiskey in his glass and refilled it. "Welcome to our happy family, Hannah."

She stiffened at his mockery. "Thank you."

"You're welcome." His mouth formed a cold smile. "She's a polite little beauty, Quinn. You could always get 'em, couldn't you?" He waved the crystal glass in the air. "The most beautiful women in the land, falling at the almighty Quinn Landry's feet."

"It wasn't like that, Elliott, and you know it."

"The hell it wasn't."

"Sarah was prettier than most."

The glass hurled against the fireplace. "Sarah was a whining *bitch!*"

Hannah flinched.

"She was as fine a ranch wife as a man could find," Quinn shot back. "She loved you." He strode forward, his bitterness, four years worth, straining to burst free. "Why did you kill her? If you hated me so much, why did you kill *her?*"

Elliott glared at him, a look of the devil himself. He took a gulp of whiskey, straight from the bottle. "I didn't intend to at first. It just happened."

"You planned to overdose me with Manny's medicine that night at the hotel. You started early, slowly, increasing the dosages as the night wore on." He took a step closer to the desk. To Elliott.

The revolver jerked. Hannah emitted a whimper of alarm. Quinn disregarded both reactions.

"How much did you pay the barmaid, my dear brother, to sedate me with so much bromide my heart would stop beating?" Quinn said with a snarl, a feral sound in the confines of the room. "What was it worth to you?"

"It was a bargain!" Elliott yelled. "She was the best damned deal I'd ever made."

Quinn steeled himself against the pain those words inflicted. "But you failed, didn't you? I didn't get enough of the bromide. Sarah interrupted your plan to finish me off in my room. You raped her, and then you killed her. And Humphrey, too."

"No!" Elliott leaned forward, his eyes bloodshot, glazed. "I never killed Humphrey."

"Yes, you did. You killed him because of what you did to Sarah. He saw everything."

"You can't pin the old man's death on me."

"The hell I can't."

"You're lying."

Quinn was relentless. "Stephen Larson supplied you with the sedatives. You paid him well for his trouble."

"How do you know that?"

"Then you hired a shyster lawyer from the East to manipulate the evidence and send me to prison. And you finished the job by paying James Steadman to print the story—*your* version of it—in all the papers."

Elliott's throat bobbed. He'd grown pale in the shadow-streaked room. "No one will believe you. You're a convicted murderer. Your reputation is ruined. No one will *believe* you, damn it!"

"I'll *make* them believe it." Quinn spat the vow. "I have the evidence."

Panic flashed across Elliott's features, his control fast slipping in the light of Quinn's revelations. "What evidence?"

He tossed the black flannel bag onto the desktop.

"Everything is there. George Larson's coroner's report on Sarah. His notes on me. On Manny. All the information on bromide any judge and jury will ever want to know." Quinn tossed the money bag aside and leaned against the desk, gripping the edges tight. "Everything."

Sweat beaded on Elliott's brow. He fell back against his chair. "How did you get this?"

"It's called survival, big brother." He pushed away from the desk in disgust.

Elliott's breaths came in quick pants. "You're just saying this to scare me."

"Open the bag. Read what's inside."

"I'll destroy everything."

"Go ahead. Jody has copies."

Elliott swore, flitted a wild glance over Hannah, and finished off the last of the whiskey in one gulp.

"I ought to kill you right now," he said hoarsely, giving the revolver an unsteady swing. "Both of you."

Quinn faced him squarely. "Are you going to kill everyone who gets in your way? You won't win. Not this time."

"You think you have all the answers, don't you?" he sneered.

"Most of them." He watched Elliott closely, tried to gauge how long before he'd break. "There's one thing I don't know."

Sweating, Elliott waited.

"Rosa had Manny with her on the day she died. After she was thrown from her horse, did you hit him?"

He appeared taken aback. For a long moment, he didn't reply.

"He was crying," Elliott finally said, the words slurred. "Rosa had taken the horse—a mare we were trying to breed. I was angry she'd taken it. The kid wouldn't stop crying. Christ, he wouldn't stop, and so I thumped him on the head." He lifted his eyes to Quinn. "Just a little thump."

Tears snaked down his unshaven cheeks. Quinn gaped at him.

"Then he started having those damned seizures. I knew it was my fault he went insane—"

"Insane?" Quinn frowned. "It was the epilepsy."

315

"He wasn't normal, I tell you!" Elliott grew agitated again. "He was touched in the head! He belonged in an asylum, but you were determined to take care of him. You and Sarah. And then Sarah started whining to have a baby of her own." A strangled sound wrenched from his throat. "What if she had one like Manny? Another lunatic?"

"He wasn't a lunatic!" Quinn roared.

Hannah flew to him. "Quinn, please."

"So you quit giving him his medicine?" he demanded, incredulous, furious.

"How the hell did I know he'd die from one of those attacks of his?" Elliott snapped, chest heaving. He swiped his coat sleeve across his cheek. "It wasn't my fault he died!"

"Yes! It was!"

"And I suppose it's my fault this damned ranch is falling apart. And my fault that T. J. loved you more than he *ever* loved me. Christ, the sun rose and set on you, y'know that? Sometimes, it made me so sick to see him look at you, I'd have to go somewhere and puke."

Quinn swallowed, stunned.

"He didn't even want me calling him Pa. Bet you never knew that, did you? Made me call him T. J., like everyone else. God, he was a hard-hearted sonovabitch!"

His pain, all the more powerful for the years he'd kept it locked inside, rocked Quinn.

Suddenly, Elliott bolted to his feet. He whirled toward Hannah, a wild man, frenzied and panicked. He jabbed the revolver toward the door.

"Get him out of here," he ordered with a snarl.

She made a sound of distress and tugged on Quinn's arm. "Let's go, Quinn."

Quinn shook her off, not ready to leave Elliott, not trusting him.

"Give me the gun first," he ordered.

"Go. Now, damn it!"

"Not until you give me the gun."

Quinn lunged, reaching across the desk to wrest the revolver from his brother's hand, but too quickly, Elliott jumped back and produced another from the gun-belt strapped to his hip.

Both weapons shook visibly, their barrels ominous in their point of aim.

"You win, just like you always do," he choked. "Get out of here, Quinn. Leave me alone. Take Hannah with you. You can have the damned ranch, too. I don't want it anymore. Do you hear me?" His voice raised to a shrill pitch. *"I don't want it!"*

"Quinn, we have to leave." Frantic, Hannah yanked hard on his arm, and he stumbled back. "He'll kill you! Can't you see that?"

"No," he said, still resisting, still afraid to leave.

From some herculean force dredged up within her, Hannah pulled him from the office and slammed the door closed, only moments before something hurtled after them. It sounded like the black bag crashing on the other side.

They fell together against the wall. Hannah was trembling and crying, and Quinn hauled her to his chest, holding her hard.

"He's very sick," she whispered. "He needs help. There's nothing you can do for him. We'll find the doctors he needs, Quinn. They're the only ones who can help him."

"I have to go back in there," he said, hating the revenge he'd been compelled to seek and tortured by a sense of dread so overwhelming he was forced to defy the risks. "He can't be alone."

"Oh, God. No." Raw fear paled her expression.

Resolutely, he pushed her away. "Run out to the barns and find someone, Hannah," he ordered. "As many men as you can round up. Send them in here. Fast."

She pivoted to obey the command, but before she could take a step, before either of them could, a single gunshot thundered through the house.

And with it, the muffled sound of a man's body toppling lifeless to the floor.

Chapter Twenty-one

Word of Elliott Landry's suicide hit the newspapers with all the sensationalism of a popular dime novel. Except this time, the gory details were all true.

Neighboring cattlemen and scores of Amarillo citizenry streamed to the Star L ranch for the funeral, more out of respect and curiosity for Quinn's return than grief for Elliott's tragic passing. He was buried in the family plot, next to the father he'd despised and the wife he'd killed.

The event made for some fascinating ruminating in front-room parlors and back-room saloons.

And the story sold newspapers. Stacks of them.

While waiting for a haircut and shave, Roger Fenwick read the well-thumbed issue of the weekly *Amarillo Champion* with more zeal than most. Though the incident had happened nearly a month before, the most recent account of it engrossed him as if it had happened only yesterday.

Pam Crooks

"Them Landry boys gave folks plenty to talk about, didn't they?" The amiable barber, his hair parted down the middle and slicked with tonic, gestured Fenwick into the velvet-cushioned chair. "Reckon if ol' T. J. were alive today, he'd be none too pleased. He hated scandal."

Fenwick could care less about T. J. Landry. Or Elliott, for that matter.

Only Quinn interested him.

"Folks were mighty surprised to learn Quinn came back with a wife at his side. Word is he plucked her right out of a nunnery. Holed up with some Mexican banditos, then married her."

The barber draped him and tilted the chair back; Fenwick set his booted feet on the foot rest. He hid his surprise at the news of the nuptials and lifted his chin to allow the barber to lather his cheeks and throat.

"Pretty thing she is, with those red curls and hazel eyes. Saw her once, after the funeral. Slender as a willow reed. Landry won't hardly let her out of his sight." He chuckled and wielded the straight razor with the ease of a man who'd performed the task a thousand times over. "Can't blame him. She's all he's got left in this world. Her and that huge ranch of his."

Fenwick let him talk while his brain sorted through the information.

"Yes, sir. Those two make a fine pair. Anyone can see they're as happy as twin bear cubs with a honey pot."

The razor halted near Fenwick's lower lip and the angry scar left there from the swing of Landry's club the night he broke out of Briggs's penitentiary.

The night he destroyed Fenwick's Solution.

320

"Nasty scar you got there." The barber maneuvered the blade with extra care. "Get it from a fall?"

"Yes," Fenwick lied.

"Gonna remind you every time you look at it."

Fenwick didn't need the scar to be *reminded* of his hate for Quinn Landry or all he'd lost because of him. The opportunity to test his solution on Brigg's inmates was forever gone; a small fortune and years of experiments wasted.

After the shave was finished, the barber wiped off the remaining soap with a warm, damp towel, adjusted the chair and reached for his scissors.

"You say Landry's got a ranch around these parts?" Fenwick asked.

"Yep. Damned near a quarter-million acres up north a spell. The Star L spread. Can't believe you've never heard of it."

"I don't recall him mentioning the place."

"You're acquainted with Mr. Landry, then?"

"Yes," Fenwick said smoothly. "We're acquainted. And I'd be obliged if you'd give me directions out. I'd like to pay him a call. To express my condolences, of course."

The barber readily complied, and after leaving the chair, Fenwick paid him, tossing in an extra two bits for the pleasure of his conversation.

Outside, he halted on the boardwalk and squinted into the morning sunshine. He'd have to find Briggs and that no-good guard of his and wrangle them away from whatever saloon and floozy they'd found to entertain them. Briggs would be keen on the news he'd gleaned and quick to lend his assistance to Fenwick's plan for revenge. The warden had a vendetta of his own against Landry's wife.

But it would be he, Roger Fenwick, who would make her husband pay.

He wasn't so foolish as to think Landry would go back to prison. Not now, with the truth of his brother's crimes out in all the papers. The warden would be most disappointed about that.

No, indeed. But Landry was far from being vindicated. He still owed for Fenwick's Solution.

Giving the *Champion* article a final glance, he tossed the newspaper onto a bench situated outside the barber shop door and went in search of Briggs.

A quick step onto the boardwalk sent the rowels on the concho spurs spinning. On the bench, the newspaper fluttered in the breeze, the printed words shadowed by the broad brim of a beaded sombrero.

The Mexican picked up the paper, read the headline and the article beneath. Black eyes narrowed and watched Roger Fenwick enter a cantina and emerge shortly thereafter with another gringo wearing a scar on his face. Soon, a third followed.

Frank Briggs.

The Mexican sucked in a breath.

At last, the long wait had ended.

Chapter Twenty-two

Quinn was late again.

Hannah sighed in wifely exasperation and set the heavy pot of stew onto a back burner to simmer. She opened the oven door, removed the pan of golden sourdough biscuits, and set them next to the stew.

Supper was ready, but Quinn wasn't.

She glanced at the clock. Most likely, eating was the farthest thing from his mind. The approach of calving season absorbed most of his waking hours and, she suspected, a portion of his sleeping ones, too. He worked long and hard to salvage the herds Elliott had allowed to dwindle. By bringing the cows in off the range, where they could be watched during calving, he hoped to save each newborn and then begin the long process of building the herds up again.

Yet when he wasn't thinking of the ranch, she mused as she arranged plates and silverware on the table, he was thinking of her. No matter how grueling his day, he hungered for her at its end. Their lovemaking was fierce and passionate and driven by the need to consume each other's souls and bodies, to saturate themselves with the truth of their love.

Elliott had done that for them. Showed them the fragility of life, the permanence of death, and how happiness could so easily be ripped apart.

And glory, she *was* happy. Happier than she ever thought any woman could be.

She felt guilty for it, sometimes. She didn't deserve the happiness, had not repented nearly long enough for her past sins. Or Pa's.

Sometimes Hannah longed to confide in Mother Superior and be consoled with her wisdom and gentle advice. Too often lately, she thought of the old abbess and the test she'd given Hannah to decide her destiny.

But to see Mother Superior, she must return to the convent. With Quinn, or without him.

Hannah could not ask it of him now. Not so soon after his homecoming. Elliott's death had affected him deeply, had swept away the years of hate and bitterness to leave a part of him forever empty.

No, he was still healing, and she could not leave him.

The ranch needed him.

She needed him.

With the table setting complete, her glance inspected the tidy kitchen. It was hers now, and oh, she was proud of it. She delighted in cooking for Quinn, pleasing him, making this house a home with him.

It was something Pa had never been able to give her. A home. Hannah hadn't known how much it meant to have one.

She glanced at the clock again and worriedly peered

out the window. She saw no sign of his lean, hard body sitting erect in the saddle as he rode in from the range with his men gathered respectfully around him.

Her mouth pursed. Perhaps he'd sent word of their delay to Juan Rameriz, Manny's grandfather, the old Mexican who had been foreman under T. J.'s leadership. Juan prepared the meals for all the cowboys who worked the Star L. If anyone knew when they'd return, Juan would.

Hannah left the room and headed for the front door to speak with him. But footsteps in the kitchen stopped her, and she pivoted to retrace her steps. She shook her head in wry amusement that he'd come home after all, despite her attentiveness at the window.

"Quinn Landry, it's about time you—"

Roger Fenwick and Frank Briggs stormed into the room with vicious expressions and their rifles drawn.

A scream rose in her throat. She whirled and bolted down the hall to escape them, but the front door flung open and Titus burst inside.

Terror numbed her ability to think. To react.

Oh, God.

Titus closed his meaty hand around her arm and jerked her back into the kitchen.

"Where's Landry?" Briggs snarled.

They crowded the room, filled it with their suffocating presence.

"He's upstairs," she said, her bosom heaving. "Cleaning up for supper. He'll be down any minute."

"You're lyin' to me, woman!" Briggs raised a hand and slashed it across her cheek. Pain exploded inside her head, and she stumbled back from the force of the blow.

"Don't play us for fools, Mrs. Landry." Roger Fenwick glared down his thin nose, the nostrils flaring with fury.

"He'll never let you get away with this." Hannah sucked in air, refused to let them see how they terrified her. Her swollen lip pounded with an ache.

"Reckon he ain't gonna have a choice," Titus said. He yanked a portion of hot biscuit from the pan and stuffed it greedily into his mouth.

"Shut up, Titus!" Briggs shot him a look of disgust.

"Answer the warden's question," Fenwick ordered. "We're not schoolboys to be toyed with."

Hannah knew only too well the brand of men they were. Ruthless. Without mercy. And if Quinn had once frightened her with his savagery, these men did doubly so.

"He's out on the range. Sundown Valley," she said finally. "He'll be back any minute."

"Alone?" Briggs demanded.

She nodded, knowing he wasn't, that he'd be with some of the most loyal men in the Star L outfit. She tried to remember the direction in which he'd left this morning, could only hope he'd return the same way. "Cows are due to calve soon. He wanted to bring them in."

The warden exchanged a glance with Fenwick, as if unsure they should believe her.

"You want to see him again, don't you?" he demanded.

"Yes," she whispered.

Briggs jabbed the barrel of his Winchester into her ribs.

"Then take us to the valley you're talkin' about. This spread is too damned big to waste time huntin' for it ourselves. But I'm warnin' you, woman. Try anything funny, and I'll kill you before we find him. You know I will, don't you?"

She refused to speak the answer he wanted. She would not give him the satisfaction of knowing she was powerless against him. Against the three of them.

He leered.

"Too bad them friends of yours weren't as smart as you." He shoved her toward the door. "Never had an inkling they'd get a bullet in their backs for interferin' in our affairs."

The rage rose within her with such speed she had no time to control it. She whirled, her hand lashing out to claw him with her nails, but he was too quick and caught her arm behind her back.

And twisted.

She was sure he'd break it. She gritted her teeth to keep from crying out.

"You drew my blood once, woman. You won't do it again. I'll shoot you first!"

"I hope you burn in hell for their deaths," she grated.

"Watch that tongue of yours! I'll cut it out. Don't think I won't!"

"And then you'll shoot me?"

"Damn right! And smile when I'm doin' it!" He twisted harder.

She winced. Pain swam before her eyes. "We know everything. How you killed Sister Evangeline and Father Donovan and planned to accuse me of it. We heard you plan it with Titus. We were right there, in the water, listening to you."

The grip faltered. "What're you talkin' about?"

"My husband has influential friends. A lawyer,

among them. He's prepared to bring charges against you."

The warden released her abruptly. Hannah fought to keep from falling. Swearing, he cocked his rifle and aimed the muzzle inches from her head.

"Briggs! No!" Fenwick barked. "Shoot her now, and we'll have half the damned ranch to fight off. We need her to find Landry."

"She's lyin'. Lyin' about everything!"

"She's tellin' the truth, Warden. The dogs knew they was there that day. And you was talkin' fast and free by that stream. I remember we stopped there to have a smoke." Accusation darkened Titus' expression. "She's not lyin' at all."

"I told you to shut up!" Briggs yelled at him.

Titus's scar quivered. Suppressed wrath glinted from the hooded eyes, but he said nothing. He ripped off another chunk of biscuit from the pan and stalked from the kitchen.

"We're wasting time," Fenwick said to Briggs. "The longer we're here, the sooner someone will find us."

Briggs pushed Hannah forward, but Fenwick gripped her chin, halting her again.

The slender fingers dug into her flesh. His sinister gaze drifted over her.

"You've come to mean a great deal to him, haven't you?" he asked.

She squirmed against his grip, but the fingers merely tightened.

"You'll raise the ante. That's good. Very good." His thin lips curved in an oily smile.

"My husband is a powerful man," she said. "Don't underestimate him."

He made a dismissive sound and released her. "A king will give up his kingdom because of a woman." He gestured toward the door. "Landry will be no different."

Briggs hauled her outside, and she stumbled to a stop near his horse. Titus waited, a rope in his hand, then bound and gagged her.

The three men mounted. Briggs sheathed the rifle. He took the end of the rope in one hand; in the other, a cat o'nine tails he'd uncoiled from the saddle horn. He bettered his grip on the rawhide handle.

His smile was cold. Ice cold.

"Lead the way to them suffering cows, Mrs. Landry," he said. "And you'd better be a-hopin' your husband is with them."

She stared at the whip, at the nine knotted cords of leather.

And a new kind of horror locked her within its clutches.

Quinn glanced up at the sky and grimaced.

He'd never make it on time.

"She gonna hold supper for you?" Bobby asked, eyeing him knowingly beneath the sweat-stained brim of his Stetson. "Or make you eat it in the barn?"

Quinn took the ribbing. He'd been late too many times not to.

"Reckon she might do both," he said.

Bobby Ralston grinned. He was the top foreman of the Star L and enjoyed a friendship with Quinn based on mutual respect and dedication to the ranch. Quinn was fortunate to have him on the payroll.

"Naw, she won't," Bobby drawled. "Hannah's too

Pam Crooks

crazy about you. She'll slide that plate steamin' hot under your nose and not complain a bit you made her wait two hours to do it."

A slow smile curved Quinn's mouth. He didn't need to be reminded he was a lucky man. "I'd wager you're right about that, Bobby."

Suddenly impatient to get home to her, Quinn shifted in the saddle. It'd been a long day. Too long. He'd have to cut himself some slack, spend a little more time with Hannah. She might appreciate having him around.

He narrowed an eye at the small herd of cows plodding toward them, a hundred head by his estimation. Several Star L cowboys urged them along, patient but persistent to settle them in closer to the ranch. The pregnant cows made for a slow trip. They were reluctant to move at all.

Quinn reached into his shirt pocket and withdrew a pair of rolled cigarettes. Flicking his thumbnail over a match tip, he lighted one and handed it to Bobby. The foreman accepted with a nod. Quinn lit the second cigarette and inhaled deeply.

"Ed can handle it from here," he decided, speaking of the cowhand riding flank with the herd. Ed Simpson was the most experienced of the trio. "We'll head on over to the ranch and let Juan know they're coming."

Bobby agreed. "What's Hannah plannin' for supper?"

"Stew and biscuits, I think." Amused, Quinn glanced over at him. He wasn't blind to the foreman's change of topic or his way of thinking. "Want to join us?"

"No, thanks." He sighed.

"She's got mince pie for dessert."

Hannah's Vow

Bobby glanced at him beneath the Stetson's brim. "Mince, eh?"

"Peach, too."

His windburned face reflected temptation. "Reckon if I had a wife like her, I wouldn't want to share her company. I'll eat at the bunkhouse."

"She'd be pleased to have you with us." Quinn's gaze roamed the horizon. He pulled in another drag from the cigarette. "The invitation stands. I won't ask a second time, Bobby."

Three horses descended into the valley. With them, someone on foot.

He hardly heard his foreman's response. Quinn exhaled, leaned forward in the saddle, strained to see into the distance.

"That look like a woman to you?" His muscles coiled, one by one.

Bobby pulled his attention from the herd. He studied the group hard. "She's leashed to 'em. Like a dog."

"It's Hannah. Christ." Quinn flung the cigarette into the dirt. He rose up in the stirrups, slid a sharp, piercing whistle through his teeth. Ed and the two cowboys rode up immediately. One look into the valley, and they knew there was trouble.

Quinn unshucked his rifle from the scabbard. The men reached for theirs. "Whatever happens, I don't want her hurt. Hear me?"

Their somber nods assured him, and Quinn kicked his horse into a run, the others close behind. The iron hooves thundered down the hill. Hannah's head lifted. She bolted toward Quinn, but the length of rope jerked her back, the gag muffling her cry.

Quinn halted with a savage yank on the reins. Bobby

331

Pam Crooks

and the others fanned out on either side of him. The simultaneous cocking of their rifles split the air.

"You lousy sons-of-bitches," Quinn said with a snarl.

"We meet again, Mr. Landry," Fenwick said, signalling the others to pull up. "And my, my, it is a pleasure."

Quinn longed to ram his fist down the man's sarcastic throat. "Untie her!"

"In time, in time." A smile, cool and lethal, spread across Fenwick's face. "But, of course, that won't be possible until all your men have put down their weapons."

He'd expected the ultimatum. Fenwick was no fool.

"This has nothing to do with Hannah. Let her go," Quinn ordered. "It's me you want."

"I do, indeed, want you, Mr. Landry," Fenwick said softly. Deceptively.

"She ain't goin' nowhere, and you're stupid if you think she is!" Briggs spat. "Now let's cut to the chase and have your men put them damned rifles away."

"I'll handle this, Warden," Fenwick snapped.

"All this pussy-footin' around ain't gettin' us nowhere!"

"I *said* I'd handle it!"

The two men glared at each other. Between them, Hannah fidgeted, her anxiety to be free pulling at Quinn.

"I want her set loose," he said. "My men will take her out of the valley. Then we'll settle this your way."

"*Our* way, Mr. Landry, includes your lovely wife. Removing her from the situation is not part of the plan," Fenwick said.

"I'll come to you unarmed." Quinn spoke between his clenched teeth. "I'll send the others back to the ranch."

Titus leaned forward. "I say let her go, like he wants. He'd be defenseless. We'd have the advantage."

Briggs and Fenwick stared at him.

"Will you just keep your damned fool mouth shut, Titus?" Briggs shouted.

The scar leapt on the guard's cheek. Abruptly, he hurtled from the saddle, stepped around Briggs's horse and snatched Hannah by the arm.

"I'm sick of you yellin' at me to shut up, Warden," he screamed. "This woman ain't guilty of nothin'! Now give her over so's we can take care of Landry and be done with it!"

He yanked on Hannah, but Briggs kept the rope taut, and she swayed like a marionnette on strings.

The warden swore and moved for his Winchester. The rope loosened, and Hannah leapt forward, but Fenwick reached down and grabbed a handful of the auburn curls on her head, jerking her back. He pressed his rifle to her temple.

Quinn's heart forgot to beat. Briggs cocked his gun and fired. Titus spun and fell to the ground, writhing, blood spurting across the front of his chest.

Lightning quick, Bobby and the rest of the cowboys leveled their weapons on Briggs.

"No!" Quinn roared. "I don't want Hannah hit!"

The warden fired again, and his guard lay motionless.

A tremor went through Quinn. It could have been Hannah lying in the tall grass.

Sweet Jesus. It could have been Hannah.

Resolutely, he tossed his rifle to the ground. He commanded the others to follow suit.

"You crazy, Quinn?" Bobby hissed under his breath.

"Drop 'em!" He swung out of the saddle, taking his gloves with him on the way down.

One after the other, the grim-faced men discarded their rifles.

"Now get back." Quinn kept Briggs and Fenwick in his range of vision. He pulled the gloves on, snug over each finger. "Do it, Bobby."

He lifted his hands into the air and stepped forward cautiously. He didn't look back to see if his men obeyed. The muffled trod of retreating hooves told him they did.

"All right. You've got me," he said. His glance darted over Fenwick and Briggs. "I'm unarmed. My men won't interfere. Now let Hannah go."

A cold, mirthless laugh left Fenwick's throat. "I've been waiting a long time to destroy you, Mr. Landry."

"She had nothing to do with your damned drug. Don't hold her accountable for something I did."

"How much is she worth to you?" he demanded. "As much as my Solution?"

"More." The word rumbled from the cavern of his chest.

"I thought so." He jerked harder on Hannah's curls, yanked her head at an awkward angle and kept the gun at her temple. "My Solution meant a fortune to me. You knew that, didn't you? A fortune."

Quinn said nothing.

"Fifty thousand, at least. Maybe a hundred."

Hannah whimpered, squeezed her eyes tight.

"The Star L ranch is worth that, don't you think?"

Quinn thought of John Mahoney's ledgers, of the accounts Elliott had squandered.

"I don't know," he hedged.

Hannah's Vow

"Quarter-million acres," Fenwick went on. "That's a helluva lot of land. Sell them acres off, one after another. You'd be a rich man." His lip curled. "Or should I say, *I* would." He yanked again on the silky curls. "Is she worth a quarter-million acres, Mr. Landry?"

"Yes." There was no hesitation in his answer.

Hannah's eyes flew open again. She shook her head vehemently, twisting beneath Fenwick's grip. Hazel-green eyes beseeched him to refuse.

"The Star L is yours," Quinn said. "Just give me my wife back."

"He's lyin' to you, Fenwick," Briggs snapped. His features contorted with disdain. "He ain't gonna give up his ranch that easy. Don't think that he is."

Briggs tossed the end of the rope onto Fenwick's lap. His fingers flexed over the handle on the cat o'nine tails.

Slowly, he rode the horse forward. The knotted ends of the "cat" dragged along the grass.

Quinn eyed the warden closely, the nightmare of the whip still vivid in his memory. Fear gnawed at his belly that Hannah would feel its sting, that her soft flesh would be ripped open by the slash of the leather.

He moved. Away from Titus's dead body. Away from Hannah.

The whip cracked, sent the tops of the grass flying.

"I know your kind, Landry," Briggs jeered. "I spent half of my life in that stinkin' prison with men just like you. You're lyin' to us, ain't you? You got no intention of givin' us a dime. Not even for that pretty wife of yours."

"You won't know until you hand her over to me, will you?" Quinn pulled his Stetson from his head, threw it aside.

Pam Crooks

"You toyin' with me, boy?"

"Just laying a few ground rules."

"You always was an arrogant cuss, wasn't you? Better than anybody else in that prison. Like the rest of us was horseshit."

"Yes," Quinn said darkly. "Horseshit."

The warden snarled and lifted his arm. The "cat" snaked through the air, bit across Quinn's shoulder and chest.

He hissed in a breath at the pain searing through his shirt, across his nerve endings.

Briggs kept the horse moving.

Stalking him.

"You like the feel of that, Landry?" he taunted. "Show your wife what it's like to have a whip across your back. Just so she knows what it's like when it's her turn."

"She's a mite smaller than you, Briggs," Quinn rumbled. "Makes you feel good to overpower a woman, doesn't it? Especially when she can't defend herself."

"Shut up, Landry!"

The whip slashed again, a deafening crack in his ears.

But this time, Quinn knew just how far the "cat" would reach, how many fractions of a second Briggs needed to use it. His body swiveled, and the whip missed its mark.

Briggs let out a bellow of rage.

"I'm gonna make you pay for breakin' out my prison, Landry. And she's gonna pay for helpin' you do it!"

His arm flung back again. Quinn lunged and met the "cat" as it was coming down. His gloved palms stung from the union, curled around the leather tight.

He gritted his teeth and hung on. Briggs dug his heels

into the stirrups, stood up straight-legged to wrestle the whip free. But where Quinn clung with both hands, the warden had only one, and he was nearly pulled from the saddle for his efforts.

He swore viciously. The rifle in the other hand raised, leveled over Quinn.

A shot exploded behind Briggs. He jerked. His eyes bulged. His mouth fell open in surprise. The "cat" fell free, and Quinn stumbled back from the unexpectedness of it.

Briggs toppled from his horse—dead in a pool of blood.

The Star L rifles still lay in the grass. Quinn whirled in search of the man who fired the shot.

Bobby and the others twisted in their saddles, searching, too.

But no one searched harder than Fenwick. His Winchester trembled in his hand, Hannah forgotten in his quest to find the unseen killer.

She bolted. The cowboys raced toward her, enclosing her in a protective circle, shielding her with their horses and bodies. Quinn grabbed for the rifles, tossing one to each of them, taking the last for himself.

Riders streamed down the hill at the opposite end of the valley. They were led by one man, dressed in black and wearing a beaded sombrero.

Fenwick went white. His gaze raked over the bodies lying on the ground.

He stood alone against them all. Quinn and the Star L cowboys in front of him. A band of Mexican bandeleros in back. All heavily armed.

He seemed panicked, unsure whom to shoot at first. He yanked the reins in one direction, then the other.

The horse whinnied and pranced at his indecision.

The Mexican leader rode toward him. Fenwick licked his thin lips and took aim.

But the bandelero was ready for him. His horse never broke stride as he fired the shot.

It took only one bullet to the heart. Fenwick fell to the ground with the others and went limp.

Relief thundered through Quinn. Bobby bent over and undid the kerchief stretched across Hannah's mouth, then untied the rope binding her wrists. The circle of horses parted, and she ran to Quinn's side. He rasped her name and held her hard against him.

A carriage appeared on the horizon. Black and gold and gleaming with elegance. One of the bandeleros left the band and escorted the rig closer. The leader slowed, letting them catch up.

The snaggle-toothed Mexican, Miguel, braked the rig to a stop. Beside him, Ramon Huerta held a tiny bundle in his arms. Tomas Huerta took the bundle, held it affectionately against him, and rode toward the leader.

Together they rode toward Quinn and Hannah. They paused only to flit their dark-eyed glances over the dead bodies. Then, the leader tossed back his sombrero onto its chin cord.

Long, black hair tumbled from inside the crown. Sophia smiled, proud and motherly. Tomas leaned over and set the bundle into her waiting arms.

"At last, *mi precioso bebe,*" she said. She opened the blanket, pressed a tender kiss to the baby-soft forehead inside. "Frank Briggs is dead, and he will never chase us again."

Chapter Twenty-three

"I could not rest until I knew they were dead," Sophia said, strolling with Hannah through the newly-planted flower garden in the Landry's back yard. "I had to see them with my own eyes—their bodies in the dirt, their hearts no longer pumping the lifeblood through them. Only then could I raise my son without fear."

"Yes," said Hannah somberly, understanding.

After the pass into their hideout had been blasted shut, the Huertas and the bandeleros had hidden in the hills until Frank Briggs, Titus and Roger Fenwick were long gone. They returned for the rustled cattle and wild mustangs, then herded them south. On the journey, Sophia's baby was born.

Thinking of him, Hannah turned and rested her gaze on the wicker basket on the porch where the little one slept, oblivious to the danger his parents had endured for his sake.

"I feared Briggs would find Tomas and take him from

me again," Sophia said, bending to touch a vibrant red rosebud. "And from our son. Always, the fear was there, and I tired of it." She straightened again, her dark eyes showing no remorse for what she'd done. "So we headed north to Amarillo. I wanted to find you and Senor Landry. I knew Frank Briggs would want to find you, too." She shrugged. "Then I knew it would only be a matter of time."

"I can't bear to think of what might have happened if you'd arrived too late." Hannah shuddered at the terror she'd endured with Quinn in Sundown Valley. "God forgive me, but those men's deaths are a relief to everyone."

"Si." Sophia paused, and in a rare show of affection, took Hannah's hands into hers. "I am pleased with my matchmaking. You are very happy with your new husband, eh?"

Hannah's throat welled with emotion. "More than you can imagine."

"So there will be a baby in your arms when I see you again."

A baby. Sudden tears filled Hannah's eyes. How could she possibly think of having Quinn's child some day?

"What's this?" A slender finger brushed a stubborn drop of moisture from Hannah's cheek. "Something is wrong. Tell me."

She blinked furiously. "I cannot stay here."

"What?" Sophia was astounded. "But you have just told me you are very happy with Senor Landry."

"I am. But—but I have taken vows at the convent, Sophia. Because of them, I should not have married Quinn. I must return to Mother Superior."

"Oh, I see."

Hannah's misery deepened at the seriousness in Sophia's tone.

"He will not let you go," Sophia said with conviction.

Unable to speak, Hannah could only nod.

"But you must go back. This I understand."

"Yes."

Impulsively, Sophia wrapped her arms around Hannah's shoulders. Hannah clung to her strength.

"Por Dios. It will not be easy for you. But you must promise me this." She drew back and cupped Hannah's cheek. "Return to the convent when the time is right in your heart. Only then will you be able to decide your future with a clear conscience."

Hannah clutched the small leather pouch in her palm. It held enough coins to buy her a ticket to the convent. The Huertas had long since left, and a thousand times she'd recalled Sophia's advice.

Now, the time was right in her heart. Hannah could delay the trip no longer.

Calving season was over, and the promise of large herds roaming Star L rangeland gratified Quinn, as well as John Mahoney. The ranch accounts showed signs of stabilizing, and Quinn's prominence as a cattleman remained strong.

He'd brought her to Amarillo for a few days of shopping and visiting with newfound friends. But he had gone on to a neighboring cattleman's ranch farther east, taking Bobby with him to consider the purchase of some fine-blooded bulls to breed with Star L stock.

He'd left just this morning. She could still taste his kisses on her lips.

He promised her an elegant evening out when he returned. Dinner. The theater. And, afterward, as much fiery lovemaking as she could give him in their big hotel bed.

She wouldn't be here when he came back. She would do none of those things with him.

Hannah dabbed a lace handkerchief to the corner of her eye and grew impatient with the emotion that rose when she least expected it. She cried too often of late. She had to be strong.

A knock sounded on the hotel door. She blew her nose quickly, dabbed a cool washcloth to her eyes, and drew in a long, steadying breath.

"Come in," she said.

Jody stepped inside, punctual as usual. Quinn had asked him to take her to lunch and entrusted her to his care while he was gone. There were few to whom he would have given the privilege, and Jody had been quick to accept.

He removed his bowler and grinned a wolfish grin.

"At last, pretty lady. I have you all to myself now that that rutting stag you call your husband is gone."

Her lip quivered.

He frowned, stepped closer. "What's the matter, Hannah? I was only teasing."

"I have to leave," she blurted.

"What?"

"I'm leaving Quinn. At—at least for now."

"You're *what?*"

"A stagecoach will depart within the hour. I'll be on it."

"Are you *crazy?*" His jaw dropped. "What happened? Did you two fight? Did he lose that temper of his again?"

"No, no. Nothing like that."

He stared. "Quinn doesn't know you're going, does he?"

She shook her head; her lip quivered anew.

"He'll be furious."

"He'll understand. He knows—he's known all along that it would come to this."

Jody peered at her doubtfully. "So you're going to just take off when he least expects it."

The words stung. "He would never agree any other way. You know that."

"And you want me to just let you go?"

"You have no choice."

"He'll *kill* me!" Jody raked a hand through his hair, began to pace the hotel room. He stopped. "When are you coming back?"

"I—I don't know."

"Wait a couple of days," he pleaded. "Talk it over with him."

"We've talked before, Jody. He promised me once he'd take me back. A long time ago. But now"—she halted, miserable—"now the deal's off."

Everything had changed. Quinn had fallen in love with her. She'd fallen in love with him. Glory, their lives were different than they were when they'd made their bargain that day at the stream.

"You can't ask this of me, Hannah," Jody grated.

She gathered her resolve about her and clung tight.

"I'm not asking you. I'm telling you. And you must promise not to send word to Quinn. He'll find out soon enough."

"And then it will be too late," he said in despair.

Hannah closed her eyes, turned away so he wouldn't see her own despair.

"Yes," she said. "By then, it will be too late."

Jody's office door burst open. He'd been expecting it to. For three long days.

"Where is she?" Quinn demanded.

Jody set the pen down, carefully moved the letter he'd been writing aside to dry.

"Gone," he said.

"I *know* that." Quinn choked the words out. "Wesley said she left the hotel with you and never came back."

"Yes. Would you like a drink, Quinn?"

"No, I don't want a drink," he thundered. *"I want my wife!"*

Jody went to the cabinet anyway and poured them both a couple of stiff whiskeys.

"She went to the convent, didn't she?" Quinn seemed on the edge of control.

"Yes."

"Alone?"

"Your wife is a very determined lady."

Quinn took the glass, threw back a gulp. "Christ."

Jody waited, let him work through the pain.

"We were happy. I never thought she'd do it. With Briggs and Fenwick gone, our lives were perfect. Why did she have to ruin everything?"

"She had her reasons. It wasn't easy for her. She was hurting as much as you are now."

"No." Quinn's lip curled, and his fingers tightened over the crystal. "She can't possibly hurt as much."

Jody moved away from the cabinet.

"When you stop feeling sorry for yourself, you can go after her." He set his glass down on the desktop, opened a drawer and removed a map. "This is a sketch of the fastest route to the convent. There'll be fresh horses waiting for you at the locations I've marked. Take the big bay tethered out front. He'll get you started. There's food and a change of clothes in the saddlebags."

Quinn stared at the map.

"I've arranged for a carriage to take you to the convent. We can't have Hannah riding back on a tired horse, can we?"

His throat worked. "She might not come back. She—"

"You won't know until you ask."

"God, Jody."

He'd never seen Quinn so unsure. So afraid.

"If I have to leave her behind, if she refuses—" He halted, shuddering.

Jody gripped his shoulder, turned him toward the door. "You're wasting time, Landry. She's got three days on you."

"It was always there, in the back of my mind, you know. Hannah leaving me."

He pulled the whiskey glass from Quinn's unresisting fingers. "She's probably watching out her window right now. Looking for you."

Quinn frowned, dubious, but he started walking, his stride growing longer with each step.

"I'll let Bobby know," Jody called after him. "And Quinn?"

He halted at the door, his hand on the knob.

"There's a razor in the saddle bag. Use it. You'll look

345

Pam Crooks

like hell at the end of the ride. It wouldn't do to scare the nuns when you come calling. They might not give her back. We wouldn't want that, would we?"

A slow grin curved Quinn's mouth.

"No," he said. "We wouldn't. Thanks, Jody."

He disappeared behind the door and slammed it shut.

Jody leaned against the wall in his office, and for the first time in three very long days, he grinned, too.

Within moments of her arrival at the convent, Hannah knew everything was the same. The austere walls. The plain stone floors. The dim halls.

The silence.

Why hadn't she noticed the starkness of it all before?

Sister Mary Margaret answered the bell tolling at the gate and ushered Hannah into Mother Superior's barren office. If the young, shy nun recognized her, she gave no indication, but kept her eyes downcast. She seated Hannah politely, and with her sandals echoing her departure, she hastened to fetch Mother Superior.

Hannah clasped her hands in her lap and tried not to think of all she'd left behind.

Soon, the door opened, and the abbess walked in. Her brow furrowed beneath her wimple.

"Hannah?" she asked. "Hannah Benning?"

Hannah's heart lifted, and she rose, embracing the old nun warmly. She smelled clean, like starch and freshly laundered wool.

"Yes, Mother," Hannah said softly. "It's me. I've come back."

The abbess pressed a hand to her bosom. "You gave me a start. I hardly recognized you."

Her gaze dragged over Hannah's travelling cloak, silver-gray *vigogne* trimmed in deep red velvet. It had been expensive, a gift from Quinn, and Hannah endured a twinge of guilt for wearing it.

"I've thought of you so often," Mother Superior said fervently. "Oh, how I've worried for you."

Hannah hesitated. "You know of Warden Briggs's accusations?"

Her lips thinned in blatant disapproval. "Yes."

"Surely you believed I was innocent, that I couldn't possibly have killed Sister Evangeline and Father Donovan?"

"Did you think I didn't believe in you? For a single moment?" The abbess appeared astounded. "I have long known of the warden's black soul, my child. When he came storming into this convent to tell me what happened and that *you* were responsible, why I—" She drew herself up, regained her usual calm. "I'm afraid I lost my temper and threw him out. I spent many hours in the chapel after that, I must tell you, seeking forgiveness for my actions."

Hannah's head lowered. "I've been guilty of many crimes in my life. I thought . . . I was afraid—"

The abbess made a sound of compassion. "It was an unnecessary penance for you to endure. I have *always* believed in you, my dear Hannah."

She was moved beyond words. "Thank you, Mother."

The abbess smiled and indicated a plain wooden chair. "Tell me about that horrible night at the penitentiary and everything since."

Hannah poured out her soul, then, about Quinn's desperation in taking her hostage, their fight to survive, their forced marriage. Briggs and Fenwick. Elliott and Jody and Loretta.

The abbess listened patiently, lovingly.

"Now you are married in the eyes of God," she said when Hannah had finished. "You say your husband loves you, and you love him. Forgive me if I don't understand, but . . ." She hesitated, as if choosing her words with care. "Why are you here? You've shared the vows of matrimony with him. Do you wish to divorce?"

She sounded perplexed, and though she spoke in her calm, even voice, the question seemed harsh to Hannah.

Divorce Quinn?

She left her chair and stood at the window. Null their marriage and end the happiness he'd given her?

Her heart constricted. Glory. How could she think it?

"I was content here, Mother," she said softly. "There is great peace within these walls. A serenity that I have not found anywhere else. I felt my place was here with you."

"And now?"

"I don't know," she whispered.

Mother Superior's gentle hand rested on Hannah's shoulder. "You are not the same girl who came to us all those months ago. You were frightened, then. And grieving for your father. You were tormented from the life you'd led with him and the crimes you committed together." She shrugged. "That was a long time ago."

"Have I failed the test you gave me, Mother? Am I not to be a Daughter of Perpetual Glory?"

"It is not for me to say, my child. You must say it to yourself."

Hannah bit her lip. "But I've taken vows to be a novitiate here."

"Temporary vows. They allow you to follow the calling in your heart, whatever it might be. But realize, Hannah, your decision must be firm. If you decide to stay at the convent, you cannot go back to your husband and his ranch. Ever. The solemn vows taken here are a perpetual obligation. Whatever you decide, you will have truly earned the name of Sister Ariel."

Hannah swallowed down a knot of misery. Who did she want to be?

Sister Ariel?

Or Hannah Landry?

"Stay with us as long as you must, my child. You are welcome. Who knows? The decision may be easier than you think."

Hannah peered at the older woman doubtfully and wished it would be so.

Serene, Mother Superior gently took her arm. "Come, my child. I will show you to your room. I have kept it ready for your return."

Hannah knelt in the garden and plucked at the young weeds daring to grow between the tender plants of spinach, peas, beans and tomatoes. The perfectly cultivated grounds within the high walls of the convent promised to be lovely. Another month, and the roses, peonies and lilies would bloom in riotous color.

She didn't think of next month, next week, or even tomorrow. She could only think of today. Of this hour.

An endless series of Divine Offices left her weary. Restless. She seemed always on the verge of tears, and the peace she'd sought in the nuns' humble routine proved frustratingly elusive.

She didn't belong within these walls anymore. Only now, after her time here, did she know the certainty of it.

She missed Quinn, more than she'd ever dreamed. She ached to run her hands along the contours of his hard, muscled body, to feel his arms tight about her. She wanted his kisses and the pleasure of waking up next to him each morning. She wanted to hear bawling calves and smell manure and see cowboys hard at work outside her kitchen window.

The convent could give her none of those things.

As if it floated down gently on angel's wings, her decision came. Hannah stopped weeding and stood. Once, Mother Superior and her gentle nuns had been the center of her world, her focus on living. Their peace and serenity had healed the wounds of her past.

Now, Quinn was her future.

The aroma of simmering vegetables wafted through the quiet garden. It would be time for lunch soon, meatless and simple as usual, and the nuns had prepared squash.

Again.

Her belly lurched alarmingly at the thought. Hannah pressed her fingers to her mouth and fought the nausea. A clammy sweat broke out on her forehead.

Her eyes widened.

Glory. Oh, glory.

She clutched her belly. The nausea and despair dissipated like clouds following rain. In their place, exhilaration swept through her.

Outside the block walls, a carriage rumbled to a stop. Hannah clung to the sound, a rarity for the convent. Her steps quickened through the back door, the kitchen and past the sleeping quarters. She lifted her skirt hems and broke into a run down the hall.

The bell tolled, once, twice, and she flung the door open wide.

Quinn stood at the gate, tall and powerful and handsome in his black suit and white cotton shirt. He'd recently shaved. His hair was still damp from a washing.

His dark eyes melted with hers.

Her heart leapt at the glorious sight of him, swelled with a joy so supreme she feared she'd burst.

"Oh, Quinn," she cried. "We're going to have a baby!"

"A baby!" he said, clearly stunned by her greeting.

His fingers closed over the iron bars, yanked on them hard, as if he meant to wrench them apart to get to her. Laughing, she threw the gate open wide and spared him the trouble. She hurtled into his arms.

"Yes, a baby, my love. A darling little baby!" She peppered his face with ardent kisses.

"Let's go home, Hannah," he said, his voice ragged between his own kisses. "Now. This minute."

"Yes, yes," she said and reluctantly pushed away. "Stay here, Quinn. Don't move. I'll be right back."

Mother Superior appeared at the entrance way, her eyes twinkling.

"Is this the savage prisoner who took you as his hostage, Hannah?" she teased.

"Yes. Isn't he wonderful? Watch him, Mother. Don't let him out of your sight. I have to get my things."

She bolted into the convent, and returned a short

Pam Crooks

time later with her satchel and new travelling cloak. The nuns followed her out, a sea of brown wool and wimples, all of them curious and smiling.

Hannah bade them each good-bye with fervent hugs and kisses and returned to Quinn beaming and radiant. He opened the door to the carriage, an elegant brougham in deep plum, trimmed in gold. A grinning driver waited patiently on the box.

Hannah paused and turned to the abbess.

"Have I passed the test, Mother?" she asked, breathless.

The wimpled head bowed. "With top marks, my child."

Waves of pleasure and satisfaction soared through Hannah. She embraced the abbess one last time and stepped into the rig.

Quinn moved to join her, but Mother Superior laid a gentle hand on his arm.

"She is a treasure, Mr. Landry. The convent has never seen such exuberance." Intense and wise, she gazed up at him. "You must honor your vows with her. She deserves to feel safe again."

"I want her more than anything. She's my reason for living." He covered her hand with his. "If not for you, I would never have known her."

"It was her calling to go to the penitentiary. I played only a small part in her test."

He hesitated. "The deaths of Sister Evangeline and Father Donovan—"

"—are difficult to understand." The abbess showed no sadness. "They are in a better place. We should envy them. They're watching us now, you know. And they are happy for both of you."

Smiling, he inclined his head. "Thank you. For everything."

Hannah made room for him on her seat, and he latched the carriage door shut. The driver pulled away, and they left the convent behind forever.

Quinn pulled the woven curtains over the windows. In the privacy of the coach, amidst the lulling sway of the ride, he loved her with his body and his heart, and Hannah knew, with glorious certainty, he would keep her safe and secure.

Always.

AUTHOR'S NOTE

Dear Readers,

A trip by my parents to Roswell, New Mexico, and the Poor Clare Monastery of Our Lady of Guadalupe proved to be an unexpected inspiration for *Hannah's Vow*.

My parents' friends had a daughter entering the monastery. They would never see her again, would never hug or kiss her after she took the final, solemn vows and retreated behind the monastic walls. What kind of woman would leave her family and the modern world to live a life of almost constant prayer, of obedience, poverty and chastity.

One who craves serenity and peace, but most of all oneness with God.

These questions and answers spurred my imagination. And Hannah Benning was born.

The Order of Poor Clare Nuns was founded in Assisi, Italy by St. Francis and St. Clare in 1212, and has grown to about 18,000 nuns in monasteries throughout the world. Their daily routine varies little from what I've depicted in this book.

I hope you've enjoyed Hannah's story.

Best,

Pam Crooks

Lady
Gypsy
Pam Crooks

When an exotic Gypsy with flowing red tresses steals Reese Carrison's prized stallion, he gallops after her—straight into a tornado. It is not the twister that threatens to ravage him, though, but the woman who tames his horse. For in the eye of the storm, her soothing touch incites a whirlwind of passion he is helpless to resist. Liza longs only to escape the hated world of the non-Gypsy—the Gaje. Instead she finds herself wrapped in the sheltering embrace of a powerful Gajo man—a man who incites traitorous desires. A man whose sensuality strips away her defenses and whose caresses touch down on her heart, leaving in their wake not destruction, but love. A love that says she belongs in his arms, a love that makes her his Lady Gypsy.

___4911-2 $4.99 US/$5.99 CAN

WYOMING WILDFLOWER
PAM CROOKS

Armed with an arsenal of book knowledge on ranching,
Sonnie returns to the Rocking M Ranch determined to prove
that despite her sex she can be the son her father has always
wanted. Lance Harmon has beaten her to the punch, though.
She rides in on her high horse, determined to unseat him.
But Lance knows Sonnie toppled him years ago, for he has
always been head over heels in love with the rancher's
youngest daughter. And yet, he plans to chase her away.
Trouble on the range demands it. Sonnie doesn't shy away
when danger comes rustling through, though, proving to
Lance that the one thing that means more to him than the
only home he's ever known, is the only woman he's ever
loved, his . . . Wyoming Wildflower.

__4843-4 $4.99 US/$5.99 CAN